Acclaim for *Highways to a War*

"Here is a mystery that is not a mystery, an adventure that is very much more than that, a subtle unfolding of character and history camouflaged in battle-dress. *Highways to a War* is an absorbing portrait of lives lived at the edges of terror and beauty . . . Ly Keang's febrile vibrancy, in particular, seems to stand for everything lovely and lost in her overrun country. At the centre of it all is Mike Langford . . . a hero of the kind that has become unfashionable. But Koch has endowed his creation with a soul: his disembodied voice, captured in his diary, reaches out to the reader. . . . Koch is a powerful writer and this is a fine book."

— Erica Wagner, *The Times* (London)

"A quite outstanding novel about the Indochina War, the best I have read since Graham Greene's *The Quiet American*. Koch . . . has brilliantly captured the mood and atmosphere of the times. He describes with almost uncanny accuracy people, places and incidents that are part of my own experience. It is a vivid, exciting and finally tragic story about a courageous man and two women, one of them French-Vietnamese, the other Cambodian, both brilliantly brought to life."

— Richard West, *Literary Review* (London)

"Mike Langford . . . is an obsessive idealist of the kind Koch has made his specialty: like Billy Kwan in *The Year of Living Dangerously*, he has the gift (or curse) of total identification . . . The elder stateswoman of Franco-Vietnamese style, the lover from Battambang, the seedy secret servicemen . . . have the air of characters in Greene, the compass of characters in James. The prose is so carefully tooled, you hardly notice how well it works. . . . The narcotic attraction of the wars in Vietnam and Cambodia produced masterly fiction . . . Christopher Koch's magnificent new novel takes its rightful place beside these masterpieces: in its humanity and honesty, and the maturity of its storytelling, it belongs with the finest products of that sad and wasteful history."

"This is not only a pulse- . . . e journalists who cover it, but such a . . . china that it will have many a retired . . . eer."

— . . . *day* (London)

"Koch has long been regarded as one of Australia's finest writers, praised for his sensitive use of language and meticulous attention to detail . . . These qualities are abundantly apparent in this, his fifth novel. . . . Above all, the book is rewarding because it brings alive a world that increasingly large numbers of readers will never have experienced and which others are beginning to forget. This is the author's most striking achievement."
—Milton Osborne, *The New York Herald Tribune*

"Koch contributes powerfully to the imaginative literature of a period and place that history will ponder for generations. The book's publication is an important event."　　—Frank Devine, *The Australian*

PENGUIN BOOKS

HIGHWAYS TO A WAR

Christopher J. Koch is the author of several novels, including *The Year of Living Dangerously*, which was made into a film starring Mel Gibson and Sigourney Weaver. An Australian who has both worked and traveled extensively in Southeast Asia, he currently makes his home in Tasmania.

Also by Christopher J. Koch

NOVELS

The Boys in the Island
Across the Sea Wall
The Year of Living Dangerously
The Doubleman

ESSAYS

Crossing the Gap

CHRISTOPHER J. KOCH

PENGUIN BOOKS

HIGHWAYS
TO A WAR

PENGUIN BOOKS

Published by the Penguin Group

Penguin Books USA Inc., 375 Hudson Street, New York, New York 10014, U.S.A.

Penguin Books Ltd, 27 Wrights Lane, London W8 5TZ, England

Penguin Books Australia Ltd, Ringwood, Victoria, Australia

Penguin Books Canada Ltd, 10 Alcorn Avenue, Toronto, Ontario, Canada M4V 3B2

Penguin Books (N.Z.) Ltd, 182–190 Wairau Road, Auckland 10, New Zealand

Penguin Books Ltd, Registered Offices: Harmondsworth, Middlesex, England

First published in the United States of America by Viking Penguin,
a division of Penguin Books USA Inc. 1995
Published in Penguin Books 1996

10 9 8 7 6 5 4 3 2 1

PUBLISHER'S NOTE
This is a work of fiction. Names, characters, places, and incidents either are the product of the author's imagination or are used fictitiously, and any resemblance to actual persons, living or dead, events, or locales is entirely coincidental.

Grateful acknowledgment is made for permission to reprint excerpts from the following copyrighted works:
"Warning" from *Collected Poems* by James McAuley. Reprinted by permission of HarperCollins Publishers Australia.
"The Slowly, Slowly Poem" and "At White Deer Spring" from *Pilgrim of the Clouds* by Yüan Hung-tao, translated by Jonathan Chaves. Reprinted by permission of Weatherhill.
"Myself" by Po Chü-I, translated by L. Cranmer-Byng from *A Feast of Lanterns*. Reprinted by permission of John Murray (Publishers) Ltd.
"Ting: The Cauldron" from *The I Ching or Book of Changes*. The Richard Wilhelm translation rendered into English by Cary F. Baynes, Bollingen Series XIX. Copyright 1950, 1967, © renewed 1977 by Princeton University Press. Reprinted by permission of Princeton University Press.
Number nine of "Seventeen Old Poems" from *Chinese Poems* edited and translated by Arthur Waley. Reprinted by permission of HarperCollins Publishers.

THE LIBRARY OF CONGRESS HAS CATALOGUED THE HARDCOVER AS FOLLOWS:
Koch, Christopher J.
Highways to a war/by Christopher J. Koch.
p. cm.
ISBN 0-670-86155-3 (hc.)
ISBN 0 14 02.4757 2 (pbk.)
1. Vietnamese Conflict, 1961–1975—Fiction. 2. War photographers—Australia—Fiction.
3. War photographers—Cambodia—Fiction. 4. Missing persons—Cambodia—Fiction.
I. Title.
PR9619.3.K64H54 1995
823—dc20   94–34603

Printed in the United States of America
Set in Granjon
Designed by Ann Gold

For Cynthia Blanche, who believed in it.
For Carl and Kim Robinson and James Gerrand,
who took me to the War.
And in memory of my friend Bill Pinwill,
who did not go gentle into that good night.

Beware of the past;
Within it lie
Dark haunted pools
That lure the eye
To drown in grief or madness.
Things that are gone,
Or never were,
The Adversary
Weaves to a snare,
The mystery of sadness.

James McAuley, *Warning*

AUTHOR'S NOTE

This book is one of a related pair: a diptych. The second will follow shortly.

Each can be read without reference to the other, and each stands on its own as a story. But there are correspondences and factual links: the principal link being that Mike Langford is the illegitimate great-great-grandson of Robert Devereux, whose story is told in the second novel.

Which order the books are read in isn't important. The order in which they're currently appearing places the present before the past; but ultimately their sequence can be a matter of taste—depending on whether the reader prefers to see the present carrying messages from the past, or the past delivering messages to the present.

Being in battle, like being in love, is one of the fundamental human experiences, and without the many conversations I've had with correspondents and cameramen who covered the war in Vietnam and Cambodia, I could not have written *Highways to a War*. When my characters speak of battle, it's in the voices of these friends and acquaintances, who were unstintingly generous with their time. Many voices speak through me in this book, and I've tried to be faithful to them.

Among the war photographers, I owe thanks in particular to James Gerrand, David Brill, Hubert Van Es, Derek Williams and the late Yosep (Joe) Lee.

Among those former foreign correspondents whose talk has been invaluable to me, and who covered both the Indochina war and the old Southeast Asia of the sixties and seventies, I'm particularly indebted to Carl Robinson, Tim Bowden, Peter Barnett, Barry Wain, the late William Pinwill, and my brother Philip Koch.

Two authors and scholars who are experts on Cambodia were also very generous with their time and knowledge: Professor David Chandler, of Monash University, and Dr. Milton Osborne. My sincere thanks to them both.

The conflicts in Vietnam and Cambodia form the background here for a work of fiction. The characters and the events portrayed are inventions, and should be seen as such. Only the historical events are true.

Few wars have divided our society as the Vietnam War did, and these divisions are reflected among my fictitious correspondents, who range in their political opinions through the spectrum from Left to Right. None of their opinions is necessarily the author's—and I make no claims to any sort of wisdom about that long and bitter saga which did so much to dominate the second half of this century. A novelist's commitment, in my view, should not be to the prescriptions of ideology, but to the conflicts and ethical dilemmas that grip his characters. Those here are of a kind that I hope go beyond the fabricated questions and answers of politics, as they do in life.

In the interests of background accuracy, I've read as widely as possible. Two superb works on the wars in Vietnam and Cambodia respectively have never been far from my hand, and should be acknowledged: *A Bright Shining Lie*, by Neil Sheehan, and *Sideshow*, by William Shawcross. I should also state my indebtedness to the correspondent Kate Webb's remarkable book, *On the Other Side*—an account of her capture by the Viet Cong. This provided some valuable physical detail for the chapter *The Common Pot*, which principally took its inspiration from conversations I once had with the late Joe Lee, a Korean cameraman who was captured by the North Vietnamese Army while filming battle in Cambodia in 1970.

Finally, the influence and inspiration of two other books must be acknowledged: *One Crowded Hour*, Tim Bowden's account of the life of the combat cameraman Neil Davis, and *Page After Page*, the autobiography of the cameraman and stills photographer Tim Page.

The late Neil Davis, my fellow-Tasmanian and schoolmate at Hobart High, who covered combat for a decade in Indochina, and was killed covering a minor Thai coup in 1985, may be seen by those who knew him as the model for Mike Langford. In this they will be partly right—but only partly. Mike Langford's legend is similar to Davis's, and Mike carries the nickname that was once Neil's: "the Lucky One." But as is usually the case with characters in novels, Langford is a composite: mostly invented, and inspired as well by other war photographers—some of them friends, others men whom I've never met. And despite his Tasmanian origins, Langford's family background is entirely different from Davis's. So too are all his personal relationships, the crucial events of his life, and his eventual fate. All are essentially fictions.

There is one exception: although even here, I'm afraid, fiction has played fast and loose with fact. On the day after the fall of Saigon, Mike Langford waits inside the grounds of the Presidential Palace as Neil Davis did, to find himself filming the arrival of the first North Vietnamese tank through the gates. But Mike is taking still pictures, not shooting film, no real-life equivalent of Jim Feng was there at all, and the personal circumstances underlying this sequence are also fictitious.

Excerpts from six poems appear in the narrative.

The first, quoted by Aubrey Hardwick, is from *The Widow at Windsor* by Rudyard Kipling. The second, quoted by Madame

Phan, comes from *At White Deer Spring*, by the Ming poet Yüan Hung-tao. The third, quoted by Dmitri Volkov, comes from Alexander Blok's *The Twelve*. The fourth, which Jim Feng recalls, is from Arthur Waley's translation: number nine of *Seventeen Old Poems*. The fifth, given to Jim Feng by Captain Nguyen Van Danh, is *The Fish in Water*, by the Vietnamese revolutionary poet To Huu. The sixth, quoted by Aubrey Hardwick, comes from *Waiting for the Barbarians*, by C. P. Cavafy.

—C.J.K.

CONTENTS

HIGHWAYS TO A WAR

I. MISSING

The bright moon slowly, slowly rises,
The green mountains slowly, slowly descend . . .
We are low in society
in the days of our greatest health,
our pleasure comes when we are no longer young.
The Goddess of Good Luck
and the Dark Lady of Bad Luck
are with us every step we take.

YÜAN HUNG-TAO, "The Slowly, Slowly Poem,"
translated by Jonathan Chaves

ONE
A LOCKED ROOM

1.

In April 1976, my friend Michael Langford disappeared inside Cambodia. Twelve months earlier the Khmer Rouge had taken power, erasing the past and restarting the world from the beginning. We were now at the end of Year Zero.

Langford was forty years old, and at the height of his reputation as a war photographer. He'd first left Australia at the age of twenty-nine, and had spent the rest of his life in Asia. Now, it seemed, Asia had swallowed him.

The story was carried by the international media on the evening of Thursday, April 8th. I got it in advance from Rex Lockhart, who phoned me from the *Launceston Courier* in midafternoon.

"Mike Langford's missing," he said. His tone made it sound like my responsibility; but Lockhart was like that. I asked him for details, but he didn't want to give them on the phone.

"We'll be running it tomorrow morning," he said. "But I think we should discuss this tonight. Come over for dinner."

It was still light when I drove from my office to the Lockharts' place at Trevallyn. Nowhere's far, in Launceston, and it took me about ten minutes.

Climbing at low speed up the winding ascent to Longview Road, I glanced at the eastern hills: rim of the gray blue bowl that contains the town. There was snow on Mount Barrow, but it was perfect autumn weather, the air thin and still. At the end of the road, on the summit of the hill, I halted the car outside the Lockharts' brown picket fence and tile-roofed garage; but I didn't immediately get out. I wasn't deeply worried at that stage: not consciously, at any rate. Langford had dropped out of sight before and had turned up again: he was known as a survivor.

Sunset had begun, and I sat on in the car, squinting through the windscreen against the long, slanting rays. On a latitude as far south as ours they linger for a long time, transfiguring roofs, distant roads and gold slopes of grass beyond the last suburbs: a light whose counterpart I've found only in Greece. Early electric lights were coming on. Launceston touched me with its smallness, as it never fails to do.

"He's done this trick before," Diana said. "We all started writing his obituaries that time he was wounded in Vietnam, remember? He'll turn up."

Rex was delayed at the paper, and she and I sat on stools on each side of the counter in the kitchen: a refuge that we often made for while one of the Lockhart Saturday night parties thundered from the living room, since we lacked the stamina to stay with the heroic drinking and singing that went on into the small hours. The counter's top was of dark-stained Tasmanian blackwood: rather handsome, but scarred by drunken cigarettes. Diana had produced a bottle of Riesling, and I topped up our glasses. I asked her whether Rex had given her any more details about Langford than he had me.

"No," she said. "You know what Lockhart's like." She generally called him Lockhart or Locko, as his friends did. "He'll announce it all when he gets here," she said.

She sipped her wine, the dark brown hair she still wore long hanging on each side of her face. She had on a close-fitting, jade green cashmere dress she'd probably been wearing during the day: she'd only just got home from the boutique she ran in St. John Street. I was fond of Diana, as I was of Rex. She was forty-six, and looked younger; her oval face with its strong, straight nose and transparent skin had been bequeathed by the Scots ancestors quite a few of us have in Launceston. I remembered her in her early twenties, when she was one of the most beautiful girls in town: the daughter of Angus Campbell, owner of our largest department store.

"I haven't taken much interest in Cambodia," she said. "What do they call it now? Kampuchea? What's actually happening there?"

I told her what I knew of the Khmer Rouge. "But it's all just rumors," I said. "No one really knows what's going on, not even the press."

She frowned at me. "So it really wasn't sensible of Mike to go in there," she said. "Why would he do it?"

I shrugged. "The story, I suppose," I said.

I heard the back door bang, and Rex's tread in the hall. He entered the kitchen without smiling, dropping his battered satchel on a chair, and came around the counter to kiss Diana on the cheek; then he looked at me, his arm about her shoulders. "Ray," he said. "Glad you could come."

He sighted the bottle, searched out a glass, and poured himself some of the white. Diana watched him and waited; then she asked: "Has anything else come through?"

Glass in hand, Lockhart looked at her and frowned, eyes narrow, cheeks heavy with portent. He tended to create such moments of hiatus and apprehension—his moods, like those of most drinkers, being unpredictable. Now in his mid-fifties, he was a big, heavy man who still had the remnants of handsomeness, and who always held himself well. He still had a head of thick sandy hair, streaked with gray, and his mustache—a relic of his days in the RAF in World War Two—was a foxy color. He pulled up a stool, loosened his tie, took his first sip of wine, and at the same time fumbled in the inside pocket of his tweed sports coat. Finally he pulled out a sheet of paper, which he spread on the counter.

"Better read this," he said.

Diana and I read it together: it had been torn from a teleprinter.

1800 hrs.

MISSING

Reuter Bangkok, 8 April

Noted Australian-born war photographer Michael Langford has disappeared inside Cambodia: now Democratic Kampuchea. Grave fears are held for his safety.

James Feng, bureau chief for British Telenews in Bangkok, has drawn attention to Langford's disappearance.

Mr. Feng, a close friend and colleague of Langford's, has told the Australian embassy in Bangkok that he believes Langford to be a prisoner in the hands of the Khmer Rouge. According to Feng, Langford crossed the Thai-Cambodian border illegally five days ago, despite the fact that Communist Kampuchea is now closed to all foreigners.

Michael Langford achieved international fame with his daring coverage of the Indochina war, both on film and in still pictures.

Published collections of his photographs are regarded as among the best that record the Vietnam conflict, and he has won a number of important prizes for photojournalism.

"Langford must have snapped his twig to do this," Lockhart said.

"He's got out of bad situations before," I said. "He presumably knew there was a way out of this one."

Lockhart lit a cigarette and looked at me sideways, waving the match out. "One would hope so, mate, yes," he said. "But I assume you do know the situation. The country absolutely sealed. No telephones, no post, no air links except with Peking, no foreigners allowed in at all, and that means no journalists either. And mass purges going on. So what did he think he was doing, for Christ's sake?"

6

Diana's expression had now grown mildly fearful; but when she spoke it was to attempt once again to reject any serious concern. "Ray's right," she said. "Michael's always taken risks he knew how to handle. There must be a reason."

Lockhart looked back at her without expression, and their eyes continued to hold in a married way I couldn't read. To break the silence, I said: "He may have made a deal with the Khmer Rouge for safe conduct."

Lockhart turned to me, his cigarette suspended halfway to his mouth. "With the Khmer Rouge?" he said. "I'm sorry, Ray. How much do you know about them? No one makes deals with the Khmer Rouge: not even Langford."

There was a brutal note in his voice that puzzled me. Lockhart had been deeply fond of Mike in the old days, to the point of sentimentality; yet the only hint of emotion I could detect in him now was repressed anger. Perhaps it was the only one he trusted himself to release. He needed his veneer; he was a man of too many feelings, underneath.

There was nothing about Langford on the seven o'clock ABS newscast on television, which we watched before dinner. Afterwards we sat over coffee and brandy in the living room, waiting for the second newscast, at nine o'clock.

The Lockharts' house always seemed to me to smell of the 1930s. One of those chiming clocks from the period sat in the center of the mantelpiece, its bow-shaped wooden case matching the dark timber trimmings in the room. Above it hung a black-and-white photograph of Lockhart's wartime Lancaster in flight, and next to the clock were more framed photographs: a portrait of Diana, a studio picture of their two daughters as children, and a snapshot of three young journalists—the young Lockhart one of them—standing outside a hotel in Singapore. After being demobbed from the RAF, Lockhart had become a foreign correspondent, working both in Europe and in Asia, and I'd never understood why he'd come home in his mid-thirties to bury himself as news editor on our modest local daily.

The clock now showed eight forty-five; we'd been sitting in silence for some time. Lockhart looked across at me from his armchair.

"You're his oldest friend, really," he said. "Isn't that right? And he used to say that you were his solicitor."

"Yes. But I've never acted for him," I said. "He wasn't the sort of man who has legal problems. He never even owned a house, as far as I know."

"Did he leave a will?"

"Not with me."

"Oh, for God's *sake!*" Diana was sitting stiffly upright, staring at us with what looked like anger. "Will you stop talking as though he's dead," she said. She seemed frozen, one hand spread stiffly on the arm of the chair, the other holding her brandy suspended in front of her.

"I'm sorry, Di." Lockhart's voice dropped so that it could only just be heard. "But the possibility does exist. You do see that."

He drained his brandy, and lit a cigarette; then he looked at me again. "Unless definite news about him breaks tomorrow, I suspect Foreign Affairs in Canberra will get in touch with his relatives," he said. "And maybe with you too, Raymond, if Mike's left instructions that way."

The clock began chiming nine. Lockhart got up immediately and moved across to the television set in a corner of the room: a newsreader in thick-framed glasses looked at us from his studio desk in Sydney. He ran through the headlines.

"In the United States primaries, Democrat Jimmy Carter has retained his front-runner status. Howard Hughes has left a fortune of two thousand million dollars. The whole Government of Democratic Kampuchea resigned yesterday, and will be replaced by appointees of the new National Assembly of workers, peasants and soldiers. And we bring you a story on the disappearance inside Kampuchea of Australian war photographer Michael Langford . . ."

We watched in silence as the first two items were dealt with. When the item on Langford came up, the announcer adopted the grave expression usually worn when dealing with a death, and went through much the same detail as we had in the Reuters report. It quickly became apparent that there was no new information—but this report was somewhat fuller.

"According to his friend James Feng, Mr. Langford entered Cambodia illegally five days ago, giving no explanation for his action, but saying that he would be back within twenty-four hours. If he was not, Langford said, he could be assumed to have been detained by the Communist authorities."

A blow-up color photograph of Langford had been projected behind the newsreader's desk, and we stared at it as though at a piece of magic. Out of the corner of my eye, I saw that Diana had clasped her hands in her lap, her face reflecting the light from the screen. Langford looked nearer to twenty-eight than forty, I thought—unless you took in a subtle hardening about the eyes. Otherwise the looks of his youth were unmarred, the blond hair a young man's.

He already looks dead, I thought.

Instantly, I tried to dismiss the thought; to disbelieve it. But it did seem to me that Mike's face had the final, fixed, historic quality of the dead. The newsreader continued, and the picture of Langford disappeared, to be replaced by film clips of black-clad Khmer Rouge soldiers with automatic rifles, marching through paddy fields and villages.

"Violent purges within the country are reported to be continuing, and any Western journalist apprehended entering the country could expect immediate arrest and detention. However, Australian embassy officials in Bangkok have received no report of Langford's arrest. Enquiries concerning his whereabouts directed to the Government of Democratic Kampuchea have received no response, and the embassy is treating his disappearance as serious.

"Michael Langford began as a news cinecameraman for the Australian Broadcasting Service and British Telenews, covering the Vietnam War. Later he specialized in war photography for magazines such as Life, Time, *and* Newsweek, *winning a number of awards. He has been described as one of the best war photographers of his generation."*

The item ended; another began; Lockhart got up and switched

off the set. He turned, standing in front of it with his hands behind his back, contemplating us both. His mustache twitched; he cleared his throat, but said nothing.

Diana was frowning at the gray, extinct television screen, her hands still locked in her lap; she seemed to expect some further image to spring into life there that would change what had gone before. Then she drew in a breath, and shook her head. "No. Not Mike. He'll be all right," she said. Her tone was matter-of-fact. "If he wasn't, I'd know," she said.

"Would you, Di? Yes, I suppose you would." Lockhart surveyed her with an expression that resembled sympathy; but something in his face made me uncomfortable, and wish to draw his attention away from her.

"There must still be a reasonable chance," I said. "Surely."

He looked at me quickly. "A chance? There's always a chance, mate. But it's as simple as this, I'm afraid: he'd have to have high-level contacts with the Khmer Rouge to survive there for five minutes. And since they're said to arrest anyone with Western connections, that seems a bit unlikely, doesn't it? So we have to hope he didn't fall into Khmer Rouge hands. Because if he did, he's now in prison, or dead."

"Michael's not dead," Diana said.

"I hope you're right," Lockhart said. "But I was trained to take facts into account."

Diana stood up. "Bugger your facts," she said. Her tone remained calm, but her face had grown paler than usual. "Excuse me," she said, and walked out of the room.

Lockhart was still standing in front of the TV set, eyebrows raised. "She's a bit emotional," he said to me.

"I should be going," I said. "Mike survived for so long—I don't want to believe this either, Locko. Will you let me know if you hear anything?"

"Hang on a moment, Raymond: don't rush off," he said. "I'll see that Di's all right."

Left alone in the living room, I sat in my armchair and studied the picture of the Lancaster, and the group outside the hotel in Singapore. The clock ticked loudly.

I sat for a considerable time, hearing the distant murmur of their voices, probably from a bedroom. They weren't raised; their tone seemed even; muffled. Eventually the voices stopped, and I heard the bang of the back door.

I lost patience, and went out through the dim, carpeted hall with its dark-stained timber paneling and framed colonial prints. One or both of the Lockharts had gone into the garden; the situation was growing awkward, and I intended to find whoever was there and take my leave.

The house at the back looked out across the Tamar to the ranges in the east: I could make out their black outlines against gray and mauve sky. There was still no wind, stars were out, and the air now was cold and astringent. I made my way across the unmown lawn, tripping over a barrow in the darkness. There was a low back gate in the jasmine-covered paling fence at the bottom of the garden, and I made for that.

He was here, a dim figure in a white shirt, leaning on the gate, smoking. I came up and stood next to him, but he gave no sign of knowing I was here. He must have been cold without his jacket, but he didn't show it. Below us were wide, distant vacancies and lights: those of the town, and the channel beacons out in the Tamar, casting blurred reflections. When Lockhart spoke, he kept his face in profile.

"The funny thing is, Raymond, that they fooled me so well for so long. Really quite amusing, mate. It's always been a subject for jokes."

"I didn't know," I said.

"No," he said. "Nobody knew. *I* didn't know. But that's not quite true, of course. I knew and didn't want to know. When I found out for certain, he'd gone. And now he's gone again, hasn't he? The ultimate departure."

"You really think he's dead," I said.

"Of course he's bloody dead, short of a miracle." He removed the cigarette from his mouth and swung around on me suddenly, presenting me with a face the color of porridge. His eyes were red-rimmed, and I stiffened; I'd never seen Lockhart weep. "Now he can *really* be a hero and a saint," he said. "And what a lot of people will make him into one, won't they?"

"When did it start?" I asked.

"When?" He turned back to his contemplation of the dark, drawing once on his cigarette before flicking it away, its spark briefly joining the other lights. "That's where they were so romantic, Raymond: it apparently *didn't* start."

"Then I don't understand," I said.

"The three of us were always together, when Mike was on the *Courier*," he said. "All those years. I used to be pleased he was so fond of Diana. And he had no shortage of women, did he? Football stars are well supplied with female groupies. Then he got the job in Melbourne, and that was that."

"Well then, Locko," I said. "Where's the harm?"

He had placed both hands on the gate, and spoke to the darkness. "No great harm," he said. "Especially if you're the sort who believes what he wants to believe. But three years later, he came back on holiday. He'd resigned from the *Age,* remember? A month later, he was in Singapore."

"Yes," I said. "I remember that visit. I got in a lunch with him—that was all. That was the last time I ever saw him. God, Rex, it's nearly eleven years ago."

"I didn't have a meeting at all," Lockhart said. "I remember being disappointed by that—even hurt." He gave a laugh like a cough; he was attempting his tone of irony, but the jerkiness of pain had taken over. "Had to come home in the lunch hour one day. Diana was here; she hadn't gone in to the shop, I forget why. I went into the kitchen and there was a cigarette smoking in an ashtray: still alight." He stopped; then went on. "Di's never smoked. I asked her whose it was, and she said Mike had just called and had gone a few minutes ago. Still he didn't contact me, after that; I didn't see him again. I kept seeing his cigarette in the ashtray; it came back into my mind years later. Still smoking. He'd dwindled to a cigarette, you might say."

"You could be wrong," I said.

But he ignored this. "I was so bloody fond of him," he said. "That's the joke of it. But I never really knew him, I realize that now. Kind; generous: do anything for a mate. That's the Langford legend, isn't it? It's bullshit. It's what he wanted people to believe: he spent a lot of time working on that image. None of us knew him—and now we never will."

"It's such a long time ago, Locko."

This was the best I could do, and I knew it wasn't much. I began, shamefully, to want to escape.

"Wrong, Raymond. Nothing like that's a long time ago." He sounded as though he were being deprived of breath. "I still feel used," he said.

2.

The package from Bangkok reached me in the week following the dinner with the Lockharts. I postponed examining its contents until nearly midnight, on the day it came. Then I sat in my study with everything spread out in front of me, in the light of the desk lamp.

After a time, the air through the half-open window began to chill the room. I got up to close it, and a faint, almost imaginary hum of traffic drifted up out of the valley. The sharp hoot of a train came from the railway yards a mile away: icy across icy spaces. There was a fog that hadn't risen as high as the ridge of West Launceston: the town was invisible, under a quilted white lid. I came back to the desk, switched off the lamp and put on the cassette tape again, sitting in the dark.

There was a large collection of other tapes, and I'd only had time to sample a few. This one had been addressed to me as a letter: something Mike had often done, over the years. It was now the third time I'd listened to it. There was a faint hiss as it revolved in the Japanese cassette player. I watched the spindles turning, unraveling this brittle clew that stretched between death and life.

—Tape recorded in Bangkok on April Fools' Day, 1976.

When the quiet voice suddenly spoke, it was as though Mike had materialized in the dark. The recording was of high quality.

His calm country drawl was still intact, but with a bland overlay: a journalist's voice.

—Hello, mate. It's been a fair time since I sent you a letter or a tape; things have been busy. I've got a few important things to say. Important to me, that is.

A pause followed: the yawn of an eternal absence.

—Ray: I'm going to do something a bit tricky in a few days' time. I'm going over into Cambodia without permission. I should be out again within forty-eight hours: that is, by the fifth. But I reckon you know the current situation in Cambodia: not exactly a place you slip in and out of with no worries. I want you to do me a favor: I want you to be my executor, if I don't get back. If you're listening to this tape, that'll probably be the situation: I won't have made it. In which case, unless I'm merely in a lockup, this is a fond goodbye.

Another pause; then a small, matter-of-fact, throat-clearing noise. The faintly humorous delivery hadn't changed; it gave no indication that his "fond good-bye" was something he took seriously. I reached for the button; then leaned back instead. I was compelled to listen to everything again.

—I'm asking Jim Feng to send these personal things on to you if I don't get back by the tenth. He'd have to assume then that I haven't made it. Jim's now bureau chief for British Telenews here in Bangkok, and is one of my oldest mates: we've been through a lot together. I hope you'll meet him someday. He'll get the package to the Australian embassy, and they'll send it in the diplomatic bag to Foreign Affairs in Canberra, who'll send it on to you.

—I've made a will, and a copy's included in the package. I don't have much to leave. What's important are my cassette tapes, papers and photographs. I want you to have sole responsibility for them, and to deal with them as you think best. There are unpublished photographs that might be worth another book—my publishers will possibly be interested.

—I was never too keen on writing things down, as you know—that's why I've generally sent you tapes instead of letters—and over the years, I've kept a diary on tape. I sometimes think of writing up some memoirs from them, now that the war's over. I hope of course that you'll never get to listen to them—no one ever has—but if you do, they may be of interest. You always were fond of history.

Another pause.

—I've written to my brother Marcus. If I don't come back, he's to give you some family heirlooms I was going to inherit. Marcus and Cliff couldn't care less about the stuff; it's earmarked for me, and they're happy for you to have it. You'd have to go down to the farm to collect it: that should stir up some boyhood memories, mate. We had some good times, didn't we? When I wasn't shooting at you, that is. So long, Ray.

I punched the tape off. Spooled back.

—. . . hope of course that you'll never get to listen to them—no one ever has—but if you do, they may be of interest. You always were fond of history.

There was a touch of gently mocking amusement in the voice, at this point. At my expense? At his own? I switched off the machine, and sat back.

It's true I'm fond of history: it's an amateur interest that's grown. The book I published some years ago on Launceston's first years of settlement was well received in academic circles, and in the national press. Since then, and since my divorce, I've given more and more of my private time to researching the history of colonial Tasmania. Roy Wilson, my partner in our legal practice, is tolerant of this; he thinks it makes me an expert on early buildings, and thus on property values in Launceston's central business district.

I fell in love with my native place in my mid-twenties. Before that (like Mike Langford, and like so many others here), I wanted to leave the island. But after the usual pilgrimage to Europe, I came to realize that for me this would only mean unrest; and except for odd trips interstate and overseas, I seldom leave Tasmania or the town. People from elsewhere say it's a place where nothing happens. I say a hundred and fifty years have happened; but there's a sense in which they're right. Battles, revolutions, concentration camps, bombing raids and the many other consequences of history are far off in another hemisphere; the town remains untouched, dozing among its hills.

This is the sanctuary that Michael Langford long ago left behind. He was the one who got away.

3.

Diana put her coffee cup down, staring through the plate-glass window of Quigley's coffee shop into the Quadrant: the crescent at the center of town. The leaves of the birches were turning yellow, and lay scattered under the feet of midafternoon shoppers.

"If he'd ever have come back here in all these years, it wouldn't be so bad," she said. "But we all get old, Ray, and he doesn't. And now he's disappeared. Why does he have to be so bloody haunting?"

She attempted a smile, head tilted back, long-sighted eyes drained of most of their blue by the afternoon light. When she was happy, they held the mild flirtatiousness that was part of the armory of women of her generation, alternating with a humorous, analytical glint. The analytical glint was there now, oddly mixed with her distress. Her well-cut tweed suit was stiffly protective, and she'd applied her lipstick with unusual emphasis.

"I'm sorry about the other night, Ray," she said. "And sorry to have dragged you from your office. But I had to; I need to talk about him, and there's no one else I can talk to. Yes, I know: it's pointless. Especially since he's stopped being real." Then, unconsciously echoing Lockhart, she said: "Mike never was quite real."

I decided to be blunt. "You never thought of leaving Rex, back then?"

She shook her head. "No. But never love a drinker, Ray: the rages, the illness, the persecution mania. Have you ever wondered why a journalist as good as Lockhart was would come back here? Why we came back from Southeast Asia, all those years ago? We

16

were never supposed to come back. But after five years, the grog thing got out of hand. There I was in Singapore with two small daughters, and he'd disappear for a week at a time. I'd know he could be anywhere, from Kuala Lumpur to Hong Kong—but always in a bar. And eventually his paper fired him, and we came back home. He can manage, on that stupid little rag. It's easy being news editor here; people cover for him. And he's tapered off, in the last few years."

She looked away through the window, following the progress of a tow-haired young mother pushing a child in a stroller. She'd never spoken in this way before; never before uttered a serious criticism of Lockhart to me. Diana was reticent. But as is often the case with the reticent, once she'd started talking it led her deeper.

"Sometimes I think it might have been better if he'd been shot down in one of his raids over the Ruhr," she said. "That's when his life really ended."

"You don't mean that," I said; but she looked at me without remorse, her eyes fixed, both hands gripping her cup.

"He was a beautiful man, when I met him," she said. "He seemed to have the world in front of him as a journalist. I didn't understand then what the War had done to him. He'd enlisted when he was twenty in the RAAF; a year later he was in the RAF in England: a flight lieutenant at twenty-one, bombing Germany. He survived a lot of raids—and so many of them didn't. Just boys. And the terrible thing is, Ray, part of him liked it. He didn't say so, but it's true. He never really had a life he wanted after that. Journalism wasn't enough. Something stopped in him like a clock, in the War."

As she spoke, I was remembering the Lockhart of twenty years ago, when Mike Langford first started on the *Courier*. In the lounge bar of the Colonel Paterson Hotel on a Saturday night, Lockhart had presided, seated in his usual place, surrounded by a respectful circle of young reporters and photographers—Mike among them. In a town like ours, an ex–foreign correspondent was almost unknown, and had a film star glamour: the glamour of the outside world. Lockhart had many anecdotes to tell concerning his coverage during the fifties: the Korean War; the French struggle in Vietnam; the Communist insurgency in Malaya and Singapore. He was always in charge of the evening, and Mike became his most constant drinking companion.

As though hearing my thoughts, Diana said: "I wish you could understand how it was, Ray, when Mike first came to Launceston. Full of a farm boy's dreams of the world: he was appealing, and Rex got very fond of him. Maybe he saw himself in Mike, before he stuffed up everything. We had Mike home for meals all the time, and Mike was always bringing gifts. He wanted to work abroad like Lockhart; he truly admired him. But he didn't go away for a long time: six years. He enjoyed his life here: playing his club football; having his nights out with Lockhart and the rest of our crowd. But mainly he didn't go because of me."

I signaled for two more coffees.

"He'd been badly hurt," she said. "He'd lost that girl he wanted to marry. The pickers' daughter on his father's farm: I don't remember her name. I never knew what really happened, and Mike wouldn't talk about it. She just disappeared, didn't she?"

"Yes," I said. "She just disappeared."

She stirred her fresh coffee, looking into the cup. "Mike and I were in love but we didn't become lovers," she said. "At least, not until the end. He had his girlfriends—I told him to, because I'd never leave Rex and the girls. But his affairs never seemed to come to anything. All three of us were friends: Rex was like a father, and I pretended I was like a mother." She smiled. "Who did I think I was fooling? Mike was twenty-one when he first started on the *Courier,* and I was only twenty-seven. A lot younger than Rex, and I was starting to feel it. Mike and I would mostly see each other on Saturday nights in the Colonel Paterson, as part of a crowd. And afterwards the party at our place: you remember. My God, Ray, those nights in the Colonel! Like a dream repeating itself. Well, Mike escaped, in the end. From the lounge bar of the Colonel; from Launceston; from this bloody little island."

She'd been picking at the varnish on a nail, her face bitter; now she looked up and attempted a smile.

"I always knew I'd lose him, naturally. He kept inventing ways it would work out for us, without hurting Rex or the girls: ways that I'd come away with him. I could go on loving him knowing it would eventually be taken away; but he couldn't deal with that: he wanted to believe it wasn't true.

"We were alone together only once, on the day after he got the news of the job on the *Age* in Melbourne. He persuaded me to come on a day trip with him in his car—down south, to Clare. Lockhart never knew. Mike hadn't visited the farm since he left it for good. He wouldn't call in, because his father was still alive, then. He really hated his father, did you know? The only person I believe he ever did hate.

"So he parked the car a mile down the road, and took me up through the bush onto the top of one of those tall hills. He wanted to show me his home, he said. He loved that valley—but he didn't love the farm or that tedious old house. He told me once that the past used to get into his dreams at night there: bits of some life a hundred years ago that he didn't want to know about. Clare was that sort of place, I suppose.

"It was a beautiful spring day. We sat in the grass on top of the hill, and we could look down on the property and on those green hop fields. The wattle was out, and the peach and pear blossom; it was all quiet, the valley, but alive, with a wonderful humming. We both knew we were saying goodbye; he knew it too. The difference was that I could say it. But he went on playing his game; he couldn't bear not to, although we both knew that was what he was doing. After a year or two, he said, when he'd got some metropolitan experience and was ready to try his luck abroad, he'd come back and get me. I told him again that I couldn't leave Rex, however much I wanted to, but he just smiled.

"Mike was old-fashioned, don't you think? Growing up on that farm out there, it was as though he'd grown up in the last century. Even the books he'd read. A lonely kid, his brothers already grown up, getting a lot of things from books. He talked about a sentimental story of Kipling's: I forget the name of it. He saw us as lovers in that story. Well, I'll bet he's changed a bit these days: he's a tough nut, from what one hears. And he never married. What was it about him, Ray? There was something in him you could never know: something far away in him that made you at peace."

She looked past me, out the window. It was after five o'clock now, and the shadows were long in the Quadrant.

"He left for Melbourne the next week," she said. "And he phoned me regularly at the shop for the next eighteen months. Then, one January, he suddenly arrived in Launceston. We met twice, alone. But only to talk: once at the house during the day, when Rex nearly caught us; once in town when we said goodbye.

"He'd quit the *Age,* he said; he had references to papers in London, and he was going there to try his luck. He wanted me to come with him, just like that; to finally cut the rope and join him. He was going in a week. And of course I couldn't, and he knew I couldn't: it was still the game."

She looked back at me, her face empty. "I'd better stop talking. I'm sorry, Ray."

"Don't be," I said.

"That's all gone," she said. "But you have to *find* him. That's why I wanted to see you."

"Find him?"

"You could go up to Bangkok. Talk to the Australian embassy people; the journalists. No one's *doing* anything."

She wanted to believe he was alive. Her eyes had regained their color, in the fading light: young eyes in her middle-aged face, looking at me with the hunger of hope.

4.

I'd reached the Derwent Valley, and the hop fields had begun. The narrow, winding side road to Clare was two miles out from the township of New Norfolk; the white signpost was still here, and I took the turn.

Mike Langford belonged to this southern zone of the island, with its towering hills, extinct volcanic peaks and Roaring Forties winds. I belong to the north: to open, pastoral distances and kinder weather. The north-south difference is as real here as in other regions of the world, and our two small cities have been locked in rivalry since the island's name was Van Diemen's Land. But here the difference stands on its head. Southern Hobart, the capital, once the center of the nineteenth-century penal administration that continues to frown in our collective memory, is the last city before Antarctica, its spirit cold and forbidding. Northern Launceston, founded as an innocent market town, is more light-hearted: closer to the continent, looking to the warmer latitudes across Bass Strait. So when Mike came north as a boy, he was making his first move towards the world beyond the island: I imagine he heard it throbbing on the breeze.

It was late afternoon. Getting down to the south had been only a matter of two hours or so, on today's highways. It used to be a day trip: the island has shrunk, since my childhood. But the side road taking me into the long corridor of the valleys hadn't changed: it was still unpaved, throwing up white dust, and it was taking me back thirty-odd years.

I'd forgotten the height of these hills. Enclosing, steep, almost overwhelming, they rose above the road on my left and right: bush-covered, dark olive, glowing in patches with dreaming sienna tints in the last hour of sun. The grass beside a small weatherboard farmhouse sitting on a knoll was dark green as grass in a storybook Northern Hemisphere, and scattered with yellow wildflowers; black Angus cattle grazed, but there was no other sign of life. The valleys still felt remote, and utterly self-sufficient: intimate, claustrophobic, brooding, shut in forever by their beautiful but jealous hills. Not an easy place in which to hide anything; not an easy place to escape. Of all the Langfords, only Mike did.

Here were the upright golden flames of the poplars lining the road, and the willows yellowing down by the creek. Here were the hop fields, and elms and pines and cedars: the country of early settlement, rich and Europeanized. Driving over the white wooden bridge that led to the farm, I found I was nursing an odd, melancholy excitement. I swung the Mazda to a halt in front of the gate, and the white dust billowed up the way it used to do in front of my father's old Buick. In the field on the other side of the road, the stripped wires and poles, bare of hops, were like ruined structures in a war zone, and I wondered why it all looked so desolate.

Then I realized that it was always summer when I came down here as a boy, and that time was constantly rerun. The English oak trees in the drive were always out in leaf, and powdered with the road's white dust, like the roadside poplars. The ancient, baby voices of crows complained always in the heat, and white cabbage butterflies were jerked as though on strings above the bush grass and wildflowers.

The last time I was here was in the summer of 1952, when Michael Langford and I were sixteen years old. There were six summer holidays before that: the first when he and I were ten, at the end of the Second World War. The holidays were a return of hospitality, in a way. Because old John Langford had gone to boarding school in Launceston, he'd insisted on sending his sons up there as well, instead of educating them in Hobart; Mike and I became friends at school, and I often had him to stay at my parents' house on weekends. But another reason the Langfords asked me to the farm, I suspect, was that Mike's three brothers were grown up, and his parents wanted him to have company of his own age out here: a surrogate brother. Surrogate brothers was what we became—to my benefit more than his, as I had no brothers of my own—and we were probably closer, since siblings tend to fight, and we never did.

There were only two Langfords left now: Cliff and Marcus. Old John Langford and his wife, Ingrid, had been dead for years. The gate of the property was still the same color: dried blood. The board was still fixed to the top rail, with the name *Clare* cut into it, picked out in black paint. It was one of the oldest hop farms in the Derwent Valley, and this minor valley took its name from it. It had been in the Langford family for over a hundred years, and I recalled Mike telling me it used convict labor, in the early days. But no one could ever tell me why the property was called Clare. Mike had the notion that this might have been the name of one of the pioneer women in the family; but I think he just made that up to satisfy my curiosity. History never much interested him.

The house too looked unchanged. It was rambling, single-storied, and built of the ochre bricks that we know in Tasmania as "convict bricks," since they were handmade by the early felons; it stood on a low rise about thirty yards from the road, its red-painted iron roof and tall chimneys half hidden by cedars and the line of oaks in the drive. The cedars, with which most of the early settlers screened their farmhouses, darkened Clare's front rooms, I remembered, and added to an air of somber secrecy there. An odd, still atmosphere always hung about the place: a heaviness which I wasn't able to fathom.

Perhaps it had something to do with the fact that the house was full of forbidden zones—most of them laid out by John Langford. I discovered this almost immediately, on my first, ten-year-old visit. One of these zones was the hop kiln.

Come and see the hop kiln, Mike said.

We crossed the farmyard from the house to approach a six-sided, medieval-looking tower of convict brick. I'd never seen a building quite like it. The steeple was of gray wooden shingles, topped by a structure like a dovecote, also six-sided, with wooden vents in it. The tower had only two small windows in each of the six sections, high up and low down, and was connected to a barnlike building, also built of the ochre brick. At ground level, in the tower, a series of big fireplaces led into tunnels: unlit, with old coal dust in them. I followed Mike inside.

He led the way into the tower and up a steep wooden stairway to the upper story, and we emerged into a deserted chamber with a floor of sacking, filled with a single, overwhelming smell. It was sharp and piercingly pungent: half sweet, half sour; half enticing, half forbidding. When I exclaimed at it, Mike raised his high-arched brows in polite surprise.

That's from the hops, he said.

I asked him what the fireplaces were for, and he looked at me with an expression of sleepy amusement; he had heavy white eyelids. They're from the old days. They used to roast convicts in them, he said.

I stared, not knowing whether to believe him or not. He winked, and I knew I'd been fooled. I would come to recognize this wink, which I'd find all the Langford brothers employed: a country wink, to be used on townies like me. Then he smiled; but his smile was without mockery or malice. No, he said, just bullshitting. This is where they dry the hops. He spoke softly, as though any loudness here would call down trouble. We're not really supposed to come up here, he said. But I thought you'd like to see it.

He wore old khaki overalls, and his yellow hair was shaggy and long for the holidays; yet he somehow appeared cleaner than other people. His eyes were wide-set, and his long face was fair-skinned: seen from certain angles it had an almost feminine prettiness. But this impression would vanish when you looked at him again, to be replaced by ordinary, even hard good looks, and his full lower lip projected in a way that warned you to be careful. I found his face chimerical, its different aspects blending and separating and blending again. It was a little the same with his character. Unlike most ten-year-old boys, Mike Langford was always kindly, I'd find, with a sameness that was not monotonous; and his voice was always quiet and even. We'd confide, as we got to know each other; and yet I'd always feel that he kept things back; that he could never quite be known. Secrecy infected that whole household; it permeated the farm like the hop smell; it was in Mike's bloodstream.

I stared about the large, dim loft with its small windows. The ceiling was of steeply sloping planks and beams, and the floor's woven horsehair sacking was stretched across slats, on which a few pale brown pods lay scattered. Baskets and antique-looking wooden rakes stood about; a small door led into another bare room, where a large iron press stood. It was very dry and quiet here, and uncomfortably warm. It seemed like a strange church. Streaks and shafts of sun leaked through the windows, and lay like syrup on the sacking.

And a queer feeling came over me. The whole world outside

was shut out, and the invisible afternoon was going on without us. We were cut off from the farm, and from the whole softly murmuring country; we even seemed to be cut off from today altogether, and to be nowhere. I began to have a sense of being stifled, as though we were sealed in a box, and of trespassing on something invisible; something very old and sad, hanging like the smell of last year's hops in the big, warm quiet.

As though reading my thoughts, Mike said: We'd better go down now, Ray.

When we came out into the simple glare and warmth of the farmyard, where a big old ash tree gave shade, and hens pecked and drawled in the gray dust, it was as though we'd escaped from something; and we smiled at each other to signal that we knew it. But nothing was said.

The forbidden zones at Clare came to seem natural.

Like many nineteenth-century farmhouses in Tasmania, it contained two distinct regions: two spirits. What was forbidden mostly lay in the first region. This was the territory of the floor-oil-smelling entrance hall, of the bedrooms, and of the sitting room. That dim, formal chamber, with its drawn, floor-length red curtains and nineteenth-century cedar furniture, was like an empty stage set, waiting for some momentous action to begin. No action ever did; and Mike and I were not encouraged to go in there.

This was still a time of chamber pots under beds; of marble-topped washstands in bedrooms, on which stood china jugs and basins, decorated with the last century's sentimental roses. There was electric light at Clare, but not in all the rooms: the sleepout at the end of the front verandah, which Mike and I shared, was lit by candles. There was no sewerage: a gray weatherboard lavatory Mike called *the dunny* stood in a small glade of plum trees at the side of the house. The rambling roses climbing over its roof could not disguise the dunny's profoundly serious stench—which came, in my mind, not just from the shit of the present but from somewhere in the dark old century that had gone.

The second region of the house was at the back, and was utterly opposite to the first. This was the true farmhouse, where life was lived: a territory full of good cheer, based on the kitchen and on the long back verandah with its posts of rough, undressed cyprus and its jumble of old hats, milk cans, dogs and mewing kittens. The big, hall-shaped kitchen, dominated by a long pine table at which nearly all meals took place, had a black, wood-burning stove at the far end that never went out. This was the house's center of power and warmth, controlled by Mike's mother, Ingrid Langford. Mike's father and his three brothers walked through constantly, with a bang of the screen door that led onto the verandah.

Marcus was the eldest brother; then came Ken, then Cliff. They were all in their twenties: men, in my eyes. Marcus was usually silent: a stocky man with flat black hair and a private smile. Ken and Cliff were fair-haired, friendly, and talked a lot. At tea with them all in the kitchen on my first night there, I learned about another of the house's prohibited zones.

John Langford, at the head of the table, cleared his throat.

I don't know whether Michael's told you this, Raymond—but you're not to go near the pickers' huts, he said. Some of those people are pretty rough. They're here to work, not to be made friends with.

He had a soft, precise voice that made everything he said sound official, and he was shorter than his three grown sons; but he appeared big because of his powerful shoulders and upright posture. The sleeves of his clean khaki shirt were rolled above the elbows, and his tanned forearms, planted on the table, were heavily muscled from hard work. But the head was scholarly: large, bald and tanned, with a few strands of darkish hair, oiled and slicked back, a narrow nose and a very thin mouth. He wore sinister rimless spectacles, and had the potential to become frightening.

Across the table, Ken looked at me and winked, swallowing his glass of hop beer. Big and lean, with his father's long, narrow nose and with thick, lank hair the color of rancid butter, he sat very straight, and his eyes had an amused gleam. He'd just come back from the war in New Guinea, which he'd volunteered for, while his brothers had stayed on the farm. He worked about the place now in the green Army trousers he'd worn for jungle fighting, and his broad-brimmed AIF Digger hat with the badge removed—getting some wear out of them, he said. He'd been decorated for bravery on the Kokoda Trail, and Mike admired him uncritically; if there was anyone on whom he modeled himself, it was Ken.

Better do as Dad says, young Ray, Ken told me. And another thing. When you go out in the bush, there's a funny-looking critter you might find wandering about. Whatever you do, keep away from it, because it's dangerous, and no good to anyone. It's called a Politician.

Cliff, smaller and curly-haired, seated next to Ken, gave a snort of laughter. That's right, son, he said. Steer clear of it. It'll tell you a whole lot of lies.

I was puzzled; I'd never heard of a Politician. But then Ken gave me the wink.

Don't tease the boy, Cliff. He'll never go out in the bush, if he listens to you.

Ingrid Langford's voice was deep and slow; she spoke seldom, but when she did, all the men listened. Her lips were pursed now, as she surveyed her sons, and she wasn't smiling; but then I saw a gleam in her eyes that I guessed to be amusement.

She was a tall, big-boned woman whose straight blond hair was faded, and tinged with gray. Her firm jaw slanted sideways, and her large, deep-set eyes seemed often to be staring at something in the distance. Before her marriage to John Langford, she'd been an Olsen, from Moogara: one of a clan of Norwegian-descended timber-getters famous throughout the island. Many of them were champion axemen: her father and then her brothers had won Australian wood-chopping titles at the Sydney Show for many years running. Ingrid Langford herself would split wood for the kitchen stove like a man, wielding the axe at the wood-heap by the barn with cold precision. She was up at six each morning to milk a small herd of cows that seemed to be her responsibility, and she kept a large number of fowls that ran free about the yard: the usual mixture of black Orpingtons, white Leg-horns and bantams. She gave them names, and when I've remem-bered her over the years I've usually seen her standing in the yard in one of her faded, short-sleeved print dresses, serious and mon-umental as a Viking matron, scattering wheat to her hens from a battered tin saucepan. While Mike and I watched, she would frown judiciously, distributing the wheat with long sweeps of her serious white arms, the feathered crowd jostling hysterically about her feet.

Come along, ladies. Don't push. You'll all get your turn.

Mike was far-eyed Mrs. Langford's chick: her youngest, the baby of the family, for whom she had a special fondness. She seldom demonstrated feeling of any kind; but once, as we watched her feed the hens, she put her hand briefly on Mike's head, not looking at him, before reaching into the pot again; and I saw in his quick upward glance a complete and serene admiration.

When we were fifteen, we were always hanging about the hop fields. Whenever we were free from our chores on the farm, Mike's feet would lead us in that direction. For a time, I won-dered why.

We weren't allowed to do any picking: that was the job of the skilled tribe of strangers with whom we were forbidden to fraternize. But in the hop fields, we could observe them at work without opposition from Mr. Langford. They seemed to be of growing interest to Mike, in that year.

The hop fields were like nowhere else. Leaving the summer blaze outside, Mike and I wandered through infinite, ordered glades of deep cool, as though under water. It was another climate here, and a differently colored world, where the pungent, beer-like smell I'd first met in the kiln was all around us. No green in the olive and tawny-colored countryside around New Norfolk was like that of the hops, which was the green of another hemi-sphere, brought here and planted by Langfords of long ago. Mov-ing down the aisles of rustic poles, under the strict, strange wires, Mike and I were walled in by green and roofed over by green:

the very light was green, the glades like the emerald-glowing church of an unknown sect.

Far off, at the end of one of the rows, in the hard, unpitying sun of day, old John Langford presided like a king, attended by Ken. Cliff drove a four-wheeled cart pulled by two draft horses called Duke and Prince, taking away load after load up to the kiln; and in among the glades, the quiet brother Marcus moved, in his gray felt hat and dark blue shirt.

Marcus, like his father, never quite looked like a farmer to me, as Ken and Cliff did. There was something almost monk-like about him: a sort of saturnine refinement and inwardness. He supervised the pickers like a high official, carrying a long, medieval-looking pole with a sickle on the end. This was for pulling down the hopbines from the wires; and it was Marcus who supervised the weighing of the hops from the pickers' bins on a set of scales, recording the names and bin numbers. He was followed by two acolytes: young hired men in overalls and straw hats, who loaded the bags onto the scales. When the hops were weighed, dirty picking was sometimes found out: stones and other rubbish would appear, with which dishonest pickers weighted their sacks. None of this escaped Marcus, who rummaged sternly in the piles. The pickers would go quiet then, giving him quick glances; sometimes one of them would argue, but mostly they were good-humored. There was no use their arguing with Marcus; a dark glance or a frown would still them.

The pickers came every summer when the hops were ripe: families of itinerant workers who moved about the island like gypsies. They arrived in crazy, battered cars on whose roofs swayed bursting suitcases and kitchen utensils, and they took up residence in a row of weatherboard huts on the south side of the property, on a dry, grassy slope near the dam. The huts were little more than sheds, with no glass in the windows; but the pickers seemed satisfied with them. They had no fixed homes, Mike told me; they trapped rabbits, and picked different crops in season, doing whatever they could find. Their children hardly ever went to school, and the authorities seldom caught up with them, since the pickers were always moving on.

Wish I could go with them, Mike would say.

He was fascinated by the pickers, and would ignore his father's prohibition: we'd often walk by their huts in the evening, enjoying the thrill of the forbidden. Kerosene lanterns would glow from the doorways and windows; men would stand outside smoking; women would gossip in groups; wild children would play and shout. They all looked at first glance like other people, but little touches gave them away: a strange dark blue cap like a seaman's; a scarf knotted at the throat in a way we'd never seen before; women in strange hats of felt and straw, like those in old pictures; small girls in their mothers' dresses, with ragged hems trailing the ground.

Lately, Mike had kept leading us past a particular hut, where I always noticed a red-haired girl of about our own age, standing with a group of others. She wore a white linen sun hat and a green cotton dress that was too big for her—probably an older sister's—but nothing could disguise her prettiness, which was of the white-skinned, freckled kind. She had prominent cheekbones, and her blue eyes were wide-set and somewhat slanting: an unusual feature which I decided was explained by her being a picker. At fifteen, I still thought of the pickers as an alien tribe.

Once, as we passed, the girl smiled at us, showing prominent front teeth. She seemed to be looking at Mike, and when I glanced sideways at him, I found that his face had gone pink: he always flushed easily. He said nothing, and neither did I; we walked on. Behind us rose the laughter of the group of girls, mingling with the piping of plover in the dusk.

Now the voices of the pickers were all around us, coming from among the hop leaves: fathers, mothers, children, all working. They tore the rustling pods off in handfuls, picking at great speed, their brown arms covered in scratches from the bines. Somewhere, in nests beside the poles, babies cried; but the sound was diminished (as all sounds were in these green aisles), and seemed to go ignored, like the wails of changelings. And as Mike and I patrolled the aisles, we always seemed to pass a particular family group which included the red-haired girl.

Today as always she wore the white linen sun hat and green

dress. She peered from among the leaves, and I saw her eyes meet Mike's. This time they looked at each other without smiling: he returned her gaze boldly, with a steady seriousness I admired. Then we walked on, saying nothing, kicking at clods of earth.

From beyond the hop fields, somewhere near the creek, a half-heard whirring came. It seemed to me to sound from the heart of the summer, and to contain a deeper meaning than summer itself: the true secret of Clare and of the land. This secret had an essence, I thought; and sometimes I imagined it to be concentrated in a particular room in the house I'd never visited.

I thought the room to be imaginary; but that summer, Mike took me there.

The sleepout was built into the end of the front verandah, with walls of vertical boards and sliding windows on the outer side. We lay in narrow stretcher beds placed at right angles, and read by the light of two candles.

Mike read a good deal. He was naturally more active and athletic than I was, and had he lived in town, I doubt that he would have read so much. But we had few other entertainments, except when one of his brothers took us in to the cinema in New Norfolk, on a Saturday afternoon. Hobart was only thirty-odd miles down the highway, but country people traveled to town less, in those days; cars were slower, and less readily used. A shopping trip to Hobart, in Mr. Langford's big blue Dodge, was a major expedition.

Mike's reading was indiscriminate, ranging from current Westerns and thrillers to more serious British books from the period before we were born, at the height of the Empire. He had a big supply of these in an old wardrobe here—many of them dating back to his father's boyhood; some to his late grandfather's. They came from a hemisphere and a past that were both intimate and remote to us, and included the Sherlock Holmes stories and works by such writers as Kipling, Rider Haggard, Captain Marryat and R. M. Ballantyne.

But more interesting to us than any of these books was a big set of papers in the bottom of the wardrobe. This was a collection of weekly colored supplements from an American newspaper, and featured serialized comic strips. It was called *Wags,* and I can still smell the pungent American newsprint. Somebody (Ken perhaps, or Marcus), had bought *Wags* over a period of some ten years, from the mid 1930s to the early 1940s, and had hoarded it; and now Mike regarded these papers as his personal treasure. Television hadn't arrived; this was still the great age of the comic strip, and all the classics were here: Tarzan, The Phantom, The Captain and the Kids, Dick Tracy, Flash Gordon.

Few of these strip cartoons were actually comic. They seemed in fact to be aimed at adults, but we knew that many adults disapproved of them. American culture wasn't much liked by our elders: it was seen as vulgar and often suggestive, and they preferred that we feed our imaginations on approved books from parental England. So two Northern Hemisphere cultures competed for our interest; and *Wags* drew us, like a forbidden maze. At ten, we'd found it both enigmatic and shocking. The sadistic gangsters and the graphically depicted bloodletting in *Dick Tracy* appalled and fascinated us, since spilled blood was seldom shown then for entertainment. Neither Mike nor I had really understood these strips when we were young; but each summer, we understood a little more. From the big newsprint pages of *Wags* came the reek of a world of machines, of violence, and of sexual mysteries. Even the lurid colors were violent. Beautiful women appeared here, stripped at times to their underwear, but mostly clad in the sleek gowns of the just-missed 1930s, when Mike and I had been infants. The cars and biplanes of the thirties roared through the strip cartoon frames, no less modern and glamorous for being a decade out of date.

One strip fascinated Mike more than any other, to the point of obsession: Milton Caniff's *Terry and the Pirates,* set on what was then called the China Coast. He would lie on his bed studying it for hours. We would read it together, when we were ten, carried along by the pictures, struggling to understand the speeches in the balloons. We were really studying these texts for clues to an alarming and seductive adult cosmos that was waiting in the future, and many of the more puzzling speeches I can still remember, as an archaeologist might remember hieroglyphics he once spent years deciphering. *("You're the Dragon Lady? The woman pirate?" "It is so! And thanks to the fair-skinned one, I look myself again!")* The American boy Terry was clearly Mike's alter ego, and we followed his life, from his boyhood in the South China Sea of the thirties, when Chinese pirates were the villains, to his manhood in World War Two, when Colonel Flip Corkin of the U.S. Air Force became a leading figure, and the villains were our villains: the Japanese. That Mike would one day go to the China Coast to lead the life of Terry (in that weird Far East which was not east for us, but north), I always took for granted.

Now that we were adolescent, the stories had come into focus; and what had been enigmas in our early years were comprehended. We pretended to be casual, now; we weren't children any more, and *Terry and the Pirates* was just a comic strip. But we still sometimes read *Wags* in the sleepout, as a ritual to pass time, and Terry's spell persisted, especially for Mike. And we couldn't be casual about its women, who had now altered their dimensions for us. There was a blond and beautiful American adventuress called Burma, and an equally beautiful villainess (to use the terminology of the time), called the Dragon Lady. That Dragon Lady, Mike would say, and he'd shake his head and grin. I think he was in love with the Dragon Lady: a Eurasian who was as alien to us, in our Anglo-Saxon island, as a being from another planet. And certainly we were both in love with Burma.

When he wasn't reading in the sleepout, Mike would listen to a green portable radio on the chest of drawers next to his bed. He liked Country and Western music, and newscasts. At such times, his face deeply shadowed in the candlelight, he appeared older than fifteen: his heavy white eyelids were like seashells, exaggerated in a way that made him unfamiliar. He lived an interior life that he didn't talk about, and I guessed that some of it had to do with the Second World War, as well as with *Terry and the Pirates*. He still admired his brother Ken without reserve, and greatly regretted that the War had ended before he could go too.

It'd be good to serve your country, he said, and stared into the candle, lying with his hands behind his head.

Even at fifteen, I privately found the direct expression of such

33

a sentiment quaint and old-fashioned; and I glimpsed for a moment the degree to which the books in the wardrobe must be influencing him, as well as *Wags*. No doubt his hero worship of Ken played a part too—although Ken's personal influence on him wasn't calculated to make war desirable; rather the reverse, as I'd seen long ago over the guns.

When we were younger, we'd played a silly game with .22 rifles. Ken used to take us rabbiting and wallaby-shooting, and had lent us each a .22 for our personal use. Without his knowledge, at Mike's suggestion, we began a stalking game with them: a version of our juvenile games of cowboys and Indians to which an element of realism was added. Recalling this now, I'm half appalled.

There were rules. We fired over each other's heads, or well to the side. And knowing the alarm it would have caused had we been found out, we played the game well away from the farmyard, on the steep, grassy hill behind the pickers' huts, on the other side of the wire fence that marked the boundary of the Langford property. There, among yellow tussocks and gray boulders coated with lichen, on the edge of a forest of gums, we stalked each other. And it was there, I often think, as well as on the football field, that Michael first began to develop the uncanny skills that would stand him in such good stead on the battlefields of Indochina.

We took turns at being the hunter and the hunted. Given a short start, and limited to an agreed area of bush, you had to try to evade discovery. If you were spotted, a shot was fired directly over your head, and you then had to freeze and surrender. I was good enough at the game to keep Mike interested; but I was never as good as he was. When I hunted him, crawling or stumbling along through the prickly undergrowth between the gum trees and black wattle, it was like hunting something gone insubstantial. If his bright blond head hadn't given me a small advantage in spotting him, I might have had to give up altogether.

When Mike hunted me, I would wriggle on my belly along the bush's floor, breathing in the sharp, papery smells of eucalyptus, fallen bark and ants: waiting for his shot to ring out. Once, the bullet thudded into the trunk of a blue-gum six inches above my head, and I laughed hysterically, raising my arms in surrender.

It was on that afternoon that we suddenly heard Ken's mighty shout. It came from down the hill: his tall figure was toiling up towards us through the grass, and soon he stood over us, hands on hips. He still wore the Digger hat, stained and bent and faded so that it was just an old hat, now. His eyes seemed darker blue and more wide open than usual.

You stupid young buggers, he said. For once, his big grin was missing.

Just firing a few potshots, Mike said.

Ken held out his hand. Give us those twenty-twos, he said.

We knew better than to argue, and handed them to him. He sat down on a small boulder a few feet away, the rifles across his knees.

Mike looked contrite. We're sorry, Ken, he said. We won't do it again.

You won't get a chance to, Ken said. He shook his head. Bloody hell.

Mike tried grinning at him, but Ken didn't grin back. He sat in silence, and we sat down next to him, as long shadows put their fingers across the valley, and the sun left the red roof of the house and the white road between the poplars. Far off, we could hear the voices of pickers among the hops, and the barking of John Langford's collie dog, Angus. When Ken spoke again, he seemed to be talking to himself, looking out over the valley.

You pick up a rifle and it gives you big ideas, he said. You think it makes a man of you, holding a gun. That's all bullshit, boys. You don't feel quite so good after you've used it on someone. Only mad bastards find that enjoyable.

Tell us how it was in New Guinea, Ken, Mike said. He was always trying to get Ken to talk about the action he'd seen, but Ken never would.

Not now, Chick, Ken said. But suddenly he looked at us, and said: You want to know how I killed my first Japanese? All right, I'll tell you.

I glanced at Mike. His expression was utterly intent; he'd waited years for this.

It was just after I got to New Guinea, Ken said. I was twenty-one; I'd never seen action. The blokes up the trail ahead of us had knocked out a Japanese machine-gun post, and we were told not to take prisoners. We couldn't; we were outnumbered. There was one Jap still alive, with a bullet in his guts, and our sergeant told me to kill him. "Shoot him, Ken." That's what he said to me.

He shook his head, and let out a quick breath through his nose that might have denoted amusement, but didn't. "Shoot him, Ken." He repeated the words wonderingly, as though they contained the key to something: a puzzle he'd been trying to solve for a long time. So I picked up my .303, and put a bullet through him, he said. He was the first man I'd ever shot. Then I went behind a tree and threw up.

He thought for a moment, while we kept absolutely quiet, waiting.

He was just lying there, looking at me, this Jap, he said. He was quite a young bloke. Sometimes I still see him looking at me before I go to sleep. I killed a lot of other Japanese in the fighting after that, and it got easier. But he was different. He was in cold blood. I don't reckon that bloody sergeant should have made me do it. No, I don't reckon he should have.

He glanced at us; but the glance told us nothing. Then his face softened a little, and became almost friendly; he seemed to be coming back to us. So don't you young blokes think it's fun, killing people, he said. It's no bloody fun at all.

He stood up, holding the guns. I'll keep these for now, he said.

He turned and walked off down the hill, erect as though marching, pulling the battered Digger hat low over his eyes, not looking back.

Mike blew his candle out, and I did the same.

Sometimes Ken has bad dreams, Mike told me. I've heard

him sing out, at night. He still thinks about the War, now and then. And he lost his girlfriend Peggy by going to the War. He was engaged to her, and she broke it off, while he was up in New Guinea. Married someone else.

Why would she do that? I asked. Any girl'd want Ken.

Selfish, Mum reckons. All those Stantons are selfish.

There was silence for a while; then his voice came softer, out of the dark. Hey: you got a girl yet?

No, I said, I hadn't got a girl. Had he?

Yeah, I've got a girl, he said. Don't tell anyone this, Ray. It's one of the pickers.

I laughed. I know, I said. That red-haired girl.

Don't laugh, Ray, he said. I'm in love with her. His voice was low and fervent: he was clearly serious, and although he was only fifteen, he had the dignity of youthful maturity. Her name's Maureen Maguire, he said; and he divulged it like a deadly secret.

We'd reached the age where the hop fields and the hills and the whole flowering land were filled with a buzz and murmur of desire. But this was still the era of sexual reticence and innocence, and although we'd exchanged inadequate information on human coupling, and occasionally told each other dirty jokes, girls and women were an almost total mystery, whom Mike in particular contemplated with reverence. So to me, and no doubt to Mike, the red-haired picker in her hand-me-down dress and faded linen sun hat was a nymph of the glades. To think of her being Mike's girl pierced me with pleasurable envy; but I told myself that it was Mike who deserved her. He had the daring to woo her; I didn't.

My amusement had been caused by the fact that he thought I hadn't been aware of his feeling, simply because he'd never said anything. He'd imagined I was unaware of his secret life.

But I knew about it. I'd caught glimpses of it, but had been tactful enough not to mention it to him. He would disappear at times, particularly in the early evenings, making it plain he wanted to get away on his own. Left to my own devices, I'd gone walking about the property; and one evening, venturing past the pickers' huts, I'd seen an extraordinary domestic picture. In one of the glassless windows, a family was framed in kerosene lamp-light, sitting around their table over a meal: a middle-aged man and woman, the red-haired girl (plainly their daughter, since the woman had similar red hair), two small boys, and Mike. He was laughing and talking with them easily, gesturing with one hand, a cup of tea in the other. They were all smiling at him, and the parents had pleasant, kindly faces. The young squire among his tenants, I thought. I'd reached the age of such silly witticisms; and as I've said, I envied him.

I was also awed. He was trespassing into one of John Langford's most seriously forbidden zones. What if his father found out? I put this question to him now.

He won't find out, Mike said. To hell with him if he does. Those pickers are good people; and they've got so bloody little, Ray. Dad says they thieve things; but the Maguires would never do that. I've started taking them eggs and vegetables that Mum lets me have.

Wouldn't your mother tell your father? I asked.

No, he said. She won't tell him. Only Luke Goddard might tell him.

Luke Goddard was a hermit. He had lived for years, with John Langford's permission, in a dilapidated shack on the boundary of the property, not far from the pickers' huts. No one knew what he had been or where he'd originally come from. He was a tall old man with a mane of white hair and deep-sunk, pale eyes whose stare was both shocked and shocking; I for one couldn't meet it. He seemed always to be walking about, head bent, dressed in a Tasmanian bluey: the dark pea jacket worn by bush workers.

There used to be many such hermits in the country, and legends were invented giving them illustrious or tragic origins. Luke Goddard was variously said to have been a wealthy farmer who'd been ruined; an ex-sailor; a jilted lover; the disgraced son of an English nobleman. But no one really knew, since he seldom spoke, except in monosyllables, and ignored most greetings. Mike and I had seen him in conversation with the pickers, but old Goddard barely spoke to members of the Langford family—despite the fact that he sometimes wandered across the property. For some reason,

John Langford tolerated him; even seemed to be amused by him. Mike and I would laugh at him as he went by when we were younger, and he would sometimes turn on us, waving his fist and shouting words that we couldn't understand, making us afraid of him.

Luke Goddard? Why would Luke Goddard tell him? I asked. That's crazy. He never talks to anyone. He wouldn't talk to your father. Even if he did, your father wouldn't listen to him.

Wouldn't he? Mike's tone was bitter. He'd sooner listen to Luke Goddard than me, he said.

The next night, we lay silent for a time. A high wind, an early warning of autumn, had come up outside, mourning through Clare's front verandah and bumping into the door of our little closet.

It was a wind I associated with Luke Goddard: a wind of great loneliness. It had come out of the steep, dark hills of this country: the ranges that enclosed the town of New Norfolk and the valley of the Derwent. It had come from places like the Black Hills and Moogara, where the farms were few and poor; it had come from farther still, howling out of the valley of the Ouse, and from beyond Lake Echo; from the empty Highlands, the snow country, with its hundreds of lakes and tarns, cold, abstract mountains, and button-grass plains where nobody went.

Ray? You awake?

It was Mike. I'll tell you something about my old man, he said. He's got a locked room, where no one's allowed to go. A storeroom. No one gets in there.

Where is it? I asked.

Down the end of the hall, Mike said; and I knew immediately which room he meant. A small hallway ran off at right angles from the main one that connected the two zones of the house. The sitting room was entered from this secondary hallway, and two of the bedrooms; and it ended at a dark-stained cedar door that was always closed. I had sometimes regarded the door with faint curiosity, but had never asked what its purpose was.

What does he keep in there?

He just says family papers.

Sounds boring.

Yes, he said. But why should he keep it locked?

I had no answer to this.

Listen, Mike said. I know how to get in there. I know where he keeps the keys. You want to come?

We went in the early afternoon, when the men were all down in the hop fields. It was around two-thirty: a bad time of day, I reflected later.

Two-thirty was a time of blank arrest; a time of tedium, with all the dangers tedium carries at its heart. Two-thirty on a hot January afternoon was a time when I no longer loved the farm. The bright dance of morning was gone, and the inviting shadows of deep afternoon had yet to appear. It was a passage without possibilities; a time when the stale, glaring exterior world promised nothing, and the mind recoiled. Tedium, almost visible, brooded in the glum little gully on the western side of the house, where stinging nettles grew: dark, malicious weeds that people were said to have eaten, in the other hemisphere. Tedium squatted in the yard on the wood-heap, where the sun gleamed dully on the abandoned axe. The axe, and all the other objects about the farmyard, appeared to be lying here for eternity, and to be stuck in a congealed light like fat. Inside tedium was no still center, but something else: something brutally restless and vicious, which occasionally caused grown men and women out here to become mad. Two years ago, it had caused Don Maxfield, on the next farm up the road, to batter old Arthur Baker to death with a crowbar in a quarrel over the sale of some stock. That would have happened, I felt sure, at around two-thirty. Yet this was the time that we chose to go into John Langford's storeroom.

The key was on a ring with a number of others which Mike had watched his father push into a drawer in a rolltop desk in the sitting room. It was a simple matter (as one of the stories in his British boys' books would have put it) for him to slip in there, get the keys, and bring them down the half-dark passage to the locked door of the storeroom. Deliberate and unhurried, he tried them one after another in the lock under the white, nineteenth-century china handle.

When he'd found the one that fitted, and we'd hurried inside, he quickly closed the door after us. There was a sort of glowing dimness in here that was strange; but superficially, nothing in the room appeared unusual. It simply looked like what it was: a store-room, with tin trunks and cardboard cartons stacked against one wall, old pieces of furniture standing about haphazardly, and a long walnut table in the center piled with papers, files and books. But I knew immediately that we'd found the core of the house's secrecy: the cell which contained its essence.

Secrecy sang in the static air, like an old valve radio with the volume turned down. It was air that seemed to have been trapped in here for decades, and which smelled of mildew. The faded wallpaper looked very old, and had a pattern of English wild-flowers. The glow was created by a faded, parchment-yellow holland blind drawn over a single tall window at the far end, sealing the place completely. The sun of two-thirty, trying vainly to get in, was filtered and transmuted into a thick yellow substance like mustard: a half-light which I guessed was the only natural one the room ever knew. There was no electric bulb in the high ceiling; a kerosene lamp with a china base stood on the table by the books, and I imagined John Langford lighting it.

The thought of Mr. Langford made me nervous; but this nervousness, and the sense of trespassing, was not the only effect the room had on me. The past, I see now, waits always for us to open its doors; and once having done so, we can choose to open our spirits to its thin, helpless voices, or else turn away. Both choices have their consequences. Mike was indifferent; I was in-terested; and that was when the past enrolled me in its service.

At first, moving cautiously about beside Mike, I thought my-self indifferent too—if not to the room's atmosphere, at least to its contents, which were the sorts of objects that filled us with instant boredom. We fingered the files on the table, most of which contained depressing-looking documents and business letters we had no desire to read. There were mountains of old magazines —*The Bulletin* and *The Land*—which were of no interest either.

What bloody junk, Mike said. He looked disgusted.

There must be *something* here, I said. Otherwise why should he lock it?

Mike looked at me appreciatively; he lived in the hope of intrigue. Right, mate. Let's keep looking.

We began now to rummage about independently; and edging past the long table towards the right-hand corner of the room, I came on a painting. It was large—about four feet by two—in a heavy walnut frame, and stood propped on a small cedar table against the wall: a portrait of a man in his early thirties, in the clothing of the last century. The thick, filtered sun through the blind fell on it in such a way that the eyes and the skin had something of the gloss of life. Like all paintings of its period, it had a veiled quality, as though it were covered in dark gauze. Yet it was very real, being technically accomplished enough to resemble a photograph.

The man wasn't looking at the viewer directly: he stared steadily past my shoulder to the right of the frame, which was my left. He wore a cravat and a dark, sober suit with wide lapels. His long brown hair was parted on the left, like that of a man of today, but grew so far down the sides that it covered his ears. His face appeared modern, being clean-shaven. His head was cocked a little to one side, his lips faintly smiling. At the same time, his full lower lip projected in a way that warned you to be careful. He looked from under his eyebrows, which were low-set, and the shrewd, humorous glint in his dark blue eyes made me feel that if I studied him long enough, I'd discover what he was thinking. His face was lean, his nose straight and narrow.

Who's this? I asked.

Mike looked at the picture with little interest. Him? One of the great-grandfathers. I'm not sure which one.

He wandered off to the other side of the room; but I lingered. There was something not ordinary about the man: an intensity, coming out of the picture, that I hadn't the knowledge to diagnose, at that age. Looked at in one way, he had the musing, neurasthenically refined expression of a Victorian poet. But then this began to seem wrong: the face had a blade-like readiness for action that I didn't associate with poets: more with sportsmen or military officers, or the leading actors in films. Both possibilities existed, and strangely blended. He would be a man capable of lightheartedness; of all sorts of fancies—but one who would not tolerate fools, or fail to challenge annoyance. Getting closer, I saw the family likeness. Except for the color of his hair, the man was an adult version of Michael, and also resembled Ken. The eyes were the same blue, and the narrow nose was the Langford nose.

Faintly, through the closed window, I could hear the barking of Angus. It didn't occur to me to wonder why Angus was up from the fields; I'd lost interest in the picture now, and was looking elsewhere. Michael had wandered off to pick up an old Minties tin with comic pictures on the side, and had began to chuckle at it.

There was an old-fashioned box standing on the table in front of the painting. It was about fifteen inches wide, of polished wood, and bound with brass clasps. Its top sloped, so that it looked rather like a miniature writing desk without legs. I couldn't imagine its purpose, never having heard of a writing-slope, but it attracted me. I fingered it, and discovered that the top was secured by a brass lock. Turning the key in it, I was able to push the lid back. There were many compartments inside. Some of the small ones were ink-stained, and I realized that these had been for ink bottles and pens. In the main compartment were two very old-looking notebooks bound in calfskin; nothing else.

And here, coming up to me from the box's interior, was the smell of the past.

It was a worrying smell; even faintly alarming. Since then, I've learned not to be deceived by it. The odor that comes up from that deep, dry shaft isn't what you should attend to if you want to see the past as it really is. Nor am I misled any more by the faded, crimped and dried-up appearance of old objects. These provoke sadness, but that isn't how things were, back then; we're merely looking at corpses. The past is alive, and full of juices. It continues in a dimension which neither human wishes nor human indifference can affect, even if the relics it leaves behind are dead—just as our own precious objects will soon, soon be dead. But on that hot afternoon, as I fingered one of the notebooks, it was another matter; I felt vaguely threatened by the past, and was affected by its melancholy: a faint, dry perfume that came not only from the writing-slope, but seemed also to hang in the room itself—its likely point of origin being the drawn holland blind. Melancholy was given off like a constant shimmering from the blind's warm surface; and the blatant sun of today, passing through that brittle linen, was being transformed; was turning into the dense mustard glow of the past itself.

I'd just begun to flick through one of the notebooks when I heard the door handle rattle.

Terror jolted through me, and I pushed the book back into the polished box, and slammed its lid shut. I had some notion of warning Mike, but it was too late. The door opened, and John Langford stood looking at us, holding the china handle. He wore his usual clean khaki shirt, and had on the rimless glasses he used only in the house, from behind which his slitted brown eyes examined us like those of a headmaster. He frowned.

Mike stood quite still, holding the Minties tin; I couldn't see fear in his face: just surprise.

When Mr. Langford finally spoke, it was more softly than usual. What are you doing here, Michael?

Mike didn't answer; and in those moments, he slowly flushed. The flush was astounding: it crept up his neck like a stain from inside his sky-blue shirt; soon the face that looked back at his father achieved a shade of bright scarlet that I'd never seen in any human face before—except, perhaps, in the faces of aged drunks.

John Langford contemplated this phenomenon without expression; then he began to put a series of questions to us both. Few of his actual words come back now, perhaps because I was half deafened by fear; but I remember that I had the impression, even inside fear, that he was angry not merely at Mike and me, but at something else: something in the storeroom.

What in particular were we looking for? he wanted to know. What had been important enough to make Michael steal his keys?

Getting no satisfactory answers, he stared at us both in silence again, his thin mouth growing thinner. Then he said: What you've both been doing is prying.

He looked at me. You will go back to Launceston as soon as possible, Raymond. I'll ring your father tonight. Now you can get out, while I deal with Michael.

Slowly, hot with confusion, I moved to the door, leaving Michael and his father staring at each other. I feared for him, and not without reason.

When he was younger, he'd been beaten with a leather strap for any misdemeanors John Langford regarded as serious: a bad school report; tasks around the farm neglected. These beatings were administered on the bare legs, and were savage: he'd once shown me the welts. Since the age of thirteen, the beatings had stopped; but for entering the storeroom, his punishment was to do heavy farm work ten hours a day until school went back, with half-hour meal breaks and no break at the weekends.

It seemed excessive, and I said so when he told me. He looked at me for a moment without comment. Then he said something I've always remembered, his pale face expressionless.

Sometimes I don't think I'm his son, he said. I think I'm the son of someone better.

Only those who have not been tied to the land can romanticize it. I loved Clare because I could escape it. Mike could only dream of escape; meanwhile, he'd found a way of escaping reality by transforming it.

The device that made this possible would eventually be his passport to the world. Ken had once given him a box Brownie camera, and Mike became more and more interested in photography. He photographed everything, and I still have the prints he gave me: his brothers working at the plow, or supervising the picking; Duke and Prince; the old blacksmith's shop in New Norfolk where they still shoed horses, and where big old Percy Maynard, hammer in hand, grins at Mike's camera from the forge: an afterimage from the nineteenth century.

The small, crude black-and-white pictures are surprisingly good; it was as though he saw these ordinary things as strange, and made the camera show it. And the light in the pictures, despite the box Brownie's limitations, was different from the flat light in the snapshots I took: he seemed to have chosen moments when it defined things.

I thought his interest merely a passing craze, at the time. I still see him focusing on something, peering into the tiny viewfinder, earnestly bent; the tip of his tongue would creep out of the corner of his mouth. He had no conscious idea then of where this would lead, I'm sure; but from his absolute seriousness, I can see now that he knew it unconsciously. We always do.

At the end of the visit that John Langford had cut short, on the night when I was leaving the farm, Mike gave me a present: a leather-covered album of his snapshots. We were standing on the front verandah, watching for the lights of my father's car.

Here, he said. Something to remember the place.

I looked through the book, and found that he'd mounted a set of his photographs. The pickers; Percy at his forge; Ken plowing in his Digger hat. Strangely, there was also a picture of Luke Goddard, striding through tussock grass at evening in his dark bluey: head down, outraged eyes fixed, white stubble on his chin, his long shadow behind him. Mike must have snapped him from hiding; and I suspected now that he didn't just fear the old man: he was unaccountably fascinated by him.

In the front of the album, he'd written: *From your friend Mike.*

The next summer, when he and I were sixteen, I was invited again. But this would be the last time. I didn't know it then, but there'd be no more holidays at Clare: Mike and I would drift apart when he left school the following year.

Two deaths hung over the place now, and the heart had gone out of the house. Both deaths had occurred the year before, not long after John Langford had cut short my visit.

Mike had told me about it at school. But he'd given no details, and I'd asked for none. His face had a stricken emptiness; and I knew, even at that age, that I was looking at shock.

He'd lost the two members of his family he loved most. Ken had died first; then his mother.

He only talked about it when I arrived at the farm. It was the middle of a warm afternoon: we were loitering in the barn, where Mike had been feeding the horses. We now spent little time in the house, which seemed permanently cold. A hired girl from a nearby farm did the cooking, and the men sat silent around the table at meals, knives clicking on plates. Much more was locked up in that house than the storeroom at its core. Hearts were locked; the Langfords wouldn't show grief except through silence.

Long, amber stalks of sun grew to the barn's rafters; there were smells of chaff and machine oil here that had once excited me, and I knew we were saying goodbye to boyhood. The two big Clydesdales ate in their stalls, blowing through their nostrils, and Mike stood patting Prince's brown flank as he talked.

Ken had been killed in a motorbike accident on the road to Hobart, at nine o'clock in the morning. The bike was Cliff's; Ken had borrowed it to go in to the city. He'd come around a blind bend near Bridgewater to find himself meeting a car that had passed a truck and was still on the wrong side of the road. He'd swerved to avoid it and had gone down a bank, pitching over the handlebars and breaking his neck.

On the evening before it happened, Mike told me, Ken's former girlfriend Peggy Stanton had phoned from Hobart. She'd broken up with her husband, who'd treated her badly, and she wanted Ken to come and see her. The whole family had heard the conversation: the old wall phone was in the hall outside the kitchen, so that no calls were really private.

I could tell from Ken's voice that he was really pleased, Mike said. He'd never got over losing Peggy. He told her he'd come in the next day, and he asked the old man for the day off, and wanted to borrow the Dodge. But Dad said they were too busy to spare him; told him to wait a few days. Then there was a row. Ken did his block and called Dad a mean old bastard. Told him to stick his car up his arse; he'd borrow Cliff's bike.

Next morning when Ken left, I was sitting at breakfast with Mum in the kitchen, Mike said. Ken came through wearing a leather jacket and Cliff's motorbike helmet; he had a clean collar and tie under the jacket, and he didn't look the same. Different: his face kind of hollow, and his eyes staring—as though he was ready to jump off the edge of something. And I had this feeling that maybe something terrible would be there when he jumped. I remember Mum looked up, and she told him to take care. Ken winked at her and smiled and told her he would; he was always very fond of Mum. But then he looked real serious again, and said: "He's not going to bugger my life up any more. He can keep my bloody share of the place, if he likes. He can cut me out of it." And Mum said: "It won't come to that, Ken. You just go to her."

A few moments later we heard the bike start up in the yard, Mike said, and then it went down the drive. Mum and I didn't talk, and we could hear the bike's engine going down the road to New Norfolk, getting smaller and smaller, like a bee. I'd decide I couldn't hear it any more, and then I'd pick the sound up again.

His quiet voice stopped short. He left off patting Prince and came and sat down on a bale of hay, not looking at me. Prince stamped, in the barn's quiet.

If Dad had lent him the car, it wouldn't have happened, Mike said. His gaze was remote, looking at the horses. The old man killed him, he said softly. And that killed Mum. They said she died of a heart attack—but I reckon she died of a broken heart. She hardly ever said another word to Dad after that. She wouldn't talk to anyone about Ken; but she talked once to me about him, on the day of his funeral. I came into the kitchen and she was sitting there at the table by herself, waiting for Dad and the others: in a few minutes we'd all get in the car to go in to Saint Matthew's in New Norfolk for the service. She had a black suit on I'd never seen, and a white blouse. She looked me over and told me I looked nice for Ken's funeral.

He paused; then he went on. I wished that he wouldn't, but he seemed compelled.

I'd never seen Mum cry, he said. She was tough, Mum was. But that day in the kitchen she cried. She had her elbow propped on the table, and she was reaching up with one hand, as though she was blind, and trying to take hold of something in the air. I thought how red and rough her hand was, from all the work she'd done, and I took hold of it. She held mine pretty hard; Mum had quite a grip. For a while she couldn't seem to speak; she just sat sucking in breath, blinking away tears. When she did speak, she was looking past me, as though she was talking to someone else: someone who was to blame for Ken dying. Her eyes got really fierce, and she said: "Ken was the best of all you boys. He came right through the War, just to be killed on that damned motorbike. That's not right, Chick. That's not right."

He stopped, and dug in the earth floor with a stick. His own eyes were dry.

She died a month later, he said. It was me who found her. She died feeding the fowls. It was around teatime, and she hadn't come back from the yard; the old man told me to go out and look for her. It was dark; I came around the corner of the barn here, and what I saw first was the spilled pot of wheat and her hand lying near it. Just her hand, where the light from the house caught it.

He was silent again for a moment. Then he said: The old man came and carried her inside. He laid her on the kitchen table while he called the doctor. Can you imagine that? On the bloody kitchen table.

He looked at me now, his face a pale egg, his eyes drained light blue by an anger that worried me. Then his usual calm came back, and he drifted to the door of the barn, hands in pockets. I followed.

From across in the evening kitchen we could hear the radio playing, tuned to the Country and Western station it stayed on all the time. Hank Locklin was singing "Send Me the Pillow that You Dream On."

Ken always liked that song, Mike said. His tone was gentle. He used to whistle it, he said.

Afterwards, at dusk, we wandered up the hillside past the pickers' huts, reaching the spot among the boulders where Ken had confiscated the guns when we were boys. There was a clear, dark sky. It was still light enough to see the house, a plowed field, and the white of the road; but already the valley was cooled by stars. We stood looking out, not speaking, and I was remembering Ken plowing down there.

On Saturday mornings, when Mike and I would lie in later than usual in the sleepout, we'd listen to the sounds of the waking farm: the warbling of magpies would rise through the blue like bursting bubbles, and Ken's voice would come up from the paddocks across the road.

Prince! Git over there! Git over!

His shouts would fill the whole valley, echoing from the dark green hills of bush. He'd be plowing with the Clydesdales, and they'd be wandering out of the furrows. Dwindled by distance, comical in its wrath since it came from good-humored Ken, the deep voice would rise higher.

Duke! Duke! Stay *in that bloody furrow! Duke—you—*bastard!

We'd chuckle with delight. That Ken, Mike would say. He certainly can yell.

Now the acres where Ken's voice had rung out were numbed into silence. But I told myself that this sly, rich landscape secreted all the joys, sadnesses and jokes of the Langfords forever, holding them like absorbent cloth, and that Ken would always be down there, plowing in the field by the hop glades.

At sixteen, I was able to make myself believe this.

I was Mike's first close friend; and friends were to be of great importance to him, all his life. I would hear this many times, in Asia. But our friendship didn't survive boyhood. As young men, we lost all track of each other.

This was mainly because when Mike left school, he went back to work on the farm, and I moved to Hobart to study for my law degree. I heard nothing from him for years, and I decided, when I thought about him, that by now he'd be a farmer, and nothing else. That would be his life, as it was for his brothers. I could have phoned Clare, I suppose. I'm not entirely sure why I didn't, in all those years; but I'd learned that meeting the friends made in childhood usually proves disappointing; even a little embarrassing. Each has become someone else, and neither finds this very attractive.

But when we were both twenty-one, I ran into him unexpectedly on a street in Hobart, and we stopped and talked. I'd just begun work as a solicitor with a Hobart legal firm, and I told him I was driving up to Launceston the next day to pick up some effects.

Then he surprised me. He'd left the farm some time ago, he told me, and was hoping to be taken on by the *Launceston Courier* as a cadet news photographer. He had to go north himself in a few days, for a final interview.

By the end of the conversation, it was agreed he'd travel up with me in my car.

We left in the late afternoon. I was driving a battered Volkswagen that had got me through student days; beside me, in his bucket seat, Langford seemed a little too large for the vehicle. He'd become as tall as Ken, with the well-muscled body of an athlete, and I learned that he played Australian Rules football with a Hobart club. He spoke about his football as though it would interest me; it didn't, and we lapsed into silence. He was even less articulate than he used to be, I thought; I found his long silences baffling, and I told myself that he'd become quite dull.

The Beetle buzzed at its modest top speed up the Midlands Highway, which is built on the track of the nineteenth-century coaching road. Soon we were entering the pastoral Midlands: an ancient, dried-up lake floor whose small, gold-grassed hills are occasional and rounded, their trees few. Open grazing country extended into the distance, the mountains blue on its rim, and still Langford's silence continued. But finally he turned and asked me about my new job.

I could tell he was merely being polite: I sensed that he could scarcely imagine why anyone would want to be a lawyer, and I answered briefly. Then I asked him about news photography. Why did he want to do it?

He cogitated, squinting judiciously through the windscreen in

51

the country manner. Then he said: "I like photography: I'm good at it. And I'd like to cover the trouble spots abroad."

He didn't enlarge on this, and his silence enfolded us again. But as he'd spoken, I'd caught something in his expression that reminded me of the way he'd looked when he listened to newscasts on his radio in the sleepout, or studied *Terry and the Pirates:* a quick, fervent gleam. Perhaps he hadn't grown dull, after all. His face had the strong planes of adulthood, and yet it was still very boyish: it still had the dreamy, almost infantile calm peculiar to the blond. Faintly smiling, he seemed to be gazing into the distances of some mythical sea: a place where I couldn't follow him.

By the time we drove across the old stone bridge that's the entrance to the village of Ross, it was growing dark; and here I broke another silence, and asked him why he'd left the farm.

But his face closed up; he peered out at the passing stone front of the Man o' Ross Hotel, and simply didn't answer. We were well outside the town before he spoke.

"Something bad happened, mate." His voice was just audible, and he lit a cigarette before continuing. "I had a row with the old man. I walked off the farm. I've been doing odd jobs ever since."

"I'm sorry," I said. "Can't it be made up?"

He shook his head. "It'll never be made up. I don't want to make it up. He's cut me out of his will like he was going to do with Ken. The old bastard could be dying, and I wouldn't make it up. I'll never go back."

I asked him if he wanted to tell me about it, but he shook his head again. "It's history now, Ray. I never wanted to go farming, anyway."

I didn't press him, and the next silence must have lasted half an hour. Then, somewhere in the long straight run through Epping Forest, he spoke again, his voice only just audible above the noisy little engine.

"It was about Maureen Maguire," he said.

And now he began to talk. His face, always in profile, showed little expression when I glanced at it. But it was illuminated only fleetingly by passing headlights, and I may not have seen all that showed on it.

The muted pain in his voice was another matter. It seemed to fill the car; to be one with the buzzing of the engine.

He'd wanted to marry her, he said. All through his teenage years, he'd waited for her every summer, when the pickers came. He'd proposed when he was nineteen, and she'd accepted.

"But nothing would make the old man agree to it," he said. "He was a bloody snob: he said pickers were rubbish, and no daughter of a picker was good enough to marry. That wasn't true; they were good people. And Maureen was a Catholic, and he had no time for Catholics. I hated the old man for that. There was no way he was going to stop me marrying her—but we agreed to wait until I was old enough to leave the farm."

He paused; then he began again, and there were no more pauses after that. He was talking about Luke Goddard.

It's a long time ago now, and I can't reproduce the rest of his words exactly. The things that come back to me most vividly may not always be the things he laid most emphasis on himself; and it seems to me now that he kept coming back to the nettles in the gully. The stinging nettles and Luke Goddard seemed oddly connected in his mind—and I thought I could half understand this. Like stained and mildewed cloth, their smell itself stained, the dark green weeds recalled something terrible: something in an ancient life that had to be paid for.

He'd followed Luke Goddard about when he was young, Mike said. This was at eleven and twelve years old, before he took up with Maureen. After that the position would be reversed, and it would be Goddard who would follow them. Since Goddard was said to be mad, he was a diversion; and Mike had the idea at eleven that a mad adult might reveal secrets that sane ones hid from children. But the hermit rarely spoke, except occasionally to turn and abuse him, in that gabbling language of his that could scarcely be understood. Or maybe the words were too difficult, Mike said: his father had once said that Goddard had been "an educated man"—speaking of him in the past tense, as though he were a corpse.

He told me how he'd once peered through the door of Goddard's gray weatherboard hut, when the hermit was out. He'd seen unclean bedding, and piles of junk; there was a smell like the den of an animal, and he was afraid to go in.

The old man had led him over those spaces of grass that were green as Wales, and beyond into the bush grass I remembered: territories wan as paper. And then Goddard went down into the gully: a place of fear and gloom. That was where the stinging nettles were: spiteful, stained weeds from an older, stained century, an older country, making Mike know he'd come too far. He somehow conveyed the notion to me that when he entered this gully he trespassed into the nineteenth century, when the farm had been founded. And he'd come to see Goddard too as coming from that century. I don't think it was an idea he'd thought out very clearly; but it seemed to be real to him.

The hermit had suddenly stopped, one day, and had quickly looked at Mike over his shoulder. His white face was spiteful, threatening and suggestive. It could be seen to know about things that were old and filthy; there was old spittle in the corners of the mouth, and Mike had turned and run up the slope of the gully. But the old man had shouted after him, and this time the words had been clear.

You! You're nothing but a bloody farmer's boy! Do you know who I am? A prince! I'm a prince!

When Goddard wasn't looking, Michael had photographed him. And when the photographs were developed, the figure that appeared was much more remarkable than the one that he'd focused his camera on. Luke Goddard in these pictures seemed not to be human, but instead to be a black spirit in the landscape, passing with bent head.

In this form, in his dark jacket, he came into Mike's dreams. He came through the window of the sleepout and tugged at the counterpane, trying to draw Mike out into the night of a hundred years ago. And now his stern face had changed: it was young, noble and refined: a dark prince of the air.

Over the years, on their evening walks in the bush and along the creek, Mike and Maureen would catch glimpses of Goddard following them, at a distance. Or he would be standing under a tree as though by accident. For some time, Langford told me, they took little notice.

But one evening he'd appeared to them from behind a tree, holding what appeared to be a white, upright candle in front of his black coat. Then Mike had turned on him.

Piss off! You hear me, you filthy old bastard? Piss off!

But Goddard had shouted after them, his words suddenly clear.

I'll go to your father! I'll tell him what you're doing! I'll tell him!

Mike had advanced on him, fist raised, and the old man had begun to scuttle away into the trees. But as Goddard went, he shouted again. *I know! I know what you're doing! Getting into her pants!* Hidden, going down a gully, the hermit had shouted obscenities: just single words, without logic or reason, echoing in the bush like dismal eruptions from the earth itself. After that, Mike said, he and Maureen had met in the hop kiln at night.

I could see them, lying on the sacking floor of the drying room, clinging together with an intensity like fear, the hop smell all around them. Sometimes they'd hear a creaking or shuffling down below, Mike said: even a creaking on the steps. It's him, Maureen would say. He's down there. Go and look, Mike. I'm scared of him.

But Mike had never found Goddard there, and had ceased to take him seriously. Nothing was serious but their love. He didn't even take it seriously when she told him Goddard had exposed himself to her again, meeting her alone by the huts. Langford saw the hermit as a foul clown; nothing more.

Just a pathetic old bastard swinging his mutton, he said. That's how I saw him. I was that bloody stupid. Now I still have dreams about it, he said: always the same. Maureen and I are standing at the end of the drying room, holding each other the way we used to do. There's the stink of last year's hops, in the dream, and the smell's part of the fear. The place is like a jail: you remember it, Ray. The old brick walls; small windows; half dark. Maureen used to say it was scary there, and it was, in a way. It always felt as though there was someone else in there somewhere: someone you couldn't see. And I always know in the dream that there really is someone—someone else is in the kiln besides us, even though I can't see anyone.

In the dream, I'm always asking Maureen to come out of the kiln; but she's hanging on to me and begging me to stay. Stay, she says. Don't make me go back. I only want to be with you.

The stronger the smell gets, the more I want to get out, he said. But she won't come; she's crying and hanging on to me. Then I wake up, and I know it's too late to save her.

He lit another cigarette and stopped talking, trying to stretch his legs. I waited, and after a time, he went on.

It happened when I was away in Melbourne for three days, he said. Cliff and I went there on a trip: one of the few times the old man ever gave us a holiday from the farm. Goddard must have been stronger than he looked. But Maureen wasn't a big girl. He not only raped her, he knocked her about, I was told—I don't know how badly. And I never saw her after it happened. When I came back and found out about it, the Maguires had packed up and gone. It had all happened in those few days; the family had disappeared, and Goddard was gone too. I never found out where he went, and he was never even arrested or questioned.

Then my father talked to me. He said Goddard was too crazy to know what he was doing. He'd driven him off the property. But he made out that Maureen had probably invited it.

I wanted to kill him for that, Langford said. I said things he'll never forgive, before I went. I left the farm that night, and got a ride into Hobart; I've never been back.

He turned to me. His face, in the white lights of the oncoming cars, suddenly looked older: I had the illusion of looking at a haggard middle-aged man. She didn't wait for me, he said. I've searched for her everywhere, but she and her family just disappeared. She didn't wait for me to come back. I'll never understand that, Ray.

I tried to offer explanations, drawing on my brief legal experience. Timid girls like Maureen, with nobody to back them, were always reluctant to testify to being raped, I said. They feared with good reason that police and defense lawyers would humiliate them, and hint that they'd brought it on themselves—just as old Langford had done. And maybe his father had even let the Maguires know that this was his suspicion: and his word with the police would have carried more weight than theirs. Maureen's family would have feared John Langford, and feared the police too: didn't pickers see police as natural enemies? So flight had been the only answer for them.

But none of this satisfied Mike. He shook his head, staring dumbly through the windscreen, and relapsed into silence again.

I'd conveyed to him how appalled I was; but I found I wasn't really surprised. Goddard had always been the carrier of some malicious intention. It would have been two-thirty on a hot afternoon when he did it, I thought. Yes, it would have been then: the time of tedium and madness, when the light was like congealed fat; when murder moved in the wood-heap.

"It's good of you to let me have this stuff," I said.

"It's what Mike wanted," Marcus said. "He told us in the last letter he sent us." His dark eyes rested on me for a moment; then they shifted.

Nothing had changed in the storeroom. Its objects all appeared to be in their original positions; there was a tricycle added, no doubt belonging to one of Cliff's children. Nor had the silent, mildewed air changed. The only real difference was that the afternoon light, coming through the holland blind (whose edges now were frayed and crumbling), seemed less intense. Perhaps the glow was diminished by the autumn.

We were standing beside the table in the center of the room. Letters Mike had written to his brothers, packed into a shoebox, sat at the end nearest us. There was also a little pile of black-and-white news-style photographs of Mike and other cameramen and journalists, taken in various parts of Asia. Some were copies of those I already had; others were new to me.

"I put these together for you," Marcus said. "Mike wrote to

Cliff and me at least once a fortnight, all these years. He was very good with letters. He told us all about his life over there, and the political situations in the countries he worked in. We learned a lot. I thought you might like to borrow them."

I listened to the hushed, slow voice I'd heard so seldom. It was like hearing a man speak who was unaccustomed to speaking at all; who'd always been thought to be dumb. I'd never really known Marcus, the quiet brother. Walking through the hop fields with his staff and tally-book, he'd moved in another dimension, like someone imagined rather than seen; now he stood here politely, his brown, work-blunted fingers curled at his sides. He was still a bachelor; and he was actually a relatively simple countryman, I saw, for whom talking was difficult, and who'd nailed up the fence of bachelorhood as such men often do, moving always in his private gullies of quietness. He'd changed little, in his fifties, except that his flat, neatly brushed hair was no longer black but gray, and the sockets of his deep-set eyes seemed even deeper. He wore a clean blue shirt and striped tie, in honor of my visit.

"We didn't realize how much everyone thought of Mike," he said. "There've been phone calls from places like New York and Hong Kong." He shook his head. "But there's not much Cliff and I can tell these people. A lot of them are asking about his papers and records. I'm glad he sent them to you, Ray—you can handle this sort of thing better than we can. Probably they should be published—don't you reckon?"

"Probably," I said. "I'll do my best with it." There was a short pause; then I put the question I'd been saving up. "Why do you think he did it?"

Marcus looked at me sideways. "Why did he take that risk, you mean? I don't reckon we'll ever know." His face contained regret, but not the depth of feeling I expected: not the frank sorrow and distress that Cliff and his wife, Helen, had showed when I arrived. Perhaps Marcus's wasn't the sort of face that could express real grief; or perhaps in Marcus's quiet world there were no emotions that strong.

"Do you believe there's any hope he's alive?" I asked.

Marcus fell silent, staring towards the blind at the end of the room; then he shook his head. "Not from what we've been told, Ray: no. I've talked to those Government people in Canberra on the phone about it, and I reckon he's gone." This was said, or rather half sung, in an elegiac tone common in the country; and he repeated it, as country people do when the mood is elegy. "Yes; I reckon he's gone."

Now it was my turn to be silent, and to look about the room. I found myself staring at the portrait, which was still propped on the cedar table. The writing-slope still sat there too. A handsome piece of work: I found myself hoping that it was included in Mike's bequest to me.

"I see you're looking at Mr. Devereux," Marcus said. "Well, he's yours now. That's the picture Mike wanted you to have."

"Is that his name? I'd assumed it was Langford."

"No; he was on the maternal side, I reckon. So far back, not much is known. I've never heard of any other Devereux relatives. The family must have died out, or moved to the mainland."

"It's a fine painting," I said.

It was; and I nursed a quiet excitement at taking possession of such an excellent piece of colonial portraiture: an excitement I prudently tried to hide, in case Marcus should change his mind.

The picture was even better executed than my memory of it, and had the power to hint at its subject's spirit. I bent and squinted at the signature, which my fifteen-year-old self hadn't thought of doing. *N. Howard:* I'd heard of no such colonial painter; no doubt he was forgotten, or had been in Van Diemen's Land only briefly. I'd have to check with the Museum. Howard's subject, hidden here all this time, continued to ruminate ironically on something to the right of the frame, which was my left. Certainly he was a handsome man: my memory here had proved correct. But he appeared more youthful now, with his mane of brown hair, than he'd done twenty-five years ago. After all, he was now something like ten years younger than I, instead of some fifteen years older. And the intensity and play of opposites in this face were not things that my young self had merely imagined. I also saw now the things I'd failed to do at fifteen: humor, sensitivity and arrogance mingled, and an underlying aggressiveness whose nature couldn't be guessed. The likeness to Mike—and, more distantly, to Ken—struck me again.

"The picture belongs to all three of us, strictly speaking," Marcus said. "But Mike knew Cliff and I had no interest in old pictures. Not much interest in ancestors either. Cliff and I hardly know anything about this bloke. So Mike wanted you to have it as a gift, you being so interested in history. That and the old diaries this great-great-grandfather Devereux kept, which Cliff and I aren't interested in either. Never read them, to tell you the truth, so I don't know what's in them. Dad read them, but he didn't talk about them much, except he said there was a lot of politics and filth in them. So it's all a last present to you from Mike, you might say. Of course, if he turns up, you can give them back to him. Here."

He turned the key of the writing-slope, pulled back the lid, and drew out the two calfskin-covered notebooks. He handed them to me somewhat awkwardly, watching my face. I flicked open the first few pages of the top one: pages I hadn't had time to read, at fifteen.

Journal, 1848–1850
Commenced on board the hulk "Medway," at Bermuda. Continued on board the transport "Sir Stamford Raffles" and at Van Diemen's Land.   *Robert Devereux*

June 21st 1848. Aboard the hulk "Medway." They are talking about me, through the wall . . .

I closed the book again, pretending that my interest was cursory; my heart was racing at the prospect of possession of such archives, and I was fearful that Marcus would change his mind about handing them over. "Yes. Interesting," I said. "I'll give them a good read at home. I'm honored Mike's left me these things."

He smiled; and I saw his sly streak. "Not much of an honor," he said. "Haven't you wondered why the old Dad kept his great-

great-grandfather hidden away in here, instead of hanging him over the mantelpiece?"

He had a secret to impart, I saw, and he was enjoying it. Yes, I said, I had wondered why.

"For the reason people always used to hide ancestors in Tasmania, Ray. He was a convict."

"I see." I stared at the picture in surprise. The opening pages of the journal were explained—or partly. I'd assumed Devereux was a colonial official, or military man: a guard, in other words, not a prisoner. Now, before I could check myself, I found myself using the old nineteenth-century cliché. "The stain," I said.

Marcus's amused grin widened, and he nodded. "The stain," he agreed. "And this Devereux must have been a bad bugger. The old Dad was terribly ashamed of it. I don't give a stuff, myself—I'm not such a snob as the old man was. But you know how it used to be, Ray: it was always the big disgrace, having convicts in the family, wasn't it? People never wanted to know anything about their great-grandparents, for fear they'd find one."

Yes, I said, I knew.

In old John Langford's generation the discovery would have been much more disturbing than it was now; and the truth was that it still created mixed feelings, despite our current declarations that the discovery of convict ancestors should be a matter for pride. For John Langford, it would have been the greatest shame imaginable. *Convict stock:* now I understood his anger. The threat all Tasmanians secretly feared: it had come up through the fathoms of the years to violate him, to disgrace and diminish him: to enlist him in its squalid and gloomy ranks forever. And he had wanted simply to reject it; he had locked it away and hidden it, as his father and grandfather had done. But he could not hide it from himself. It had always been here, like evidence of an hereditary illness.

"It's a wonder he didn't burn these diaries," I said.

"He was too bloody mean," Marcus said. "He thought they might be valuable—even though Devereux was a convict. Apparently this feller was a cut above the average. Good family, and all that."

"He doesn't look like a criminal," I said. "What did he do?"

"Dad said it was something political. He was Irish. Always made trouble, the Irish, didn't they? You'll probably find out in the diaries, if you can get through 'em. Maybe you'll publish them, Ray."

He was fingering the writing-slope, and now he grinned sideways at me, with a flash of country cunning. "You don't get this letter case, though. The old man used to reckon it was Devereux's, so it's pretty old. Nice workmanship: mahogany and brass. Worth a bit, wouldn't you say?"

"Yes. It's a nice heirloom," I said. "I wonder how a convict would manage to bring a thing like that out with him. Do you mind if I have a look?"

He nodded somewhat reluctantly, and I began to examine the interior. "These writing-slopes usually have secret drawers," I said. "They're not hard to find."

I proved to be right; it pulled back on a spring in the usual way, and Marcus looked at me sharply. "Well, well," he said. "We never knew that was there." He moved closer, as though fearing I'd purloin the contents, and peered into the drawer. "Anything valuable in there?"

There were only some personal letters. I unfolded one of them; it plainly came from the same period as the diaries, and was signed *Catherine*. My heart raced again; these letters had been undisturbed and unread for over a hundred years, and I lusted after them. "They seem to be from his wife," I said. "Can I put them with the diaries?"

"Take them," Marcus said. "They've got no interest for me."

His expression was glum; he'd perhaps been expecting money, and he looked around the storeroom now as though wondering why he was here. This had been a lot of talking for Marcus. The light through the blind was going, and his features were indistinct, his eyes lost in their deep sockets. When he spoke again, it seemed to me that he took on the dark authority of his youth, when he'd moved through the hop fields with his staff and tally-book.

"Some people carry the past on their backs like a saddle," he said. "My father did. It ate into his hide. I reckon this stuff affected him, sitting in here. Let's get it bundled up, Ray."

I put the journals and letters carefully into my briefcase; then I picked up the set of news photographs, and I was held for a moment by the one on top.

Mike walked in a line of South Vietnamese soldiers through a paddy field in the Mekong Delta. They were marching on a dyke above the rice field's shallow water; young shoots could be seen. A small cinecamera was slung from Langford's wrist by a strap; he wore cotton military fatigues and jungle boots like the soldiers. But unlike the soldiers, he had no helmet, and his blond hair was bright against the background of water and trees. He looked very tall, among the smaller Vietnamese men, but their faces were engraved with histories of experience that made his face look childlike. He was young; it was the sixties; he had a beauty that made him a little unreal. The war would always go on, and he would never die. He smiled with cool amusement, his lower lip pushed out.

The photograph, like that decade, like the war, like the nineteenth-century portrait on the table, was dead, and gave off the subtle scent of all dead objects. And I reminded myself once again that Mike himself was almost certainly dead. Yet he and the man in the painting both resumed life as I looked at them, their smiles one smile, repeated on two different faces.

5.

I switched the desk lamp off, and sat in darkness.

Forty, I said. Maybe you've only made it to forty. No further ever, now. Four months younger than me. November child and July child. You the arrow in the air; I the crab under the rock. Now I've got your hoard, under my rock. What am I going to do with it?

Over the past two weeks, most of us had continued to maintain that Langford must still be alive. But this week something had happened to reduce our hopes. It had also made me decide to do as Diana Lockhart had suggested: I'd go up to Bangkok to see what I could find out for myself. I'd written to Jim Feng to arrange a meeting with him, and was booked on a flight from Melbourne in ten days.

A number of English-speaking papers around the world, while hedging their bets about Langford's fate, had this week published what amounted to obituaries. A final assessment was being made of his achievement, and of what the papers were now calling his "legend." All this because of an unsubstantiated report that had come in from the Thai-Cambodian border.

Even the *New York Times* had run a three-column story, and tributes had flowed in from journalists in North America, Europe and Asia. Foreign correspondents seemed more or less unanimous in regarding him as one of the best war photographers produced by the Vietnam conflict; he even had hero-worshipers who'd declared him one of the best of all time. I'd been startled by the upsurge of sentiment; Mike seemed to have been liked—even loved—by just about everyone he'd ever worked with. He'd come to belong to the fraternity of international journalists rather than to a country; but the Australian press was claiming him as its own, and was striking organ-notes of sentimental pride in feature articles. At the same time, it was able to revel in a mystery, and to hint that Langford could still reappear.

Like Lockhart, I'd never thought that could be counted on, considering the nature of the Khmer Rouge regime. Yet our hopes had been kept alive until now by Langford's colleagues of the press in Asia.

"Langford can't have bought it," one of them said. He was a cheerful, middle-aged Australian broadcasting correspondent working in Bangkok: one of Mike's drinking mates, interviewed on television. "Not Snow," he said. "He'll turn up, and buy us all drinks in the Foxhole Bar."

But then the report of Mike's death came in.

It had originated with a new batch of Khmer refugees who'd got across the border, and it was vague about details. The exact way in which Langford was supposed to have died remained uncertain, since the refugees hadn't witnessed it, but had got it by word of mouth. On one thing they were unanimous, though: a Western correspondent answering to his description had been taken prisoner by the Khmer Rouge—and this man was said to have been executed.

—I sometimes think of writing up some memoirs from them, now that the war's over. I hope of course that you'll never get to listen to them—no one ever has—but if you do, they may be of interest. You always were fond of history. . . .

I punched off the letter-tape again. Did he really want me to "write up" these memoirs for him? He didn't say so directly; he was always a little sly like that. But I thought he did want it; and if he proved to be lost irrevocably, I'd do it: I knew that already. So did he, standing behind my shoulder.

The taped diaries, nearly all of which I'd now heard, had surprised me deeply. Mike's silences had always made me see him as inarticulate; even unimaginative. But not on tape, it had turned out: not when he was alone, speaking into his machine. Was it old John Langford's beatings that froze him outwardly? His mother's early death? There was an inner life I'd half suspected, but had seldom been given a glimpse of; now it was all in my hands, more complex and intense than I would have thought possible—to be dealt with as I wished.

There'd be a great deal to be sorted through, if I were to do this properly. What I'd have to do first would be to organize all the material into categories: tapes, photographs, work diaries, notebooks, reports and the letters Marcus had given me. There was a small mountain of material: eventually I'd have to start reference cards. I was thinking of a text illustrated with his photographs: a memorial.

The work would be extensive, but not difficult. His notebooks and papers were well organized and barely travel-stained—like the effects of a fastidious bachelor whose existence was completely stable; even dull. Yes: it was all in surprisingly good condition for the personal effects of a war photographer who moved constantly from country to country and battle zone to battle zone, his existence seen as utterly fluid, rootless and dangerous—especially by certain kinds of safe, wistful men who openly envied him, and who questioned me about him with a common expression of naked yearning on their faces: men who lived as Mike did only in their fantasies, and who wouldn't have found his reality tolerable, even for a day.

The work diaries interested me least, containing as they did a bare professional record of assignments covered, costs of film stock, and expenses claimed. But they all had one feature in common that did interest me. Each one of them had the same epigraph written in the flyleaf, in Langford's small, careful hand:

> *You have never lived*
> *Until you almost died;*
> *And for those who fight for them*
> *Life and freedom have a flavor*
> *The protected will never know.*

No author was given. Where did he hit upon it? When I'd first read it, I'd been touched and embarrassed, as though I'd uncovered something no one was meant to see; and I reflected that when a man of action revealed the secrets of his spirit, he was apt to seem jejune. There was something almost schoolboyish about his having faithfully entered that inscription into the work diary every year. But now, looking at it again, I no longer felt so patronizing. This was the creed he'd lived by, and had probably died for. He'd earned the right to inscribe it in his work diaries —even though it did make me see him as incurably young. At thirty and at forty he'd been the same young man, hitting himself each day with the elixir of risk, and writing into the book of each new year the same magic rune that made it all worthwhile. Well, why not? He'd probably lived more intensely in any two weeks than I'd done in a lifetime.

The notebooks had at first appeared to be personal journals, but had proved on examination not to be. Each of them carried the title "Contact Notes," and these contact notebooks dealt entirely with other people—mostly political, military and business leaders in Indochina. They took the form of running diaries, detailing Langford's meetings with the subjects of the entries. Until I'd listened to the tapes, it had been hard for me to see why a war photographer would want background material of such detail, or would record these meetings so meticulously.

It had taken many evenings to carry out this audition of what I'll call his audio diary. He had each cassette neatly labeled, and they dated from February 1965 to the week preceding the fall of Saigon—just over a year ago.

It was clear that in many of these recorded diary entries he had in mind his projected memoirs. There was a good deal of analysis of the progress of the Vietnam War, records of his experiences of battle, and impressions of military and political leaders. Such passages recorded a life lived on the plane of momentous public events; life as history. He certainly documented it well. And I'd begun to suspect that he'd seen himself as living inside his own preplotted story from the time he'd first arrived in Singapore. But many other passages were highly personal. These, as he'd indicated in his taped letter, were pretty clearly records made only for himself. Electrical recording has made this fatally easy to do: much easier than confiding to a written diary. But even in such passages, intimate though they were, I found that Langford still remained somehow a little removed, as he used to do in life; and I wondered if there were once even franker passages that he'd decided to wipe.

The narrative I'd decided I might attempt wouldn't be quite the sort of book he'd planned to do himself. I'd take the liberty of expanding on the account in the audio diary where I felt I had the knowledge or insight to do so—and where his friends might add to the record, when I got up to Bangkok. I might even take some of the liberties of the novelist—some, but not too many. If the result proved more revealing than he might have anticipated, I'd have to hope that he'd forgive me; but it was the inner story, after all, that was the one most worth telling.

In portraying the outer story, I'd be helped by his photographs: the two books on the Indochina war published in New

York and London, and the unpublished prints, negatives and transparencies he'd left in my hands.

I drew some of these out now: black-and-white prints from a package labeled *The Delta*. Images of the Vietnam War accumulated and flowered in the circle of light on the desk—most of them taken by Langford, some by his fellow cameramen or by friends, since these featured Mike himself. South Vietnamese troops in steel helmets slogged thigh-deep through the water of a rice paddy, on patrol: small, wiry men, their faces set with fatigue. They rested on a bank, automatic rifles stacked beside them. They lay flat, under fire. I pulled out more, and the desk was covered with black-and-white glimpses of that long, fruitless conflict which a year ago had slid into history, with all the other wars. Langford's war: the center of his life.

I continued to sort and sample.

At some irrational level, he didn't believe he could die: I knew enough now to feel certain of this. How else to explain his habit of standing up to film under fire, when the troops around him were flat on their bellies? Or his practice of filming in the front line, and even beyond the front line? He never seemed to grow older; well, he might well be safe from age now: might be locked in the frozen youth of the soldier.

He waited, in the darkness behind my chair. The calm voice waited on the tapes, and my grief was ambiguous. Reason said he was probably dead, but emotion said he might still be alive: it was just possible, and the mixture of affection and bafflement that he'd stirred in me as a boy was back again. It reached out to me now from that tropical kingdom of Dis he was lost in, beyond the Thai border.

TWO
THE BELLY OF THE CARP

1.

AUDIO DIARY: LANGFORD

TAPE 1: SINGAPORE, FEBRUARY 22ND, 1965

    —In order to conserve my capital, I've decided to live poor. I've taken a room in a Chinese shophouse: I like the idea of getting to know Singapore from underneath. I have one bag of clothes, this new tape recorder, and the Leica that I hope's going to make my fortune.

    —Came here to do some freelance work. Arranged this with the *Age* before I left: pics for a series of articles they're planning to run on independent Singapore. I also have a reference I can show to the people at the *Straits Times*.

    —I intended eventually to go on to London. But now I'm not sure that I will.

In the first moments of waking, he looks up in puzzlement at the aged ceiling fan revolving above his bed. It's a strange device to him, and makes a noise like a motor boat. Then it says *Singapore,* and he remembers where he is. His wristwatch says ten past seven.

I see him here, in Wu Tak Seng's shophouse: he describes it in loving detail. At twenty-nine, he's still in the peak physical condition of an athlete; he runs five miles a day religiously, and no doubt comes to consciousness with the sense of his body purring in neutral: perfectly tuned and ready to serve him. The single sheet on the bed has been kicked off during the night; he finds himself naked in the dense, humid warmth of Asia.

A strong shaft of sun comes through a doorway framing sky. He contemplates this for a moment and then stretches, beginning to hear a set of novel sounds. There's a trilling and whistling of many small birds, as though he's in an aviary. Half-chanting Chinese voices float up to him and always seem to break off on a note of question, and someone lengthily hawks and spits. Strange mechanical hoots and a persistent, hollow tapping come from somewhere below. He arrived at Paya Lebar airport yesterday evening, on a Qantas 707 from Sydney, and now, as he lies here, the road from the airport unravels again in his head.

His taxi was a rattling Morris Oxford driven by a Sikh, and in the headlights, Asia was disclosed to him for the first time, like a video show arranged for his pleasure. Dim and shadowy, the old road from Paya Lebar was very different from the freeway that brings the air traveler of today into Singapore from Changi: it was a glowing and teeming tunnel of life, walled and roofed over by the dim fronds of palms, and by giant, snake-limbed banyans and rain trees. Dusk became blue-tinged darkness there: *malam,* the big Malay night, flaring and glimmering with the little mysteries of kerosene and oil lamps. These lit up the humble thatch-and-bamboo matting of kampongs; it was a rural road, Langford says, and that appealed to him immediately. Along it, in endless, festive crowds, flowed the figures of three races: Malay, Indian and Chinese. Slow, creaking bullock carts impeded the Sikh's taxi, and the turbaned figure at the wheel cursed as though they were not extraordinary. Toy-tiny roadside stalls with awnings the color of paper were memories from another existence: a life of medieval simplicity, always known about, yet forgotten until now. The stream of warm air through the taxi's open window carried vast vegetable smells; Indians in dhotis pulled hand-carts; Chinese in singlets and baggy shorts rode bicycles. There were few cars, then.

Sometimes the course of a life is set by an experience that's both undemanding and unexpected. A simple drive from the airport had apparently begun this process for Langford, and the voice on the tape develops a soft fervor.

—This is the place I've always been waiting for. If there's any way to stay here, I'm going to do it.

He sits up on the edge of the bed, and begins to look for his clothes.

The room, for which he pays only ten Straits dollars a day, is on the third and topmost floor of a Chinese shophouse on Boat Quay, owned by a merchant called Wu Tak Seng. The two rooms next door are divided into cubicles accommodating whole Chinese families: six or eight people in each. The place is of a kind that very few Europeans in Singapore except the most desperate would ever contemplate renting, even for a few nights. The furnishings are like those in a hostel for derelicts: two metal chairs; a Laminex-topped table; a bare electric bulb. For a wardrobe, there's a hanging-space in one corner, behind a ragged floral curtain. Yet what Langford proposes to do is to make it his home for the next month. What arrangements there were in the way of showers and lavatories in Wu Tak Seng's building he doesn't record; but probably they wouldn't have been as daunting to him as to someone city-bred. After all, he'd spent most of his life in comfortable familiarity with the outdoor dunny on the farm, and its ancient, somber stink; and he'd taken his regular turn at removing the can, and burying the family shit. His upbringing had made him in many ways indifferent to the comforts and luxuries of this century; it would stand him in good stead, in Asia.

The only source of light and air is the doorway at the end of the bed, opening onto a tiny balcony. Two louvered shutter doors, painted a faded and flaking sky blue, stand permanently open; one of them has a broken hinge, and hangs at an angle. He describes a balcony with a balustrade of crumbling stucco, on which sits a struggling jade plant in an earthenware pot. A bare bamboo washing-pole, angled like the bowsprit of a yacht, projects above the street. Dressed, he walks out there, into sun which pours over him like a thick, scalding soup.

The whistling and trilling he heard on waking is explained: many bamboo cages containing pet birds hang bathed in sunlight above the balconies on both sides. Mingled with their sound is that of a radio playing Chinese music, raised Cantonese voices, chugging marine engines, hooting of river craft, roaring trucks, jingling bicycle bells, and the sounds of many feet: clicking shoes, clacking sandals, and the whisper of feet that are bare. There's also a dry, rattling noise, subtle as the sound of the naked feet: in the spreading trees that line the Quay, big black pods are shaken by a faint breeze; a sound that will be stitched into his life here.

The radio is quite close, and a female Chinese voice is singing, high and wailing and plaintive as a child's, yet sexually tantalizing, hovering on the edges of both discord and sweetness: the melody a blend of Chinese and Western. He's never before heard a Cantonese love song, and it flowers for him as that most telling of all hybrids, beauty crossed with strangeness. Together with these sounds, a wave of smells comes up to him: cooking rice and pork, rotting cabbage, rubber, the sweetness of sandalwood, and a strong stink of the tidal inlet. He puts both hands on the warm stucco of the balustrade and breathes in Singapore.

He's perched above the widest part of the river's tidal basin, its brown water jammed with slipper-shaped sampans. Boat Quay's curve follows the curve of Singapore River, and lines of misshapen, tile-roofed godowns and shophouses like Wu Tak Seng's follow this curve into distance, leaning on each other like drunks. The wrought-iron British arch of Elgin Bridge is opposite his balcony; Cavanagh Bridge is visible downriver. A little beyond, he knows, is Singapore harbor, whose space is invisible yet tangible, thrilling as a wind behind the heat.

Just below him, opposite Wu Tak Seng's doorway, Indian coolies in shorts and singlets are unloading bales of rubber from a low, flat bumboat in the river, on whose bow is a painted eye.

The hollow, wooden tapping comes up to him again: a small Chinese boy clad in a singlet and outsize blue shorts is making his way among the crowd, carrying a polished length of bamboo and a little wooden rod. He has a wide grin and a cast in one eye; he taps with the rod in different sequences, and is summoned by Chinese men in shophouse doorways, who hold him in conversation.

This is puzzling; but today, Langford says, he likes it to be puzzling. On a set of old stone ferry steps going down into the water, tidal debris and garbage lie, and he views even this with pleasure: the mysterious litter of Asia.

He dwells a good deal on this moment. It confirms what he learned on his ride from the airport: that his life's new direction lies here.

2.

"Really nothing I can do for you, I'm afraid."

Mr. Chand looked at Langford across the desk with an expression resembling faint surprise. He drew deeply on a cigarette, stubbing it afterwards in an ashtray which held an extraordinary number of butts.

He was Chief of Staff of the *Straits Times:* a thin, ascetic-looking Indian of about forty, whom Langford would never see again; yet he's carefully described in the audio diary. I can understand why: in that special time when everything lay ahead, Mr. Chand was guardian of the gate to a fabled land. He's thus transfigured forever in the lens of youthful hope, with his throaty voice, thick black hair going gray, and the deep lines in his cheeks. His serious, fatigued air was that of many senior journalists, Langford says—as though the tensions and corruptions of the world had reduced him to cynical despair, yet had hardened his resolution to carry on.

Despite the heat, Mr. Chand wore a crisp white business shirt and a narrow, striped tie, and did not perspire. He made Langford feel sweaty and untidy. A number of metal paperweights held down memos, sheets of copy and galley proofs on the desk; edges of paper fluttered like trapped birds in the breeze from an overhead ceiling fan, whose smooth whipping was enviable after the loud chugging of the one in the shophouse. One of the galley proofs read: AMBUSH IN SARAWAK. *Malaysian and British Security Forces Trap Indonesian Raiders.*

Langford liked this office. The tired rattan chairs reminded him of old Hollywood movies about the East, he says. He was filled with a heady longing for the office and Mr. Chand to accept him; to let him stay. The clatter of typewriters came through the open door, and there was the familiar and welcoming smell of printer's ink. He'd walked into this white colonial building without an appointment, and had got in to see Mr. Chand simply by announcing himself at the desk downstairs and requesting an interview. He'd produced a copy of a general reference from the Melbourne *Age,* headed *To Whom It May Concern.* But Mr. Chand had barely glanced at it.

"We have no vacancies for photographers at present," Mr. Chand said. "And even if we did—" He opened his hands and then folded them. "Forgive me for pointing this out, Mr. Langford, but since independence, we like to hire Singapore nationals: people who understand this country. The days when British and Australian news people could blow in here and pick up jobs are gone, I'm afraid."

He could understand that, Langford said. But he wanted to stay in Singapore: he'd taken a great liking to the city.

Mr. Chand's sober face became a shade more friendly. "Not so pleasant just now," he said, "with this bloody Indonesian Confrontation. Difficult times here." He picked up a fresh packet of Players cigarettes and offered one. Langford took it, his hopes beginning to rise.

"You've never been out of Australia before?" Mr. Chand asked. "You simply landed here on spec? A bit rash, wasn't it? But perhaps you have private means."

He had enough to survive a month or so, Langford said. He lit Mr. Chand's cigarette and then his own.

Mr. Chand looked through the fresh smoke with narrowed

eyes. "You are not running away from something in Australia? No? Then my advice to you, old chap, is to go back. Or on to Britain, perhaps. Much easier for you there."

He held out his thin, weary hand. "Goodbye, Mr. Langford."

A black-and-white picture of Wu Tak Seng's shophouse survives. It also shows a stretch of Boat Quay, with the iron arch of Elgin Bridge in the background. Wu Tak Seng himself is sitting on a varnished wooden chair in his doorway, in singlet and baggy shorts. He's framed by the sinister shapes of hanging sharks' fins.

This is one of a number of pictures that Langford shot around the streets of Singapore in that time—some taken for his *Age* feature articles; others purely for pleasure. They're becoming historic, now.

Old Singapore, old colonial Asia, had lingered here just long enough for him to capture it in black and white. Soon it would be replaced by a sanitized metropolis of the late twentieth century: a place where there would be little left of Asia. Glass shopping palaces would sell Japanese transistors and designer jeans, and the last of the crumbling old godowns would cower along the river, waiting to be bulldozed. But in 1965, early in the Johnson era, it was all still there: the Singapore of Raffles, Somerset Maugham and Rex Lockhart. It was newly independent, but still part of Malaysia until August, and it remained for a little longer the city that Rex and Diana had known, in the days when they lived at the Cockpit: the old airline pilots' hotel on Oxley Rise, favored before the War by Qantas Empire Airways flying boat captains, and a favorite now with correspondents on expenses. The Cockpit was where Langford had promised himself he'd move to, when his fortunes turned around.

And the dying British Empire's military reach also remained, in that year. Singapore was still Britain's major naval and air base in Southeast Asia, and from here, at the Far East Land Forces Headquarters at Phoenix Park, the region was still policed. The drawling, confident English voices were sounding for a little while longer in the Long Bar at Raffles and in the Tanglin Club, and the shadow of British authority persisted, in this Chinese city on the equator—just as it had long persisted in Tasmania.

He felt at home here, Langford says.

He couldn't have been farther from home; but I think I understand. Rex Lockhart's stories of his Singapore heyday had filled out a dream begun in the sleepout, so that Singapore, before it was ever seen, had a private and occult meaning. This emerges in passages in the audio diary.

The first diary entries were no doubt recorded on an impulse, in odd hours in his room in the shophouse. Confiding in the cassette machine must have been a solace, at a time when he was a good deal on his own; and what was at first a comfort evidently became a habit. His first, spoken meditation on Singapore needn't be quoted. It's clear to me that the city's real significance for him lay in areas he found too rarefied to express: his efforts to do so are clumsy, and a little embarrassing. Words weren't Langford's medium: his love affair with Singapore is in his pictures, and the pictures are wonderful.

Meanwhile, he nearly starved, after that first month. He became quite ill in the end; yet still he refused to go on to London. The audio diary documents his plight; but he doesn't reveal his difficulties in his letters home to Marcus and Cliff. He never even asks them for a loan.

But Jim Feng remembered Langford's situation, when he and I talked in Bangkok.

Mike came into the bar of the York looking thinner each week, he told me. Yes, a little bit thinner every time, he said: a bit more hungry-looking. Not many people manage to do that now, do they? To starve, I mean. Not from your country, anyway. But Mike did. Jesus, he was thin. He laughed: a soft Chinese laugh that might have been sardonic or affectionate—or both.

The old York Hotel (demolished now) was a favorite with journalists, both as a residence and as an unofficial press club, and was patronized as well by Australian jockeys and trainers, who came up to Asia to make fortunes at the tracks in Singapore,

Kuala Lumpur and Hong Kong. Somehow Langford found his way here in his third week in town.

Although he knew no one, he'd learned that the York was a journalists' hangout. It was on Scott's Road, next door to the much grander and more expensive Goodwood Park. His photograph of the place sits in front of me: like the Goodwood, it was reached through formal gates, and had a drive going up to its entrance. But whereas the Goodwood, remote and haughty on its rise, had a long and impressive driveway, the drive of the York was humbly short, and crossed an open and dangerous monsoon drain. A rambling, tile-roofed old Chinese house that had seen better days, it still had its dignity: two-storied, with black lines of mildew down its dim stucco front, like bloodstains seeping through bandages. Tall old palms stood in tatters, rustling and sighing by the Sino-Greek pillars of the entrance. Batwing doors from a Wild West saloon led into the main bar, which was paneled in beautifully carved Siamese teak.

It was long, cool and cavernous here; customers sat at small round tables, also of teak. Fans flapped and turned in twilit, unlikely heights near the ceiling. There were vast mirrors in gilt frames behind the bar, painted with Chinese birds and flowers, and earthenware spittoons stood in corners, filled with evil black liquid and butts. An aged Hainanese barman in baggy blue trousers and wooden platform sandals shuffled among the tables with drinks, or chopped up ice loudly behind the bar. He had a wise, patient smile, slicked-back gray hair and the flat-backed head of the natives of Hainan island; he made constant loud nose-clearing noises for which he was famous, and was known to the press as Old Charlie. Remembering afternoons in the York, Jim Feng spoke nostalgically of the scuffing of Old Charlie's sandals on the tiles, and of the sound of the ice being chopped.

At first, Jim said, Mike hung out with the jockeys rather than the correspondents. Maybe because his tight situation embarrassed him. One of them, Les Lonergan, was from Hobart; so Mike got a big welcome. There aren't so many Tasmanians in the world, are there? They were noisy, friendly little guys, those jockeys—fond of jokes, like Mike. One of Les Lonergan's party tricks was to disappear inside one of the Shanghai jars in the foyer and make horrible noises; another was to come fast through the batwing doors and then reverse, going out backwards before they closed, like on a rubber band. All those jockeys were making lots of money. Some rode for the trainers who had brought them here; others rode for Singapore stables, and for the Malayan sultans. Les Lonergan rode for the Sultan of Johore.

They offered to lend Mike money, but he refused; instead, he got good tips from them, asking them how their horses were going to go. You know how he always liked to bet. At that time, gambling helped him to survive.

I didn't meet Mike immediately; but you couldn't help noticing him. Very big, among all those little jockeys: they called him "Snow" because of his hair, which was how his nickname got started. Seemed to make a mascot of him: maybe they liked that country look about him. He always looked clean, but his clothes were in terrible taste: cowboy shirts, very loud colors, with piping around the pockets. Always wore those things, didn't he? I wondered what he was doing here. I thought he was a horse trainer, perhaps. Always looked happy, always looked easy. By and by he was very thin, and not so healthy—but he was still cheerful; still seemed to be enjoying himself. I think he wasn't doing so well with the betting, then. He told me he lost a packet on a horse Les Lonergan rode in Singapore; he backed it straight out, but Les came in second.

That was when Donald Mills got interested in Mike. Donald was Second Secretary at the Australian embassy. He used to drink in the York quite a lot. One of the jockeys told Donald that Mike was an Australian, and he went up and started talking to him. And that was how I met Mike myself.

Friday: the long lunch hour at the York. Standing at the bar, Langford felt a touch on his elbow.

Turning, he found a man in his thirties, whose jut-jawed, faintly pugnacious face was set in an expression of cheerful good will. Mills had a ruddy complexion, narrow blue eyes and a high clump of springy bronze hair; he wore a bone-colored safari suit with perfect, knife-edged creases. He had a companion who was Chinese, also in his thirties, wearing a short-sleeved khaki bush shirt faded almost white, and brown, ankle-high boots that were polished to a military brilliance. Jim Feng's smile had a warmth that Mills's seemed to lack.

Mills put out his hand, his arm at full length. "I hear you're fresh from home. That calls for a drink, wouldn't you say?"

He led the way to a table, moving with a high-elbowed briskness that Langford describes as worrying to look at. Jim Feng signaled to Old Charlie, who shuffled forward.

"Busy time, Mr. Jim?"

"Always running, Charlie. Your family are well?" Feng ordered gin-tonics, and then leaned towards Langford.

"I believe you are a cameraman," he said. "I too. Maybe I can be of help, if you're still settling in." His voice was low yet distinct. He was tall and big-boned, with the light ivory skin, well-cut features and long head of North China: a type that Langford says he'd never seen before, knowing only the stocky Cantonese of Singapore and Australia. Feng's hair was slicked straight back from his high, broad forehead in a style that vaguely recalled the film actors of the 1930s.

Langford asked him what newspaper he was on.

"None. I am a news cinecameraman with British Telenews —based here."

"They call him Crazy Jim Feng," Mills said. "He likes working in war zones. Likes being shot at. Can't keep him away from Saigon, and the Borneo border."

Feng's smile widened. "We had a good firefight between the Malaysians and Indonesians in the Bau district last night. But it's bogging down there, now. Vietnam is the place to be." He offered a pack of American cigarettes, and Langford took one.

Mills immediately held out a lighter; but he didn't take a cigarette himself. Then he asked: "Have you got anything going, up here?"

Langford told him he'd been freelancing for the Melbourne *Age,* and had hopes of getting work here for some of the London dailies. While he spoke, he says, he was aware that Mills and Feng were studying him; he describes their faces as showing the concern that people exhibit who have just discovered that a man is seriously ill.

Jim Feng spoke first. "Not easy. Not easy, Mike, selling pics to the Brits from a place like this. They send their own guys if it's something hot. You really need to be with an organization yourself. And film work's better than stills."

He'd never done any news cinecamera work, Langford said.

"You could learn," Feng said.

Mills spoke now. "Have you got a work permit?"

No, Langford told him. Just a tourist visa.

"I might be able to help you," Mills said.

Langford asked Mills what he did here.

"I'm with the Australian embassy."

Jim Feng nodded, grinning with a look of encouragement. "A handy fellow to know," he said.

Mills glanced at his watch. "I have to be pushing along," he said. He stood, draining his glass. "There's someone I believe can help you more than I can," he told Langford. "Also a diplomat, but a lot senior to me. I'll talk to him, if you like. His name's Aubrey Hardwick. He has a lot of contacts." He smiled suddenly, as though confiding a secret. "Yes: you must meet Uncle Aubrey. He'll get you fixed."

AUDIO DIARY: LANGFORD

TAPE 1: MARCH 17TH, 1965

—Early each morning I come out of the shophouse and head for a swimming pool in the city. I did a regular twenty laps there until recently. Now the starvation diet is beginning to slow me down. But I'm still taking pictures.

He loved this time of day, he says, walking through the big fast sunrise and warm air along Boat Quay, finding that the river and the city had been awake before him. His Leica was always around his neck, his camera bag slung from his shoulder. The stuccoed shophouses were pink with dawn, and the dark, spicy cave-mouths in their ground floors were already quick with business.

Chinese merchants drank first cups of tea. Motorized barges, sampans and lighters were moving on the water. The food stalls were open, selling noodles, satay, and the omelette called Foo Yung that was usually Langford's breakfast, together with coffee of a pungency he'd never known before.

There was a Chinese shoeshine boy operating in the shade of a banyan tree by the steps that went down into the river, and Langford always stopped for a shine, paying too much. The picture he took of the boy is one of the best of his Singapore series. The shoeshine boy had spiky hair, a big grin and a cast in one eye: he was the same boy Langford had first seen tapping his way along the Quay with his rod and piece of bamboo. He worked part-time for a Boat Quay trader, taking orders from customers. The number and rhythm of the taps signaled the goods for sale: chopsticks; woks; rice; radios. Langford was trying to learn this tap-language, and each morning he leaned down and knocked on the box in different sequences.

"Listen, tap-tap boy. What's this?"

"Chopsticks! Chopsticks!"

"And this?"

"Nothing, Mr. Mike. That nothing!"

They both laughed. The tap-tap boy looked forward to this game: he was the first of Langford's many street-kid disciples.

—I believe I could spend a lifetime getting Boat Quay and the people and the river into my camera. Life was always hidden behind curtains and doors, at home. But the whole of life's on the streets here.

—I've done all the pictures for the *Age*; what I'm shooting now is just on spec. Don't know how many rolls of Tri-X I've gone through; I'm spending nearly all my money on film. But I don't always get things as they really looked: as I saw them at the time. That's what makes me hurry, in spite of the heat. There's always a more perfect shot than any I've got that's waiting around a corner, or down some steps. Just now and then a shot comes out right, and then it's all worth it. I'm still learning.

—It's all to do with light, I realize that more and more. What light does to things: to surfaces, faces, small objects, distances. Light's everything. Light's my greatest tool. What else is a camera but a light-box?

He moved about Singapore in a long waking dream, shooting pictures he'd never sell, in the grip of that fatal obsession which refuses to let things go. He wouldn't let them dissolve; wouldn't let them die; wouldn't ever resign himself to seeing them drift away on the stream. He would capture them all in his light-box.

He wandered; wandered on.

At the back of Boat Quay was Chinatown, stretching to Collyer Quay and the harbor. Nankin Street, Market Street, Fish Street, Pekin Street, Pagoda Street, Sago Lane: he was lost in dense hot mazes, assailed by the startling stinks of South China, and by all South China's sounds: the wailing of children and of Shanghai opera; Cantonese pop music; banging of metal; gargling shouts. He drifted through a Singapore that's gone, but which all lies in front of me now in his pictures. Old Change Alley's tunnel of trading booths, the merchants in their doorways hissing and cajoling in English, Arabic, Tamil and Cantonese; the white colonial bungalows in Orchard Road, with their deep verandahs and gardens dense as jungles; the warm, thatched nests of the kampongs, threaded through the outskirts. All gone; all captured forever in Langford's light-box.

This was the end of the wet season, and he sheltered in doorways from the brief storms of the northeast monsoon.

Towering, mile-high, ink blue curtains flew together in the sky at extraordinary speed: as he watched, they met beyond Collyer Quay and its roadstead, and over flat infinities of harbor. Then the day went black, except for a tarnished band of light along the horizon. The shophouses, rice mills and crumbling godowns cowered; the hundreds of ships in the harbor, near and far, were dwindled to toys; thunder crashed like gunfire; the gutters and alleys became roaring silver rivers, and the upstairs shutter doors of Chinatown banged shut: crimson; green; celestial blue.

But it all ceased in moments. The sun struck out again after last heavy drops, and colors brilliantly returned. A dripping sky-blue shutter or the red flowers of a flame-of-the-forest tree were images exploding on the vision after blindness. He wandered on, through steaming calm.

Old amahs in black pantaloons lit joss sticks in wayside temples, and prayed for prosperity. Young Indian pimps with faces like sly schoolmasters sidled up and murmured to him of virgins, and nice clean English ladies. And Langford talked to everyone: a convention of the Tasmanian countryside which he never thought of abandoning.

He began to be known. Chinese traders greeted him by name, and chatted with him. Malay shopkeepers and their tribes of assistants, who often had no English at all, crowded about him in the alleys where he shot pictures. They would bring out a chair onto the path for him to sit on. Enthroned, he would pass around cigarettes. I see him there, among the broad, smiling brown faces, waving his hands in the way that he had when he was trying to communicate: an outlandish guest in his 1950s cowboy shirt, perfectly happy.

As time goes on, the audio diary and the pictures dwell extensively on the food in the streets.

Spitting, bare-chested, chain-smoking cooks stir sizzling iron cauldrons over open flames, among deadlocked smells of urine and sandalwood, stale cabbage and spices. Honey-glazed roast ducks hang in doorways beside weird sea slugs and dried fish. There are pictures of giant crabs and prawns; of mighty platters of chopped vegetables; of colored Chinese cakes behind glass: a child's vision of plenty. And no doubt his vision was sharpened by hunger—since for all their cheapness, most of these things had come to be beyond his pocket.

In the first month here he'd eaten well, in the restaurants along Orchard Road; he'd even had curry in the Tiffin Room at Raffles. But now, as the money ran out, he'd taken to eating in the humble open-air places around Boat Quay that catered for poor waterhands. Serenaded by a loud radio broadcasting strangled arias from Shanghai opera, stooped over a wooden table of kindergarten size, like a boy sent to a lower grade for punishment, he was surrounded by coolies in ragged singlets and shorts who shoveled the food fast into their mouths, bent low over their bowls, and stared at him curiously, since no Europeans ever came here. Hungrily, still clumsy with his chopsticks, he devoured his own beans and rice and few shreds of pork, and drank the cheap black Chinese tea.

By the end of March, all he could afford any more was the *makan* cart.

AUDIO DIARY: LANGFORD

TAPE 2: MARCH 25TH, 1965

—Now that my money's almost gone, I wait every evening on the balcony for the woman with the *makan* cart. It rides on bicycle wheels; there are lots of these little mobile food stalls stationed along Boat Quay, making tours at regular intervals. Each one specializes in a particular cheap dish. Hers is noodle soup, with chicken and prawns: sustaining. I've decided to live on that, until the *Age* check comes: one meal a day.

—I look forward to seeing the *makan* woman, and not just for the food. She cheers me up. She's a very short, stocky young Chinese with a snub-nosed face a bit like a Pekingese dog's: but it's an attractive face, with a lot of humor in it. She wears a faded blue jacket, black pantaloons and old-style coolie hat; she shuffles along in wooden platform clogs. There seems to be a tribe of these Chinese women hawkers around the Quay, all dressed alike. A small girl trails after her with two buckets to wash the bowls: I listen for the buckets and the clogs, and the *makan* woman's voice calling her wares in Chinese. She thinks it's very funny that I bring my bowl to her to be filled, like the rest of the people here; she laughs and makes jokes that I don't understand.

Langford was expecting a second check from the *Age* at this time: when it arrived, he hoped to live normally again. He talks of phone calls to a stringer for the London *Daily Mail* in Kuala Lumpur, who was promising him casual work; but whether it ever eventuated he doesn't say. At such times, we come to depend on recurring figures that reassure—and it's surely a measure of the lonely extremity of his position that he waited as he did for the *makan* woman.

Wu Tak Seng had noticed his frequent descents to the noodle soup cart. For a few dollars, he sold him a device that was used by some of the other tenants: a wicker tray attached to a rope, which Langford was able to let down from the balcony with his bowl and his money. And the tray proved its worth, Langford says, because shortly after purchasing it he fell ill, and grew too weak to get downstairs.

He had a strong stomach, and had not until now caught one of the gastric complaints that most Europeans went through after arrival here. But inevitably, his visits to the cheap eating places along Boat Quay had caught up with him. What he seems to have contracted was no ordinary gastritis but a form of Asian influenza. This was in the week after his meeting with Donald Mills and Jim Feng in the York.

Diarrhea and vomiting kept him to the room: his condition grew worse, and soon he was too weak to get up very much at all. He lay on his narrow iron bed, whose cheap cotton slip was decorated with repeated figures of Donald Duck. The yellow plaster walls had enormous damp-stains; and these, he says, began to take on frightening shapes: he began to hallucinate. Black tea, which he kept by his bed in a big vacuum flask, and his bowl of noodle soup in the evening, were all he could keep down; and after three days he could no longer manage the soup.

There came a time when he drifted, unaware of the passing hours, and only just conscious of day and night. There was no plumbing in his room, so that his situation must now have become unpleasant. He mentions a bucket with a lid which he had to take out and empty, in intervals when he felt strong enough.

And the passages in the audio diary begin now to be more and more disjointed. Spoken in a voice that grows slower and more feeble—coming at times from the edges of delirium—they end by being quite strange. I'm surprised that he didn't wipe them.

TAPE 2: MARCH 27TH

—The *Age* check still hasn't come. If it doesn't turn up soon, I'll be in trouble.

—Getting light-headed, and afraid this may be more than just a gastric wog. Wu Tak Seng just came up to see me. He's never done this before, but he came to tell me there was no mail for me. Maybe he's worried about the rent. More likely he's concerned I'll get seriously ill, and cause some sort of trouble. He started hinting at this: stood in the doorway in those baggy navy shorts of his, bowlegged. Queer, seeing him here instead of downstairs in the grocery, where he sits all day at the desk with his abacus. He has a big square head, shaven almost bald; lots of gold teeth. He asked me if I wanted help.

—You wa' me to ge' do'tor?

—Cantonese have an accent like Cockney: swallow the ends of their words. I told him I was OK, but he still stood there. He was looking at Diana's picture, which I keep on the table by the bed. After a while, he said: You nice young gen'leman. Wrong here. Need be'er place.

—Gentleman! I laughed, and told him I liked it here, and that I'd be fine. But he just shook his head, sucked his teeth and shuffled out. Poor Mr. Wu: he's been kind to me. I hope he doesn't ask me to go.

MARCH 28th

—Very weak. Should I let Mr. Wu call a doctor? Can't afford to pay one.

—Voices in my head sometimes; voices outside it. Talking into this machine helps keep my head clear; keeps things real.

—Giant red cockroaches walking up the walls, and even on my table. They're bloody monsters: never saw any of such a size. Had a dream of being locked in a room even worse than this one, and the bastards were crawling everywhere, eating me. Horrible: I woke yelling out, like Ken used to do.

—The sounds down on Boat Quay are very distinct: especially the rustling pods on the trees. There goes my mate the tap-tap boy, tapping on his bamboo cylinder. Woks. Radios. This room feels like a coffin, but most of the sounds here are good sounds, and I concentrate on feeling better. Singapore outside is like a good taste in my mouth. I think about the spaces of the harbor and the Malacca Strait, and it keeps me cool. Sometimes I think about the hop fields at home; but that's not such a good idea.

MARCH 29th

—Weak. Have been very bad, and can hardly get downstairs to empty the bucket and fetch more tea. Must have liquid. No food for days: how many? Delirious. Dreamed about Luke Goddard. Hunted him down and shot him in the chest with a .303, but he wouldn't die: he went on running through the bush in his black overcoat, laughing at me.

—The *makan* woman went by through the room, pushing her cart, the wheels squeaking. Her smile. Wanted her to stay.

—*Tiger Balm:* the sign winking out the door. Would it help? What is it? Do you drink it? Rub it in?

—Diana was here.

MARCH 30th

—Better; head clear, but can't eat much. Wu Tak Seng brought me tea and some rice. Still urges me to get a doctor.

—Dreamed of Diana again. Does she still go to Quigley's for coffee, at four in the afternoon? I saw her sitting there, in her green tartan dress. And saw her on the corner of Tamar Street, her face white under the dark beret, saying goodbye. Strain making her eyes big, tears making her mascara run.

—Goodbye. Behind us in the dark was that two-storied, red-brick building with bay windows that I never used to notice much, where Harwood the dentist has his surgery. Now I remember every bloody detail.

—Mum was here for a while, too. She sat quietly on the steel chair, looking sad. She spoke only once.

—Take care of yourself, Chick. I've lost Ken—I don't want to lose you.

3.

I could not believe how he was living, Jim said. Like a poor Chinese. Letting down a basket for his food from the *makan* cart.

Crazy! I didn't know then that he could have written home for money—that he was too proud to do it. Well, the only thing Mike ever cadged was cigarettes.

A Chinese boy took us to him: a street kid. Mike was a Pied Piper for such kids, from the beginning.

The sun had gone down behind Sumatra. The silent, orange and white tingling of hundreds of ships' lights had broken out in the roads and the Singapore Strait: in that space beyond the city's heated mazes that was cool in Langford's head. His doors framed spicy darkness, and a night he couldn't join; a neon tiger leaped and leaped again above a godown around the Quay, a sign beneath it winking on and off, saying: *Tiger Balm.*

He dwells on this sign a lot: it seems to have mesmerized him, as he fought to hold reality in focus.

"Mr. Mike? Here are friends."

He opened his eyes. The tap-tap boy with the crooked gaze stood in the open doorway, grinning as usual. Behind him stood Jim Feng and Donald Mills. Langford struggled to sit up, and couldn't.

A conversation seemed to have begun; he didn't take in the beginning of it, he says.

"You can't stay here," Jim Feng was saying. His long, ivory face was sober yet concerned.

The boy had gone, and Donald Mills was examining the room—which Jim Feng was too polite to do. Someone had switched on the weak electric bulb, and Mills glanced sharply about at the sordid fittings, his expression both inquisitive and appalled; he wrinkled his nose at the bucket with its lid, his perfect safari jacket shining in the gloom like phosphorescence. Finally he looked back at Langford, who lay under a sheet on the narrow mattress with the grimy Donald Duck slip.

"Christ," Mills said quietly. "We'll have to get you out of here, mate."

It wasn't their responsibility, Langford told them. He'd be all right; he was getting better. He asked them how they'd found him.

"Mr. Wu let us come up," Jim Feng said. "One of the jockeys told me you lived along Boat Quay, so we asked around. When you stopped showing up in the York, we got a little bit concerned."

"You weren't hard to find," Mills put in. "You seem pretty popular around here. The boy knew who we meant straightaway."

"Sorry about crashing in," Jim Feng said. "You don't mind?"

No, Langford said, but he couldn't offer them much hospitality.

Mills picked up one of the metal chairs, turned it around, set it close to the bed, and straddled it. "Listen, Mike. You may think this is just Delhi Belly you've caught, but it's obviously not. If you get much weaker, there are nastier bugs."

Langford told him he wasn't worried; he'd had his shots.

"Against everything? Hepatitis? Meningitis? No. So be sensible," Mills said. "I don't want to pry into your affairs, but I assume you're pretty broke."

He was expecting a check, Langford said.

"And after that?"

Langford said nothing. He'd begun to find it difficult to talk, and was drifting off again.

"Okay, this is none of my business," Mills said. "If you like, Jim and I will walk out of here. But if you go completely broke, or get seriously ill, it'll probably become our business, at the embassy. We'll have to get you home."

No, Langford said. That wouldn't arise. He had enough money to survive, and he wasn't going home.

"All right," Mills said. "But it's reasonable your embassy should look after you through this. Later, you can pay us back. Meanwhile, I've brought you some good news." He folded his arms on the back of the chair. "My friend Aubrey Hardwick believes he can help you. But first we've got to get you on your feet." He looked at Diana's picture in its vinyl frame, propped against the flask of tea. "Your girlfriend?"

Just a friend, Langford told him.

"Very beautiful woman. You must miss her." Mills stood up. "I can be back here with an embassy car for you inside an hour.

Jim'll help you pack. We'll take you around to the Cockpit, and settle you in there. Tomorrow I'll get our doctor to have a look at you."

Looking at Langford over Mills's shoulder, Jim Feng nodded, and seemed to wink.

Langford lay back on his single pillow, staring at them both. He was still light-headed.

—I wondered whether they were actually in the room at all.

He woke to find himself in Singapore of the 1930s.

He was lying back on pillows that smelled sweetly of ironing: the linen of the Cockpit Hotel, whose gates he'd peered through wistfully on his wanderings. Somewhere, an air-conditioning unit throbbed softly, maintaining the climate of a cool-temperate zone. Last night, Mills had given him a battery of tablets that had evidently been effective: he was still weak, he says, but his fever and the griping pains in his gut were gone.

Beyond red curtains that stood open at the foot of the bed, windows with glass louvers framed a tropical garden of great beauty. Purple bougainvillea blazed, making him blink; banyan trees, fan palms and jacarandas cast shadows on a green lawn, and an old Indian gardener in an orange turban and black waistcoat was sweeping up blossoms from the grass. Strayed onto the lawn out of 1935, he seemed to inhabit some territory of memory rather than the present, and Langford watched him, hypnotized.

This garden (now gone into history, with the old Cockpit itself), extended behind the main building. A small row of tile-roofed bungalows stood there, with front doors painted Chinese red, and Langford had been put into a suite in one of these bungalows. Apart from the air-conditioning unit, its decor belonged entirely to British Singapore of the pre–World War Two period. There was a good deal more Chinese red in the room: a red-lacquered writing desk, a glossy red door to the bathroom; black-lacquered Chinese chairs with red upholstery. There were prints on the walls of fox-hunting scenes, and English easy chairs with chintz covers and cushions.

A phone rang on the red-lacquered table beside his bed.

He jumped; he'd been drifting off. The brisk, loud voice that came from the instrument sounded like that of a British military officer, and brought him fully awake.

"Good morning. Am I speaking with Michael Langford? Excellent. My name is Hardwick—Aubrey Hardwick. Donald will have spoken to you about me. How are you this morning?"

Langford said that he was better. Collecting his wits, he made a speech thanking the Australian embassy for its generosity. He apologized for the inconvenience.

"Oh, you'll make it up to us," the voice said. "Don't worry about that." There was a throaty laugh. "Meanwhile, just relax and get better. You *sound* all right, I must say: you must be a very fit guy to come back so fast. May I offer some advice? When you put this phone down, pick it up again, dial room service, and order black tea and dry toast. The Cockpit will provide. Our doctor should get to you around midday. Obey his orders."

Langford told him he appreciated all that was being done, but that he couldn't stay here. The accommodation was out of his range.

"Do what you're told, please, until you're cured," Hardwick said. "Don't worry about the bills—you'll be well able to pay for them soon. That's what you and I have to discuss. Meet me for dinner at the Goodwood Park Hotel on Friday evening: are you free? Good. The Gordon Grill Room: seven-thirty."

Langford tried to ask Hardwick what he had in mind. But the military voice cut him off. "Patience. All will be explained, old fellow, as soon as you get to the Goodwood."

The phone was abruptly hung up.

"How is the Scotch fillet?" Hardwick asked. "Done as you wanted?"

—I told him it was perfect. My first steak in months was a pretty intense experience.

The audio diary entry describes the Gordon Grill Room in appreciative detail: tartan wallpaper, soft light from tartan-shaded table lamps, starched white tablecloths, and a platoon of Chinese waitresses in navy tunics, every one of them pretty. A number of British and Australian correspondents were dining at other tables, and Hardwick pointed out some of the well-known identities.

The entry also goes into some detail in describing Hardwick himself. He'd asked Langford immediately to call him Aubrey, and he's referred to as Aubrey from this point on. He wore a single-breasted, lightweight khaki suit, and a striped tie that Langford assumed was a regimental one, since Hardwick's style and appearance suggested a military past. But Langford began to revise the notion as an almost theatrical vivaciousness emerged: he couldn't quite see Aubrey as a soldier, despite the martial erectness and the blond-white, brutally crew-cut hair—which he describes as resembling the fur of a short-haired dog. He also makes mention of Aubrey's light, unwinking eyes, calling them "watchful." The word's apt, from what others have told me. No photograph of Aubrey exists.

—I thought he was a bullshit artist, at first. No wonder Mills calls him Uncle Aubrey. But I humored him—and I was bloody glad I did. There's a lot more to him than that.

"Have a little more Bordeaux," Aubrey said. "I'll say this for the French, they do get it right with wine. We go on about those Barossa and Hunter River reds of ours, but really! No. There's no comparison, in my mind. But I'm a Francophile; I spent a good deal of my youth there."

This speech surprised Langford; he'd assumed Aubrey to be British, not Australian, and he asked what years Hardwick had been in France.

"Ah-ha, Michael, you're trying to find out how antique I am. Well, the answer is: *very* antique. I was there before the War, at about your age, doing postgraduate study at the Sorbonne."

This was another surprise, Langford says. He'd assumed Aubrey to be around forty; but it seemed he was over fifty.

"Then it all blew up," Aubrey was saying, sawing neatly at his steak. "The Krauts made their tank-dash to Paris, and that lovely time was over. An age was over, as you probably dimly know. Interesting times began for me then, as they did for quite a few others. But enough of my youth. Here you are with *your* youth on the wing, and we have to do something for you."

Chewing, he put down his knife and fork and looked directly at Langford for some fifteen seconds before continuing. "I understand that you want to work here as a news cameraman. What I propose to do is to get you started with British Telenews, working with Jim Feng. They're looking for an extra man, since there are now two big stories escalating at once: Indonesia's confrontation of Malaysia, and the conflict in Vietnam. This means you'd be covering battle."

He examined Langford with a questioning expression, pausing again as though to give him an opportunity to object. When Langford merely waited, he picked up his knife and fork and went on.

"Now that President Johnson has begun this bombing campaign against the North Vietnamese, and American forces are coming into the South in serious numbers, the demand for coverage will grow. The Vietnam War's at a new stage: a very interesting one. Does this appeal to you?"

At first, Langford seems to have been disbelieving. Yes, he said, it appealed to him very much. But there'd be dozens of trained news cameramen running after a job like that when it was advertised: why should Telenews give it to him?

"Ah, but perhaps it need *not* be advertised." Aubrey smiled and leaned forward. "Do you know much about Telenews? It's a London-based newsfilm company. It offers stuff to the television networks that gives them a different angle from the American one. The BBC are shareholders—and so is the Australian Broadcasting Service. And here in Singapore, Telenews shares the ABS office, which is administered by ABS's Southeast Asian chief. Arthur Noonan has the power to hire and fire; and Arthur happens to be a pal of mine."

He sat back, smiling with an air of innocent pleasure, brows raised, watching Langford's face; and Langford began to see that he stood on the brink of everything he'd ever wanted: that he had only to walk through the door.

"Jim Feng will train you," Aubrey was saying. "Great guy,

Jim: the son of a mandarin. The family fled to Hong Kong just after the War, when the Communists were coming to power. As well that they did—or they would have been liquidated. So our Jim's a member of a vanished class of people. Sad, don't you think? But he's good at his job—and he'll show you all you need to know about covering combat."

He smiled, and raised his glass. "To your future as a combat cameraman."

Most of the correspondents had gone now; the room was half empty. Softly, on the piped music system, Gertrude Lawrence was singing "Someday I'll Find You." Aubrey sipped his brandy, nursing the balloon in both hands and studying Langford openly. He was now a little drunk, and so was Langford.

"You look Irish. Is that your ancestry? Sorry, I'm being rather personal, but these things interest me. I flatter myself I can pick people's origins."

Langford told him that his ancestors were English and Norwegian. One great-great-grandfather was Protestant Irish.

"Ah-ha! The Ascendancy," Aubrey said. "Yes, I see it now: the elongated face, and the less flamboyant charm than the Paddies exert. Now I *am* being personal. A strange lot, the Anglo-Irish; a bit fey and decadent. But look who they gave us. Swift; Wilde; Shaw; Yeats. But I doubt that you're interested in literature. Action's more your line, isn't it?" He didn't wait for an answer, but went on. "When I hear you talk, Michael, I hear myself at your age. In my day, as soon as we'd come of age, we hopped onto a ship to Europe to make direct contact with history. You've come to Asia instead; you've sensed that the vortex is here. You're right, and I admire you for that—especially since you seem to have come with no guarantee of survival. History's a game that's played for keeps, in my sort of work—and it will be in yours. But for most Australians, it's a dimension of reality that's only found on TV—don't you agree? The reason Australia's half asleep is that it's *outside* history. The Japanese nearly woke us up, but they didn't quite get there. So we went on sleeping. I wonder who *will* wake us up? What do you think? Sukarno? The Communists in Asia? Is the domino theory true or false?"

Langford makes no record of his answers. It's Hardwick's talk, not his own, that he obviously wants to record, and the detail with which he does so is evidence of the effect that Aubrey had on him. Despite his amusement at the older man's dated style and theatricality, he plainly found him intriguing— although he doesn't record a clear judgment of him. The only direct comment he makes is that Aubrey gave the impression of being close to the sources of events—and perhaps of being able to tinker with their mechanisms. But when he asked Aubrey what work he was engaged in, the answers he was given were very general.

"I was a diplomat—but not any more, alas. I now work for our Department of Defense, based in Melbourne. I've been seconded to Foreign Affairs, and attached to the embassy here in a temporary capacity. Examining the ramifications of British military withdrawal from Singapore. Liaising with foreign ministers, discussing policy decisions—that sort of thing." He took out a packet of cigars, and passed one to Langford. "But let's get back to history."

His cigar lit, he drew deeply; then he gestured with it towards a window that framed the tall palm trees at the entrance of the Goodwood. "Consider, Michael. When Britain does pull out of here—when Phoenix Park closes down—that will be the final end of the Empire. Funny: I believe an Australian of my generation finds this more bloody poignant than the Brits themselves do; *they've* lost interest, or numbed themselves. But the facts are the facts. The most successful empire since Rome's: finally gone. And Australia naked: our shield in Asia taken away. It's only the Brits, really, who are holding back Sukarno. Without the Canberra jets on standby at Kuching, without the British Marines and the Gurkhas in Borneo, he'd have invaded Malaysia long ago. Britain still holds up this part of the world—not America. But it's almost over: this is the last act. I wonder what the shade of Stamford Raffles thinks—that marvelous man who built this place out of a swamp, and brought British freedom and justice to the eastern seas."

He drained his brandy, and signaled for two more. They had

both drunk quite a few now, Langford says; Aubrey's voice had taken on a rhetorical boom, and was very faintly slurred. "Let's see," he said. "You're twenty-nine, didn't you say?"

Langford hadn't said; but he nodded.

"Then you're old enough to remember the maps where most of the world was colored imperial red. Yes? You're of the last generation of children of the British Empire. Do you remember your Kipling?

> " 'Take 'old o' the Wings o' the Mornin',
> An' flop round the earth till you're dead;
> But you won't get away from the tune that they play
> To the bloomin' old rag over'ead.' "

He laughed, picked up his brandy, and raised it. "No longer true, alas. Here's to the Empire on which the sun is finally setting. How can the Brits know what *we* feel, we children of the old Dominions? It was always like unrequited love; and now the beloved is departing!"

It was impossible to tell whether this was satire or sentiment, Langford says; but he drank the toast. He makes no record of his own sentiments at this point; nor of what he said in reply. But he registers no objection to that "we"; and I believe I catch a whiff of the books in the sleepout.

Hardwick glanced at his watch. "We'll talk again, Michael." He stood, swaying. "My God, I'm tiddly. Haven't the stamina of you young chaps. Oh, for a dose of your lovely youth, that will take you to so many bloody marvelous things." His hand on Langford's shoulder, he began to negotiate a path for them towards the door.

Uncle Aubrey was the envoy of the future, smiling at the entrance to the world. He swung the door open and Langford hurried through, without a second's thought.

4.

The combined Telenews-ABS office was in a ferroconcrete building that Langford describes as smelling of ink and latrines, standing on a rise in Peck Hay Road.

Aubrey's friend Arthur Noonan, the ABS bureau chief, was an elderly, permanently drunk Australian of huge girth and flaming complexion. He flew the national flag by appearing always in elastic-sided bush boots, and was usually to be found in the bars or at the Tanglin Club instead of in the office. An efficient Chinese accountant and his staff handled the administration. Noonan took Langford to the York for a long, alcoholic lunch, delivering a hoarse lecture about the conditions of the job; after which, Langford says, the chief had little more to do with him.

Transient Australian and British broadcasting correspondents were the aristocrats here, Langford found: a cameraman was given the use of a small desk in a corner as a favor. But he sat there in a state of bliss, savoring his good fortune. He'd been hired on trial as a stringer, with the freedom to travel to any country in the region.

—I'd have taken a table in the toilet, if they wanted. It all seems too good to be true.

—Jim Feng's teaching me how to use two different cinecameras: the heavy Auricon, which you use with a soundman, and the little, spring-loaded Bell and Howell. I like the Bell and Howell: it lets you move easily, without a soundman.

—Jim's very courteous and generous with his time. He went to a British school when he arrived in Hong Kong at the age of fourteen; he speaks English well but a bit too correctly, and he uses American slang as well as British. No sweat, he'll say, in that Hong Kong–British accent: it amuses me. His real name is Feng Ming Chi: he took the name Jim to Anglicize himself. Remembering what Aubrey told me about his background, I sometimes feel a bit sad for him—but he always seems in good spirits.

—Singapore's basically a rest place for correspondents: a service station, not a news center. The focus is further east: Saigon; Vientiane; Phnom

Penh. There's a Telenews office in Saigon, and Jim spends most of his time up there, when he's not in Borneo. He took me to Sarawak last week, and we filmed some Indonesian prisoners being brought in. But no fighting; it's all pretty quiet there.

—I'll be glad when Jim thinks I'm ready to cover in Vietnam: I want to get up there soon. I'm afraid the war there may not last.

"They say that revolution's what's needed in Southeast Asia—that only Marxist dictatorship will deliver the people from their cycle of misery," Aubrey said. "This is very sad nonsense, Michael. The lessons of the French Revolution seem to have been forgotten."

He and Langford were walking around Boat Quay together, following the curve of the river that the Chinese call the Belly of the Carp. I hear Aubrey pitching his voice above the hubbub: engines; horns; bicycle bells. They met to take these walks often, Langford says, in the early mornings before work; and once again he records Aubrey's remarks with remarkable faithfulness. Yet he never makes clear the purpose of their meetings—or whether they had any purpose at all. Nor does he make any judgment or comment on Aubrey's discourses—even though they seem like the discourses of a mentor.

"Revolution does *not* spring from the people, but from power-drunk and obsessive intellectuals who despise the people," Aubrey said. "Such creatures always move immediately to limit freedom. Yet you can't create freedom out of unfreedom, can you? The intellectually rigid seem never to take that in."

Langford pictures Hardwick halting in the shade of a banyan, running a hand over his head's whitish blond stubble. Musing on the river and its traffic, his well-pressed, faded khaki bush shirt like a relic of colonial Malaya, Hardwick seemed to belong here, Langford says, in a way that most transient Europeans didn't.

"You should study the French and Russian revolutions," Aubrey said, "if you're to cover what's going on in this part of the world. Revolution: colonizing Europe's most poisonous departing gift to Asia! The irony is that it's largely been left to the Americans to deal with the effects of the poison. But the military intervention in Vietnam is only what you *see:* a good deal goes on under the surface. And the stakes really do matter."

Now they had turned into Chinatown, and were moving down its narrow, teeming gullies, under strings of paper flowers. The throaty voice grew confiding, competing with the wail of Cantonese singers from radios, and Aubrey took Langford's arm, guiding him around piles of rotting vegetables.

—He talked about a hidden war in Indochina, not known to the public. Cross-border operations; a secret American air war in Laos. And he said that this secret war would decide the outcome of the open one.

"There are pretty big changes coming in this part of the world," Aubrey said. "And they won't all go our way. I'm speaking of Australia, Michael. We must learn when to adapt and when to resist, or be swallowed up. That's where you could be involved: you could be very valuable, if you wanted to be. You'll soon see what I mean when you get to Vietnam. Now that our troops are arriving to back the Americans, the balloon's going up there: and I can tell you in confidence, we're going to be ten times more involved in this war than most people think. You're off to Saigon soon? Good. I can give you a few contacts there. So can Donald Mills: he's going there next month as Second Secretary. He'll be briefing Canberra on the situation in Vietnam as it develops. You do see the importance."

He stopped, and let go of Langford's arm—which Langford says he found something of a relief; he wasn't used to these old-fashioned intimacies. Aubrey took out a notebook and began to write down an address.

"It's very important you look up this lady," he said. "A French Vietnamese friend of mine from Paris days—very dear to me, and a brilliant woman. Claudine knows everyone in Saigon. Her husband runs a trading company, and has connections on both sides: there's a bit of a mystery about his whereabouts just now. Whatever you do, look her up immediately: she'll be expecting it. And keep in touch with Mills: he'll give you a lot of leads. You'll be able to help him too, if you feel inclined. Let him know from time to time the way you see things going in the country: a cameraman's in a wonderful position to do that. Just give him the flavor and feel—I know he'll be eternally grateful."

—I said I'd try to help where I could, and that I appreciated all he'd done for me.

"You'll show your appreciation eventually, dear boy, I've no doubt of it," Aubrey said. "There's a *quid pro quo* for everything in this life: haven't you noticed that yet?"

THREE
THE DELTA

1.

I have in front of me a picture of Langford with Jim Feng, taken somewhere in Vietnam in 1965. No details are given on the back. They're seated in the topless Jeep they called the Big Budgie, pulled over at the side of a highway.

Both men are in combat fatigues. Jim Feng is laughing: long hands resting on the wheel, long head thrown back, long horse teeth gleaming, backswept hair shining and perfect—a Chinese army officer in an old newsreel. Langford is pointing at him, his face in profile miming shock-horror: a lost joke.

The picture—like most of the others Mike left me—is a black-and-white news-style photograph, six inches by eight. So the Budgie's flamboyant blues and yellows can't be seen, and the fabled vehicle looks like any other dilapidated Jeep with the top cut off. The photograph is typical of a good many others taken at this time: pictures that Langford and Jim Feng and their CBS competitor Dmitri Volkov shot of each other for amusement in the field, in periods of waiting. They're laughing in nearly all these pictures.

Vietnam in the sixties was the peak of their youth. Middle

age and the war in Cambodia were scarcely visible on the horizon, and laughter was like breathing. But Vietnam was also the place where their youth casually vanished. It vanished while they shot the action; vanished while they joked. Jokes were their food: more necessary than whiskey, or the many other stimulants the region and the period had to offer. They were high on everything, in those years, but their greatest high was risk: that sprint along the near edge of death they never tired of repeating.

The surviving combat cameramen who were Langford's friends continue to chase stories, in their middle age—but the big story is over for them. They linger in Hong Kong; Bangkok; Singapore. Each year, their cumbersome gear has been getting a little heavier for the cinecameramen to carry, and the stills photographers find their wind growing shorter, their reflexes slowing. They're like those aging gunmen in the Western movies that Mike and I watched in the little cinema in New Norfolk, on Saturday afternoons. It's time for them to hang up their irons.

But how can they do that? The greatest high of all will be gone then: the one presided over by Dis, commander of the dead, whose other name is Meaning.

He arrived in Vietnam in the May of Rolling Thunder, coming in, as everybody did, through Tan Son Nhut.

The Pan American Boeing 707 banked as it prepared to land, leaning at an angle that passenger aircraft didn't usually attempt: a precaution against Viet Cong snipers on the ground. The landscape tilted on its side, filling the whole porthole, and Langford was looking at flat, sack-brown spaces, thin dark lines of trees and long silver canals, rushing upwards. The plane dropped lower, returning to the horizontal, and the airfield appeared.

In this year, the United States Military Assistance Command in Vietnam had transformed a sleepy civil airport into one of the busiest on earth. Lined and teeming and glittering with aircraft, Tan Son Nhut had become a military citadel, with taxiways, high-speed turnoffs, operations buildings, mess halls and barracks, its air-conditioned PX stores and commissaries carrying every necessity of American life from ice cream to stereo systems. Aircraft landed and took off without cease, so that seldom less than a dozen were airborne at one time. Concrete runways stretched to the horizon.

The 707 taxied in between rows of screens painted military green, where pierced-steel planking flashed in the sun. Scores of American servicemen in olive fatigue caps and T-shirts tended Phantoms, Thunderchiefs and Super Sabres: fighter-bombers molded so exquisitely for speed that they seemed to breathe not death but exhilaration: lovely darts, crafted to puncture reality's barrier, and then go on. Beside them were Hercules transports like winged barns, and the helicopter transports and gunships of the new age: the Shawnees, Hueys and Chinooks that were changing the style of war.

Tan Son Nhut was the imperial platform from which the war was being directed. From here, the United States had just launched Operation Rolling Thunder: the full-scale bombing of the North which was intended to end the struggle. But it would not end the struggle; the war was merely beginning.

Coming down the gangway, squinting in the blinding heat that rebounded from the tarmac, greeted by smells of aviation fuel and the roar of afterburners, Leica around his neck, camera bag over his shoulder, Langford was entering his future: that war whose remorseless sequences would devour the rest of his life.

The Big Budgie's blue and cream color scheme was intended to advertise the fact that it was no longer a military vehicle. According to Jim Feng, this dissuaded the Viet Cong guerrillas in the city from bombing it. Or he hoped that it did: you could never be sure. He kept the Budgie parked in the garage of the Continental Palace Hotel on Tu Do Street, where he and Langford were sharing a room.

At the wheel of the Budgie now, with Langford beside him, Jim drove with hair-raising skill, swinging and weaving through Tu Do's evening traffic. Both men wore garlands of wild jasmine, sold to them by child hawkers who worked the front of the Continental. Four of these street children rode in the back of the Jeep: three boys, and a long-haired teenaged girl who was crippled. A single crutch propped on the seat beside her, she sat up proudly, a tray slung from her neck displaying her wares: cigarettes and flowers.

Little Renault taxis painted blue and cream like the Budgie —aged survivors from the French days—scurried and buzzed and hooted among U.S. Army trucks and big-finned Chevrolets and Fords from the 1950s. The traffic jam was permanent, complex, and brutally loud. Trishaws the French had called cyclos were pedaled through pandemonium by wiry men in straw hats and nineteenth-century sun helmets, their bells ringing like alarm clocks. These and an insect swarm of bicycles, motorcyclos, and Italian and Japanese motor scooters moved in hundreds down Tu Do Street's narrow channel. At its top end were the red brick Cathedral of Our Lady of Peace and the white, baroque public buildings of the French, with their orange-tiled roofs. At the bottom end, near the Saigon River, where the Budgie was now headed, was the newly expanding zone of bars catering to the American troops.

Even though Rolling Thunder was beginning to strangle it, Saigon still had echoes in this year of a dozing town in Provence. Stuccoed colonial buildings with French shutters and overhanging balconies were painted in pale pastels; fading enameled advertising signs fastened to moldering walls were still French: *Michelin; Pernod; Le Journal d'Extrême-Orient.* But above dark doorways, new signs and neons were appearing: *Chicago Bar; Saigon Express; Massage; The Bunny.* Bougainvillea flared and climbed on concertinas of barbed wire thrown up by the Americans to protect clubs and hotels from Viet Cong bomb attack. Lines of spreading tamarind trees with bright green feathery leaves and dark trunks whitewashed at the bottoms survived like afterimages from the street's colonial days, when its name was rue Catinat.

The jeep was nearing the river, and now every second doorway seemed to be a bar. Tu Do here became a carnival alley, its primary odors beer, urine and perfume. GIs in cotton khakis or Hawaiian shirts wandered in the humid heat: coarse and alien giants, white and black, badgered and pursued by a race of refined, ivory-skinned gnomes who waved mutilated limbs at them, or tried to sell them copies of *Time*, and *Stars and Stripes*.

One of the street children on board the Budgie was a crew-cut nine-year-old with an old man's face and a Batman T-shirt. He leaned out now and snatched a camera from the hands of a young GI on the curb who was taking a picture. Then, fast as a gull, he dropped from the Jeep and raced into the crowd. The soldier shouted after him, his pink, outraged face more childlike than his attacker's. But Jim Feng drove on, glancing at Langford deadpan, with raised eyebrows.

"That kid is lightning," he said. Then he yelled sternly at the remaining child passengers. "Off, all of you! I told you, no more stealing when you ride the Budgie!"

He slowed in front of a neon that said *Texas Happy Bar,* and the children began to drop off. Racing into the crowd, the boys called cheery farewells. "Sorry, Mr. Jim!" "Goodbye, goodbye!" "You Number One Saigon man!"

The girl peddler with the tray jerked after them on her single crutch, jaunty and confident in the traffic, and Langford stared after her. Her face was exquisite, he says, framed by her shining black hair: a flower. He'd never seen a face so beautiful. But one foot was twisted and withered to a mere flap of flesh. It was hard to look at it.

"Welcome, brother, to the Pearl of the Orient."

Harvey Drummond had a gentle, ceremonious air, and his well-modulated voice was a professional broadcaster's. He extended a huge hand to Langford, swinging around on his barstool. He was thirty-five: an Australian Broadcasting Service correspondent who divided his time between Saigon and Singapore, often doing television news stories for which Jim Feng shot the film. From behind their glasses, enlarged gray eyes asked Langford to prepare for jokes. He was wearing the type of safari suit currently popular among correspondents in Asia, and doomed to become a sartorial cliché in the next few years: olive, with huge patch pockets and epaulets.

Langford and Feng took stools on either side of him, and

Harvey signaled to one of the two white-shirted Vietnamese barmen. His large finger was seen immediately: seated, he was as tall as some of the men here who were standing, being somewhere around six feet six. At first glance, he resembled a truck driver, or perhaps a mercenary soldier. But his shoulders were stooped and sedentary from years over a typewriter; his monumental head, with its high, balding forehead, curly brown hair and Victorian side-whiskers, was that of an old-style Anglican cleric, and there was a touch of clerical sing-song in his voice.

He passed Langford a Scotch. "I'm glad Jim's shown you the way here, Mike," he said. "The Texas Happy Bar has ebullience without being frantic—wouldn't you say so, Jim? And so far no playful VC has thrown a bomb in here."

"Right," Jim said. "The Happy Bar feels OK. You get to know."

"You get to know," Harvey echoed, and nodded at Langford. "I am a cautious journalist, Mike—I am not a crazy cameraman. Gun-happy types are everywhere in this town, and I pay due heed: I don't want to die. I walk out of bars that don't feel right. If someone stands next to me with a bag, I move away. I don't like it when the barman is too smart; I leave such bars. I like around me dumb barmen and respectful customers. Smart-arse barmen end up dead: they are probably not paying enough kickback to the Viet Cong." He drank half his whiskey at a gulp and pointed at Langford's chest, his sing-song voice taking on a sermonizing cadence. "We have every sort of bar on Tu Do, brother. Loud bars; bars where you can get laid; bars where you can get thumped; and there are bars down lanes where the Special Forces gentlemen put their M-16s and UZIs on the counter. But the Happy Bar is where we like to be. Here's where a sensitive correspondent can get sensitively *drunk*."

The place was narrow, crowded, and in semidarkness, lit by shaded lamps on the polished wooden counter of the bar. A pair of buffalo horns and a cowboy hat were set above backlit, multicolored bottles on shelves. There was a large framed picture of John Wayne, six-guns drawn; Country and Western music was playing on the music system. Apart from a sprinkling of correspondents, most of the customers were American military officers, some in starched khaki service dress, others in civilian outfits, with a small number of GIs among them. The aroma of their cigars mingled with a rumor of fish sauce. Some sat on stools at the bar; others were in a line of banquettes along the wall that were upholstered in lurid green vinyl. Most of these soldiers were white; Langford would discover that black GIs had their own bars, where whites weren't welcome, and where soul music, Bo Diddley's guitar and rich laughter flowed out through the doors.

Looking around him, he was aware of a constant, watchful tension, he says. Any new customer was discreetly scrutinized by the two barmen, and examined less discreetly by the officers and GIs. When the newcomer was passed as harmless, they relaxed and turned back to their drinks. Nearly all the customers were male; but a number of Vietnamese girls sat perched in a row on stools along the bar, and others sat on the knees of soldiers in the banquettes.

Out on Tu Do, Langford had been captivated by the beauty of young Vietnamese women: a common response among newly arrived males in Saigon. They rode sidesaddle on the backs of motor scooters as though on magic steeds from Annamese legend, all in their national dress: the clinging, semitransparent *ao dai,* with its tunic and matching pantaloons—mauve, green, red, white. Straight-backed, dignified and ethereal, black hair streaming, silk gowns fluttering, they'd passed with eyes averted, with the modesty of another time, their small, pointed faces delicate and remote. But their sisters here in the Happy Bar were different. Most had used so much mascara and lipstick that their faces were like those of clowns; and instead of the *ao dai,* they wore grotesquely brief miniskirts, low-cut blouses and colored camisoles—their small breasts enlarged with padded bras to please the Americans.

Langford's response to one of these bar girls was something that Harvey Drummond remembered about that night, when he and I talked. This and the incident of the bomb.

Old-fashioned isn't really an accurate term for my first impression of Langford: but it was something close to that. I think it had to do with the way he treated the bar girl.

For what they called Saigon Tea—the colored water in tiny cups that you bought for them at $1.50 a throw—those bar girls would give you nothing but the pleasure of their company. Jim Feng and I found it a pointless exercise, and didn't encourage them. Jim chased more promising Vietnamese women, being single, but I was that amazing anachronism among correspondents, a happily married man—and although my wife was in Singapore, I didn't look for diversion in the fleshpots of Tu Do, as a lot of my colleagues did. For me, the bar girls were a frieze in the background, and its colors would alter from pathetic to tragic as the war went on. Few of them saw themselves as prostitutes, and some actually weren't—although many of them could be hired after-hours, if you wanted to pay a large enough sum. They took pride in their status as amateurs; it made them a sort of elite, in their own eyes, among the tribes in the city that were now living off the Americans. Most of the girls were peasants from the countryside; their villages had probably been bombed or torched, and their families were either killed or living in the shantytowns on Saigon's outskirts. But some of them were from once-prosperous Vietnamese families wiped out by the war.

One of them slid off her stool now and came around to Langford: she'd probably noticed he was new. She was a model of bar girl elegance: emerald green blouse; black miniskirt of fake leather.

"If you buy me Saigon Tea, I can stay and talk," she said; and she gave him her seductive smile.

"Not tonight, thanks," Langford told her. "Maybe some other time." He was pleasant and politely regretful, his voice soft.

Her own smile switched off immediately, and she changed to a big pout. "You fucking cheap Charlie," she said, and sauntered back to her friends, swinging her little handbag.

Jim and I laughed; it was one of their standard bits of repartee.

Langford stood looking after her, not laughing. His face was always placid, and it stayed that way now; but I caught a fleeting expression I found arresting and at the same time puzzling. I couldn't really read it; but when I got to know him, I'd understand it in retrospect. I'm sure he already saw the bar girls as damsels in distress, whom he had to do something about—in the same way as he'd decide to do something about the street kids who hung around the Continental Palace, and the crippled girl who sold flowers. It began on that very first night.

But then I forgot about it, as Jim and I began to fill him in on business here.

Dmitri Volkov was due in soon, and Volkov needed a little preparing for—particularly since he was opposition. He was working for American CBS, and he and Jim Feng scooped each other whenever they could, with no love lost; but they were the best of friends off-duty. That was how it was with most cameramen.

For Jim though—and for me too, when I scripted the pieces we did together for ABS—it was a pretty unequal contest with the Americans. The American networks had given their cameramen advantages in Saigon that Telenews and ABS simply couldn't match. CBS and NBC had headquarters in the city with lavish facilities, making Telenews look rudimentary. CBS had taken over half a floor of the Caravelle, the modern high-rise hotel opposite the old Continental—and they'd been known to charter every aircraft in Saigon in order to beat the opposition out with their film. They even had U.S. military cooperation to get their film out to Tokyo and Bangkok with the wounded, on medevac flights. We were resigned to this now: it was a fact of life like taxation or the weather, and we explained it to Mike.

"So the Yanks can scoop us any time," he said. He was looking thoughtful.

"Don't worry," Jim told him. "The good news is that we come out on top when we get the crumbs the Yanks miss."

At about this point, Volkov came in.

He was still in dirty combat fatigues, and looked dead beat: he'd obviously come straight here from Tan Son Nhut, stopping only to drop off his film and his gear at the CBS office. He took a stool between Mike and Jim Feng, and he had to look up slightly at Langford as they shook hands, being a smaller man. This, and the fact that Mike was a competitor, seemed to get Dmitri edgy: his face went entirely deadpan.

Told where Mike came from, he said: "Tasmania? Jesus, do they have *people* there?"

Langford said nothing. He just smiled amiably, looking at Volkov with that sleepy stare he had, as though waiting for something; and Volkov stared back. They were sniffing each other out like dogs, those two.

"Come on, Count," Jim said. "Get a drink into you and get friendly with the opposition." And he signaled to the barman.

Volkov didn't much like being called "Count." But he'd once let slip that his grandfather, who'd brought the family out of Russia to Paris after the Bolshevik revolution, had been Count Volkov, and we assumed that Dmitri's father would have succeeded to the title, had history not intervened. So we decided that Dmitri would ultimately have succeeded to it too. Counts were a penny a dozen in czarist Russia, I understand, and I'm not sure that in fact it *was* a hereditary title there; but we liked the idea, and liked getting a rise out of Dmitri, and the nickname stuck. And he did look like our idea of a Russian aristocrat: thin, blond, and rather small-boned, with light blue Tartar eyes and a small military mustache. Despite his slightness, he was pretty strong, as most combat cameramen had to be in those days, when the gear they handled was punishingly heavy. But you'll have seen pictures of him.

He'd got his whiskey now, and propped one elbow on the bar; then he began to shoot questions at Langford as though to put him through some test. What background did he have in news photography? What papers had he worked for? What did he think of the current television coverage of the war? Dmitri's English—learned in post-War Paris in his adolescence—was good but erratic. The definite article was inclined to appear in strange places, and to disappear from other places where it should have been. He carried a French passport, but he was sometimes taken for an American, because of his accent. He'd added the American component to it when he worked on a paper in New York.

Langford answered all his questions good-humoredly. But Dmitri's Tartar stare remained unimpressed.

"Well, good luck, Bud," he said. "You're going to need it, as a matter of fact, working for Brits on their lousy budget. My outfit doesn't care what it costs to get stuff out first."

Langford cocked his head. He surveyed the Count now from head to foot, adopting an expression of simpleminded awe. "Jesus, mate, I can see I should start worrying," he said. "And how will I ever scoop a bloke who looks like Errol Flynn?"

He glanced aside at Jim and me and winked. It was the rural Australian style of put-down, and done without malice; but I could see that Volkov didn't know how to take it, and I decided to divert his attention. Dmitri's moods always went up and down a lot—the famous Russian temperament—but high spirits usually prevailed, and I'd begun to realize that something was wrong tonight. I knew he'd been in the Central Highlands for the past few days, so I asked him how it had gone.

He shook his head, lighting a cigarette and grimacing to expel smoke through his teeth. "Not very jolly, Harvey," he said.

I asked him where he'd been.

"Route 19," Volkov said. "There has been an ambush in the Mang Yang Pass, between Qui Nhon and Pleiku. VC have managed to destroy a whole Special Forces convoy there."

"You were *there,* Count?" Jim Feng had turned sideways, suddenly alert; even in the half-dark, I could see his gaze get hungry.

"Not when it happened, baby, or I would not be here now," Volkov said. "I have been up coast at Qui Nhon. Hitched a ride on a Huey to the new A-Team fort at An Khe, near the Pass. They had just got the news. So I went on a Jeep to scene of disaster." He drew on the cigarette, staring unseeingly at the bar girls. "A real butcher's shop, James. Two Americans dead, and many Montagnards. The Charles has amused himself with sniper fire at us all the way back."

Fresh whiskeys arrived, and Volkov pushed one into Langford's hand without looking at him, the action neither friendly nor unfriendly.

"Lucky. You always were lucky, Count," Jim Feng said. "So what's wrong? Didn't you get the film?"

"I got good film, James. But it doesn't amuse me to contemplate deceased gentlemen from Green Berets with their balls stuffed into their mouths."

There was a short silence, during which I noticed that Volkov was being listened to by a British correspondent who'd moved alongside us: a *Manchester Guardian* man I'd run into a few times before, but whom the others didn't know. Trevor Griffiths was Welsh, and his appearance, like his temperament, was dark Celtic. He had the build of the former Rugby player, and his dead white, unhealthy-looking complexion went strangely with this vigorous appearance: it made Trevor appear to be suffering from some secret illness, and it also caused him to have a five o'clock shadow like Richard Nixon's—a similarity I enjoyed drawing his attention to, since he was a man of dedicated left-wing views.

"Sounds like a nasty scene for our friends in the Special Forces," he said. He had a measured, strong voice, and something of a BBC accent: very little Welsh in it.

Volkov looked at him. "Nasty would be one way of putting it, Bud."

"But somewhat appropriate, I should have thought," Griffiths said.

"What?" Volkov said.

"Appropriate," Griffiths repeated. He swayed; he was slightly drunk, and his voice grew more resonant. "Just the sort of fate to make those cowboys understand what they're meddling in."

"And what is that, exactly?" Volkov asked.

"A war of liberation that's none of their business," Griffiths said. "One that John Wayne can't win."

Volkov smiled. He had a strange smile sometimes: open mouth stretched as though through an act of will; light eyes empty. "You know what is wrong with you, Limey?"

"No, Yank. What's wrong with me?"

"You lost your bloody Empire. That's why you hate Americans who have replaced you. But that is none of my business; your shitty politics don't interest me. What interests me is that you have no pity for men whose bodies have been mutilated. Maybe *your* balls should be stuffed in mouth."

He slid off his stool, hands open, palms outwards.

Griffiths took a step backwards, frowning at him in disbelief, and some nearby GIs had begun to turn around, sensing a fight. But Jim Feng put a hand on Volkov's shoulder.

"Come on, Count, you can't deck him in here. There isn't the room." He leaned towards Griffiths and said softly: "I would go, if I were you. He's a little strung out."

Griffiths put his glass on the bar, lips tight, looking whiter. "I can see that," he said. "I'll leave him in your charge. I don't drink with psychopaths."

Watching him go, Volkov began to laugh. He climbed back on his stool, wiping one of his eyes with the back of his hand. "Buy me a whiskey," he told Jim. "Now you've cheated me out of a fight, James, this is least you can do."

We were all rather drunk now, and for some reason the bar began to appear sinister to me. Saigon could have that effect.

A barman was staring at us. He had one of those unreadable Sino-Vietnamese faces, and kept looking at his wristwatch while he picked his teeth. This was making me paranoid; I decided he knew something, and that if he suddenly left, we must leave too.

I should perhaps explain that we were all more jumpy than usual in that month. Viet Cong agents were everywhere in the city: they were impossible to identify, and could be standing next to you. And down at this end of Tu Do Street, near the river, a number of restaurants had recently been wrecked by parcel bombs. There had also been the big explosion at the American embassy a month or so ago, which had killed or injured over two hundred people. This had tended to bring home the fact that the Americans weren't even able to safeguard their own embassy, let alone the city of Saigon. One began to worry.

So when the thin Vietnamese with the parcel came in, our reaction was immediate. It was Volkov who spotted him first.

"We have a character with parcel," he said.

He jerked his head, and I was hit by a jarring chill. The man was the sort of small wheeler-dealer you saw everywhere in the streets, peddling goods stolen from the American PX stores, or various forms of sad commercial sex: thin as a stick, with long hair, a crafty face and a pencil mustache, wearing a baseball cap. He slid into one of the banquettes down at the other end, near the door to the street. It was occupied by two bar girls; the three of them exchanged smiles and greetings, and he put the parcel carefully on the table between them. It was about the size of a box of chocolates, and wrapped in brown paper. No one else in the bar seemed to have noticed, although parcels were usually suspect. It was like one of those situations in sleep where you can't run, although you badly want to.

But then I saw Volkov relax. "It's OK," he said. "He doesn't go through to the john, and girls are looking happy. It's just a parcel."

We understood. The standard technique, when a VC booby-trapped a bar, was to move straight through to the toilets before the parcel went off, and escape out the back. So we picked up our drinks and relaxed.

But then Jim Feng tapped me on the shoulder. "We have spoken too soon," he said.

The man in the baseball cap was moving through the crowd towards us. He passed by and vanished through a bead-curtained doorway that led to the Happy Bar's Augean toilets. The parcel still lay on the table, and both girls had stood up.

I stood up too. I was pouring with sweat, and my head was spinning. It wasn't the whiskey: I knew I was going to die. The bomb was between us and the exit; it would probably blow in a moment, and wreck the whole bar. I'd never seen this happen, but I'd been told about it often enough. Still no one had registered the parcel's existence except our group; only seconds had gone by, and now I heard Volkov shout, and saw him pointing at the banquette.

"Bomb! Everybody out!"

All around us, servicemen and civilians began throwing themselves flat on the floor. Down in the area by the fatal table, they began to lurch through the exit, shouting warnings. Bar girls were screaming, and trying to fight their way past us. Trying to run myself, I saw that Langford had charged ahead of the three of us, heading towards the door.

He wove through the crowd very fast, shouldering and elbowing people aside, graceful as a professional footballer—which I believe he once was. And in that moment, terrified as I was myself, I had a flash of disappointment at seeing what I assumed to be fear driving him so hard. Then he reached the banquette, and without a pause, scooped up the parcel in his right hand and raced on. This and his next movement also reminded me of football. He plunged through the open door and pitched the parcel over the heads of the crowd into the middle of the road. But there was no explosion.

Out in the warm dark on the pavement, surrounded by American servicemen and a crowd of curious Vietnamese, we found Langford staring at the traffic: cyclos, motor scooters, and an old, rickety bus from the country, painted in carnival colors. The GIs were saying things like: *"Fuckin' bomb." "Guy threw it." "Hey buddy, where's the fuckin' bomb?"* Then the old bus had gone by, and we all saw the burst parcel in the middle of the road. The wrappings had come off: it was a shattered transistor radio.

Dmitri and Jim and I began to laugh, and some of the American servicemen joined in. Volkov staggered about the pavement, pointing, bent double, while Langford smiled and scratched his head. Then one of the bar girls from the banquette appeared, small and angry and vivid in a purple camisole and skimpy black shorts, frowning up at Langford.

"Dumb GI bastard," she shouted. "You smash my radio. Why?"

Volkov pushed a handful of bills into her hand. "Buy yourself another one, darling." While she stood counting the money, he turned and slapped Langford on the back, his pale eyes alight with joy. "What were you trying to do, Aussie? Blow up whole goddamn street?"

Langford asked him for a cigarette. Taking it, leaning to the flame of Volkov's lighter, he said: "Less people in the road than in the bar." He looked apologetic, but unruffled.

Volkov turned to Jim and me. "This man becomes interesting," he said. "He is genuinely crazy. I want to see what tricks he plays with grenades." A Slavonic hundred-degree turn had taken place: he'd decided to like Mike unreservedly.

Yes, Langford had become interesting; but also a little disturbing, I thought. I was curious to know whether he was suicidal or just foolish, and as Volkov and Feng headed across the pavement to the Budgie, I hung back and took his arm.

What had that been about? I asked him. Had he really wanted to die before he even got into the field?

He gave me a sidelong look, and didn't answer for a moment. Then he said: "It had to be a radio. That little bloke had been in the bar selling them half an hour before. You guys didn't notice him." He gave me his country wink. "Don't tell Volkov," he said.

We ended the evening on the roof of the Caravelle Hotel.

We'd eaten at a French-Vietnamese restaurant near the river, and had drunk a large quantity of French wine. When we left, Volkov was reeling from a mixture of liquor and exhaustion, but he remained in high good humor.

A curfew began at midnight for Vietnamese civilians and U.S. military: what we called Cinderella Time, when the bar girls disappeared. The roof garden of the Caravelle was one of the few places where drinks could still be had. And from there, you could watch the war.

It was dark, quiet and half empty this evening. A few lamps put an aquarium light on the leaves of the potted shrubs and trees; there was a scent of frangipani. A small number of Europeans and Americans lingered here, wandering out from the cocktail bar inside, drinks in hand: staff from the various embassies; diplomatic wives; hotel guests; U.S. Army officers; other correspondents. The darkness and space made us all speak in undertones. Saigon is very flat, and at ten stories, the Caravelle was its tallest building: from here, a good deal of the city could be seen. In one direction were the grubby ferroconcrete apartment blocks of modern Southeast Asia, with their teeming balconies. In another was the traffic-clotted channel of Tu Do Street, whose ornate, nineteenth-century public buildings always looked forlorn to me. The white clock tower of the City Hall should have been veiled by the rain of some French provincial town, I thought—not trapped here, in this heavy Asian heat.

We wandered around to the side that faced towards the river, and stood in a line by the parapet. From here, looking southeast, you could see intermittent flashes in the dark. This was South Vietnamese artillery fire in the Rung Sat Special Zone: an area of mangrove swamp at the mouth of the Saigon River, where the South Vietnamese Government had military outposts. The Viet Cong also had bases there, and tried to sink the boats coming in through the shipping channels. They were probably attacking a South Vietnamese outpost now, and at this distance, the flashes looked not ominous but serene. I suppose that sounds odd.

"There you are, Mike." Volkov's voice, like all others here, was pitched low. "There is your war," he said.

"This close," Langford said.

"This close, as a matter of fact. And getting closer all the time."

Suddenly, out above the southeastern horizon, parachute flares flowered, lighting up the landscape like daytime. They were dropped from old DC-3s to light up VC positions, and fields and lines of trees sprang into sight from nowhere: tan-and-olive tapestries in a black frame. A chorus of murmurs went up on the roof—some of them delighted, like the exclamations of children at a fireworks display. One of them carried clearly: a young American woman's. "Hey, wow. Isn't that just beautiful?"

Below his breath, Jim Feng muttered: "Beautiful for some, lady. Not so beautiful for others."

Standing by the parapet, we were all like people on the bridge of a ship. We could only just see each other's faces, and now we fell silent, staring into the dark. Then Mike said: "I thought the Yanks were turning it around this year. This doesn't look much like it."

"Give them time," Volkov said. "Their troops only arrive now in real numbers."

Jim Feng's voice came out of the dark. "True, Count. But there are some people here who think the war's already lost."

"Crap," Volkov said. "Left-wing crap, James. Wait and see what happens when Marines dig in."

"Maybe," Jim said. "But the GIs are right: the night belongs to Charlie." He turned to Mike, and pointed. "Out there in the Delta, Victor Charles is in charge at night. You want to travel the highways out of the city by Jeep, you only do it in the daytime: and Saigon officers need an armed convoy. Sometimes we wonder if it's only a matter of time before just the city is left—like an island in the sea."

"Feng, you are being very negative tonight, you will make the Michael depressed," Volkov said. "Yank airpower will win in the end: how can it not?"

"The rainy season's coming," Jim said. "More difficult for planes to fly. Soon the VC will hit hard again."

But Volkov was addressing himself to Langford. "This is a helicopter war, baby. It will be won in my opinion by the sweet little gunships." He turned from the parapet to face us all, swaying a little, his voice more slurred than before. His eyes, almost white in the dark, were unfocused and red-rimmed, and his face had taken on a tender, exalted expression; he'd obviously reached a point of exhaustion that created both euphoria and mild derangement. This was alarming only if you hadn't grown used to him.

"Amazing machines," he said. "I recognize they are instruments of destruction, and in nice moral moments I do not approve of them—but I tell you, I am also in love with them, the Chinooks and the little Hueys. They have beauty. I think this term can be used of them. Yes: a Huey is beautiful. The gunships are like nothing else before them. You may think so too, Michael, when you ride a Huey into combat zone. But of course you may not turn out to be bloody war-freak like us."

"Speak for yourself, Count," Jim said. But his voice was soft and tolerant.

Volkov grinned. "You are not a war-freak, James? Why else do they call you Crazy Jim Feng? Hah?"

Jim smiled without answering; then both of them looked at Langford.

They wore an identical expression now: one that people wear who watch someone wandering into an area that's shaped their lives, and whose consequences the other can't foresee.

"Of course we are not bloody war-freaks," Jim said. "I know I am not. I just like to shoot the bang-bang stories."

Volkov gave a shout of laughter. "That's right," he said. "Never mind who wins or loses: in the end, it's not our problem. James has summed it up. We like to shoot the bang-bangs."

2.

AUDIO DIARY: LANGFORD

TAPE 4: MAY 12TH, 1965

—Jim Feng and I nearly died this afternoon. I didn't expect to run into a situation like this on my second day here.

Headed back towards Saigon at four in the afternoon, the Budgie buzzed along the straight metal ribbon of Highway 1: the road that links South Vietnam and Cambodia. Jim Feng drove; Langford sat beside him. They were twenty-five kilometers north of the city, swerving among bicycles, cars and military traffic, and occasionally circumnavigating tall wooden oxcarts that were piloted by old men in straw hats: vehicles that seemed to move at the invisible pace of clock hands, oblivious of the century and the war. It was the beginning of the southeast monsoon, and on each side of the road, peasants were transplanting rice shoots into the paddy fields.

Langford studied the scene with rural eyes. It was still novel to him, he says, and the tree line on the horizon of this level, heat-sunk country contained no species that he recognized except coconut palms. Crisscrossed by a grid of canals and dykes, the newly flooded, cloud-reflecting paddies resembled a shallow, land-locked sea, and the small, tough green shoots of life, sticking up from the surface, looked deceptively frail to him, like things left behind from some casual children's game: unlikely to survive. Far out on these water-plains, between the long green horizontals of the dykes, figures in black pajamas and straw hats stooped and straightened and stooped again, hypnotically. Water buffalo stood motionless.

—We were coming back from Cu Chi, which is only thirty kilometers down Highway 1. Jim had taken me out to have a look at the big American base there: the Twenty-fifth Infantry Division. We'd put a sound camera and a Bell and Howell in the back in case we ran into some action—which Jim said was always possible. The Viet Cong were active around Cu Chi, he told me, and the region's not entirely safe—even though it's commuting distance from Saigon, and pretty much controlled by the Americans and the Government.

—This morning, Jim had seen me through the process of getting my accreditation: the two press passes, American and Vietnamese, that you have to have if you even want to get on a military aircraft here. So I'm now a *bao chi*: a member of the Saigon press corps. He'd taken me to the Khu Dan black market in the city and helped me buy the gear I'll need when I go out in the field: combat fatigues, canteens, jungle boots. Then, after lunch, we'd headed up the highway.

—Just a little outing, Jim said, to see what's cooking. We'll be back in Saigon before evening—no sweat.

—We were dressed in sports gear, as though for an outing in the city: I wore a bright red shirt, which I'll never do again. It's a crazy situation for correspondents at present, and Jim says it can't last much longer. The Americans will soon tighten up, he says, and the only way we'll get to the front then is by being attached to an American or South Vietnamese unit with our names ticked off on a list. But that's not how it is just now. All you have to do is jump in some kind of vehicle and head off down the highway.

—The road passed between stands of tall green bamboo, as though entering a tunnel. Ahead of us was a line of slow-moving military trucks filled with South Vietnamese soldiers: small men wearing outsize steel pot helmets. Jim increased speed. He wanted to get past the convoy, he said. You could get in trouble traveling with them, especially this late in the day: they attracted Viet Cong attention.

—We overtook the trucks, leaving the other traffic behind. Once we got past, the jeep came out of the tunnel of bamboos, and the distances of the paddy fields opened up again on each side of the road. Then we heard an explosion.

—We looked back and found that the lead truck in the convoy had been blown up. It sat stalled, the cabin shattered, with a column of black smoke rising from it. Vietnamese troops were spilling onto the road from the back of it, and from the trucks banked up behind it. A rattle of gunfire had begun.

—Jim increased speed. Remote-controlled mine, he said. That means VC are here.

—I grabbed my Bell and Howell to try and shoot film; but we were going too fast for it to be much good. The road ahead was suddenly empty: there was no one here but us, and this made Jim look worried.

—No oncoming traffic, he said. Something else is happening up ahead.

—We came around a bend, and soon found out why the oncoming traffic had stopped. Another South Vietnamese military truck had been blown up. It was slewed across the middle of the road, the front of it smashed and blackened, black smoke climbing from it, the driver and his mate dead in the cabin. About fifteen dead and wounded South Vietnamese soldiers lay on the highway, automatic rifles beside them, their uniforms and the bitumen patched with blood. One or two were moving and crying out; a couple were crouched in the ditch by the road; most were still. Out in the flooded paddy, a group of a dozen or so peasants in black pajamas stood by a dyke, staring at the truck. They had objects in their hands, but I didn't focus on what these were.

—We slowed almost to a halt. We were looking at a South Vietnamese officer in a peaked cap who was lying against the trunk of a banana tree at the roadside. He was holding his stomach, and staring back at us. He had a small mustache that looked false against the dead yellow color of his face. Blood blackened his shirt and welled between his fingers; he called out, asking us for help, and I saw that his entrails were coming out. It made me feel very bad not to be able to help him.

—I started to get out of the Jeep, but Jim pulled me back. No! he shouted. Get down, Snow!

—When I asked him why, he pointed to the peasants in the rice field. Because of them, he said.

—He gunned the Budgie, and headed past the truck at top speed.

Then I heard a sharp, fast cracking, and looked towards the paddy field. The people in black I'd thought were peasants were moving forward through the water, shin-deep, firing burst after burst with automatic rifles. They were firing at us: the Budgie's colors weren't protecting us.

—I seemed to have seen them before, in some other situation I couldn't quite recall; but I didn't have much time to think about it just then. Jim had his foot on the floor, swinging around potholes, driving like a maniac. We were all alone on this road, absolutely exposed, the only sounds here the roar of the Budgie's engine and the fading gunfire. From somewhere by the truck, the few Vietnamese soldiers left alive were now firing back.

—We both had our heads down as low as possible. Bullets were passing quite close overhead, and one ricocheted off a front mudguard. They sounded just like the bullets in the old Western movies, and I half wanted to laugh. I was sweating like a pig and my heart was thudding, but I got out my Bell and Howell again, twisted in the seat, and tried to shoot film of the VC backwards, on long lens. For a moment I had them in my viewfinder, and I felt no more fear at all; all I wanted to do was to capture them. That was all that was real: what was inside the frame.

—But Jim yelled at me to stop. Forget the bloody film, he shouted. They're targeting that bloody red shirt of yours!

—Tall bamboos appeared beside the highway again, and a settlement with low wooden shops, and thatched huts like haystacks. The open paddy fields and the Viet Cong were gone.

—A heavy monsoon shower began, wetting us through, and we both started to laugh.

—I doubt that I'd ever be able to find that little noodle shop again. I only know it was somewhere in a side road, where Highway 1 comes into Saigon. We stopped there to have a quick coffee before going on into the city; but we found we didn't want to leave. We ended by eating dinner there, and getting pretty drunk.

—I still felt light, when we first sat down; I'd felt light ever since we got away, and I was still trembling. They'd tried to kill us and we were still alive, and I kept wanting to laugh.

—The rain had stopped. The Budgie was parked where we could keep an eye on it through the entrance door, in this muddy side road that was lined with long wooden shop buildings like sheds, with rusty iron roofs. Children and chickens ran about, and purple bougainvillea hung from the coffee shop's red canvas awning. The coffee came in cups with aluminum drip filters; no coffee ever tasted so good, and I said so to Jim.

—He looked at me with a humorous expression. Everything tastes better after action, he said. Food; beer; dope; making love to a woman. Now you have found that out, Snow.

—Then he got serious. You have also found out about the VC, he said. You can never tell whether they are there or not: they dress the same as the peasants; hide in the villages. You can be next to them and not know it: remember that. The peasants call them the Black Ghosts. They also call them the People Over There.

—I asked him why they'd hit the trucks.

—Probably because they wanted to move a large unit across the highway further north, he said: it would have been closed, after that convoy was shot up. The VC have invisible roads through the paddy fields.

—Then he pointed at me. I should have realized sooner what was happening, he said. That was my mistake. You know what your mistakes were, Snow? One: you wanted to help that ARVN officer. A cameraman can't do that: you can't get involved. Two: you went into the Cameraman's Daydream. That's what the Count calls it. When you were trying to shoot the VC, you were forgetting your situation. You thought that what was in your viewfinder wasn't quite real: that you were watching your own movie. That you couldn't be touched. Right?

—Right, I said, and Jim nodded.

—We all have to fight it, he said. Never let it take over. That's how you get your arse shot off. And please don't wear that shirt again. Then he laughed, and I joined in. We were still laughing a lot; we knew how lucky we'd been.

—There were no other foreigners in the noodle shop: there was nothing here for them. Just three or four cyclo boys: young men in their twenties, tired from pushing their machines, smoking and drinking beer. Maybe they were VC, but I don't think so: they didn't seem to mind us. The round wooden table we were sitting at was very low, like a table for children, and the chairs were old cane ones like some we had on the verandah at home. It was like being in a private house: children's toys were stacked in a china cabinet; a little boy played with a truck on the tiles; a white cat was asleep on a chair. Behind the bar counter, you could see the living area, with an old woman in black pajamas asleep on a bed, and a man in a cotton army hat mending a bicycle. Red candles and incense sticks burned in a little shrine.

—Through the door the afternoon faded, and we began to drink Ba Muòi Ba: the same Vietnamese beer the cyclo boys were drinking. It came crammed with ice: beer on the rocks, Jim said, the way the Vietnamese like it. The latest rain shower had stopped, and an orange, smoky sunset came on. And I felt I was being hypnotized: by the thick light out there; by the smells of camphor smoke and *nuoc mam,* the fish sauce they put into everything; by the Vietnamese music coming from a radio that sat on the red bar counter at the back of the room. It was a woman singer, high-voiced like a very young girl, the way their singers always are, and her songs went on and on, to a very slow, rocking beat, unwinding like a stream, like one continuous song that wouldn't end: slow, slow, with sexy, high-calling, wailing notes that made my nerves jump. The darkness came down now, and inside this dark were people who could kill you. The VC guerrillas were in charge, out in these suburbs at night. But I was confident we wouldn't die today: that had already been proved.

—After we'd eaten a cheap but good Vietnamese meal served in clay pots, we went on drinking beer. We really liked it here, and had no desire to move.

—I think you will be OK, Snow, when it comes to your first bang-bang, Jim said. No sweat. I have taught you all I can. Just remember to take the lens cap off.

—He laughed, and punched my shoulder. We were both getting pretty smashed now, and it was the first time I'd seen Jim actually look drunk: eyes half closed and eyebrows raised. He signaled for two more bottles of Ba Muòi Ba. The young woman who brought them had a warm, smiling face, and Jim tried to chat her up, the way he always did pretty women. He turned to me with a question, when she'd gone.

—Do you have a girl back home, Snow?

—No, I said. Not now.

—I had a girl in Hong Kong, Jim said. Very attractive and intelligent young woman. We were engaged; but she broke it off last year. Her parents didn't want her to marry a man who was likely to be killed at any time. Parents have a strong influence, in Chinese families. And I guess they were right. A man who covers combat is not a good marriage bet. Most people say your luck runs out after three years: three years of covering battle full-time is enough. And I have done five, in various places.

—He carefully poured more beer, spilling a little; then he suddenly looked up at me and shook his head and frowned. I am thirty-two and I have been in love with a number of women, he said. For a time. Sometimes I'm afraid I will never find the woman I can stay with. I get bored, Mike —I get bored with many people; many situations. So I run away from them. I leave.

—I told him I understood. I'd been running away myself, when I came to Asia.

—Hearing this, he didn't go on immediately, but stared at me with a Chinese look I couldn't read. When he spoke again, his voice was more soft and gentle than usual. It always has a rise and fall that's good to listen to; now, perhaps because of the beer, it had a sort of extra rhythm to it.

—I thought that might be, he said. He leaned forward across the table and pointed a finger. I get bored, he said, and I run from this terrible boredom that is the opposite of life. But I never become bored with battle. Never. Please understand, Snow, I don't approve of this war, or any other. I don't enjoy seeing men mutilated. But still I have to tell you: I can't keep away from battle.

—I asked him why.

—Because in battle everything matters, he said. Every little thing is clear, as though you see it for the first time, like a child. And in battle, you are all drawn together. You are close to those around you in a special way: you see the best in everyone. Afterwards, ordinary life seems unimportant: business; politics; all the things people get worked up about: unimportant.

—He lit a cigarette, looking out the door. Everything was a perfect mix: the slow Vietnamese music, still going on; the quiet-talking cyclo boys at the next table; the cat on the chair; the burning dark out the door.

—I'm telling you this because I think you may become like me, Jim said. You are the type. You could come to like war too much, and be good for nothing else. Look at Dmitri: he's like that. He has had one failed marriage, and no woman stays with him for long. You will want a wife and children someday, and so will I. So do the job well, Snow, but don't do it too long—that is my advice.

—I'll give it up when you do, I told him, and that made him laugh. Besides, I said, this looks like too good a war to miss.

—He shook his head, glanced aside at the cyclo boys, and his voice dropped. Great to cover; but a bad war, he said. In Saigon, the South Vietnamese are making money out of it while the Americans try to save them. Their generals grow rich on graft instead of fighting, and waste the lives of their men. And the Viets really don't want the Americans here, did you know that? They call them crude. They hate their rock and roll music; and they say the Americans are oversexed, with cocks too big for a Vietnamese woman. They would rather have the French back, they say. At least the French had style and good manners—and nicer music. The people of Saigon are living in the past, Mike, and that is a dangerous place to live. I know all about that; my father's class were doing it in China, before Mao came. And now they are gone, and old China is gone.

—He stubbed out his cigarette and was silent again, staring past my shoulder, and I knew he had memories too strange for me to get into: probably memories of Peking and his boyhood. He looked more Chinese than usual, and very serious and dignified, even though he was drunk. I liked him a lot now; ever since the VC had fired on us, I'd known that Jim and I would probably be friends for life.

—He leaned forward, speaking even lower, holding his beer glass in both hands. My father was never very practical, he said. He is a scholar. Once he was an important public official, and had a small estate; now he teaches in a Chinese school in Hong Kong. He taught us classical poetry, myself and my brothers. He made us learn a lot of poetry by heart, but I have forgotten most: I was never the scholarly type, which disappointed him. My two brothers were brighter than me. I am very fond of my father, and I know he is honest. He has no time for the Communists: he told me once how Mao Tse-tung boasted that he executed forty-six thousand scholars. So the Communists destroyed our best minds, as well as killing greedy landlords. Not many people want to hear this—or they won't believe it. But even my father says that his class was no longer fit to rule. They had failed the people; they did too little to stop the suffering. They had lost what the emperors had lost: the Mandate of Heaven.

—And now it was all happening here in Vietnam, I said.

—Yes; and because I know how it was in China, I understand the rulers here in South Vietnam, Jim said. I'm afraid they may lose here for the same reasons.

—I asked him whether he ever went out in the field with the South Vietnamese Army.

—With the ARVN? No, he said. Nobody in the press wants to. Some of them fight well, but their bad leadership puts you at too great a risk. And when Charlie engages the ARVN, the ARVN either fight their way out or die—and that means you die too, if they lose.

—So it's easier with the Yanks, I said.

—Of course. They lay it all on for us, he said. Air transport there and back guaranteed: same day. Purified water. Fresh food and ice cream flown into combat zones: even pizzas. And you're back in the Continental that evening.

—So no one was covering the South Vietnamese Army, I said.

—You are thinking of doing it? You are serious? he said.

—Why not? I said. You say we get scooped with everything else.

—But Jim shook his head. Christ, he said. Do one patrol, Mike. I don't think you will do a second. But if you must do it, find a good commander.

—He stood up. He was swaying, and quite drunk now. We had better get back to the Continental, he said. There are VC out here, and I don't want to dodge being shot up again.

—When we came outside, it was black and spooky. Most of the kids had gone, and a dog was eating garbage from a pile by a stall. Kerosene lamps had come on under awnings, glowing in that murky way they do, like treacle, and lighting up the faces of some passing men. They didn't look at us. We checked the Budgie to see that no VC had wired it to explode. Jim's method was to throw a rock onto the accelerator pedal. He missed a few times, he was so drunk, and we started laughing and couldn't stop, staggering around in the mud. But it was OK, and we drove away with no problems.

—I'd really like to go to that noodle shop again, but I don't think I could find it. I guess there are places that you're only meant to be in once.

3.

AUDIO DIARY: LANGFORD

TAPE 5: MAY 20TH, 1965

—Last night I had dinner at Madame Claudine Phan's. When I phoned her, I found she'd been expecting to hear from me. Donald Mills had contacted her, and told her I was in Saigon. He doesn't waste much time.

The Phan villa was in a narrow residential street of high stone walls and spreading tamarind trees, running off the top of Tu Do near the Cathedral. Langford arrived there after dark, riding in a cyclo.

The cyclo boy knew where the house was immediately, without being given the address. He was a long-haired young man with a thin, sly face, wearing a long-billed American fatigue cap. He'd already asked Langford his name and occupation, and Langford had answered his questions warily; he'd been told by Jim Feng that many cyclo boys were Viet Cong. As the young man bent forward to pedal, his mouth was brought conveniently close to Langford's ear, since the passenger seat in the cyclo was in front.

"You are friend of Madame Phan, Mr. Mike?" The voice from behind was hushed and intimate.

No, Langford said, he was just about to meet her.

"Everybody know Madame Phan," the voice murmured. "She is a dragon lady. Important business every place. Her husband Mr. Phan Le Dang also important—but I think he is never in Saigon now. Some say Phan Le Dang is killed by the Communists. Why do you visit Madame Phan, Mr. Mike?"

Just business, Langford said.

Silence followed, in which the squeaking of the cyclo's pedals sounded like a protest at Langford's brusqueness. Then the machine stopped beside tall iron gates with white, grimy pillars. The cyclo boy wanted to wait, but Langford told him to go, and paid him off. The boy pedaled slowly away under the streetlights, looking back with lingering reproach.

As Langford approached the gates, a small, fantastically narrow figure materialized in the darkness on the other side, coming from behind an orange tree. At first, he says, he thought it was a child. But it was a young Vietnamese woman, little more than five feet tall. She wore a white *ao dai,* the silk tunic and pantaloons outlining her body from throat to hip, and her face was an inverted triangle, peering at him through the bars.

—Like a fairy looking out of a cave.

She unlocked the gates and swung one open to admit him. *"Bonsoir, monsieur."* Her piping voice was only just audible. He summoned up his school French to return the greeting, and she led him up a short set of stone steps to the main entrance, pushing open tall, heavy double doors that he calls "historic-looking," their carved wood the color of dead leaves. The villa was French colonial, with a basement area below the steps, two stories above, and many windows with faded blue shutters. The girl brought him inside and then vanished, as though into a crevice.

He found himself in the semidarkness of a sort of anteroom. In front of him, light came from a remarkable number of candles on shelves and low tables, their flickering causing the whole interior to dance with a golden glow. He smelled sandalwood and spices, and was startled by the sound of a piano; a European piece was being played that he identifies only as "classical." He took a couple of paces forward, his eyes adjusting to the light.

The piano was an old upright, situated at the far end of the chamber; it was played by a woman who sat with her back to him. Her black hair was drawn back in a chignon; she wore a high-collared Chinese blouse of midnight blue, and a black slit skirt. At first he thought she was unaware of him, but then she turned and smiled over her shoulder—as though they'd already met, and shared some intimate joke. She went on playing, one prominent cheekbone dusted orange by the candlelight.

It was the last kind of scene he would have expected to confront him in Southeast Asia: a cameo from nineteenth-century

Europe—or rather, a kitsch idea of nineteenth-century Europe: a painting on a chocolate box. He found it absurdly stagy, and was partly embarrassed, partly amused. Yet he was also impressed: perhaps because the staging was so effective. He waited politely, among gilded Chinese cabinets and carved tables: all of them aflame like altars, all of them laden with dimly seen busts, statuettes and vases. "Crowded with junk" is how he describes the place—not yet knowing (as he would do eventually) that he was looking at Khmer, Cham and Chinese artifacts centuries old: some of them of great value. He had an impression of museum dustiness, and the closeness in here made the heavy Saigon heat almost suffocating. Sweat ran down his face, and he mopped it away with his handkerchief. There seemed to be no electric fans—as though in this papier-mâché Europe they were thought to be not needed.

The woman brought the piece to an end, and stood up. He guessed her to be somewhere in her late thirties. She was slim, but much more substantial than the servant girl had been, her physical scale European rather than Vietnamese. Moving towards him, hand outstretched, she gave off an aura of vigor and physical well-being. The silk blouse, worked with a design of red peonies, shone like porcelain; so did a heavy gold chain around her neck that was set with rubies. He describes the chain with some awe.

"Do you like Chopin, Mr. Langford? Yes? Forgive the romantic candlelight: we've had a power failure." Her speech was rapid, her voice somewhat deep, and her accent French. The pressure of her hand was firm.

A single color photograph of her has survived among Langford's effects: a portrait with the name of a Saigon studio on the back. It was probably taken around this time, when she still had her youth, and it's easy to see that she was as attractive as Langford claims she was. But it's an unconventional attractiveness, and one he does little to describe. The face is dominated by the eyes, which look directly and challengingly at the camera. They have the Vietnamese almond shape, but the French side of her ancestry has made them a surprising gray green.

"No electric fans, either," she was saying. "So we are melting.

That's bloody Saigon for you. We melt." She took Langford's arm. "Come on. My girls have still found a way to cook dinner —under my supervision, of course. I don't want to disappoint you. I'm sure Aubrey Hardwick will have told you about our cooking. Perhaps that's why he sent you here—for a good meal. Yes? But Aubrey never has *one* reason for doing anything. You've found that out?"

Langford told her that he didn't know Aubrey well enough to make a judgment.

She laughed as though what he'd said had been witty. Her laugh was a gleeful, exuberant shout, her deep voice making it almost masculine. It made him laugh too, and she looked at him with quick warmth. "Yes," she said. "Good. You have understood that Aubrey needs a lot of study. True. He does."

She slid back a curtain of heavy red velvet that screened a door beside the piano, and led him through.

They sat at a round table covered with a lace cloth. The room was large, and less stuffy than the other, but the warmth was still heavy. Folding bamboo fans sat beside their plates, and they both made use of these. There were even more candles in here than in the anteroom: the same golden flares and areas of shadow. The room was imposing—but it was not, to his mind, like the dining room of a wealthy household.

High and square and somber, its white walls dim and grimy, it was more like the shabby-genteel salon of cultivated people whose country had been occupied and impoverished: somewhere in Central Europe, perhaps. Its fans hung stalled above them like the wheels of an extinct machine. Eventually he'd discover that this had been the house of Madame Phan's late father, a French colonial official. It belonged to Asia and Europe at the same time, and the effect was odd and troubling. There were huge stuffed armchairs from the 1930s, their backs draped with antimacassars; dark French dressers; a library of books in French, Vietnamese and English. More Asian objets d'art, some of which Madame Phan identified for him, sat on shelves: stone heads of Buddha; a bronze statue of Shiva; a stone bas-relief of the naked Cambodian nymphs called *apsarases*, dancing with serene smiles.

But Langford has more to say about the cooking than he does about the art works. Aubrey had been right: it was quite simply the best meal he'd ever eaten. There were little spring rolls and spiced chicken wings; hearty French onion soup; then a chicken casserole with rice, accompanied by a delicate Beaujolais. The casserole was French, yet with a coloring of Indochina, the flavors mysterious and novel. It had come in individual clay pots, carried in from the kitchen by two young women who Langford assumed were servants, yet who didn't look like servants: he describes them as "refined." Both were formal and elegant in the traditional white *ao dai;* one of them was the girl who had opened the gate.

He complimented Madame Phan on the meal with an enthusiasm that made her smile; and she shook her head.

"No, I'm afraid it's quite crude," she said. "Forgive me, but things are always rushed these days: since I've had to take charge of my husband's trading company, I have too little time for important things like cuisine. Aubrey will have told you that my husband disappeared? Yes. Six months ago, he was captured by the Communists near Tay Ninh, on the Cambodian border. He was visiting one of our trading posts there, and never came back. We trade into Cambodia: watches; electrical equipment; food: everything. One of our agents there says the Viet Cong were trying to extract too much protection money, and my husband refused. I expected an approach for ransom for a long time, but nothing happened. So now we have little hope. And I don't really know whether I'm a widow or not." She smiled faintly.

Langford said he was sorry.

She shrugged, her face suddenly blank, and sipped her wine. Then she said: "This country is built on bribery, my dear—you've learned that? Our pure-minded Communists are no different; they want their share of the graft: all for the Party, of course. My agents at every depot on the Mekong need a constant supply of bribe money—to pay off the Viet Cong, and to pay off the criminals who burn our warehouses and raid our ships. Everyone thinks the Phans have a bag of money with no bottom. But it isn't true. Like all businesses, we run on credit; we take risks; nothing is certain."

She looked drolly despairing; then she smiled. She was never serious for long, he says.

Over a second bottle of Beaujolais, they began to talk more easily. Already she was Claudine, and he was Michael—but not Mike. She had the gift of achieving a sort of light intimacy without in any way losing a final formality and privacy; and he'd already sensed that failure to recognize these boundaries would be a mistake. She questioned him about his life and his background, and he pictures her listening with absolute intentness, one elbow propped on the table to rest her chin on her hand, the other hand slowly flapping her bamboo fan.

"So why are you here, Michael?"

For a moment he thought that his visit was being challenged, and he stared at her in confusion. But he had misunderstood, and she laughed.

"I'm sorry: I meant why have you come to Vietnam? You are very welcome in my house."

He told her he was here for Telenews.

"Of course I know this," she said. "But why have you come to Indochina in the first place? That's what interests me."

He seems to have answered in a deliberately prosaic way. Because it was the best place to be at present for any correspondent or news photographer, he said: the best story going.

But she pursed her lips as he spoke and shook her head slowly in mock reproach, matching it to the rhythm of her fan. "You are giving me careful answers," she said. "I think that you are an interesting man who wants to hide the fact that he is interesting. You forget that I have learned a little about you from Aubrey. When he found you in Singapore you were starving. Now why would a healthy, attractive young guy like you want to starve in Singapore? To punish himself?" She shook her head. "No; you don't look the type. On the run from something? Maybe. I think so. Yes?"

Cocking her head, she snapped the fan shut and pointed it at him. Then she laughed: the same frank shout that he'd first heard in the anteroom. It invited him to join in, and he did. He saw that she wanted to know him, and to make him like her—but not to flirt. Her sexual presence was strong, and had a quality that was formidable rather than seductive. He saw this as non-Western; baffling.

"Am I being nosy? Yes; I am nosy," she said. "That's me; that's Claudine Phan. Everyone knows that. If I want to find out, I ask; if I think something is so, I say it. The Saigon bourgeoisie find me appalling. I'm a rude bloody *frog,* they say." She laughed again, briefly: a statement in two syllables. "You can stop me asking you these questions if you like, *mon cher.* But because Aubrey has sent you to me, I'm being absolutely frank with you, and I would like to be your friend. So you and I must be truthful with each other: no secrets. Our secrets have to be from other people—you understand? Aubrey and I have trust, and I want to have trust with you too, Michael. But I cannot be anyone's friend unless I know him."

He said that he'd value her friendship, and would value her help. And he must have given her his smile, because she nodded and said: "Yes. You know how to charm, Michael; good. But still I'd like to know what made you change your life. Why did you come to Asia?"

—I told her. Told her everything: things I've discussed with no one else. I thought it was the wine, last night; now I think it was only Claudine. It's the way she listens: listens without speaking. I felt she understood everything, and didn't judge me.

He gives no detail at all of what he said. But it's clear that he talked not only of his hopes and ambitions, but of his relationship with Diana Lockhart. He doesn't even do this in the audio diary: he never looks backward. And in someone as private as Langford, I find the bare fact of this confession remarkable. Nothing could make clearer the way in which Madame Phan had won his confidence. And while his own side of the dialogue is lost, everything she said is recorded in full.

"I think you will be very successful as a war photographer.

You are the kind who will be good at it: you are cool, aren't you? But I think you must leave your pain behind. Not just about this woman, but the guilt over your friend. Because there's nothing to be done, is there? You did a bad thing—to yourself as well as him—but it's all gone. Gone. And now you are doing what you really want to do, and you are where you are meant to be." Suddenly, her voice grew humorously hard; almost coarse. "So never mind."

She laughed at his expression, which must have been disconcerted.

"Never mind, baby—never mind. Everyone says that in Asia: here in Vietnam we say *không xấu,* and where you just came from, they say *t'id-apa,* right? 'Never mind; not to worry.' The same in Vietnamese and Malay and in all Asian languages. When nothing can be done, we say *không xấu,* and walk away. You are going to have to learn to do that too, Michael. I think you have been like Rip Van Winkle. You were asleep; in a dream over this woman, and time went by. Perhaps that's why you look so young—and you are not really so young, are you? Nearly thirty; that's quite old, in this country. Yes; you nearly lost your youth. But then, one day you woke up in Singapore. And now you commence living the life you were meant for."

She began to laugh again. Laughter, he saw, was a release for the extraordinary, electric energy that brimmed inside this woman.

The young woman who'd opened the gate to him came back noiselessly into the room, passing Madame Phan's chair with coffee and cognac on a tray. She stooped, setting the tray down, and Claudine put a hand around her narrow waist, detaining her. At the same time she looked across at Langford with a confiding smile.

"You should find a nice Vietnamese girl," she said. "They are very beautiful, don't you think? This one especially."

The young woman stood still, waiting and smiling: small as a child in her glimmering white silk. Her head remained bowed, her eyes averted, and still Claudine held her waist.

"Don't worry," Claudine said. "She speaks no English. Her

name is Khanh Ha." She spoke to the girl in French, too fast for Langford to follow; but he heard his own name.

He greeted the girl again in his rudimentary French, and told her how good the meal had been.

"Merci bien, monsieur." Her voice was only just audible. Released, she glided away again across the tiles.

"Khanh Ha is from a town in the Delta," Claudine said. "Her parents, brothers and sisters are all dead: killed in an American air strike. I'm very fond of her. I have a number of girls like her in the house, many from middle-class families. They are not just servants, they are like my own family: I call them my orphans. They don't want to become bar girls and prostitutes—which is what so many have to do." She looked at him with narrowed eyes. "But perhaps this is your loss. Perhaps you will like to spend your spare time laying bar girls—like other correspondents."

He still had enough rural conservatism to find this directness startling. No, he said; that didn't appeal to him.

"I'm glad to hear it," she said. "Now tell me how I can help you. Aubrey has asked me to; and when Aubrey asks, we don't question."

He told her that he wanted to go out on patrol with the Army of South Vietnam. He'd be grateful for her help with this.

"Really? With the ARVN? Believe me, *mon cher,* it's much safer with the Americans—and more comfortable."

He explained, as he'd done to Jim Feng. Surely their war should be reported, he said.

"Mon Dieu, I believe he's an idealist," she said.

—I said I hoped I was. The South had to win, didn't it?

She ignored his question. "Joining the ARVN should be simple for you to do. You have accreditation, no? So how do you need my help?"

He needed to find a good company, he said, with a good commander.

"Aha. Yes; that's important," she said. "A commander who will not get you killed, you mean. Yes—I can do that. I have a cousin who is a company commander in the Delta—a good man. A rarity. I'll arrange it."

She swirled the brandy in her glass, and then set it down. For a moment, her ebullience and vivacity had gone. When she spoke, it was to answer the question she'd previously ignored. " 'They have to win,' you said. Oh yes, they have to—but without the Americans they won't. And perhaps not even with them."

You can't believe that, he said. You'd lose everything.

"Yes, that's true. But we are used to that idea. Today we have; tomorrow we have not. That's how we live, in Saigon." She drained her glass. "I am glad you are an idealist," she said. "You and my cousin Trung will get on well. He is one too, poor fellow."

Her deep laughter was released again, and he found himself joining in.

—

4.

Down in the Mekong Delta, that country of water, Michael Langford had a second birth.

There seems to have been no single moment of revelation. It was a gradual process, as he waded and stumbled hour by hour and day by day through the marshes and flooded paddies, soaked by the monsoon downpours and by his own pouring sweat; seldom dry, and seldom halting except for brief hours of sleep. All that he'd eventually become had its origins in those early field patrols with Captain Le Tan Trung, whose unit was tracked faithfully by death. Death was there week after week and month after month, waiting with a cocked Kalashnikov across each paddy dyke. In the region called the Cradle, it was always prowling close to them, behind or in front, and Trung and his men were what they were because of it.

Down there in the Cradle, a life began which Langford saw as his true one. It was a life that would last for a decade, and die with the war.

—At six in the morning, I caught an Air Vietnam flight from Tan Son Nhut to My Tho, the chief provincial town of the northern Delta. That's where the ARVN Seventh Division has its headquarters, in an old French barracks. I had an appointment there at eight with Captain Le Tan Trung: Madame Phan's cousin.

The office was large, and languidly warm; there were a number of green metal desks in it, and maps on the walls. Young ARVN officers in tailored green uniforms came and went, carrying files. Langford sat in front of Captain Trung's desk, and Captain Trung studied him without smiling, leaning back in a swivel chair. He hadn't smiled when they shook hands.

"We leave in half an hour," he said. "I am taking a company down to Kien Hoa Province. American helicopters will drop us at our forward base to relieve others who are there."

His English was stiff and educated, and his voice low and courteous, but without detectable warmth. He was dressed for the field in combat fatigues and jungle boots; he had crew-cut hair like an American, and was taller than the average Vietnamese. Relatively young—around Langford's age—he looked older. Experience, presumably harsh, had prematurely tightened Trung's face, and emphasized the hollows under his cheekbones. On the wall behind the desk hung a framed map of the Delta region with little flags stuck in it; he swung around now and stood up to point at it.

"This area where we go is called the Cradle," he said. He looked hard at Langford over his shoulder. "It is called the Cradle because it is the birthplace of the Viet Cong. Nearly all is in their hands. No American troops fight there. Only we. Our company makes sweeps from the base, staying in the field for four, five days. You would be with us all the time: not just one day, like your people are with the Americans."

He turned back and leaned towards Langford, his hands on the desk.

"That whole countryside is full of booby traps. You understand, Mr. Langford? Just to move through it is dangerous. I lose troops all the time that way. There is no resupply in the field like Americans have. Often no artillery or air support, even if we are overrun. We can radio for help, but this doesn't mean it will come; we are often too far out of range. No foreign journalist has ever come out with us." He paused, as though expecting Langford to say something; when Langford didn't, he went on. "Madame Phan has asked that I help you, and I am happy to do so. But I will not be responsible if you are killed."

Langford told him that he understood. The responsibility was his own, he said. Whatever risks Captain Trung and his men were taking, he was happy to take too.

The captain compressed his lips and frowned; then he looked resigned, and nodded. "Okay," he said. He jerked his head for Langford to follow, and led the way out of the office.

The floor that Langford sat on was of diamond-patterned aluminum; his camera bag and his pack were between his legs. The Vietnamese soldiers on each side of him looked at him curiously; in their outsize American helmets and baggy combat fatigues, they seemed like boys playing at soldiers. The roar of the engines and the thumping of the rotor blades was terrific: his teeth vibrated. There was a reek of hot metal and of the fuel called JP-4: a smell he would come to know as the universal odor of the war.

He was airborne in a Bell UH-1: the transport-cum-gunship that Dmitri Volkov had waxed so poetic about. Ten of these small helicopters had taken off together from the airfield at My Tho, piloted by Americans, with about eight ARVN soldiers in each: the whole of Captain Trung's fresh company. Some of the soldiers were sitting on their helmets, and Langford sat on a thick paperback book he'd put in his pack. Captain Trung had informed him that VC snipers often tried their luck from the ground, and this made him acutely conscious of his rectum, he says: he imagined a bullet coming through the floor and neatly finding its mark. But after a few more minutes, he forgot about it.

The doors of the Huey stood open, and the rush of air was exhilarating. Poised on the edge of space in the doorway nearest to him, an American gunner in his harness squatted over an M-60 machine gun. Looking past him, Langford saw four other Hueys strung out across hazy, radiant sky, riding in a perfect, unstoppable line. They were like a new kind of creature: light, evanescent, frivolous and absolutely predatory.

—I felt free in a new way. I was so happy I felt drunk.

He brings his circumstances back like a high memory of childhood. A bright day, despite the onset of the monsoon, and below him, Vietnam: this bitterly contested country that was seldom much more than a hundred miles wide, but which seemed now to extend to mirage-like infinities, deep green and cigarette-smoke blue, its checkerboard of mangrove swamps, coconut groves and paddy fields invisibly patrolled by the Black Ghosts. The gleaming, flooded rice fields made the land here like a chain of islands; long, thread-like canals ran between the coconut groves, and the vast silver bends of the Mekong flashed in the sun, dotted with sampans and the blunt, brutal shapes of gunboats. The tall, flat-topped towers of thunderhead clouds stood reflected in the river.

This was the Cradle: the country of violent birth and violent death. But even the hidden threat down there was part of its beauty for him.

—The big American door gunner caught my eye. He patted his down-tilted M-60 and grinned, as though he knew what I was thinking. I liked his face; it reminded me of Ken's. I wonder if he'll make it through his tour of duty?

He waded shin-deep in water, with the slow-motion gait of a man wading through a dream. The mud beneath the surface dragged at his boots, which seemed to be weighted with lead.

At this time of the year, most of the country here was flooded, and heavy downpours punctuated the day. Endless gray liquid extended under a high dome of silence, and Langford had never been so tired in his life. He wanted only to drop and lie still, but knew there was no hope of this until Captain Trung called a halt.

This was the third day of the sweep. Two ARVN companies, marching far apart, were crossing a flooded plain of marsh weed. Langford marched in the company led by Captain Trung. The small Vietnamese soldiers were burdened with their weapons and ammunition belts, and Langford was hung about with the tools of his own trade: a Bell and Howell cinecamera attached by a strap to his wrist; a small cassette tape recorder hanging from his webbing belt; a camera bag, with its precious cargo of film stock, lens brushes and filters, slung from his shoulder. A Weston light meter in a leather case dangled from his neck like an amulet. So did his Leica, which he'd brought despite the fact that he was only employed to shoot film.

His outfit of stolen and dead men's clothing from the thieves' market in Saigon had already lost its spurious newness. The sodden green fatigue shirt steamed from the last downpour, and would never really be dry; his sweat soaked it when the rain didn't, and white deposits of salt stained it under the arms. He would wear this multinational military outfit for many years in the field, and many photographs preserve it: American fatigues, webbing belt, pack and water bottles; French canvas-sided combat boots; cotton Australian Army hat. He looks like an improperly turned-out Australian soldier in need of a haircut. He would never wear into combat zones the American helmet or heavy flak jacket that most other correspondents adopted; he preferred to reduce heat-fatigue by taking his chances without them, as the Australian infantry did.

Crossing rice fields, the patrol found dry ground by marching on the tops of the dykes. Otherwise, water was all-enveloping: an element they couldn't escape. They breathed it, waded through it, exuded it. All the muscles of Langford's legs were aching in a way no football game had ever made them do, and the effort of getting through the mud, in the immense, steam-room heat, was draining them of their strength. But his years of athletic training were standing him in good stead. There had been times in the past two days when he'd felt he'd not be able to march for ten more minutes, yet he'd always done so: had always found reserves to draw on. He was determined, he says, to give no sign of his fatigue to Captain Trung, whose thin figure marched remorselessly at the head of the leading platoon. When halts did come, Trung would glance at Langford and nod, his expression speculative. But he would hardly ever speak to him; instead, he talked to his men in Vietnamese. And with every day, Langford's admiration for the small ARVN soldiers in their oversized helmets increased.

—I'd thought them to be physically like children. But as the days went by, I found how wiry and tough they were. They kept on, with no sign of tiredness, weighted with their spare ammunition and a crazy collection of guns, most of which were too big for them: M-1 carbines from World War Two; Thompson submachine guns; Browning automatic rifles, and the new American M-16s they're being issued with now. When we crossed small streams, I'd go chest-deep, but sometimes they'd be in over their heads, packs and weapons held above the surface. But they came out laughing.

—They were farm boys like me, and we got on well. They speak little or no English, and not much French either; that's only common among the officers. So I used sign language, and got them to start teaching me Vietnamese. They hadn't had much to do with Europeans, so I was a novelty: a funny white giant, I suppose. They like to laugh.

Trung had told Langford to keep the cotton bush hat on at all times. ("VC will target that yellow hair.") He had also urged him to keep close behind the man in front: to tread in the soldier's footsteps, and imitate his every move. In this way, Trung said, Langford had a chance of avoiding the booby traps that were everywhere in Viet Cong country; sometimes mines, sometimes grenades, but most commonly bamboo *punji* stakes: fire-hardened barbs planted in the rice fields and the grass, their ends smeared with human shit. To step on one was to contract almost certain infection; and they'd been known to pierce even the soles of jungle boots.

So the patrol trod always carefully, carefully, slowed not just by mud and water, but by the thought of the barb that couldn't be seen, and Langford paid strict attention to the soldier in front of him: a young man of about twenty-two called Tho. They talked together whenever there was a halt.

Tho spoke more English than the others. He told Langford that he'd learned English in a Saigon bar where he'd worked as a general handyman. One day, out fetching ice, he'd been stopped and shanghaied for the Army by an ARVN street patrol; they did this, it seemed, if a young man's papers weren't in order. Tho didn't seem bitter about this; he was always cheerful.

—Even though he had a very Vietnamese face, he reminded me of a kid I'd been friends with in New Norfolk when I was young, who'd been fond of jokes: same wide jaw and wide-apart brown eyes. Tho liked to show off his bit of French; when I'd ask where the VC were, he'd point to the horizon and say: *"Beaucoup VC!"* It got to be a sort of joke between us. I'd say there weren't any VC, and he'd shake his head. *"Beaucoup VC!"* He helped to keep me going.

They had still not encountered the Viet Cong, after nearly three days of slogging. Tomorrow they'd start back to base, joining the rest of the brigade there; and Langford had begun to doubt that they'd make contact with the enemy at all. The company covered some twenty-four kilometers a day: three times the distance the more heavily laden American patrols could achieve. Their food at breakfast was a little dried fruit and dried fish or jerky. During the day they ate nothing. In the evening they had a thin vegetable soup, small pieces of fish, and rice. Their only drink was water. Most Westerners would have found this diet a privation: Langford seems not to have minded it.

On the first day, he says, they'd marched all afternoon and through most of the night, trudging down the aisles of the coconut groves, stumbling across sodden plains of marsh-weed and elephant grass, stopping only for snatches of sleep on patches of dry ground, or on paddy dykes. At midday on the second day they'd made a halt beside a rice field, under the emerald fans of some water palms. As Langford had sunk gratefully onto his poncho, a group of soldiers had gathered about him.

They smiled broadly, watching him unlace his boots, their stares frankly curious. He began to burn blood-filled leeches from his legs with a lit cigarette, and they laughed; but their laughter was soft; polite. Captain Trung watched from a distance. They asked him in Vietnamese if he was tired. *"Mat, khong?"* He made signs that he was; then he got them to teach him how to say it.

"Co, mat qua." Yes, very tired, they said, and laughed.

He handed around American cigarettes, and they took them appreciatively, elongated brown fingers reaching delicately into the pack; and suddenly he became aware that two of them were plucking curiously at the blond hair on his forearm, discussing it in Vietnamese.

—I felt like a bloody Gulliver.

He took some still pictures of them with his Leica, and they immediately formed groups, asking him to take more. These pictures have survived, and the faces under the outsize helmets are lit with youth's pleasure in life, the smiles carefree, as though they are on a pleasure trip. Some of them produced photographs of wives and children from their wallets and showed them to Langford. He sat talking to them with his first words of Vietnamese: happy.

Tho had gone to the edge of the paddy, and had scooped some water into his helmet. He came back with it brimming, and dropped some purification tablets into it. Few of the soldiers in this platoon carried canteens; the streams and paddies were their main source of water, and in the regular downpours, they would sometimes collect the rain in their helmets. Tho drank, and then held the helmet towards Langford, smiling and nodding.

Langford still had water in his canteens, but he accepted out of politeness, he says, and with some misgivings. Paddy water was lethal without the tablets, and risky to Westerners even with them.

"Let me take your picture."

Captain Trung had come up, helmet in one hand, rubbing his spiky hair with the other. For the first time, he smiled at Langford. He took the Leica, which he seemed familiar with, and photographed Langford as he drank.

This picture too still exists, and went into Langford's first published collection. Tho, smiling and holding the helmet from one side, is tilting it while Langford drinks, as though assisting a child. One can see why. Cotton army hat crushed in one hand, nose in the helmet, the long blond hair that the soldiers find so novel spilling forward as he drinks, Langford looks more like a twenty-two-year-old than a man of nearly thirty.

—They treated me a bit like a kid, on that first patrol: one who needed help with the simplest things. They reminded me of the country people in Tasmania, who treat strangers in the same way. I felt at home with them.

On the second day, the company had been up before dawn and had marched until sundown, passing occasional villages whose black-clad inhabitants stared at them sullenly. These were VC supporters, the men told Langford—either by conviction or because they were forced to be. After dark, they stopped and lit a small cooking fire, talking and laughing noisily. But minutes after the fire was lit, Trung called a low command; packs were picked up, rifles slung again, and they marched on, leaving the fire burning. Exhausted, hungry and baffled, Langford followed. An hour later they made camp again, this time without noise.

Trung came out of the thick, moist darkness to survey Langford with an amused expression, hands on his hips.

"You wonder what we do. We made false camp back there. Now we make a secret camp. The VC will see the fire at the other camp, and hit that. Oh yes, they are here—quite close. Always they attack at night."

But there was no attack that night.

Now, at sundown on the third day, they waded on across the paddy field, which was like every other paddy field. They were making towards the tree line, which was like every other tree line.

There was a long irrigation canal there, some three hundred yards away, walled in by a high earth dyke, on top of which was a grove of fruit trees: guava; papayas; coconut palms; the big green sails of banana trees. Behind this grove, a palm-thatched roof could be seen, and a thread of smoke: signs of a hamlet. The trees and the smoke rose against sky that had a warning tinge of sunset. Under its vast, gray curve and its towering cumulonimbus clouds, treading in their own reflections, the figures of Captain Trung's patrol seemed small and lost, toiling on without purpose. Birds whose names were unknown to Langford wheeled and called. The other company wasn't in sight; but Langford had just learned that it had reported by radio that two guerrillas had been captured trying to escape the area. The VC were here then, somewhere; but he was too weary to feel concerned or even interested.

The patrol reached a paddy dyke and climbed onto it, marching towards the grove and the hamlet. Grateful to be on semidry land, Langford trudged behind Tho, in his waterlogged boots.

The gunfire, when it began, was without echo in these big, level spaces, under this sky. It was a flat, loud stuttering, coming from behind the grove of trees on the irrigation dyke: a noise that was workmanlike rather than ominous: the sound of the Kalashnikov AK-47, the standard assault rifle of the Viet Cong. For the second time in his life, Langford found bullets whining and cracking above his head. But this time was different.

—I thought: I'm not ready. God, not now, I'm too tired. Why not in the morning?

But it was now. All along the dyke in front of him, the ARVN soldiers were leaping and splashing into the paddy water, unslinging their weapons as they went. Langford followed, Bell and Howell raised to keep it dry.

He crouched next to Tho against the slick mud of the dyke, the water up to his thighs, half wanting to get below the surface as the bullets continued to whine. The patrol was almost completely exposed here, since the dyke ran at right angles to the irrigation canal; but so far the VC were aiming too high. Rolls of thunder joined the gunfire now, like giant echoes, and it began to rain, reducing visibility. Air and water became one element, within which Captain Trung was gesturing to his troops, water streaming down his face, shouting in Vietnamese. *"Di di mau! Di di mau!"*

He was pointing to the next paddy dyke, which ran parallel to the irrigation canal; a position in which to take cover. The men waded fast through the water after him, crouching, firing short bursts towards the trees. Langford, moving beside Tho, found the noise both shattering and reassuring.

He lay half prone in the water against the protective wall of the new dyke, and began to concentrate on his technical problems, while the troops concentrated on theirs. The cloudburst was already easing, and instead of being concerned about the better visibility this gave the VC, he was grateful: now he'd get good film. He checked the light with his meter, switched on his cassette tape recorder to pick up wild sound, and began to adjust the lens aperture on the Bell and Howell. His hands were shaking slightly, but he found himself calm.

—The sunset was coming on fast, and I was more concerned about that now than the bullets; I had to get the aperture right. I also had to be economical with what I shot, since all I had was two minutes forty seconds to a roll of film, and there might not be many opportunities to get in new rolls.

—We still couldn't see the VC, and didn't know how many there were. They were dug in behind the irrigation dyke, among the trees. So they were still invisible, still ghosts: it was only their bullets that weren't ghostly. I began to move along the dyke, filming as I went.

—My tiredness had gone; all that mattered was what was in the viewfinder. I could hear Jim Feng talking in my head, teaching me all he knew about filming battle. Always look for movement; look for action. Get involved. Move. There'd be no Cameraman's Daydream this time: I knew I'd be lucky to get out of this paddy field alive. I had confidence in Trung, though, and my main aim was to capture the way the ARVN troops were handling themselves: I wanted to show them functioning out on the edge. As they watched the irrigation dyke, firing off bursts, their faces had the same look of concentration that the faces of athletes get when they push themselves to the limit; the same concentration that faces have when people do delicate and expert work. I believe I got that.

—So the cinecamera work went well. But a thing I found was that I kept wanting to freeze the frame: to capture single images that summed everything up. I wanted to get out my Leica, but there just wasn't time. You can't do both. I guess I'm a stills cameraman at heart.

The firing from the irrigation canal seemed to have stopped. Captain Trung called for the troops to advance, and they moved out across the paddy field, spraying the grove of trees with heavy fire, making for the last paddy dyke that lay between them and the canal. Langford was beside Tho, filming as he came; once, between bursts of fire with his outsize M-1, Tho grinned at him sideways.

"Beaucoup VC," he called, and Langford had a surge of deep affection for him—as though, he says, they'd known each other for years, or were blood relations.

There was no answering fire until the company came quite close to the cover of the new paddy dyke; then there were two bursts, and a bullet passed close to Langford. Crouching behind the low mud wall, he saw in his viewfinder two black-clad figures with assault rifles in the grove of trees, half obscured by broad banana leaves.

—Black Ghosts! Where had I seen them before?

As he filmed them, one dropped, and the other vanished. The hammering of the machine guns and rifles around him was continuous. Then there was silence, and Captain Trung's voice shouting a command. Langford lowered his camera and turned towards Tho.

But Tho was lying on his back in the water, clutching his rifle, his arms wide-flung. From a depthless cavity that had appeared in the front of his shirt, long red skeins crept through the water's gray.

Two soldiers stooped over him and lifted him carefully, murmuring in Vietnamese; the mud and water sucked at him, wanting to hold him there. Langford received the gaze of his wide-set, sightless brown eyes, from which all glint of humor was gone.

—I shot film of them carrying Tho away. In one way I hated doing it, but it was exactly the sort of shot I badly needed to get. So I had to shut off my feelings. That's what the trade's mostly about: I've learned that already.

The hamlet was almost deserted, except for two old women and some small children. The rest of the people had gone. It had been a VC hamlet, Trung said. Walking beside Langford, he pointed to a blue and red Liberation Front flag on a bamboo pole above one of the houses; two soldiers were climbing onto the roof to get it down.

—I got good footage of this. Also of four dead Viet Cong lying in foxholes on the irrigation dyke. Big bluebottle flies were already buzzing around their wounds; it was very quiet here, and that was the only sound. I thought of slaughtering day on the farm, when we butchered pigs; but these were men. One of them, with a square, dependable-looking face, had his belly torn open: something that shouldn't be seen. There was a stink from him you should never have to smell, either, and after I'd shot the film, I had to go and throw up. I found then that I was thinking of Ken again, and of how he did the same, when he had to kill that Jap.

—When I filmed these dead VC close up, their faces surprised me. I'd imagined them as some sort of demon, I suppose. But instead, lying there in their black pajamas and those crude rubber sandals they make out of car tires, they had faces just like those of the ARVN troops. Very young: peasant boys.

Langford and Captain Trung sat cross-legged on their ponchos under a banana tree, by the edge of the narrow dirt road that ran through the center of the village. Trung had come over and joined him, which he'd not done before. The hamlet was a small and simple place, with a mangrove swamp at its western end. The sunset there was into its final phase, deep pink and bronze, the twisted mangroves and some tall coconut palms standing out black against it. The houses that lined the little road were built of bamboo, with pitched roofs of water-palm fronds, making them look like haystacks. Lean black pigs and chickens rooted and scratched in the yards.

Many of the soldiers lay prone on their ponchos, dozing with their rifles beside them. It was the first time Langford had seen them show absolute exhaustion. Captain Trung and he smoked, easing their aching bodies and slapping at mosquitoes, at first saying little.

"We will eat well tonight," Trung said. He pointed: in the yards outside the houses, clusters of soldiers had lit pottery stoves of unglazed clay, on which they were cooking in purloined woks and pans. They had killed some pigs and chickens. The charcoal smoke from the stoves mingled pleasantly with the pungency of Vietnamese cigarettes. Underneath, faintly, was the stench of sewage.

Langford told Trung he was sorry about Tho. He had liked him, he said.

"I am sorry too. He was a good soldier. We will carry his body back to base, for burial." Trung was still looking at the soldiers grouped around the stoves; their laughter floated across, together with the murmuring of hens and the calling of birds from the swamp. He gestured towards them.

"These are mostly village boys," he said. "They get poor pay, and no R and R like the Americans. If they die, their families get no pensions. They see their sisters and girlfriends become hootch girls for the GIs. It is not easy to tell them why they fight and die."

Langford offered him a fresh cigarette. As Trung bent his head to Langford's lighter, he looked up at him with open curiosity. "You do not have to be with us," he said. "My men wonder why. Why you are not eating ice cream in the field with the Americans, and flying back to Saigon for a shower and change in the evening. I really cannot tell them." He blew out smoke, continuing to look at Langford. "They like you. You have marched very well, these last three days: I was afraid you would not be able. Claudine has said you will be different, but I didn't believe her. I have seen no other correspondent do such a thing. One has tried last year, I heard, but after a day he grew ill, and was taken out by chopper. Were you once a soldier? I hear Australians are good jungle fighters."

No, Langford said. He was just a cameraman.

Trung leaned back against the trunk of the banana tree, looking at Langford now with a mocking expression. "You will go out with the Americans next time, I think."

Yes, Langford said. He had to cover every aspect of the war. But he hoped he could come out again with Captain Trung's company.

"You still have not told me why."

Langford told him that Western news services seemed to give all their coverage to the Americans. He thought television audiences should see what the Army of South Vietnam was doing. It's your war, he said. Your country. Isn't that right, Captain?

Trung nodded slowly. "Yes—it is our war. And Americans say we do not fight. They say our commanders are dishonest. I am sorry to admit that in many cases this is true. There are commanders who live on bribes, and steal the pay of their troops. Saigon soldiers. But we are not all like this." He smiled suddenly, and the smile transformed his thin face. "Come out again with us soon, since you are crazy enough. You will be welcome. And please—call me Trung." He stretched, sniffed the cooking odors, and picked up his helmet. "Now we will eat—and tonight we sleep under cover. But we will not be allowed to sleep for long, I think."

Langford stared at him. Did he mean they'd come back?

"They always come back, Mike. So do not take your boots off when you sleep."

FOUR
SAIGON TEA

1.

So far off now, 1965! It begins to seem almost as far as 1848. Yet neither of these years is as distant as we think: unfinished roads stretch from them both, and run to where we stand.

Langford's typescripts from the sixties lie in front of me: old shot-lists for his television film stories; reports on Vietnamese political figures which might have been for his own use, but which I suspect he wrote for Aubrey Hardwick; some short statements for international magazines, to go with his pictures. The pages are yellow and fraying at the edges, like the holland blind in the storeroom; even the paper clips that hold them together are beginning to be stained with rust. And this pierces me with sadness. Absurd: but I don't want to see these papers grow so old. I have the superstitious feeling that the more they do, the more Mike dwindles—and will soon vanish. Already they give off the same aged perfume as the journals of Robert Devereux.

But this sad odor, coming up from the past's deep shaft, isn't what I ought to be attending to, if the Saigon of 1965 is to be entered. Sadness isn't how it was, back then.

..

Harvey Drummond has given me a color photograph he took at the front of Villa Volkov.

Mike and Jim Feng moved into this house of Dmitri's soon after Mike's arrival in Saigon, contributing to the rent. Harvey stayed there too, whenever he was in Saigon. It's one of a row of two-storied French colonial villas, dingy white, with a long roof of orange tiles. The street entrance is secured by an iron grille with a narrow door in it, and shaded by a big, spreading tamarind growing by the curb. In the picture, Langford, Feng and Volkov are standing under the tamarind with Monsieur Chen, the Sino-Vietnamese manager who's the Count's chief supplier of marijuana, and who also (according to Harvey) would procure girls for Dmitri, sometimes at half an hour's notice. His oblong head is brutally crew-cut, and his bent, handmade cigarette is clenched between gold-filled teeth. Not a man to fool with, Harvey said. The three cameramen, smiling at the camera for their picture, are wearing identical green safari suits.

Is this a joke? Partly; but they're fond of these outfits. These are what they call their TV suits, styled by Mr. Minh of Tu Do Street, the correspondents' tailor. The cameramen wore them not in the field but when filming or carousing around Saigon. With special slots and pockets in the sleeves for pens, notebooks and cigarettes, they were much sought after by television journalists who did stand-up pieces to camera. Harvey had one. Soon they'd be imitated all over Asia, and by fashion designers in the West; but this was in the future.

The picture gives off a vibration of the sixties: last decade of the trio's youth, and of fashionable derangement. Its newfound, illegal drugs are as easily available in Vietnam as coffee or tea; its new music roars insolent and prophetic from the Count's big speakers, and the figures in their TV suits stand bathed in the light of a life of lost action, lost laughter, lost excess: a life whose memories I seem chosen to preserve.

2.

HARVEY DRUMMOND

When I miss Saigon, I miss Villa Volkov.

It was on Cong Ly Avenue, which ran parallel to Tu Do Street; a good residential address, and very central: five minutes in the Big Budgie from the center of town. Volkov had made the place into a sort of fraternity house for *bao chi,* and it was famous among scribes and photographers for the quality of its dope: the premium stuff called Cambodian Red, unfailingly supplied by Monsieur Chen.

Villa Volkov was where we got our nerves together, coming in from covering battle; where we all recharged; where we made the jokes only we could understand, and where we looked for the meaning of Vietnam, always Vietnam, before we floated away and didn't care any more, stoned out of our brains, carried on thunderous waves from the Count's stereo system: the Beatles; Del Shannon; Jerry Lee Lewis; the early Stones.

There were often transient correspondents camped there. You stumbled over them in the living room in the mornings; they lay on canvas cots in the hall. It was rather like living with a circus troupe—an effect that was reinforced by the presence of Dmitri's animals. He had three cats, a parrot, and a monkey called Vice Marshal—named after Air Vice Marshal Ky, the Prime Minister. Dmitri claimed there was a likeness, but I could never see it. I called the creature Onan the Monk: he was forever masturbating on the bookshelf, frowning in disapproval at himself. I think he was permanently spaced out from breathing the apartment's air.

I was a paying guest, coming and going at intervals, since my wife and I maintained an apartment in Singapore. When I was in Saigon for long spells, and missing Lisa, the scene at the villa was a compensation. It was a scene that would last until 1970, when Dmitri, Mike and Jim moved their base to Phnom Penh. The villa was on the old colonial scale, with a vast sitting room whose louvered doors had brass handles, many big bedrooms, and a bathroom the size of a hallway, with a bath like a whaleboat, a French hosepipe shower and bidet, brass taps that were Parisian antiques, and a blue, child-high storage jar from the Arabian Nights standing mysteriously in a corner. The rent was expensive, but we could well afford it.

Like most of the foreign press, we were changing our dollars for piastres on the black market, through an institution known as the Bank of India. This consisted of two very nervous Indians in a tiny office in the Eden Building on Nguyen Hue Boulevard. They were located conveniently on the same floor as the Telenews office, whose facilities Mike, Jim and I were sharing. They faced prison if they were ever caught by the wrong authorities, but their web was said to involve both Peking and the CIA, and the steady inflation of the local currency was making them wealthy—as well as giving great satisfaction to us. Lying on his vast double bed in the mornings, clad in a black silk kimono he'd acquired in Tokyo, the Count would call out regularly through his open door, reminding us of our good fortune.

"Just think, gentlemen! Every time we wake up, we've made money!"

The phone was in Dmitri's bedroom, but we were allowed full use of it: his bedroom door always stood open in the royal manner, except when he had a girl there. The lease was in his name: he dealt with Monsieur Chen. The place was owned by a Paris company, and Chen and his wife managed it and doubled as servants, living downstairs. When Monsieur Chen came upstairs with his latest batch of Cambodian Red (or failing that, with Delta Green), he carried it in a plastic shoulder bag lettered *Air Vietnam,* smiling the broad smile of a benefactor. He had many interests, buzzing around Saigon on a Vespa motor scooter, and was sometimes seen at the door downstairs paying off the White Mice: the small, corrupt, unloved Vietnamese police who patrolled the city in white uniforms, with .38 revolvers on their hips and gun belts many sizes too large for them.

Feng, Volkov and Langford were always together in those days. At times they'd go out into the field together as well, unless Mike and Jim were trying to scoop Volkov, or vice-versa. Then there was no mercy. But they'd cooperate to save each other sweat, when the stories weren't too big: they'd even tell each other where the action was breaking. "This is only a small one, Count," Langford would call, as he and Jim passed Volkov's door with their cameras. "No need to get on your bike."

They went in for practical jokes, which at times could be trying. Langford in particular had a juvenile addiction to these. Once, when stoned, he got hold of an American smoke grenade and threw it onto the awning above the front door, filling Cong Ly Avenue with orange smoke. The White Mice arrived, but Monsieur Chen placated them with money. On another occasion I woke in my bed to find that a trail of lighter fluid had been poured along the sheet towards my face; Langford, urged on by Volkov, crouched next to me with his Zippo lighter aflame, ready to set the trail off.

It was Trevor Griffiths who started calling them the Soldiers Three. He didn't exactly do it fondly; there was always a touch of acid with Griffiths, and the reference to Kipling was deliberate. He saw them as too gung-ho; they were treating the war as a boy's adventure, as Trevor saw it, and had no political awareness: a common failing among cameramen. But the Soldiers Three were having too good a time in those days to care what Griffiths thought, and the nickname backfired: it came to be used admiringly rather than mockingly. This must have irritated Griffiths; but he did have the grace to be amused as well. After that first little incident in the Happy Bar, he and Dmitri had patched things up; and now Griffiths valued the quality of the Count's hash supply too much to want to be persona non grata at the villa.

My bedroom was at the back, over the garage where the Budgie was kept. I looked down onto a lane of noodle sellers and clothing stalls and some sort of tinsmith's. The old blue wooden shutters were always ajar, and when I woke in the morning, I'd hear the hawkers' cries and the banging of metal, accompanied by faint French-Vietnamese pop music from Madame Chen's kitchen downstairs, where she'd be cooking us a breakfast of eggs, hot rolls and coffee. I'd hear Dmitri shouting passionately into the telephone to someone at CBS, and smell the lingering tang of last night's Cambodian Red in the apartment, and know I was back in Saigon.

Sometimes the radio in the sitting room would be tuned to American Armed Forces radio, and Madame Chen's genteel ballads from downstairs would be drowned by the rapid babble of the disc jockey, and the thud of rock and roll. The disc jockey had a regular dedication for the listening GIs: *To all you guys out there, groovin' on the danger.* We all found this wildly funny. "Hullo," Volkov would say, looking deadpan at some newly arrived correspondent. "Are you groovin' on the danger, buddy?"

Villa Volkov: the sitting room. I remember the walls ballooning, pushed out by humidity and by a big sweet cloud of cannabis, the frontier of the Land of Other long ago crossed. Jim Feng, Trevor Griffiths and I were imprisoned by Volkov inside a single Elvis Presley ballad—"Can't Help Falling in Love"—which he insisted on playing over and over again.

He was seated in a massive, throne-like leather armchair of 1930s vintage. Here he had control of the turntable, which was on a table next to him. Vice Marshal sat frowning on an arm of the chair, occasionally reaching out a small black hand to caress his master's face. Volkov kept putting the needle back to the start of the record again, smiling like someone cooking a perfect omelette. The rest of us were sprawled on cushions scattered about the floor's raffia matting. On a coffee table near at hand were cigarette papers and a commonly owned sandalwood box filled with Monsieur Chen's precious herb. Pasted on the side of the box was a headline from a magazine: *What are you afraid of?* The room was getting dim, but no one turned on the lights. Through the open shutters of one of the front windows, I could see green sky, the top of the tamarind tree, and a ferroconcrete balcony across Cong Ly Avenue, overgrown with potted plants, where small Vietnamese figures moved about, leading useful family lives.

Dmitri had been in the Central Highlands today, covering some heavy action, and had changed into his black kimono: with his wavy blond hair and Tartar face, it made him look like a medieval boyar. Where the kimono gaped over his chest, his lucky charm could be seen: a chain to which was attached a medallion of Saint Nicholas that had been brought out of Russia by his grandmother. All the cameramen were superstitious; all of them had some emblem or other without which they believed they'd immediately be killed. Jim had a Cambodian tiger's claw, and Mike had a brass belt buckle with the Communist star: these were taken by the Americans from captured North Vietnamese soldiers, and were greatly prized.

Elvis was at fairly low volume—or else I was becoming deaf from the effect of the grass. The Beatles had sung "Eight Days a Week," Del Shannon had sung "Keep Searchin'," the Stones had sung "Little Red Rooster," and I'd managed to slip in one of my Gregorian chants. We all contributed to the LP collection, bringing records back from Singapore and Hong Kong. The others got off on my chants when they were stoned, but I hadn't been able to convert them to my Artur Schnabel Schubert Impromptus. And for now, we were stuck with Elvis, whom I was fond of, but not fond of enough to hear ten times in succession. Dmitri's lips moved devoutly as he sang along under his breath, a joint suspended in his upraised fingers.

"Wise men say
Only fools rush in . . ."

Jim Feng passed me another joint that was going from hand to hand; I took a drag, holding the smoke in my chest in the recommended way, and when I let it out, things had changed even more. I didn't really share the general devotion to grass in Villa Volkov, it made me paranoid; but not to smoke it seemed like an unfriendly act. I found the Count watching me now with his open-mouthed smile and pale blue czarist stare, the pupils so small it gave him the look of a fanatic.

"Look at the Harvey. He doesn't really approve of these illegal substances. No no, man, he says, take it away, don't rape me. But then he blows his mind anyway. You are a bloody puritan, Harvey."

Jim Feng laughed quietly: a monotone chuckling. But Trevor Griffiths didn't join in. He sat with his hands flat on the floor, looking at Volkov, blue chin set, tangled black hair falling on his forehead to meet his heavy eyebrows. In the room's twilight, his face looked more corpse-white than usual. He'd been up to the Central Coast area for the past week, doing a story on the American air strikes there. He'd mentioned this to me before we began to smoke, his dark, significant stare and compressed lips warning me that he was holding in check a tide of righteous anger. Trevor's anger, like his humor, was never far below the surface.

Now he spoke to Dmitri with artificial politeness, his resonant Welsh voice coming from his chest. "Do you think, Count, that this doleful and crude dirge of Elvis's might soon be changed? Giving way, perhaps, to the subtlety of Bob Dylan?"

Volkov gazed down on him, reclining in his leather throne; he toyed with his medallion. "Greatest thing the King has ever done," he said, and reached for the needle again.

"I beg you to change it," Griffiths said, "before I smash it."

Volkov raised his eyebrows. "It must have been a busy day, Trevor; you sound tense. I take it you filed the assassination?"

"Assassination?" Griffiths' eyes widened in alarm; hands still flat on the matting, he began to push himself up from the floor. Then he saw Volkov begin to laugh, and lowered himself again. "You bastard, Count."

It was the oldest of correspondents' jokes, but it still worked. We were all terrified of being scooped in Saigon now, since so much was breaking every day. Griffiths had been out of town for a week, and in Prime Minister Ky's new military government, anything seemed possible—especially to Trevor, who had placed the elegant Air Vice Marshal high in his pantheon of villains, close to Lyndon Johnson.

I'd come to like Griffiths, despite his uncertain temper. Whenever he appeared, large brown eyes gleaming, menacing black eyebrows clenched into one, simmering over some tidbit concerning the follies of the American Military Command here, or the perfidy of the Saigon Government, I was somehow glad to see him, agree with him or not. Trevor was passionately sincere in everything: his opinions; his pleasures; his love affairs. His sense of humor saved him from being earnest all the time, and he was generous in sharing information. His love of Dylan Thomas had caused him to memorize many of the poems, and he would intone them beautifully when drunk. For this I forgave him anything.

But tonight the grass had affected him the wrong way: he was still looking broodingly at the Count, and had begun to bark questions at him.

"Why must you always take control, Volkov? Or to put it another way, why are you such a Fascist?"

Dmitri took a drag of his joint; then he removed the needle from the disc. There was silence, and he spoke in his slurred drawl.

"Why do you show me the strong arm, Trevor? Why do you call names?"

"Just making an observation. You are a Fascist, aren't you? You even support the Ky junta."

"Anyone you don't like is a Fascist, Griffiths. The Ky is not too bad. At least he has guts, and is better than Diem."

"Good God. He's a maniac. This is a man who wants to lead a bombing raid over Hanoi just so he can blast his lost family home out of existence."

"Yanks have to work with who they can. Ky can do what he likes if he stops the Commies, so far as I am concerned. You know what your beloved Commies do when they take over, Griffiths? They build a prison and put the people inside it. Then the commissars proceed to live in luxury, like fuckin' bishops of Middle Ages, pretending to love peace and the people—whom they screw."

"And who's screwing who in South Vietnam? The Yanks are turning this country into a colony. They've transported California here for their own benefit, while they pauperize and bomb the peasants. And still they can't beat these peasants in rubber sandals, can they? Charlie's still coming down the highway."

Trevor's chest rose and fell; his fists were clenched on the matting; he was whiter still, transported with noble rage. Vice Marshal, apparently alarmed by this, leaped suddenly from his master's chair onto a dresser, and sat frowning at Griffiths from there. But Volkov, sprawled in his throne, continued to smile down with an air of insolence.

"Is that so? U.S. First Cavalry have just done all right in the Ia Drang Valley, baby. Their first engagement with the Army of North Vietnam and they won, as a matter of fact. In the end, Communists pissed off across Cambodian border. I covered. So did Mike."

"And you really think that's the way it will go? That the Yanks will win in the end? Against the North Vietnamese? These are the same people who hauled artillery through fifty miles of mountain and jungle, an inch at a time, half a mile a day, for three months, and then shafted the French at Dien Bien Phu. These are the Spartans of Asia, Volkov. And discipline and dedication will always defeat decadence—haven't you learned that?"

"Bullshit. Their artillery was courtesy of fuckin' Soviet Union. Is that what you want, Griffo? Soviet control of Southeast Asia?"

It was Trevor's turn with the joint; he inhaled, and returned to the attack.

"I've just been in Binh Dinh Province. The Yanks have designated it a 'free-bombing zone.' You know what that means? Have you seen what it bloody well entails?"

"I have seen it. Those are VC areas, and you know it. American boys are dying too; so are ARVN. And VC have no mercy. They roll grenades down floors of cinemas and blow up women and kids: does your heart bleed about that, Trevor? Do you think they'll be merciful if they win? *Mon Dieu.* I know about Commies, baby."

"Oh yes. All because your grandfather ended up driving a taxi in Paris, with no more serfs to flog."

I half expected Volkov to physically launch himself at Griffiths; but his response was still verbal, his drawl exaggerated. "We all know why you are a bloody lefty, Griffiths. You are victim of English class system." He turned to Jim and me. "A poor Welsh boy sent to English snob school; parents made sacrifices. This makes him feel deprived, and so he becomes a radical. And so he overlooks liquidation of twenty million people in Soviet Union. He prefers this to democracy, and filthy capitalism."

Dope had turned both men into cruel children; and now I expected Griffiths to slug Volkov. But instead he sat motionless, fists still clenched, still staring. For all his intelligence and commitment to ideas, I doubt whether Trevor *reflected* very much; and I doubt that Dmitri did, either. They were actually very alike. Both were men given to passionate intensities; and I believe both had taken up positions in response to old psychic wounds. Political arguments are not finally about politics, in my experience. All those abstract passions have their origins somewhere smaller, somewhere humbler: in childhood, usually, or adolescence, where some small humiliation alters us forever. So it wasn't lost Russia or broken Vietnam that had brought my two brothers to such an intoxication of rage. There's no wound so profound as the early wound to our self-esteem—or perhaps to our esteem for a parent. To be esteemed: this is surely our greatest hunger, right? All else pales.

I think there might have been some sort of punch-up eventually, despite the fact that they were both too dazed with grass to handle it. But then Mike Langford came in.

He suddenly materialized among us, standing in the middle of the room in stained combat fatigues, with a large white wound dressing taped to his forehead. He seemed pale and tired, but cheerful. He dropped his camera and camera bag onto the coffee table and put his hands on his hips, smiling around at us.

We looked back at him, adjusting to his existence. Jim Feng spoke first. "Jesus. What has happened to your head, Snow?"

Mike didn't answer; instead, he pointed a finger at Jim, and then at the rest of us. "You're stoned, James. You're all stoned. All right, where's my fix? And what's happened to the music?"

His presence dissolved all antagonism: his white and yellow blandness had a calming quality. He went to the record player, hunted through the stack of LPs beside it, and put on Bob Dylan. "It's All Over Now, Baby Blue" filled the room, and Volkov and Griffiths stopped looking at each other. Trevor lay back on his cushion, and a small smile returned.

"That man is a genius. Took his name from the great Dylan Thomas, of course. In homage."

Mike sank down beside Jim, who passed him a fresh-rolled joint. "What the hell hit you?" Jim asked. "Shrapnel?"

"Better than that, James. I was out with an ARVN patrol near Soc Trang, and Charlie overran us for a while. I saw one of them coming over the top of a dyke, and I tried to get film of him. It would have been a bloody marvelous picture, but he clubbed me with the butt of his AK as he went past."

Volkov was shaking his head. "Cameraman's Daydream, Langford. Jesus. Lucky he didn't shoot."

"You're right; you're right." Mike shook his head in mock regret; catching my eye, he gave me his wink.

Griffiths addressed him now. "Still going out with the ARVN, Snow? You're mad. You'll run out of luck eventually—and what's it all for? They're a bloody lost cause."

We all knew that Mike had become devoted to the ARVN, going out over and over again with his friend Captain Trung. He also covered quite often with the Americans; but the Army of South Vietnam was his first love. Most of us were impressed by the risks he was taking and the privations involved—risks and privations that even Feng and Volkov had no wish to share. For one thing, the ARVN just weren't the main story. Yet we all acknowledged that the film he shot of battle with the South Vietnamese was remarkable; and his stocks were high with Telenews, which was selling his footage successfully in many countries. Seeing Asian troops in battle was a novelty at that time for Western audiences, who had always been shown the Americans. And Langford was shooting closer to the action than anyone else in the business. People watching their television newscasts over dinner saw these Vietnamese soldiers dying; saw the expressions on their faces as they tended wounded comrades. To get such shots meant being right in the front line, instead of shooting with a telephoto lens from the second or third line, as most photographers did. Already one began to hear the nickname Suicide Langford; but that was either sour grapes or silly sensationalism. He judged his risks; he had an extraordinary survival instinct.

He drew on his joint now, regarding Griffiths mildly. "Oh I don't know," he said. "I reckon the ARVN'll still be fighting when the Yanks have gone. Anyway, the Count just scoops me when I cover with the Americans—so I might as well be with the ARVN."

Volkov smiled. "Bullshit will get you nowhere, Snow. But be careful, or you will die with your Captain Trung."

Griffiths looked up quickly.

"No he won't: shut up, Count. Also, accept my apology. I shouldn't have spoken about your family like that."

Volkov waved a slow hand.

"Accepted. I also have said personal things which I withdraw."

Such animosities were never maintained. We were all superstitious, at Villa Volkov.

3.

HARVEY DRUMMOND

At first, to tell you the truth, I thought Langford rather ordinary—apart from his risk taking, that is. And in many ways he *was* ordinary: ordinary at the personal level, I mean.

But I soon came to notice two things that weren't quite ordinary about him: his unchanging calm and gentleness, and the impression he gave of having a secret life. I'm sure the air of secrecy wasn't conscious; he was never pretentious. It was simply an atmosphere he created around him, probably without knowing it.

Well, there was a secret life, we know that now. But in those days I didn't take seriously the things that people like Trevor Griffiths had to say about Mike's association with Donald Mills at the Australian embassy. Mills was the resident spook for ASIS, the Australian Secret Intelligence Service, with the spook's usual cover of Second Secretary—but I never believed that he was running Mike as an agent. You'd see them drinking on the Continental terrace from time to time, and sometimes Aubrey Hardwick would be with them when he appeared in Saigon; so maybe Mike gave them a few personal impressions of the way he saw the war as going on the ground, and of some of the Vietnamese leaders he filmed interviews with for ABS—interviews that I usually conducted. No great harm in that, from a cameraman; or so I thought at the time.

I think his real secret life was more innocent, and at the same time more subtle. I believe it revolved around Claudine Phan. Whether he and she were ever lovers is something I don't know either; and I don't think anyone knows, because nobody dared ask him. For someone so easygoing, he could be quite intimidating when he closed up on you. Personally, I doubt that he and Madame Phan were ever sexually involved. She was a good deal older than he, and I see them as friends: genuine friends. They stayed friends all through the next ten years, and I find that a lot more interesting than a simple affair. Mike would never talk about her, except in the most general terms. His relationship with her was something separate in his life, existing in some private bubble. What their intimacy was based on I've no idea. No doubt she was some sort of Saigonese guide and confidante—but I don't really know what vital links held them together. All I do know is that she was important to him.

Another feature of Langford's character, which I see as being linked to his secret life, was his preoccupation with the outcast, the vulnerable, and those who were fighting for doomed causes. Some of my more cynical colleagues put it more simply: he was forever trying to help losers.

What they were mainly referring to of course was his deepening sympathy for the Army of South Vietnam. Unlike Griffiths and Volkov, Langford never grew heated in argument: his voice remained soft. But in our drunken or stoned discussions at Villa Volkov and in the Happy Bar, he came back and back to his claim that although some ARVN companies avoided battle, others were fighting heroically—and the Americans were denying them credit for it. He didn't rail, he remained good-humored; but it became a near-obsession with him. The ARVN were taking much higher losses than the Americans, he said—a fact that wasn't generally acknowledged. They fought the Viet Cong on the Viet Cong's terms, and no one brought them pizzas in the field.

"The Yanks call them gooks and slants," he said. "They don't see them as human beings. They say that they're all cowards, and that their women are all whores. That's not bloody true. Smart-arse correspondents help to put that sort of thing around—the sort that are always propped on bar-stools along Tu Do, and don't go out in the field."

There was some truth in this, of course; but most of us remained repelled by the Saigon regime's networks of graft, and by the ARVN colonels and generals who were busy becoming black market millionaires instead of fighting. Listening to Langford plead the cause of the few honest commanders, and of the ordinary troops on the ground, I began to understand that beneath his calm, he was a peculiar kind of dissident and nonconformist: one whom I began to see as well-meaning but naive. His thinking and his positions were never really political; they were tuned to some other wavelength, and he fitted into no easy mold. The fashionable position among journalists like Trevor Griffiths was to deplore both the Saigon Government and the American involvement, and to see the North Vietnamese as liberators; but Langford didn't hold this view. He seemed to take the justice of the South Vietnamese struggle for granted—but at the same time he grew more and more disenchanted with their American allies. He liked the Americans; he got on well with them when he was attached to one of their units; but he condemned their air strikes on Viet Cong–held villages. He shot footage of the effects of these strikes, which ABS didn't want to run: mothers weeping over the bodies of their children; old people wandering in shock. So in this he agreed with Griffiths, and not with Volkov. The war could only be fought on the ground, he said, as the ARVN were doing—not by the destruction of farming people from the air.

Some in the Happy Bar were amused by his insistence about this; others were reluctantly impressed. Even Griffiths didn't argue very much; he just shook his head and smiled with raised brows. Because of Langford's obvious liking for the Vietnamese, and because he shared the dangers they faced—which none of us was prepared to do—his view was respected. If the truth's told, few of us correspondents had very much to do with the Vietnamese people at all, and fewer still learned their language, as Langford was doing. He'd already become a lot more involved with the country than we had; he seemed bent on forming a bond with it, and I wonder now if this might have been one of the reasons for his affair with Kim Anh.

Of course, she was one of the outcast, to begin with. I'm not being cynical: this was a powerful brew for him, and I'm sure he was utterly sincere.

I first learned about his involvement with her on an evening when he and I met for a drink on the Continental terrace. That was quite late in the year; about October, I think.

In those early days of the war, the Continental Palace Hotel was still locked in a colonial reverie. Its yellow arches, its pillars and its latticework, its little interior garden with the ceramic elephants and the falling petals of frangipani, would seemingly never change. The aged, shuffling Chinese waiters who'd been there since before World War Two would always be there; and beside the grand staircase in the lobby, plump Monsieur Loi in his white suit would always be bowing to arriving guests. The war was a noise in the background, which eventually must go away. He always used to find a room for me: I wonder what happened to Monsieur Loi?

I sat waiting for Langford in my deep wicker chair over a chilled aperitif, close to the low stone wall that was the frontier on Tu Do Street. The terrace—or the Continental Shelf, as it was known to the press corps—was Saigon's axis: our rendezvous and refuge after a hard day in the field, just as it had been for generations of scribes and diplomats before us, and before that for the French rulers and planters. It was raised a few steps above the pavement, its privileged black and white tiles a zone nominally forbidden to the beggars, child thieves and hawkers beyond the wall. But they kept invading, and a row of boys hung over the wall now and shouted and pulled faces at me with macabre vigor, hands reaching out as though to clutch me.

"Hey you! Number One! Change money? You want boom-boom photo? You want number one fuck? You number ten!"

It was seven o'clock. Twilight was coming on fast, adding its thickness to the effluvia at ground level: petrol fumes; fish sauce; camphor smoke. Everything was the color of paper, which was the color of the heat; nothing was natural. Chaos ruled on Tu Do and the square beyond the wall: my ears rang with the cacophony made by military trucks, armed Jeeps and motor scooters. The Saigon Cowboys roared by on their Hondas, masked in criminal sunglasses, looking for watches to snatch.

Now I sighted Langford, walking up Tu Do Street towards me. It's a memory with the unaccountable staying power some small things have, while bigger incidents get vague.

Neat and spruce in his green TV suit, hair held in place by that cream he always used (he remained in the 1950s, where Brylcreem was concerned), he was coming past the old French Opera House, accompanied by a jigging crowd of street kids: his outcast tribe. Two of them held his hands, walking on each side of him, and I'd seen these two before: they both worked the front of the Continental. One was a small boy of about ten, carrying a bundle of newspapers. The other was a crippled girl I thought to be about fourteen: she was hobbling on a single crutch, a tray of cigarettes and flowers hanging about her neck. For her sake, Langford walked slowly, smiling down like a fond young father.

He fraternized a good deal with the child thieves and hawkers on Tu Do. Most of them were war orphans; some had been injured by bombs and shrapnel, and we all felt pity for them. But at the end of a hard day their insect persistence could be maddening; no foreigner could move without their chanting persecution. Yet Langford encouraged them with money and gifts much more lavish than the reluctant alms the rest of us gave; he even bought them clothes in the markets. I still hear them shouting after him: *"Mr. Mike! Mr. Mike!"* They'd sit outside our door at the Telenews office in the Eden Building, just around the corner from the Continental on Nguyen Hue Boulevard; they waited for him to come back from his trips to the Delta. Our Vietnamese secretary would chase them away, but they'd just reappear. Some of them would hang about for days—and it seemed to me that greed for handouts couldn't entirely account for this. They seemed genuinely devoted to him.

When he came up the steps onto the terrace, most of his child followers had fallen away. But the boy with the papers and the girl hawker with her tray were still with him. They'd be driven off eventually by the Chinese waiters, but for a while they'd probably be tolerated, together with other invaders from the square: the old Chinese fortune-teller with the wispy gray beard; the legless soldiers selling sentimental landscape paintings; the shoeshine boys. As Mike moved towards my table the two children left him, going off across the terrace in different directions.

The boy was simply a beggar: his bundle of newspapers was a pretext, and we called him the Newspaper Boy. He went crying his tattered wares from table to table, holding out his hand: he had a whining, jarring voice, and people shook their heads. But the girl was a genuine peddler, her flowers always fresh and attractive, and her American cigarettes—no doubt liberated from a PX store—low-priced. She went jerking and hopping among the tables on the single crutch, holding out a gardenia, smiling at Vietnamese businessmen in pastel suits, at their wives and mistresses in their Paris gowns, at Western embassy officials and correspondents, at U.S. Army officers in their khaki service dress and gold and silver insignia. Most of these people ignored her, or waved her away; but the American officers dug into their pockets, their faces kindly and uneasy.

Watching her closely for the first time, I saw that she wore a rubber sandal on her good left foot; her right leg was bent and twisted sideways, and the withered bare foot protruding from her dingy white pantaloons was a mere nub of flesh. And not for the first time, I was struck by the beauty of her face, which was framed by shoulder-length hair. It was heart-shaped, shining with intelligence and life, and simply perfect: the sort of fragile beauty that makes you want to smile and weep. Fragile! That little creature must have had a strength to survive that we can only guess at. A lot of the correspondents used to notice her; a lot of us found the sight of her hard to bear, and got uselessly angry about the war. I didn't know her name; she was generally called the Girl with the Withered Leg.

Mike sat down opposite me and signaled to a Chinese waiter who stood beside one of the terrace's yellow pillars. His hair gleamed like a big brass helmet, and he had a new sort of stillness, leaning back in his wicker chair. It seemed to me this evening that there was a subtle difference about him. He wasn't quite the same man as he'd been six months ago: not the same man that I'd met in the Happy Bar.

But anyone who has the sort of success he was now enjoying gains a different aura, I suppose—at least in the eye of the beholder.

He'd given notice at Telenews in that week. He was going freelance, to specialize in stills photography.

I'd no doubt that he'd make a living: he'd already begun to establish quite a reputation. As well as his film coverage for Telenews over the past few months, he'd managed to go out on his own account and get photographs which he'd sold through Magnum, the big photo agency here; *Paris Match* and *Life* magazines had both bought some. They were great pictures. He was born to do stills work; he always wanted to freeze the moment. Well, they're putting his moments into coffee table books on the war now.

You could get breaks very fast then, in Vietnam. The international agencies and magazines were desperate for pictures, and they'd pay anyone who was crazy enough to hitch a ride on a chopper and get dropped into battle. A lot of semiamateurs were doing it; and quite a few of them were killed. There were some pretty crazy stringers around town, some of them carrying weapons as well as cameras. Most didn't last. Mike became professional very quickly: he was always cool. And the breaks got bigger and bigger.

The *Life* spread was what did most to set him on his way internationally. After he sold a set of pictures to *Paris Match,* one of the people from *Life* went out to the airport to grab him when he got off an American transport; he'd been covering a big battle in the Central Highlands. The American 101st Airborne had just begun to engage units of the North Vietnamese Army there, and Mike told me that *Life* offered him $500 for first look at what he had. That was a lot of money then. They gave him a four-page spread, and the cover: great action pictures, taken in situations of extreme risk, when most of the platoon he was with were wiped out. He caught American GIs on the rim of death, as he did with the ARVN troops; he got the expressions on their faces in those moments. They were pictures you didn't forget: it had something to do with his magic use of contrasts, and the way the faces were transfigured. The cover picture showed a GI kneeling next to a mortally wounded buddy in the big battle of the Ia Drang Valley, his face blind and haggard with despair. You remember it? One of the great images of the war.

Mike had just got back from the Delta; he'd only been home to Villa Volkov for a quick shower and change, he told me. He swallowed his beer now in a few gulps; then, stretching his legs, he looked around the terrace at the well-pressed, laughing evening crowd with their faint odors of aftershave, cigars and perfume.

"It's all a bit unreal," he said. "Isn't it, Harvey?"

I am not a brave journalist; I avoid covering battle unless it's absolutely necessary, and dodging bullets generally results in a bad story, in my view. I leave that to the cameramen. But I'd been in the field enough to know what he was talking about. A few hours ago, he'd been in sweaty fatigues, probably up to his knees in mud, filming the South Vietnamese as they died among the reeds of the Delta, his ears full of the hammering of automatic weapons. Now, here he sat on the Continental Shelf, shaved and showered and ready for a good dinner. And few of the people at the tables around us, other than fellow correspondents, would have guessed where he'd just been. Yes, it was unreal. Even though the war was half an hour away, a lot of these people assumed that war correspondents barely moved from the Tu Do bars and restaurants except to file. And indeed, one canny New York newspaperman operated in just that way, and never saw a shot fired during his term, except by the White Mice in the city. But he was unusual.

It was full night now. The pavement hawkers down on Tu Do, squatting under the tamarinds beside their little glass cases of goods, had lit petrol lamps that glowed and flickered uncertainly in the dark, and the crippled girl had sold most of her flowers and cigarettes. She moved to a table a few feet from ours, holding out her gardenia to two middle-aged men in collars and ties and tropical lounge suits whom I placed as officials from the French embassy. One of them waved her away without looking at her.

Perhaps she didn't see this, or perhaps she chose not to. She continued to stand and smile, holding out the flower, and the official looked up at her. He was a heavy man in spectacles, the lines of whose yellowish face had been drawn and set by years of administrative severity. He now reprimanded the girl in rapid French, ending with: *"Allez! Allez!"*

She began to shift backwards, wielding her crutch, but the official signaled to one of the old Chinese waiters, who shuffled forward. The official raised his voice and began to speak even more rapidly, pointing to the girl. But now Langford stood up, and moved across to the table. He took hold of the man's shoulder in its pale blue linen, and bent over him. His expression was pleasant, but his grip must have been very painful, because the man winced and frowned, his eyes widening. The Chinese waiter stood hesitating, looking at them both, wearing the blank smile with which some Chinese cover embarrassment or perplexity.

"Don't be like that, old fellow," Langford said. "She just wants to sell you some flowers. They're very cheap. Why don't you buy some?"

He continued to hold the man's shoulder, his face brought almost level with the other's, and people at nearby tables were turning to stare. The official glanced across at them; then he looked up at Langford and attempted to remove Mike's hand, saying something low and vehement in French that I didn't catch. His expression combined anger and outrage with a dawning alarm that surprised me: an alarm presumably caused by what he saw in Langford's face. I expected him to shout for the management; but he didn't. The second French official muttered something I couldn't hear, beginning to look around for help.

But now the first official fumbled in his jacket, drew out his wallet, and threw some notes across the table to the girl. She smiled radiantly, and placed a big bunch of flowers next to him. Then the Chinese waiter came to life and shouted and waved at her, and she began to hop away.

"Thank you, monsieur, that's generous of you," Mike said. He let go of the official's shoulder and straightened up, his expression still pleasant.

"Leave us, monsieur." The official had spoken in English. He was holding his shoulder, and his face was pale. In front of those watching from other tables, he hadn't wanted to appear too miserly to buy flowers from a crippled girl. But it was also plain to me that Langford had frightened him; that he'd sensed a potential for violence that he hadn't wanted to deal with.

Langford came and sat down again; he winked at me and said nothing. The incident had been ludicrous and quite funny; but it had shown me that there was something under his calm veneer that I hadn't suspected: a hidden anger of some kind.

You should be that little girl's manager, I said to him.

"I'm going to be, mate." He sipped his beer without enlarging on this, watching her hop and jerk towards the steps. As though sensing his glance, she turned around and waved to him. Her eyes shone with affection, and her smile was a small flash of light.

"I'm planning to get her leg fixed up," he said. He spoke abruptly, as though making a confession. "I'm negotiating to send her down to Sydney. There's a top orthopedic specialist there I've found out about."

That's going to cost, I said. Where's the money coming from?

"I've got a bit together," he said. "And I'm talking to an Australian charity organization here. They've given me a rough idea of what'll be involved. A few more sales to *Life* and I should be almost there. And this specialist can really do a lot for her. I've been on the phone to Sydney." He leaned forward, one hand raised for attention: undemonstrative in every other way, he was a great one for gesturing. "They can actually rejuvenate that shriveled leg with a set of operations. It won't be perfect, but it'll be much stronger. They'll straighten it out in a cast. Then they'll fit her with a special boot and she'll be able to walk without crutches. How about that, Harvey?"

If it's true, it's great, I said. I'll kick in. And we'll pass the hat around at the villa.

"Terrific, mate." He smiled, sitting back again, and poured us more beer. Then he added casually: "I'm also planning to marry her."

I could find no words at all in answer to this: I simply sat and looked at him.

While I did so, the Newspaper Boy sidled up to our table. Holding his bundle of papers with both hands, he stared at Langford accusingly, lower lip pushed out. I couldn't like him; I was prevented by his permanently sullen air and his rodent-like face with its black fringe of hair reaching to the eyes. Other child beggars thought they had to be winning, or at least entertainingly aggressive; not the Newspaper Boy. All I could feel was pity for his filthy shirt and shorts, and his sore-encrusted legs.

"Mr. Mike? I am going now. But I need money for pantaloons," he said.

Mike and I both laughed, amused by this archaic word that had survived in Vietnam beyond its century. "Pantaloons? But I got you some clothes last week," Mike said.

"Yes, but now I am needing pantaloons," the Newspaper Boy said. He didn't smile when we laughed; instead his unpleasant voice rose to a wail. "I am needing them *now,* Mr. Mike. I need *pantaloons!*"

Mike fumbled in his pocket and produced some piastres, which he pushed into the gray, out-thrust hand. "Okay, okay," he said. "Make sure you buy them."

The Newspaper Boy retreated, watched by a severe Chinese waiter.

"He won't buy them, of course," Mike told me. "He's probably been ordered to get money for drugs, poor little bastard."

I'd now gathered enough resolve to ask him about the girl.

Had I heard him correctly? Did he really intend to marry a child?

"She's not a child," he said. "She's eighteen, although she mightn't look it."

Even so, I said. Was he serious?

He lit a cigarette, and at first didn't answer. His gaze went past my shoulder to the crowds flowing by beyond the wall. "Her name's Kim Anh," he said. "Years ago the Viet Cong bombed her village because they weren't getting cooperation from the head man. She was only a kid then. It killed her whole family except for a sister, and did that to her leg. Now she lives with a collection of people on the edge of Cholon, in one of those shanties made out of sheet-metal pallets. I go out there and visit her. There's a man who says he's her uncle: he seems to be in charge of her. I don't trust him. I think he creams off her takings. I reckon if it weren't for her leg, he'd have her set up as a bar girl. I have to get her out of there."

Could he and she communicate? I asked. Did she understand much English?

He looked faintly embarrassed. "No—she doesn't speak much English at all. We have to manage with my bit of French and Vietnamese."

But look here, brother, I said. Do you really think you're in love with her, when you can only just communicate?

I'd kept my tone tactful, I believe; but his face grew closed and stubborn, and he looked at me from under his brows, drawing on the cigarette. "I *know* her, Harvey," he said. "Talk's not the only way you get to know someone." Then he looked away over the wall again, at the passing Vietnamese faces lit by the petrol lamps, and the whirring and blaring traffic jam. "I want to look after her," he said.

At this point I made reluctant noises of approval: there seemed nothing else to do. She was certainly exquisite, I said; I could see why anyone would fall for her. And I asked him when they planned to marry. Yet even as I asked it, the question somehow seemed fantastic; unreal.

"There's no rush," he said. "First she has to have the operations. And I'll wait about a year—let her grow up a little. My friend Madame Phan has offered to take her in. She has a number of Vietnamese girls working in her villa who've been orphaned like Kim Anh. She can work there and be looked after until we marry. She's a Catholic: she'll want a proper wedding."

I saw him in a dark blue suit, as he would have been in Tasmania. I saw Kim Anh in her wedding dress, and the stiffly posed photographs. Yet I couldn't believe in what I saw.

We sat silent for a time, and crowds of drunken GIs passed beside the wall, clowning and reeling, headed down Tu Do towards the bars near the river, where neons spelled out *Chicago,* and *Fifth Avenue A Go-Go.* One of the soldiers called out: "Diamond pussy! That's what I want tonight, ole buddy: diamond pussy!"—and I wondered whether Langford could actually save Kim Anh from the future.

As though hearing my thoughts, he repeated what he'd said before, the cigarette between his lips, his voice muttering and fervent. "I have to get her out of that shantytown in Cholon, Harvey. Every time I go out there, or look for her here along Tu Do, I wonder whether I'll find her this time. Whether she'll appear again."

I asked him why he thought this way. Why shouldn't she reappear?

"Oh, I don't know, mate," he said. "What you really love usually disappears, doesn't it?"

It was an odd thing to say, I thought. He saw Kim Anh as ephemeral; perhaps not quite real. I've wondered since if he saw the other women he'd loved in the same way.

4.

HARVEY DRUMMOND

It was cold in the helicopter, with gusts of air coming through the open doors. We were coming in to a hot landing zone, and this made me even colder. I crouched among the American troops on the chopper's floor, nursing the heavy helmet they required me to wear into battle, and encased in one of their flak jackets.

Westwards through the door a dark green roof of forest rolled towards Cambodia: to the border country known as the Parrot's

Beak. The Beak was where the Ho Chi Minh Trail came through: where North Vietnamese guerrillas entered the south, to join forces with the Viet Cong. The tip of the Beak was only fifty-five kilometers or so from Saigon, and surveying this region added to my sense of foreboding. As Trevor Griffiths liked to point out, the North Vietnamese Army kept on coming, down that trail which was many trails: men and women on bicycles, in trucks and on foot, in those comic colonial sun helmets of theirs. Nothing seemed to stop them. The Americans were bombing the Trail daily, but it didn't even slow them down.

Going into a battle zone wasn't something I'd ever had any taste for, as I think I've made clear. I'd been to a number of American bases in the past year, and had witnessed a little incoming fire as a matter of professional honor; but this was different. I'd not been threatened with a serious firefight until now. The Soldiers Three had talked me into this, and I cursed them. I wished they were here to complain to; but they were on other choppers in the formation.

Perhaps I should explain how I'd been lured into this situation.

It was now November, and ever since June, the Communists had been building up their offensive in the Iron Triangle. The Triangle was their main sanctuary, and the headquarters of one of the VC Military Regions: riddled with tunnels, teeming with mines. It was a place of scrubland and marsh less than sixty-five kilometers north of Saigon. The Viet Cong were clearly poised to make their big attempt on the capital from there; so General Westmoreland had put in the 173rd Airborne to flush them out. You see the crucial nature of the story; and for some time Langford and Feng had been trying to persuade me that I should cover it at first hand. Now they'd finally shamed me into it. They'd got word of a big offensive by the Airborne this week, and Jim Feng and I were hoping to put together a television piece for ABS and Telenews that would make a splash. Volkov, who wasn't about to be scooped, had come along too.

The noise of the Huey's motors discouraged talk, and the half-dozen American troops in the cabin showed little inclination for it anyway. They stared ahead of them, and when they glanced at me they did so without curiosity; or perhaps they didn't see me. They were tough, highly trained volunteers in the Airborne, but some looked very young to me. One of them, a boy with red hair, had a bad case of adolescent skin eruptions. He was on his way to possible death in the next few minutes, so he had his own thoughts; and I had mine.

"I said: You sure will make a fuckin' big target, Aussie."

The man beside me was calling above the noise of the motors, leaning forward to look at me sideways, chewing gum. He was a sergeant called Tom Breen, with a hard, beak-nosed Irish face. He'd been assigned to me as a sort of unofficial guardian, and despite the nuisance this must have been, he was very friendly and polite.

"This is going to be a hot one," he shouted. "And that motherfuckin' Charlie is everywhere down there. So listen, Aussie. Hit the ground and run when we get down, and follow me close, OK? Or you may step on a mine." He nodded cheerfully, and pulled on his helmet.

The Huey was dropping now, heading into the nauseating spiral of a combat landing. As if I didn't feel nauseous enough already. When it leveled out, the GIs were on their feet, shouldering packs and weapons; it hovered a few feet off the ground, and they began to jump out the doors.

I did the same, running and stumbling, following Sergeant Breen with deep devotion, suddenly very glad of my helmet and flak jacket. Small-arms fire was coming from a tree line up ahead, and I was conscious of a nasty zinging and cracking in the air. The sergeant threw himself flat, shouting an order I didn't hear; the troops were all doing the same, and I followed. Some were digging with entrenching tools, like frantic gardeners. This was the dry season, and the ground was red and powdery.

I burrowed into it, feeling deep love for it, and I hoped the little furrow I'd found would protect me. I got dizzy with the smell of the dust and the noise of the gunfire, and I prayed not to faint. The GIs had opened up with their M-16s, and the machine guns in the hovering gunships were pouring fire into the tree line. They did this until nothing came back.

Sergeant Breen shouted to the troops around us to cease fire. The terrible noise stopped. The VC either were all dead or had melted away: it had seemed very quick. The sergeant turned and grinned at me, still chewing his gum. "One LZ secured," he said.

I discovered now how my heart was pounding; I was covered in sweat, and checked to see that none of it was blood. It was quiet now, and I was aware of a distant crump and boom: artillery fire from the American bases at Bien Hoa and Ben Cat, trying to clear the Triangle of the Viet Cong.

We camped with the Airborne that night: a company of about a hundred men. We bedded down on ponchos on the dry ground behind a little hill, the troops all around us in sleeping groups. The Soldiers Three soon slept, but I didn't; I lay slapping at mosquitoes and thinking of the next day, when we'd go out with the company on a search-and-destroy mission.

Midmorning. We'd marched for an hour with nothing happening, passing through old rubber plantations and areas of light scrub, not far from the Saigon River. It was a place of spindly, white-trunked trees, and stands of leaning bamboo. There were patterns of leaf-shadow on the pink, powdery ground, but not enough shade to matter. It was hot; hot.

Volkov, Feng, Langford and I were in a platoon at the rear, led by Sergeant Breen. Jim and Dmitri were burdened with the heavy sound cameras they carried on their shoulders—an Auricon and an Eclair—and were sweating heavily under their American helmets. They seemed cheerful, but I pitied them, lugging those big machines through the heat together with their other gear: they practically had to be trained athletes to manage it. Next to them, marching like prisoners in chains, were two young Vietnamese soundmen, tethered to the cameras by leads. This was the bondage that Langford was free of, having gone over to stills work: he traveled very light. In addition to his Leica, which he used for wide-angle work, he had a backup Nikon around his neck with a telephoto lens, his camera bag, and that was all. He wore no flak jacket, and no helmet either: just a cotton Australian army hat he said was lucky.

My head ached from the weight of my helmet, and the heat began to seem malignant to me, like a secret weapon of the Viet Cong. No people here; no bird calls, and I didn't like the silence. It was a place of old VC bunkers, apparently cleaned out. The GIs muttered and joked, trudging with their heavy loads of web gear and their weapons.

"Hey, man, you ready to kick Charlie's ass?"

"First you gotta find ass to kick."

When the firing broke out, it was like some utterly excessive fireworks display. Land mines had gone off, and hidden machine guns opened up at the same time. I would grasp after some moments that the lead platoon had walked into a VC ambush, just up ahead.

The noise was terrific. The lead platoon was being cut to pieces, it seemed; olive-clad figures in helmets fell and screamed and cried and swung their automatic rifles, toy-small with distance, in a flat, sunlit space between the trees. Shouted orders and exclamations rose around me but they made no sense. I stood still: an idler at an enormous accident. The troops were flattening themselves on the ground and burrowing in, and finally I gathered my wits and did the same, fear closing around me like a sheath of ice.

I looked around and saw Feng and Volkov and their soundmen lying flat too; but not Langford. Nikon at the ready, its long lens raised like a refined weapon, he was running towards the scene of the ambush, together with a small number of GIs who were led by a lieutenant. He dodged and twisted like a football player carrying the ball; when a fresh burst of machine-gun fire halted the GIs, who flattened themselves and opened up with their M-16s, he threw himself to the ground a few yards to one side and in front of them, getting off shots all the time with the Nikon. Then, when they began to move on, he was off again too, dodging, weaving, hitting the ground and rolling, seeking anything that gave him cover: even the bodies of the fallen. He was quite uncanny: very graceful and controlled, seeming always to know where the fire was coming from. I suspected that he saw himself as magically invulnerable; and because I was more frightened than

I've ever been in my life, I was gripped by an unworthy emotion. I half resented him, and I remember thinking: *He's not a photographer, he's a bloody soldier; he's hooked on this.*

Lying beside me, Feng and Volkov were shooting film, and at the same time watching Mike's progress.

"That goddamn maniac," Volkov said. "He sure can cover a firefight."

Jim Feng stood up. "They're moving," he said, and hoisted his camera on his shoulder.

He was right. The company had begun to move forward again, and we moved with them, approaching the sunny zone of chaos ahead. I deeply desired not to have to do this; but to have been left behind would have been worse.

Then came a time when I was running, not knowing where I was running to. The VC had opened fire again: bullets whined and cracked; mines continued to explode and earth to shower; the Americans shouted and cursed. Bodies of the wounded and dying were ahead of us, in the clearing. I was no longer Harvey Drummond; I was an anonymous dreamer, the landscape of whose dream kept maliciously breaking up, while he tried to get back to the place where he'd left his real life behind. Pebbles and pink dust and emerald leaves were all in bits, in disconnected fragments, bright and precise, flying by me. I'd lost the Soldiers Three, and badly wanted to find them.

Helicopter gunships had now appeared over the trees, insidiously throbbing, searching like intelligent insects, spraying the invisible VC with fire. Other choppers were dropping smoke grenades to mark the VC position, and lurid orange and yellow clouds began to fill the clearing, making it like an outrageous fairground. I heard screams, and a man calling: "Doc! Doc! Jesus, help me!" Another GI sat against a tree with one of his legs blown off, perfectly conscious, staring at the red stump and bright white splinters of bone; he had a long jaw and light, amazed eyes, and I'll never forget him.

Now I was behind the trunk of a fallen tree, and found Langford and Feng and Jim's soundman sheltering there. No sign of Volkov or his soundman.

"Come in, Harvey," Mike said.

He smiled as though we were meeting in the street, and put a calming hand on my shoulder. The air around me became almost normal, and the dust I lay on was real dust. I huddled beside him, shaking uncontrollably as though from a chill. I've never been so glad to see anyone, but I found I couldn't speak: partly from lack of breath, partly from a paralysis in my throat. Langford looked at me and saw my state. But there was no condescension in his expression, and no judgment; just serene concern. He seemed to have no fear himself, and yet he treated my fear as a reasonable phenomenon. This was a courtesy he'd extend to many others, in the years to come.

Super Sabres had arrived, roaring in over the treetops to drop napalm, and American artillery fire had begun to locate the VC position. We crouched lower as the ground shook; Langford spoke into my ear over the noise, his hand still on my shoulder as though steadying a horse, and I realized he was giving his whole attention to helping me regain my control. "No worries now, mate," he was saying. "The game's just about over. The Yanks have called in their backup, and the VC aren't going to hang about. We just have to sit tight and wait for the whistle." He squeezed my shoulder once and then let it go.

I managed to speak, and asked where Dmitri was; I was worried that he'd been hit.

Mike pointed across the log, and I saw the Count as though in some sort of vision: one that often comes back to me. He came jogging towards us out of a great screen of orange fire, like a man running out of Hell, his small soundman beside him, their silver umbilical cord connecting them. But as they neared us, I understood that it wasn't fire they ran through at all; merely another cloud from a smoke grenade.

They came in beside us, and Dmitri laid his camera down. I heard the harshness of his breath, and saw how his chest heaved. He pulled off his helmet, and his rope-yellow hair was damp with sweat.

Mike passed cigarettes to him and to the soundman. "You OK, Count?"

Volkov pointed a finger at him. "I am never coming out with you again, Langford. You draw fire."

Jim started laughing; then Langford and Volkov joined in. As the three looked at each other, I saw something between them that overrode jokes and competition: something unspoken that belonged purely to the field, close to the beating of those wings they'd once again eluded, once again captured on their rolls of film. I had a childish gladness that we were all here; but it wasn't to last.

Langford stood up. I saw Jim's lips move, questioning him; but a gunship had come over low, and I could hear nothing. Then I heard Langford say: "Need a few more shots."

"Better wait, Snow," Volkov said. "VC are still there." But Mike had gone.

Soon no more fire came from the trees where the VC were located. American voices became distinct in the clearing, talking or crying out, and the medical evacuation helicopters with their red crosses were coming in over the treetops for the wounded. But Langford didn't return, and Jim and Dmitri began to frown and mutter. They got to their feet and consulted; then they disappeared.

A short time later they came back carrying Langford between them. Dmitri held him under the arms; Jim Feng had his legs, and also carried his cameras. Sergeant Breen was walking beside them, talking into a field radio, and the thudding of the medevac choppers was the only big sound left.

My first impression was that Mike was dead. He was limp, and his whole face was covered by a shining red screen of blood that oozed and moved; it left only the white nose uncovered. His hat was gone, and there were gobbets of blood in his hair as well.

"Shrapnel," Volkov said to me. His pale eyes, looking briefly at me, had a hostile appearance; his face was pinched.

They laid Langford gently on the ground beside the fallen tree. Sergeant Breen was saying something about a medevac chopper, but not much clear speech comes back to me; I seemed to be half deaf. Then the three of us were alone with Mike, who lay still. His eyes were open, staring blue out of the red mask; there was a dark, soggy patch behind his left ear. Volkov knelt down, pulled off his sweat-scarf, and began to dab at the blood on Mike's face. The two Vietnamese soundmen stood side by side, looking on with sober expressions.

Jim Feng's prominent front teeth were bared in what looked like a grin; his eyes were unnaturally wide. "I will see what is happening about the chopper," he said. "We have to get him out right away."

Langford's lips were moving. I dropped to my knees beside Volkov and we leaned close, straining to hear.

"Somebody find my lucky hat," he said.

He'd be wounded many more times, over the years; but never as seriously as that first time. He'd taken a piece of shrapnel in the brain.

The Americans acted quickly and generously. He was transported on a medevac chopper to their field hospital at Long Binh, and Jim and Dmitri and I were allowed to ride along with him, crammed in with the wounded GIs. The Vietnamese soundmen got a ride back to Saigon, to dispatch the film.

The medics had given Mike a shot, and he was unconscious all the way. The Army surgeons at Long Binh operated immediately, despite all the badly wounded troops they had to attend to. We waited in one of the bars at the base, not wanting to go back to Saigon until we knew the worst.

But although the American surgeon we spoke to that evening was reassuring, he couldn't give us final answers. The wounds to Langford's forehead that had put all the blood on his face were superficial, he said. But the wound above the ear had been more serious. Here, a small piece of shrapnel had entered the temporal lobe of the brain. The temporal lobe could take a lot of ill treatment, he said; they'd removed the fragment, and in his opinion the area it had entered wasn't one where fundamental damage would have been done. But they could only be certain about this when Mike's responses were tested, over the next few days. They'd keep him here as long as was necessary; no less than a

week. Then he'd be taken to their hospital in Saigon for conva-
lescence.

There was nothing more we could do; Mike was still unconscious. At first, we felt hopeful. But back in Villa Volkov that
night, we began to sink into gloom.

Perhaps we were affected by fatigue; but we decided the surgeon had been giving us false comfort. Privately, I felt little hope
at all. Shrapnel in the brain! It threatened the seat of reason; of
memory and dreams.

Dmitri sat in his leather chair nursing Marshal, his face as
serious as the monkey's. "Snow has gone out one time too many,"
he said. "Jesus. Just when he was hitting the top with his work.
I did warn him, as a matter of fact. You heard, Jim."

"We must hope," Jim said. "No use to think about it tonight."
His face was blank, his voice toneless. He sat very still, smoking
one cigarette after another.

"Hope?" Dmitri said. "Our brother will live as bloody vegetable, most likely. What hope is there in that?"

"No," Jim said. His voice was stern. "Remember he asked for
his lucky hat before passing out? The brain was *working,* Count."

Volkov looked up with faint eagerness. "True," he said. "Yes,
true. You have heard, Harvey—he did ask for the hat."

The request for the hat was discussed at length, and Dmitri
swung now to absolute optimism, jumping up from his chair so
that Marshal made a leap onto the coffee table. "You're right:
Snow is the lucky type," he said. "Yes, gentlemen! The hat will
have saved him; I feel it."

Most combat cameramen, undergoing the risks they do together,
regard one another as brothers. They used the term often, in
Vietnam.

Unlike us correspondents, who could pick and choose our
risks, they had no choice. Any week could be their last, and it
made them sentimentalists as well as superstitious; it made for a
bond, even when they were in competition. But even allowing for
that, the way in which Feng and Volkov were affected by Mike's

wounding seemed to me to have an extra intensity; and I found I was affected in something of the same way myself. Believing as I did that he'd sustained irreparable brain damage, I shared in a yearning sadness that went beyond sadness. It simply wasn't tolerable to us that Langford might die, or be wiped out mentally.

Until now, I'd merely been mildly amused by the attraction he had for people: men and women alike. His unusual risk taking, his quick success, and his blond, country-style good looks were what accounted for it, I thought—nothing more. As I've said, I'd seen him as rather ordinary. But now that I'd been with him in action, I knew there was something more.

It's not easy to put into words. It had something to do with the soft-spoken, uncanny amiability which had made me feel safe behind the log, up in the Triangle. It was something he extended to everybody: a sort of low-key yet vital affection; a calm concern. But this wasn't all. Most of what I sensed about him now was crystallized in my recollection of his unconscious face as he lay on the stretcher in the medevac chopper, on the way to Long Binh. Dead white, the blood cleaned away from it, the heavy eyelids closed under their high-arched brows, it had become a different face. It resembled a piece of nineteenth-century sculpture, I thought: one of those pieces deriving from classical antiquity. It was a face that tended to change a lot: did you ever notice that? He could appear plain or good-looking; tough or sensitive: sensitive to the point of being feminine. I don't imply anything in particular by that. But there are certain apparently ordinary faces which grow extraordinary as you look at them— and Mike's was one of them.

Who can say why? I think their actual ordinariness has something to do with it—mingled with an opposite element that takes us by surprise. I'm summing this up badly, and maybe the words aren't to be found—not by a journalist, anyway. But I'll try. I think it all has to do with mortality, in the end: mortality and its opposite. I'm talking about the odd illusion one sometimes has that particular men and women are—how can I put it?—very human, yet a little more than human, in some way. They talk in an ordinary manner, these people: they eat; laugh; walk in the streets; sit in a pool of sun in a coffee shop, or the artificial light of a bar: yet nothing dissolves the film of strangeness that surrounds them. It's got nothing to do with conventional beauty; they haunt us in a way that's beyond the impact of beauty. That's the miracle of human beings, in my view. We grow old, we shrivel up, we die; we're a sad lot of creatures, ultimately; and yet certain human faces can make us disbelieve it—or at least forget it for a while. How are they different? How can I say? They seem exempt, somehow. They change our lives like music; they put time and disappointment on hold; they even make us forget the final sadness of reality, and of our miserable physical decline. You never know when or where you'll encounter them: faces that we look at in fascination, and can't say why. We're captivated by a particular shape of eye; a smile; a set of the mouth: captivated above all by the spirit behind the face: by a sort of easy daring, an always lighthearted ease with life that's magical, and that seems to speak of a connection with—what?

I'm tempted to say: with a life other than this, on some sweeter level. It's a face which in its youth—recurring in many variations, male and female—can never be devalued, never obliterated. Growing old, disappearing, it's always replaced. No telling where it will reappear, in the famous or the obscure. In the end, it's beyond analysis. It's what makes us immortal.

So what I'm saying is this: if you want to understand about Mike, I think you have to understand about that. And if you want to understand how he changed after his wound, you have to understand about the crippled girl, Kim Anh.

When they brought him back to Saigon, to the big American field hospital at Tan Son Nhut, he was supposed to spend some time there. He'd been told he'd make a full recovery; but he'd been ordered to take a lot of bed rest. He was still very weak.

But he stayed there only a few days; then he signed himself out and moved to Madame Phan's villa. She sent her car to fetch him, apparently; she even had her own Vietnamese doctor attending to him.

But now the fear that Langford had expressed to me on the Continental terrace turned out to be prophetic. Kim Anh, who'd been successfully treated in Sydney and fitted with her surgical boot, and who'd been living in Madame Phan's household for some time, should have been there to greet him. But instead, she'd disappeared.

5.

TAPE 12: NOVEMBER 16TH, 1965

—This room's on the first floor, and the shutters of the windows are always open, above the courtyard. It's as big as one of the bedrooms in the Continental, and a bit similar. But the only French furniture here is the heavy old wardrobe and the bed. The rest is Chinese, or Indochinese: a black, gold-edged cabinet; a carved camphorwood chest; a silk scroll painting of a pine tree and a bird.

—The only sounds are birds in the lychee tree outside, and the faint voices of the girls coming up from the kitchen, and the radio that they keep turned on low, playing Vietnamese pop music. Sometimes I imagine Kim Anh's down there: that one of the voices is hers. But she's still away visiting relatives.

—Once I said to Claudine that her house was sleepy. She's made a joke of it since: calls it her "sleepy house." This sleepiness is healing me. Even the room's red tiles, lukewarm under my feet when I walk across to the bathroom: they seem to heal me too. Peace: always peace in this room.

—Peace ever since the operation at Long Binh, when they opened up my skull. Keep seeing that big circular light over my head before I went out under the anesthetic, and the surgeon's face, floating like a pink saucer. Another light shone to one side: softer, but with a bigger glow. I want to be clear about this, but maybe I never can be. The light had a human shape, with tall wings. An angel? I've never thought about angels before; never taken them seriously. There were pictures of them in the Bible at home, but I don't remember the old parson at Saint Matthew's saying much about them. This figure didn't look like the pictures in the Bible or on Christmas cards. Just a shape; no face. And yet I knew it was looking at me. It made me feel safe. Loved, I suppose.

—*Elle est morte.*

—The letter's lying on the bed in front of me: my letter, unopened. My writing on the front. On the back, in ballpoint pen: *Elle est morte.* Small, neat writing, like a dull high school kid's. The uncle. It must have been the uncle.

—Today Claudine sent a servant out to Cholon for me, with the letter. I'd begun to worry, and so had Claudine; Kim Anh's been away a week. The servant was an old man who said he'd be able to find the place where she used to live. He took my letter and talked to a man there who knew her, he says; he didn't get the man's name. He tried to get this man to deliver the letter—but instead the man wrote a message on the back, and gave it back.

—*Elle est morte.*

—I won't believe it. She can't be dead.

—Can't record any more tonight.

—I've got to get out and look for Kim Anh. But I still haven't the strength. Often feel dizzy: can't walk very far. My wound itches and throbs under the dressing. The Vietnamese doctor doesn't want me to move from this room for another week.

—*Elle est morte.*

—I keep seeing that hut where she used to live, in the shanty town at Cholon: the big flat wastes like a tip, stinking of sewage and *nuoc mam,* with a maze of alleys between the sheet-metal humpies that are stamped with the names of American beer companies. At night out there weak electric bulbs hang from crazy illegal wires, and ragged people move in and out of the light like ghosts. The place is full of refugees from the bombed-out villages, and also full of drug dealers, prostitutes and black market operators with their hoards of luxury goods stolen from the PX stores. Why would she go back there? Why?

—Last night I dreamed about the place. Saw the uncle leading her away, going in and out of those sickly lights down the alleys, holding her hand. She was using her crutch again, as though she'd never had the operation, but looking more beautiful than ever. I ran after them, but I lost them, and woke up.

—Claudine tells me that a man was hanging about outside the villa a few days before Kim Anh left. Two of the servants saw him and Kim Anh talking together—but Kim Anh denied it. She denied it: that's what worries me most.

—The uncle: a man in his forties, with crooked teeth and a bad face. Is he even her uncle? She told me so; told me he looked after her when no one else did. He always wore fancy sports shirts and sunglasses: a petty crook, like so many others out there at Cholon, with their caves of stolen goods and the hootch girls they sell to the Americans. Once he was there when I visited the shanty; but he scuttled off, not speaking to me.

—I don't believe she's dead. Now that she's been fitted with the surgical shoe, and can walk without crutches, I believe the uncle's seen a use for her. He'll make her into a bar girl, selling Saigon Tea.

—Why would she have gone with him? Why?

NOVEMBER 27TH

—Claudine spends time with me every evening, after one of the girls has brought me a tray of food and I've eaten.

—She sits in a bamboo chair beside the bed, always smiling at me in the same way, strange greenish eyes looking at me from her Vietnamese face. Sometimes she'll be wearing a smart, Western-style frock; at others, just a blouse and jeans. Her hair always up in a bun. She looks quite French, then. But last night she wore the *ao dai:* mauve silk tunic and pantaloons, looking entirely Vietnamese.

—She told me more about herself than she's ever done before, last night: I think to distract me. Then she told me something else.

—She'd carried a book in, and was holding it in her lap. You're still grieving and fretting, Michael, she said. You have to stop. And if you try and get up now, you will do yourself damage. Be patient. *Không xấu,* remember?

—I have to start looking for her, I said. You don't believe she's dead, either.

—Maybe not, she said. But if she isn't, she went because she wanted to go. You did a wonderful thing for her, Michael: because of you, she walks on two feet. Now she walks off into the world. She was only a child: you wouldn't really have married her. You think so, but you wouldn't. And you never even made love to her, did you? She was a dream. Most love is a dream we wake up from.

—She opened the book. I brought this to read to you, she said. A Chinese poet, translated into English. A poet from the Ming. Men like you don't much like poetry, do they? But poetry is still important to us in Vietnam; men like you still read it here. I'm going to make you listen, Snow. This poem might teach you something—or else make you sleepy, in my sleepy house.

—Recently she started calling me Snow as a joke, when she heard that all the *bao chi* call me that; it seems to amuse her. *Snow,* she says, in that deep voice, and looks at me with a serious face before the laughter comes out.

—She read the poem to me now; it was short. Afterwards she left the book for me with the place marked. It's true I don't read poetry as a rule, but I liked this one, and I copied it out.

> *A little fishpond, just over two feet square,*
> *and not terribly deep.*
> *A pair of goldfish swim in it*
> *as freely as in a lake.*
> *Like bones of mountains among icy autumn clouds*
> *tiny stalagmites pierce the rippling surface.*
> *For the fish, it's a question of being alive—*
> *They don't worry about the depth of the water.*

—After she'd read it to me, Claudine sat quiet for a while. The room was half dark; only the little table lamp was on beside the bed, with its orange parchment shade. Then she began to talk.

—My European half's fading out as I get older, she said. I used to read French and English novels; now I read only the Chinese and Vietnamese poets. I'd rather do that now than run the business.

—And she began to tell me about her youth, when she'd studied in Paris. Her father thought she'd marry a Frenchman. He sent her to Paris four years after the War to do a degree at the Sorbonne—and also to find a husband. At first she liked the idea, and she was excited by Europe: even by the cold, she said, and by gray winter skies with an orange sun showing through. She did all the things you do in Paris: talked with her friends in cafés about films and books, and had an affair with an interesting Frenchman she liked but didn't love. That was the French half of her spirit coming out, she said. But then her father died, and she came back here to Saigon.

—Ah, Snow, she said, where we spend our childhood, that's what counts! And she told me how she'd missed her mother's people, and the tamarind trees in the streets, and the heat and noises and smells. She'd missed the monsoon, with the rain bucketing down and everything coming alive in the Delta. She'd even missed the smells of monsoon drains.

—She found now that she was most truly Vietnamese: she even became nationalistic. She wanted the French to be thrown out, which would have made her father sad, if he'd still been alive. Her husband, Phan Le Dang, was young and idealistic too, when she met him. He'd come here from Hanoi, and he was very northern and serious, she said. They were both in the same political club. They wanted the French to go, but they didn't like the Communists.

—We'd debated with enough Marxists to know that they were fanatics, she said. We weren't attracted by people who would tell us how to think and how to live. Certainly we didn't want to exchange French rule for another bloody dictatorship run by them. We wanted real freedom: but instead we got this filthy war.

—In those early years, she really loved Phan Le Dang. Helping him build the business, she found she had a talent for it. It linked her to him, and it linked her to the life here. For a South Vietnamese, life is business, she said. Yes, she said, there's bribery and corruption involved—but that's in every part of our life here: the pure-minded intellectuals are participating too. Most business people are cunning yet naive, I've found. A bit like politicians: complexity frightens them.

—For those reasons, she said, she stopped being amused by business and business people some time ago—and politicians too. And she lost her feeling for her husband. Making money had become all he wanted, and he began to do things that she couldn't agree with and didn't want to know about.

—I want to tell you something, Snow, she said. Phan Le Dang wasn't just selling watches and food over the Cambodian border. He was selling automatic rifles—and I believe he was selling them to the North Vietnamese Army. He still had family in the North, and maybe the NVA people pressured him. I think this is why he disappeared; something went wrong. You'll probably tell this to Aubrey Hardwick, won't you? But Aubrey already knows, I'm sure.

—I told her no, I wouldn't say anything to Aubrey. What she and I discussed was private. We were friends, and I wasn't on Hardwick's payroll.

—I wouldn't have told you this once, she said. Now I don't care, I'm finished with it all. Do you understand what I'm saying? Don't play those games for Aubrey, Snow. Don't trust him, or you'll eventually be sorry.

—The glow of the little orange lamp made her face like a beautiful mask: like one of her carvings downstairs. She sat up straight with folded hands, frowning at me. It was an expression I'd never seen her wear before.

—Aubrey had good-quality information from Phan Le Dang and me over the years, she said, especially about what was coming down the Ho Chi Minh Trail. But now our Uncle must be worried: he must ask himself whether Dang was misinforming him: whether Dang had links with the North all along—or whether they'd perhaps turned him. This is always a spymaster's nightmare, isn't it? Well, you can tell Aubrey that I don't know. I don't know, because for years I didn't know my husband any more. And I'll tell you something else. For all I know, it was Aubrey and his friends who arranged for my husband to disappear. That would make sense, wouldn't it? Don't look so shocked. I'm finished with secret games. They're over for me.

—She sighed then, and sat back; she looked tired.

—Business and politics and the war surround me like a bloody web, she said. I'm compelled to sit at the center of it, if only for the sake of my sons, who are still at school. They have only me to rely on. But I'm tired of it, Michael. I'd rather be reading my poetry. I'd rather run a restaurant, with my little Khanh Ha. Yes, perhaps I'll sell off the business, and turn this house into a restaurant! My orphans will help me. What do you think?

—She threw back her head and gave that loud laugh of hers; but there wasn't much amusement in it tonight.

—Time you went to sleep, Snow, she said. Then she leaned forward and kissed me on the mouth. She's never done that before: her lips seemed very soft and tired.

NOVEMBER 29TH

—This morning when I woke, my mind was like a clean sheet hung out to dry in the sun.

—This isn't happiness, but not grief either. It's the place that Claudine's taken me to. I want to remember it, and all the things she's said to me.

—Last night we talked again, and she lay on the bed beside me.

—We lay lightly together, head to head, foot to foot, holding each other. She'd come in the *ao dai* again; then she was naked, and her hair was hanging about us like a black tent. And even as we made love and I forgot everything, I knew that she could never belong to me, however much I might feel for her.

—Afterwards she spoke in my ear, while her hands kept moving over me. They seemed to explore and heal every muscle and nerve; and eventually every muscle and nerve would be made loose, and I'd float free of my body. Nothing and no one's ever made me feel like that before. For a while, she took away sadness: not just over Kim Anh: over everything.

—She lay propped on her elbow in the orange glow of the lamp, stroking my forehead and looking down at my face. She touched the wound there, and the other, behind my ear; then her finger traced the mark left on my forehead by the butt of that VC's Kalashnikov, in the Delta.

—Snow, she said, in her deep voice; but she wasn't laughing this time. So many wounds already. She shook her head, lips pursed. You nearly died, and you might not be so lucky next time. You could die down there with my cousin Trung, in some bloody Delta rice field. But you won't stop going out, will you? This means that you live in a dream. So I mustn't love you, because you're always likely to disappear.

—I told her I had no intention of disappearing. But she didn't answer; just looked at me.

—Then she said: Don't think I'm flattering you, Michael. The opposite, really. It's sad, being a warrior: and that's what you are, of course. It means you'll always be alone. You're a warrior because battle is what you want most, and the comradeship of men. Don't deny it. You really don't do it for the money, do you? Many people say that they're not interested in money, but they usually lie; especially those who can't make much. But you're truly not interested in it, I can tell: I'm an expert on that. And you're the sort of warrior other men love, because you're what they wish to be. You'd make a good father. But if you have children, they'll end up orphans, won't they? So better that your children are orphans already—like Kim Anh.

—You have a little bit of the woman in you, she said. Don't be offended, Snow, I know this is true: it's in your face. And perhaps that makes men love you more, without knowing why. As for women, they'll always want to rescue you and change you. But they won't change you, and won't possess you. And the reason I understand that is because I'm the same. I can't be possessed either, and I don't want to possess you. But we'll always be here for each other, won't we?

—Don't feel badly about losing your Kim Anh, she said. Vietnamese don't waste time on regret: regret's a bloody waste of life; you should learn that. You wouldn't have stayed with her, she said, even though you wanted to. Yes, I know how much you loved her. I was becoming a little in love with her myself, she was so beautiful. Don't look at me like that: sometimes I do love women, didn't you know? I've never met a man I care for as I care for you, but I'm not going to say I'm in love with you. And I know that I won't really lose you, because I know that you'll never leave Asia.

—I asked her how she knew that.

—Maybe I'm a bit of a witch, she said. I also know that you won't die here in Vietnam. You'll die somewhere else in Asia. Don't worry; it won't be for a long time. And remember: "For the fish, it's a question of being alive—they don't worry about the depth of the water."

—Recording all this is probably not a good idea. Maybe it's best to forget it—even though I don't want to. Maybe I'll eventually wipe this tape.

6.

HARVEY DRUMMOND

About Kim Anh I'd known almost nothing. Now she was gone, and I doubt that Langford had really known her much better than I had.

Some people see the crippled girl's disappearance (and perhaps her death, for all we'll ever know) as a major blow, and the reason he never married. I'm not so sure about that, myself: but certainly he changed from then on. Outwardly, it wasn't obvious: his easy good humor was the same, and his enjoyment of life appeared to come back as soon as he was covering the action again. But he had spells of brooding quietness, back in Villa Volkov; and he drank a lot more than before in the Tu Do bars. Usually, Volkov and Feng went with him; so did I, when I was in town. But sometimes I'd catch sight of him alone.

He must have drunk in every bar and brothel in central Saigon many times. He was searching there for Kim Anh. He didn't talk about her much, but he insisted to us that she was still alive, and in some way entrapped by the man he said posed as her uncle. He was convinced that the uncle had put her to work as a bar girl, and was living off her earnings. He searched for the uncle as well, scouring often through the shantytown near Cholon; but he never found him either.

As far as anyone knows, Langford's relationships with women for many years after that were few and transitory. The only thing that appeared constant in his life was the friendship with Madame Phan—and as I've said, I believe that was platonic. There were no other serious involvements in Vietnam; and he was never, so far as I know, involved with a Western woman again. His occasional affairs—if they really were affairs—were always with Vietnamese and Cambodian bar girls. He'd never gone to bar girls before Kim Anh disappeared. Now, when he'd appear in company with one, he'd behave to her with scrupulous courtesy and respect. This may sound hackneyed, but he really did treat the bar girls as ladies.

Some people were cynical about this, seeing it as a technique of seduction he employed; but I don't think so. In another time, he'd probably have been described as romantic. That may seem paradoxical, since we're probably talking about a very casual sex life, similar to that of many other correspondents and cameramen: men like Volkov. But Langford was always giving these young Vietnamese women lavish amounts of money: just as he did with his child beggars. I heard too that he helped some of their families—when they still had families. He had a kind of secret life now in that shantytown at Cholon; after he gave up looking for Kim Anh and her uncle, he seems to have involved himself there with helping the refugees from the bombing. He wouldn't talk about this; one picked it up in indirect ways. So when I say he was romantic about his bar girls, I mean that some sort of idealism was involved—presumably founded on pity. And pity can be romantic, wouldn't you agree? Pity can be a kind of aphrodisiac. And maybe all these girls were shadows of Kim Anh.

Having said all that—and all of it's guessing—I can't quite see Mike's loss of her as a tragedy in depth. You may disagree. But the episode had been so brief; so unreal. And the barrier of language would surely have prevented much depth of communication. He had little French, and far less command of Vietnamese then than he'd develop in the future. His acquaintance with Kim Anh, despite what he'd done for her, had been as brief as his acquaintance with Vietnam then was. So forgive me: although she was so poignantly lovely and sad, I have to see his love of her as love of an illusion. I don't want to sound callous, but I also formed the impression that Kim Anh had promised to be an answer to something for him—and now the answer had been taken away.

I've no idea what that something was.

A few months later, in the February of 1966, ABS informed me that I was being posted to London. It would be seven years before they sent me to Indochina again. So except for a few letters we exchanged over those years, and sightings of his pictures in various papers and magazines, I lost track of Langford until early in 1973, when I came back to cover the war in Cambodia.

My last sight of him in Saigon is easy to remember. It was the eve of my final departure—and also the afternoon of his extraordinary outburst at the Five O'Clock Follies.

You'll have heard of the Follies, no doubt. That was what we called the press briefing the American Military Command staged each afternoon in the Rex—a big hotel on Nguyen Hue Boulevard, conveniently opposite the Eden Building, where Telenews and other media organizations were housed. The Rex had been entirely taken over by Military Assistance Command, Vietnam (or "Macvee," as we called it), and the ground floor housed one of those many organizations of theirs that went under an acronym: JUSPAO, the Joint U.S. Public Affairs Office.

Here we entered a fully North American zone. It was air-conditioned, and crowded with hardworking military public relations people, typing and telephoning with that air of intense purpose that can make the Americans impressive or worrying, depending on your prejudices. The amount of paper pumped out in those warrens was awesome. It contained not only the vital daily intelligence that we all depended on, but an unfolding story of the war as MACV wished it to be: a sort of serialized novel whose tone was realistic yet ever positive, and whose ending was bound to be triumphant. The morning and evening press releases sat in bulging racks; we were even provided with telephones, to get the stuff through. Journalists could live almost entirely within the walls of this paper kingdom if they wanted to, and cover the war from JUSPAO, through JUSPAO's eyes.

Some did; but other *bao chi* were beginning to ask more and more skeptical questions at the Follies, and were suggesting that the paper story didn't always tally with the one they'd discovered outside. And this made Langford's performance that evening of considerable interest to his colleagues.

The conference was held in a fully equipped auditorium. Coming in there from the noise and petrol-smelling heat of Nguyen Hue Boulevard, I was always glad of the imported air-conditioning's icy fingers, and not inclined to sneer at American luxury. A hundred or so of us sat packed on tubular steel chairs, notebooks and press releases on our laps, like aging students: sullen or boisterous, as the case might be. I was sitting on an aisle opposite Trevor Griffiths; Langford was somewhere near the back. He'd come in late, as he usually did, since he used to go as well to the Army of South Vietnam's four-thirty press conference in ARVN headquarters, a little further up the boulevard. Hardly anyone went to that, and I confess I didn't either: the seating was poor, there was no air-conditioning, no microphones, no maps, and the press saw no point in it anyway. The ARVN weren't news; the Americans were running the war.

Jokes and laughs and extended coughings went up now as we waited for the briefing to begin. An Army major in starched, knife-edged khakis took the stage, pointer in hand, coming up to the lectern in front of the charts and maps. He was tall and prematurely bald, with a fringe of foxy red hair; his intense brown eyes looked honest. An elderly colonel with a steel gray crew cut stood to one side, ready to intervene if the questioning got difficult.

The major got through his briefing fairly quickly, using the Vietnam militaryspeak we all had to master to understand anything. Among other things, he spoke of continuing U.S. military assistance to the South Vietnamese forces through strategic bombing. He claimed, as usual, that the raids were successfully containing Viet Cong expansion. It was all pretty routine, and I didn't see a story this evening.

When question time came, and the soldier sitting under the stage with his tape recorder began pointing a microphone at the audience, I was surprised to hear Langford identify himself from the back. Photographers seldom asked questions, and Mike never. Turning, I found that he was on his feet, and still in combat fatigues: he must have come straight here from the field. He didn't have his cameras; he'd probably left them in the Telenews office over the way. He looked grimy and extremely tired, and his voice was very quiet: I had to strain to hear it. But his reputation, particularly through his pictures for *Newsweek* and *Paris Match,* was already becoming considerable, and the correspondents listened attentively.

"Major, I believe you said that the area south of Soc Trang has been pacified through air strikes," he said. "You also said that the VC are giving no serious trouble there. I've just got back from a week in the field with an ARVN battalion down there. They're the only forces opposing the VC on the ground in that area. No other correspondents were covering. I want to tell you that I saw no evidence that the air strikes are weakening the VC. Only that you're killing large numbers of the rural population without any military gain."

He paused, and there was a silence. People craned to stare at him, and I did the same. I was frankly surprised, and also embarrassed. Instead of asking a question, Mike was making a speech, like some novice correspondent with an antiwar line to push. It was entirely out of character, and so was his demeanor.

His fists were clenched, and his eyes were bulging slightly, as though he were drunk. But he plainly wasn't drunk; despite the softness of his voice, he seemed actually to be holding in check some sort of rage: I don't think the word's too strong. In someone so calm, the effect was eerie.

The major drew his reddish brows together, gazing at Langford as though having sincere difficulty in understanding what he was doing here. Perhaps the dirty fatigues bothered him. But when he answered, his tone remained polite. "Well, that's one man's observation, concerning a particular area. But our intelligence shows that in general our preplanned strikes to assist the South Vietnamese Government forces are working. In depriving the enemy of his village sanctuaries, we're hurting his ability to function. Did you actually have a question, Mr. Langford?"

A flush mounted in Langford's face: he went a profound pink. I'd seldom seen this happen in an adult, and it was both bizarre and distressing. But it went as quickly as it had come, leaving him very pale; and when he answered, his tone was even.

"Yes, Major, I do have a question," he said. "Will you acknowledge that a pitched battle took place this morning between the Viet Cong and ARVN forces just south of Soc Trang, in which American air support was involved? And will you confirm that this battle ended with heavy losses to the ARVN battalion, and the wiping out of an entire company?"

There were some small exclamations, and the major hesitated. Before he could reply, Langford was going on. "I was attached to that company throughout the engagement—and I'd like to ask something else. Will you confirm that the commander of the company, Captain Le Tan Trung, was killed by American fire because a U.S. helicopter pilot got his coordinates wrong? And will you also acknowledge that the VC downed two U.S. helicopter gunships, with a loss of six American lives?"

He sat down, and people began to converse loudly with one another. I should point out that the stir wasn't really about the fate of the ARVN company: an ARVN defeat in the Delta, even of this dimension, even with American losses involved, wasn't really big news, since the ARVN weren't big news. The current

American battles in the Highlands were what mattered most. What was interesting was the fact that we hadn't been told about it.

The major glanced quickly at the colonel. The colonel stepped quickly to the microphone, hands crossed neatly over his groin, and cleared his throat.

"Yes, we can confirm that this battle took place," he said. "I know nothing about the circumstances of a company commander's death by friendly fire, but I sincerely regret that, if it's true. And yes, I can confirm the downing of two UH-1 Iroquois gunships, with a loss of six American lives."

He stepped back again abruptly, as though the matter were over.

But it wasn't, of course. The briefers had been forced to admit to losses they hadn't informed us of—and that would be the story for journalists like Griffiths, who was smiling with delight, and scribbling hard in his notebook. The defeat itself, and the death of Mike's friend Captain Trung, were of small interest.

A correspondent from the *New York Times* was on his feet. He was a heavily built man called Kramer, with a dark, receding crew cut, and one of those deep bass American voices that command attention. His colleagues held him in high esteem, and MACV followed his stories with particular concern.

"My question is this, Colonel. Since your briefers left this battle out, I'm wondering what else you left out? And what credibility do we now attach to these official briefings?"

The colonel's lips tightened; he paused before replying, and I turned around again to look at Langford. But I found that he'd left the auditorium; his chair was empty.

I came out under the teak-lined awning of the Rex. I'd left as soon as I saw Mike had gone; I wanted to catch up with him. I knew that in a few moments, other correspondents might follow: they'd want to get his story.

The orange-tiled steeples of the old Town Hall at the top of Nguyen Hue were casting baroque shadows, and the tide of bicycles and motor scooters was running faster with the promise of evening. Opposite, the neon sign saying *Sanyo* winked on the ferroconcrete Eden Building, just above our office window, and I suddenly knew I was saying goodbye to Saigon; it hadn't really sunk in until now. I looked among the crowds for Langford.

I soon caught sight of his yellow head, but he was a little way off, moving south on the pavement in the direction of the river. He was going at a fast pace, in spite of his combat boots, and I hurried to try and catch up with him.

But I failed. He suddenly turned right into Le Loi Avenue, and then crossed the road among the traffic, dodging a small swarm of bicycles and cyclos. A passing convoy of military trucks and Jeeps hid him from me, and by the time it was past, he'd disappeared.

I caught a cyclo down Tu Do to the Texas Happy Bar, hoping he'd come there too. He wasn't here, but I bought a beer and settled on a stool. Dmitri Volkov was away on assignment in Cambodia, but Jim Feng and Trevor Griffiths would arrive soon: we'd arranged to meet here.

When they came, they wanted to know where Langford was: they'd assumed he'd join us, on my last evening here. So had I; but I no longer felt certain of it.

Griffiths was simmering with glee over Mike's performance; his eyes gleamed in the lamplight in the way they did when he was profoundly gratified or incensed. He'd already got his story off to the *Guardian,* and now he leaned sideways on his stool to look at me with the air of an athlete who'd run his race well.

"Superb performance of Langford's," he announced. "A clear exposure of Macvee's whitewash and evasion. I didn't know Snow had it in him. The man's a rebel, underneath, in spite of his eccentric devotion to the cause of the South Vietnamese." He drew fervently on his cigarette, savoring American disarray. "The VC will take the whole Delta soon, and Saigon next. But you won't see it, will you, Harvey? Name your drink, my son: tonight we'll toast your departure for Blighty, and buy you a fine Italian meal."

Jim Feng looked at me soberly, passing me a Scotch. "This is a sad thing for Mike," he said. "He and Captain Trung were friends: that is why he blew up. We should look for him."

I'd already phoned the Telenews office and the villa; he wasn't in either place, I told them. After a time, we left the Happy Bar and set out to check other bars where he might be. But we didn't find him, and went on to dinner at La Dolce Vita without him.

Afterwards, at about eleven-thirty, with curfew near, Griffiths went off to his hotel, and Jim went home to Villa Volkov in the Budgie. He'd expected me to come too; but I decided to linger on Tu Do for half an hour more. I still wanted to say goodbye to Langford.

I couldn't be sure that he'd turn up at the villa that night; his comings and goings had become less and less predictable lately. And I wanted to say goodbye as well to the carnival of Tu Do at night, which reached its crescendo now, in the hour before curfew. I wanted to say goodbye to Saigon: a city which might well fall before I ever got back here.

Saigon, the Pearl! It was exhausted now: debauched; doomed; threatening. Mostly I'd detested it; but now that I was leaving, I knew I'd perversely miss it. Certainly I'd miss the Soldiers Three, and Villa Volkov; I suspected I might even miss the war, and the endless hushed beating of chopper blades and the high thunder of F-4 Phantoms and Super Sabres that was the war's music. So I went on searching, with drunken obsessiveness. I'd consumed a good deal of wine, and time had got lost down a funnel.

Amplified pop music from bar doorways beat in my head like ten radios playing in a room at once. A crude canvas poster I can't forget waved above a bar, strung from bamboo poles: a Vietnamese girl got up as an American Playboy bunny. She wore the required tights and rabbit's ears and tail, but her face seemed full of woe: an ambiguous lure for the American troops who lurched across my path. All for them, these parodies of American pleasure, flowering on the grave of rue Catinat! The limbless beggars who were the war's children crawled on the pavement, trying to impede me as usual, holding up their bowls; small boys in T-shirts and shorts made ancient obscene gestures and shouted their suggestions for the last time. *"You want to boom-boom my sister?"*

I still had a conviction that Langford was here somewhere. I drifted on towards the river, wading for the last time through the swamp-dense air at Tu Do's ground level. Meanwhile, in the dark brown upper air, off beyond the fluorescent green of the tamarind tops, an occasional distant parachute flare lit up the sky: the war going on, ignored. Windows and doorways fitted with wire guards against bombs framed figures that seemed to be locked in cages. A row of GIs sat on stools with tiny Vietnamese girls on their knees. The girls were wearing the demure white tea dresses dating from colonial times; they looked like children at a party, and they stroked the Americans tentatively, as though petting unpredictable animals. I passed La Pagode and the Melody Bar and the Sporting Bar and still I couldn't find Langford.

Then I sighted him. About twenty yards ahead, he was pausing under an awning where a very old man in a coolie hat sat beside a little glass cabinet of cigarettes; Mike was buying a pack. He had his throng of child beggars with him, and he was still in his combat fatigues.

A few doors further on was the neon of the bar called La Bohème, which was known to double as a brothel. As I watched, Langford began to walk away towards it, and I saw that he was very drunk: much drunker than I was. He was weaving along as though scarcely able to stand, supporting himself with one hand on the shoulder of a sturdy boy in a ragged green T-shirt, while the Newspaper Boy, still clutching his bundle of papers, held his other arm. Even at this distance, I could see that the children wore expressions of concern. They were shouting up at him vehemently, as though trying to persuade him to do something— or not to do it, perhaps.

Before I could catch up to him, Langford began to turn into the doorway of La Bohème. I heard the voices of the children rise in remonstration at this; the boy in the green T-shirt and the Newspaper Boy both tugged at one of his arms to hold him back, while a small girl in a ragged white blouse and shorts grasped his shirt. Mike paused, looking down at them; then he gently freed himself, and squatted to bring his face to their level, his expression solemn, his eyelids drooping. All of them stared at him intently, as though trying to understand something. He spoke to them for a moment; then he got up again, raised a hand in farewell, and staggered inside La Bohème.

I didn't follow; like the street kids, I turned away. I started looking for a cyclo.

I wouldn't meet him again until we were all reunited in Phnom Penh, and he'd be different then. We'd all be a good deal older—on the edge of middle age, in fact. His youth and his pain would be left behind in the Delta, and on Tu Do Street.

II. THE PEOPLE OVER THERE

One great hour of noon with the sky-faring Rukh
I clanged on the golden dome of Heaven.
Now in the long dusk of adversity
I have found my palace of contentment, my dream pavilion;
Even the tiny twig of the little humble wren.

PO CHÜ-I, "Myself," translated by
L. Cranmer-Byng

Nine in the second place means:
There is food in the ting.
My comrades are envious,
But they cannot harm me.
Good fortune.

"Ting: The Cauldron"
From the *I CHING* or *Book of Changes*

ONE
SURVIVORS

1.

The Foxhole is long, dark and crowded. All the bars and massage parlors of Patpong Lane swarm with lights and neon, and the Foxhole's no exception: its ceiling is a firmament of colored bulbs, winking on and off. This puts bewildering rainbow effects on the faces of Jim Feng and Harvey Drummond, smiling in front of me.

"They're still living inside the war, some of these guys," Harvey says. He jerks his head at a row of men hunched on stools along the bar. Nearly all of them are in early middle age: most are dressed in a mixture of old military fatigues and combat boots.

"Right," Jim says. "Some of them don't believe it's over. Not even after a year. Sometimes I don't either, Ray."

When I first met them, Feng and Drummond were like figures from fiction who'd suddenly walked into reality. They were different from the way I'd pictured them, over the past two months. The men in Mike's photographs—pictures mostly taken in the sixties—were young, their faces always lit with expectancy. These men have lost their youth. Harvey Drummond's sparse, curling hair has turned half gray, and he's almost bald on top.

His height is as startling as I've been led to expect, but his stoop is pronounced. In contrast, Jim Feng's hair remains thick and black, and his long, refined face has the smooth, apparent agelessness of so many Chinese faces. As in the photographs, his white shirt and khaki trousers are so well pressed that he looks like a military officer. But a particular essence is gone from this face, just as it's gone from Harvey's: youth's essence is missing, making him subtly different from the figure in my archives. And there's something else.

When he first appeared, on the night of my arrival, coming up to greet me in the foyer of my hotel, I saw that he limped badly. Then, as I took in the mechanical stiffness of the action, and the way he threw the right leg forward, I realized that this leg was artificial.

I hadn't known that Jim Feng had lost a leg, and this was as shocking and pitiable to me as the mutilation of someone close to me. He told me it had happened eleven months ago. He'd been filming a Khmer Rouge attack on a Thai border village, at a point where Cambodian refugees were coming across; he'd stepped on a Khmer Rouge landmine. So he'd survived the whole war, only to be crippled by an accident.

We're standing now by an inner wall of the bar, glasses of gin and tonic on a wooden shelf beside us. The Foxhole isn't the usual girlie bar for tourists: it caters for them in a perfunctory way, with its winking bulbs and a catwalk for dancers in the middle, but for now the catwalk's empty, and the piped music is playing at a volume that favors conversation. A poster on one wall advertises a Soldiers of Fortune shooting match. A sign above it says: *There are no Atheists in Foxholes.* There's a betting board displaying horse-racing odds, and a list of propositions to bet on. *(Teddy Kennedy will run for President.)* On a notice board next to it there are photographs of boxers, and of other people I don't recognize: journalists, perhaps, since the Foxhole's an unofficial club for correspondents, war photographers, mercenary soldiers and Vietnam War veterans.

Harvey's following my gaze.

"This was Mike's home away from home," he says. "That's

why I thought you should visit it, Ray. He had a lot of friends here—as you can see."

He puts down his glass and points in the direction of the wall near the notice board, and I find myself looking at a framed black-and-white portrait photograph of Langford. It gives me a shock that's different from mere surprise.

The picture seems idealized, and has the appearance of an icon. Perhaps it is. Langford, staring across at me, looks supernaturally young, and at the same time like a man from a much earlier era. Underneath is a professionally lettered legend: *Michael (Snow) Langford, 1935–1976. The Lucky One.*

"So it's agreed in here that he's dead," I say.

"No—there are lots of people who keep on hoping," Harvey says. "And some people in the Bangkok Press Club took strong exception to those dates under the picture—but no one's bothered removing them. There's an assumption that he's dead at the official level, though—as you've probably found out."

Jim passes me a fresh gin and tonic. "You know, Ray, now that you're here, I have a feeling that we'll find him," he says. He smiles, and his face is cheerful.

I'm about to reply when a huge wave of amplified rock and roll music swamps everything, and half a dozen Thai girls file onto the catwalk, all in black tights that leave their golden buttocks bare. They begin to go through motions of dancing, holding on to the steel poles that support the ceiling, jerking mechanically. Around the bar, the sweating, red and white faces of the male tourists turn upwards in salacious worship. But the correspondents and mercenaries don't even glance aside; they continue their conversations by shouting.

During this, we're joined by two men who greet Jim and Harvey and then stand beside us, watching the dancers. Their names are Carr and Kennedy: Harvey shouts introductions above the noise, briefly explaining my association with Langford and the purpose of my trip. The two nod, and look at me with expressions that could be either sympathetic or dubious.

Finally the music ceases. The girls file off, and Carr, the newcomer standing nearest to me, addresses me abruptly.

"I'm afraid you're here on a wild-goose chase, Ray. Sorry to have to say so."

He's a correspondent for a London daily: stocky, pallid, somewhere in his fifties, with flat, rusty hair that has a wig-like appearance. His speech is precise, with a Midlands accent, and his small, tight mouth closes on his words with finality. "Mike Langford was executed," he says, "Khmer Rouge style. That's ninety percent certain, and it's not a thing you'd want to think about."

"That's if it's true," I say. "We don't seem to have firsthand evidence."

Jim Feng has been watching Carr fixedly; Harvey looks thoughtfully into his drink. Kennedy, the other newcomer, remains silent, his blank, hooded eyes seeming quietly amused by something. He's a big, powerfully built man who's running to flesh a little, with thinning fair hair and a mustache; he has a hard, pleasant face of a type I've encountered in violent criminals, and he gives off the same atmosphere of warning. He looks like a mercenary—which is more or less what he is, it seems. Harvey has murmured in my ear that Kennedy's an ex–Air America pilot, who flew arms for the CIA.

Carr is still speaking to me. "There's a constant idea among some of the press corps here that Langford's still alive," he says. "They pick up rumors from Cambodian refugees—from anyone who'll cook up a story and claims to have seen him. Some of them will say anything—especially if they're shown money. And a lot of the journalists here who were Langford's mates believe them because they want to believe them. It's bloody sad, really."

"But that's natural, Paul," Harvey Drummond says. His voice is soothing; almost placatory: a tone I'm to find is habitual. "In a situation where no death has ever been confirmed, and where a man has simply vanished—it's natural to hope, no matter how bad it looks."

Jim Feng is still looking at Carr. "*I* will not stop hoping," he says.

Carr refuses to meet Feng's stare, which is now openly hostile. "Well, Jim, you're entitled; but you know I don't agree," he says.

"I will not believe he is dead," Feng says. His voice is hushed yet strong. "I will not believe it unless I meet someone who saw it happen—someone I can trust," he says.

"If you want verification," Carr says, "go up to the refugee camps on the border, and talk to the people I talked to."

"I have already done that," Feng says. "They tell stories that other people told them. Rumors. A European picked up inside the border by the Khmer Rouge, and taken away to be executed. *Yes*. We all know that." He claps his palm down on the shelf along the wall: not very hard, but the effect is one of pent-up violence. "Nothing firsthand! No witnesses, as Ray says. Are you such a lousy bloody journalist that you make up your mind on this basis?"

Harvey Drummond puts a hand on Jim's forearm. "Come on, Jim." It's a murmur that's only just audible.

Carr rubs his nose. "No need to get offensive. The evidence is circumstantial," he says. "I'm satisfied those refugees were telling the truth. The story fits with the time he went in there; and how many Europeans would have been wandering around in the Cambodian countryside? None; no one would be crazy enough. Add to that the fact that he's been gone for two months with no word." He turns to me. "If the Khmer Rouge found him or any other foreigner inside the country, death would be pretty well automatic; we all know that. If they didn't kill him on the spot they'd try him as a spy, and then execute him—and we'd have to hope they didn't interrogate him first. I'm sorry. It just has to be accepted."

Harvey speaks quickly, before Jim can reply. "Unless he's still a prisoner, Paul. That's always possible."

"It's possible, if the story those people brought in isn't true," Carr says. "But I think it is true."

"Your opinion does not make it true," Feng says.

Carr finishes his beer and puts the glass on the shelf. "I know you two were friends a long time, Jim, but look at it this way. Maybe Mike died at the right time."

Jim has been about to light a cigarette; now he pauses without doing so. "What does that mean?" he says.

Carr speaks to the wall of the bar, not to Feng. "Langford

was a great war photographer," he says. "Don't misunderstand me. The pictures will always be there to prove it. But in one way Mike was like a lot of those stringers and freelance cameramen who had the big ride in Vietnam: some of them ended up being war-nuts, and it's hard for them now to give up the drug and move on. Hard to believe they'll never hitch a ride on a Huey into battle again." He looks at me now, his expression slyly confiding: You'll understand, the look says, even if Feng doesn't. "You see them in here all the time," he says, and gestures towards the figures at the bar. "Always talking about the war," he says. "Always in their macho combat boots. Ankle high. Zipped up. In this heat." He smiles, and there's a touch of spite at the corners of his mouth.

"You are saying all this about Mike? You are calling Mike a *war-nut?* I tell you, Carr, he was never a war-nut," Jim says. "And neither was I. We left that to the crazies; the amateurs. And amateurs got killed."

"I'm not saying he was a crazy," Carr says. "But with his reputation, he could have been working anywhere in the world: so why did he hang on here in Bangkok? With Vietnam and Cambodia locked up, and the war over, there was simply nothing here for a news photographer of his caliber. Nothing's happening in the region now that matters—you know that. It's different for you, Jim. You're a bureau chief, a man with a family; you've got a life here."

Feng slaps his artificial leg through his knife-edged khaki slacks, his eyes still gleaming with anger. "If it weren't for this, I would still be covering. I would not be flying a bloody desk for Telenews."

Carr shakes his head. "Then maybe it's just as well for that charming wife of yours that you lost the leg—or she might have lost *you.*" Before Jim can reply, he turns to Harvey. "What I'm saying, Harvey, is something you'll probably understand. Mike was forty, with no war to cover any more. What was in front of him, if he stayed in Bangkok? He was propping up the bar here in the Foxhole half the time, like so many others—or else he was up at that Khmer Serei camp on the border, doing God knows what with those shady guerrilla groups, and that military commander he was so bloody thick with: Colonel Chandara."

Feng interrupts. "Is there something wrong with Chandara? I know him: a brave man."

Carr shakes his head again. "Not my cup of tea, I'm afraid. I've heard some pretty nasty stories about him." He turns to me again. "You know what they called Mike in the press club? 'The unofficial spokesman for the Free Khmer.'"

Harvey Drummond smiles; so does the silent Kennedy. But Carr's tone now grows severe, and faintly pompous. "Mike lost his objectivity over that movement—which he'd never done before. It's a bloody lost cause, but he couldn't see it. He forgot the journalist's duty to be impartial. I didn't realize it at first. He got me interested and fed me news stories about his Free Khmer. I filed them, and my paper ran them—stories that actually affected the policies of governments. And then I found he'd gilded the lily. He did it with other correspondents too. Now that was naughty."

"Maybe he'd found something worth getting involved with," Harvey says.

"In that case he'd ceased to be a journalist," Carr says. "Suicide Langford was a good name for him: maybe he really was hooked on death." He's looking at me again; his expression is covertly mocking, and it's plain to me now that this is a man who didn't like Mike at all. "But in the end, I don't really feel I knew Mike Langford," he says. "Maybe none of us did."

He glances at his watch.

"I have an interview to do: I must go. Nice to have met you, Ray."

"Better you do go," Feng says.

Carr's face stiffens. He turns away without speaking again and edges off through the crowd, not looking back.

"A bit harsh, Jim," Harvey says.

"He is a shit," Jim says. "No one can speak about Mike like that." He turns to Kennedy. "It would be a pity if Ray listened to someone like Carr," he says. "He's here to find Mike, and I believe he will do it."

Kennedy looks at me. "Good luck," he says. "I miss having Mike around. We had some great times in places like Laos in the old days, Mike and me."

"Yes, in the White Rose," Jim says. "What a place that was, the old White Rose. Wild." He grins at Kennedy, then turns to me. "Everyone used to be there—even the Russians."

"Well, it's all gone now," Kennedy says. "And so is Mike." His tone remains entirely neutral.

"I hope not," I say.

"Oh I don't know," Kennedy says. "He had a good time."

His pleasant, hard expression hasn't changed, and at first I'm a little shocked. But then I realize that what he's said has been a kind of epitaph: probably the best that a man of his kind knows.

2.

Journalists based in Bangkok call this place the Newsroom, Harvey tells me. What its Thai name is remains a mystery. It's somewhat like an American diner: a structure on the lines of a railway car, serving cheap Thai meals. It sits on the edge of a square off Ratchadamri Road, opposite a canal called Klong Mahanak.

This is a district of up-market bazaars and big new department stores, where the British and American embassies are located. Late-model cars and Japanese motor scooters are parked around the square. A number of international news organizations have their offices in the district, and the Newsroom has become a foreign correspondents' lunch club.

British Telenews, where Jim Feng is bureau chief, is housed in a modern glass building here in the square, next to a row of shophouses with washing hanging from their balconies. And it seems that Mike Langford bought a house in this district, which I've yet to visit. It's a little way along the *klong,* Harvey tells me: the only property Mike ever owned.

Harvey and I are seated on stools at one of the white Formica-topped tables, facing each other. We've finished our lunch and are drinking coffee; Jim Feng has gone back across the square to Telenews. But Harvey's prepared to stay on: he tells me he has most of the afternoon free.

Prosperous Bangkok still has some hearty Asian odors, and there's a somewhat ill-smelling urinal just inside the entrance of the Newsroom; but once in the diner itself, this is forgotten. The food's good and the coffee's excellent, brought to us by young Thai waiters in white shirts and trousers. The long, narrow compartment, with its two rows of tables, is clean and bright, with music coming from a radio at just the right volume. The heavy heat is reduced by portable electric fans fixed upside-down in the ceiling, and a faint rumor of the urinal's odor is kept at bay by the scents of fresh flowers, hanging from the lamps. On a counter at the far end—the frontier hiding the kitchen—a telephone rings at intervals.

The calls are mostly for the correspondents and news photographers here: London, New York, Sydney and other cities around the world summon them up the aisle between the tables. Sitting behind the counter, the Chinese proprietress cries out their names and holds up the phone; when no one responds, she writes down messages. She's a plump, smiling matron in a purple blouse and upswept spectacles, and Harvey tells me she's a millionaire property investor. Her Mercedes sits in the square.

I now ask Harvey Drummond the direct question that I wasn't prepared to put to him with Jim Feng here. What's his personal opinion about Langford's disappearance? Does he agree with Jim that Mike's still alive?

Harvey takes off his glasses and polishes them with his handkerchief. Exposed, his large, fish-like gray eyes are sorrowfully blank; his freckled bald head is fortress-like yet vulnerable. "Maybe not," he says, so quietly I only just hear it. "He could be, but lately I don't feel optimistic."

I ask him why not.

"Just a feeling, Ray. I'm afraid our friend Paul Carr was right: the odds are against it."

We both sit silent for a moment. Then Harvey says: "You want to know why he did it—why he went over the border.

Nobody really knows: but I'll give you my opinion. He went to get back into the past."

I wait for him to explain.

"Cambodia was Mike's adopted country," he says. "He fell in love with it; a lot of correspondents did. Mike more than most: and he wanted that life back. Just about everything and everyone he cared about was there, including the woman he was in love with: I believe you know that. And now that the Communists had won, he was locked out of the two countries he'd made the whole point of his life. Thailand could never replace Cambodia and Vietnam for him: he didn't give a stuff about Thailand. So as Carr was asking, why did he stay here? Because this was the closest he could get: Thailand was his window on Cambodia. And he could also keep in touch with those Free Khmer of his, at Camp 008 on the border."

"Paul Carr didn't seem too enchanted with that involvement," I say.

Harvey sits studying me with his arms folded. "Most of the press corps made a hero out of Mike; but not everyone was a fan," he says. "Certainly not brother Carr—who's a good journalist, but a somewhat sour little turd. There are quite a few types like that who are critical of Langford: mainly the sort who don't like being shot at. They say he was too gung-ho; callous; a war-lover—all that stuff. And there was another side to Mike that bothered one or two people." He draws his big finger slowly around the rim of his coffee cup. "It's a long time since you really knew him, isn't it?"

"Over ten years," I say. "Except that we kept up a correspondence."

Harvey nods. "Mike was a bit in love with secrecy," he says, and watches me as he says it.

"He was like that as a kid," I say, and wait for him to elaborate.

But he doesn't; instead, he asks me another question. "You know about the association with Aubrey Hardwick? And Donald Mills? Is there stuff on that among his papers? Right: well, Donald Mills is based here in Bangkok," he says. "I think it's important you talk to him. I can give you the address of his office. He and Aubrey left the foreign service and set up a PR business here, with an end in Melbourne. Mills is the Bangkok end; Aubrey handles Melbourne, apparently. It's called Pacific Consultants. I believe they represent Asian corporations that do business in Australia. Take care of their corporate images, as they say in the trade." His smile grows sardonic, and still he watches me carefully. "Mills is always drinking in the Foxhole," he says. "I think he gives more time to drinking now than he does to PR. He might have a few things to tell you about Mike—he might even have some theories about what happened. Especially if you catch him when he's nicely primed."

He leans back and stretches, giant hands reaching towards the ceiling. "Time to go," he says. "I'd better do a stroke for ABS. We'll meet here again tomorrow, Ray, if you like." But then he shoots another question at me. "Are you really going to put Mike's memoirs together if he doesn't come back? He was always talking about those memoirs."

I say I probably will.

"Good," Harvey says. "I'm sure you'll do it well. Mike goes on fascinating people, and I believe I can see why—aside from the obvious reason of the achievements as a war photographer. When somebody attractive or daring or both is cut off in their prime, there's always the tendency not to accept it; and in this case, people don't have to. He's simply disappeared; he may not be dead after all; so we can all go on convincing ourselves he'll come back—like Baldur."

He smiles, getting up from the table, and I wonder for a moment if he's mocking Mike's fate. But I'll find as I get to know him that humor is never far off with Harvey, even over things for which he cares deeply. It's one of his methods of keeping regret at bay, and of being reassuring. He seems to look for ways to placate life.

From the table where Harvey and I have made a habit of sitting, we can look across the road to the canal. A row of little market stalls is strung along the bank there, under giant tropical trees for which I have no names.

The Newsroom has windows at table level for its full length down both sides, fitted with white-painted iron grilles instead of glass. Orange-striped blinds are drawn halfway down these grilles, protecting us from the sun, and out beyond the blinds is the white glare of Bangkok: a city choking on the exhaust fumes of its squadrons of new cars; a city never touched by the war. But in here, Harvey and I are oblivious of Bangkok and of Thailand: we've now become mental inhabitants of those two closed countries on the other side of the border.

We've met here every day this week, matching Harvey's memories with what I feel able to share with him from Langford's audio diary. Sometimes Jim Feng joins us, but he can seldom stay for long: running the Telenews office gives him less free time than Harvey seems to have as ABS correspondent here. Often, when Harvey hasn't any appointments, he and I linger here through much of the afternoon, over beers and many cups of coffee. Both of us are caffeine addicts: not the only thing we turn out to have in common.

I like good talk and a good talker, and Harvey has more than a journalist's feeling for a story: he has a nineteenth-century relish for words, and for the story inside the story. It's he who does most of the talking, but without my promptings and speculation he wouldn't continue at such length; he's never a bore. And Langford's life and disappearance is a topic we never seem to exhaust. I suppose this is because it puts out so many stems and branches—becoming in the end Harvey's story as well, and Jim Feng's, and Dmitri Volkov's, and the story of the war itself.

Today, Harvey has brought me his notes and archives, stowed in an airways bag.

"Here you are, Ray: for a ghostwriter-cum-historian. A journo's relics of Indochina: plus bits of my aborted Vietnam novel."

Pushing the bundle of papers across the white Formica, he gives me a smile that attempts lightness, but doesn't quite succeed. There are two fat folders of typescript and written notes, and a bulging, quarto-sized envelope containing press releases, news clippings and photographs: a journalist's memorabilia, together with pieces of his unfinished book.

"You see, brother, I suffer from Journalist's Paralysis," he says. "It's a condition that explains why so many of us have unfinished novels in our desks. We live *inside* things like the war in Vietnam, and novelists don't, on the whole: they tend not to have the stomach for it. And we know in the end that it's impossible to bring it back as it really was. So we give up; we get paralyzed; the pages lie in the back of the desk and turn yellow, and we go out and get pissed instead. Take it back to your hotel; keep it as long as you need. One or two things there might throw some light on Mike, and the way we all were." He raises his hand for the Thai waiter. "Let's have a beer, this time."

And now he begins to talk about Cambodia.

Cambodia was different, Harvey said. You have to understand that, for a start. It wasn't just Mike Langford who loved it; all correspondents loved it. All through the sixties, the war scarcely affected Cambodia—and Phnom Penh not at all. How can I tell you what Phnom Penh in the sixties was like?

A short ride on Royal Air Cambodge ferried us there from Saigon, leaving behind an occupied city whose virtue was lost: tangled in barbed wire, roaring with traffic and military convoys, fearful of VC bombs, filled with American troops and their attendant legions of beggars, touts and prostitutes. Coming out of this, you found yourself in a city of charmed peace, in a kingdom that had once reached to Malaya. Old Phnom Penh, which no longer exists, which will never exist again, was a French city on the Mekong colored Mediterranean pink and cream. Although it was the capital, it was only of modest size. Not a big population; very little traffic. Tamarinds and flame trees lined its grand, half-empty boulevards, and its handsome old French villas had walled gardens. The cooking was still French, the restaurants excellent, and the coffee, pastries and bread a delight. It was how Saigon must have been before the war. Intimate little nightclubs featured female Cambodian vocalists singing French-style love songs. The phones worked. Journalists loved it.

And we'd come into a land that tugged at our collective memories: a strange yet half-known country with alphabetical writing and familiar, spicy foods, recalling not only France but regions outside geography: regions that tantalized the mind, almost recalled and yet not, like a whole mislaid life. The people too were oddly familiar. Instead of the delicately made, hardworking, worldly Vietnamese, we found here a brown-skinned, strongly built, wavy-haired, pleasure-loving people who laughed easily at our jokes, and whose faces hinted at an antique India, and the Malay archipelago. The men had a coarse-grained handsomeness that sometimes seemed more Western than Asian, and the women were beautiful: figures from Indian frescoes. And no one harassed or badgered us, Harvey said, as the street hordes let loose by the war were always doing in Saigon. There was corruption and greed among the Cambodian ruling class, and in the Palace circles presided over by Prince Sihanouk; but there seemed to be very little cupidity in the ordinary people. They were farmers, knowing little or nothing of business; they left that to the enclaves of Chinese and Vietnamese. Even the Khmer bar girls were shy and amateurish: country girls, still wearing the traditional sarong, who wanted to be friends.

What lay under the surface of things we frankly didn't know, and didn't want to know. The Cambodians seemed to realize that life was to be enjoyed, we told each other; and they wanted us to enjoy it too. They didn't try to deceive us, or cajole, or work angles. They wanted to be friends, and they lived in a country at peace.

Peace in the boulevards, Harvey said, with so little traffic that sometimes it seemed that minutes went by before a car passed. Peace in the squares and the narrow lanes, where hibiscus and bougainvillea climbed over sleepy walls. Peace in the deep green country beyond the town's edges, where the big rivers met: the Mekong, the Bassac, and that other strange waterway called the Tonle Sap, which in spring flows backwards. A river city. Hot silence; and Phnom Penh's noises were the muted, magic sounds that come to you in a doze: an afternoon siesta where you're having good dreams.

A dream was what it was, Harvey said: a good dream with a bad one at its edges, waiting to invade. You know the kind? Even in your sleep, you know the other's waiting: there's the sense of something out on the perimeter; something you can't quite see. You know that if it breaks in, the terrible will arrive. Well, it finally arrived in Cambodia when the sixties ended.

He drained his beer, and looked out through the grille. Over by the *klong,* a boy in bright orange trousers and a blue shirt was squatting in the sun by a stall, sorting bunches of long green vegetables.

We used to say Cambodia wasn't serious, Harvey said. We saw it as a country of make-believe: our land of Holiday. Bloody nonsense, of course, and we half knew it—but we didn't care, in the sixties. Phnom Penh was our place to escape to from Saigon and the war: our capital of pleasure, and of opium trances at Madame Delphine's. And Mike Langford more than anyone believed in the good dream of Cambodia. He knew about the bad dream, waiting on the edges, but he wanted to believe that the good dream would continue. I think he was like a sleeper who wakes up and can't bear the dream to end, and goes back to sleep to try and get inside it again. We never can—right, brother? But he wouldn't accept that.

The bad dream had been there all the time, of course, up in the jungles on the eastern border. That was where Prince Sihanouk had allowed the North Vietnamese Army and the Viet Cong to maintain sanctuaries inside the country: bases for their drive on South Vietnam. Sihanouk was a little prince of pleasure, whose main interests were directing films, broadcasting five-hour speeches to his people, and playing in his jazz band. His family and his court were also said to run some of Phnom Penh's brothels, and to control its gambling. But he'd declared himself a Socialist prince, and a neutralist; he'd turned against the Americans, removing Cambodia from the American camp. He was a cunning politician, and he already saw the North Vietnamese Communists as winners. Perhaps he tried to forget that the sanctuaries existed up there in the jungle, and put them out of his mind.

Meanwhile, we scribes used to hunt for evidence of them: they were the great mythical scoop of the sixties for Indochina correspondents. But no one ever saw them, although I believe Mike Langford and Dmitri Volkov once got pretty close. And the U.S. Command in Saigon grew more and more obsessed with them. They claimed that the headquarters of the North Vietnamese organization known as COSVN was located there too, in those border jungles: the Central Office for South Vietnam, from which (so they said), the whole Communist war effort was being conducted. Their B-52s began secretly bombing inside Cambodia, in an effort to knock out the bases, and perhaps to knock out COSVN as well: the ultrasecret nerve center of the war. But they didn't succeed; and COSVN was never found.

Did it even exist? I still wonder. Like so much else about Cambodia and the war itself, COSVN was a secret inside a secret. The sanctuaries and the unofficial bombing both had an existence on the level of rumor, and the Central Office in the jungle lay in the realm of legend: a final secret at the heart of things, tantalizing the Americans. Perhaps if it could be found and rooted out, all the agonizing problems of the war in Vietnam could at last be solved, and victory achieved. This haunted the minds of their Special Forces men, their top military commanders and their CIA operatives—as well as the minds of humble scribes like me.

Alas, the dreams of the 1960s had to come to an end, Harvey said: everything changed with the new decade. But by then I'd been moved out of Asia: ABS had sent me to London. The devious little prince was overthrown, and went into exile with his patrons in Peking; the kingdom became a republic; the Americans and the South Vietnamese Army were sought as allies, and briefly invaded to clear out the sanctuaries. They didn't succeed; but when they pulled back across the border, the real war in Cambodia had begun, and the news media caravans rolled into Phnom Penh as they'd done into Saigon.

I wasn't with them: it was a war I'd yet to see. I read about it in the newspapers, like everyone else, or in letters from Mike; he was always a great letter writer. It wasn't until 1973, in the last week of January, that ABS sent me back to Asia. They based me in Singapore again, but I was expected to spend as much time as necessary in Phnom Penh. Lisa, who now had a job in London as a research assistant at the BBC, wasn't very happy about this; but she promised to join me in Singapore if the war situation dragged on. It certainly did: I'd be covering in Indochina for the next two years.

There was a false hope of peace in Cambodia in that week of my arrival. A cease-fire was hoped for, arranged between Hanoi and the Americans as part of the Paris peace accords. But it wouldn't happen. Out in the countryside, a new group of Communists had taken over from the North Vietnamese and the Viet Cong: and these were native Khmers.

Sihanouk had called them *les Khmers Rouges;* but most Cambodians simply called them *les autres:* the Others. No one knew anything about them. They wore black, like the Viet Cong, and when we covered engagements with them, we seldom got close enough to see their faces. They belonged to the dream at the edges too; but now they were moving to the center.

I'd been out of Indochina for nearly seven years, Harvey said. When I came back, all highways led to the war.

———

3.

HARVEY DRUMMOND

Pick any highway, I was told: all of them go to the war. I thought it was a joke, at first.

But what my colleagues were telling me was true: every one of the highways that radiated out from Phnom Penh would take you to the front. The struggle had come down to keeping them open, so that the city wouldn't die. This was a war over highways.

Will there ever be another war like it? One you could go to by taxi? On my first day there, I was taken by air-conditioned Mercedes.

The Mercedes belonged to Mike Langford. It was black,

somewhat elderly, but still handsome; he'd named it Black Bessie, after some long-ago pig on the family farm. He'd bought it cheap, he told me, from a Chinese businessman who'd recently departed Phnom Penh: one of the many members of the merchant class now fleeing the country. But I couldn't help seeing the Mercedes as a sign of Mike's mature success: one of the few obvious rewards he'd allowed himself.

On the evening of my arrival he'd come out to Pochentong Airport in Black Bessie to meet my plane. He'd come alone, since Jim Feng and Dmitri Volkov were both out of town, and I was touched.

I'd learned from Mike's letters that both Feng and Volkov had continued to work in Indochina over most of this time; but for Dmitri, there'd been a break of nearly two years. He'd married an American, an employee of the U.S. State Department based in Saigon; when she'd been moved back home, he'd gone with her to Washington, and had given up covering combat. But the marriage had ended, and for the past six months he'd been back in Cambodia, covering for CBS again. Trevor Griffiths was here as well, Mike said, after working for some years in Europe; Griffiths too had been married and divorced. Mike of course had never married. Correspondents aren't good marriage material; the way of life's against it, and I seem to be an exception. I hoped that Jim Feng would be luckier; according to Mike, he'd just become engaged to a young Chinese woman in Singapore.

There were soldiers manning sandbag emplacements all around the terminal, and the Caravelle that had got me here from Saigon kept its engines turning over for an immediate takeoff. No civil aircraft now stayed in Phnom Penh overnight, since Khmer Rouge rocket attacks on the airport were frequent. This put a certain chill in me; but I still looked forward to a reunion with my Saigon brothers. Walking across the tarmac, I tried to imagine in what way Langford would be changed by the years. But the figure waiting at the customs barrier looked exactly the same.

He stood among a small crowd of anxious-looking Cambodians who clutched outward tickets for the Caravelle. The edge of middle age didn't seem to have made a mark on him; I saw with immediate envy that the mane of yellow hair remained as thick as a twenty-year-old's. I was rather conscious of hair lately; in an era that had brought in a fashion for wearing it as long as a medieval courtier's, mine was going fast. Langford's hair, I noticed, was still cut short by current standards, with only the sideburns worn longer as a concession to the seventies.

"Harvey," he said, and put out his hand. "What took you so long to get back?"

He grinned and winked, comically contorting one side of his face: the exaggerated country wink that always conveyed a message. This one said: *You've been wasting your time all these years; there's no other story; no other place to be.* And for him of course this was true.

I'd followed his career over the past seven years through his letters and his published work. He was getting more and more famous, and he'd been briefly lured out of Indochina to cover other conflicts for leading magazines: the Chinese-Indian clash on the border of Tibet in 1967; the street fighting in Belfast in 1969; the civil war in Jordan in 1970. But he only did it for the money, his letters told me; they'd been interesting interludes, nothing more. There was only one war that mattered.

Three years ago, a New York publisher had brought out a book of his Vietnam photographs, with a text by a well-known American correspondent. It had included not only scenes of battle, but other pictures showing the plight of the peasants in the countryside, and the tribes of the displaced in the shantytowns and streets of Saigon. It had attracted a good deal of favorable attention in most of the major newspapers—and also praise from the antiwar movement, which eventually used some of his pictures as propaganda. Last year a book on the war in Cambodia had followed, with pictures of equal power. Some of the reviews had treated his collections as art, as well as documentary—which I suppose they are, now that one looks at them again. And a leading New York magazine had recently run an interview and a story on him, dwelling heavily on his reputation for unusual risk taking, and elevating him towards the edge of that plateau inhabited by celebrities.

But he had no wish to be there, apparently. Another photographer would have proceeded to enjoy the fruits of such success, basing himself in New York or London. Langford had spent time in both capitals when his books were launched; but then he'd come back to the war, and he'd based himself now in Phnom Penh. He was under contract here to a big American newsweekly, and his pictures often made its cover.

Cambodia was his home, he said.

At seven o'clock the next morning, the Mercedes rolled down Highway 5.

Its air was nicely cooled, "Tupelo Honey" was playing on its tape deck, and an icebox sat in the back, filled with bottled orange juice. So this was the way my colleagues went to war in Cambodia. It made me laugh; and I have to admit that my laughter was euphoric.

Don't misunderstand me: I didn't like the sound of this war, which was said to be killing more correspondents than any other in history. But I'd just come out of a London winter, my grateful body was clad in light cotton clothing again, and the big warmth of Asia surrounded me; I was back, and it put me on a high, that morning. So too, if I'm honest, did speeding down a highway towards the action in Langford's Mercedes, with "Tupelo Honey" coming over the speakers.

Van Morrison was a favorite with the brothers, Mike told me: he was especially good for playing on the way to a firefight. So were Creedence Clearwater Revival, and Rod Stewart. I savored this information, which had the same importance for me as learning some vital news source; it tuned me in to their lives again, and after seven years away I yearned to be tuned in. We journalists love the ephemeral, and there's no hunger so exquisite as hunger for the ephemeral; now Van Morrison belongs forever to the war in Cambodia, and the clear sunlight of the dry season. I wouldn't be this high in an hour or so, but the moment lives on, its fragile structure built on air, like all our best moments.

We were headed towards a battle. Mike's sources had told him of a probable engagement between Cambodian Government forces and the Khmer Rouge, about sixty kilometers northwest of the city. We were driven by a thin, brown-faced Cambodian of middle age called Lay Vora, whose crisp white shirt and navy trousers made him look quasiofficial. He had a thick cap of wrinkled black hair and many wrinkles in his forehead from perpetually raising his eyebrows; he smiled a lot, his eyes wistful and kindly, and had the permanently concerned air of a good family man. Vora was Langford's driver-interpreter—and also his landlord, I'd discover. He and his family lived in a three-story house near the Old Market, and they sublet the top floor to Langford. Mike and I were sitting next to him on the old-fashioned bench seat; in the back were two correspondents who were strangers to me.

Bill Wall was an American who was bureau chief here for the U.S. newsmagazine Mike took pictures for, and who wrote the stories the pictures accompanied. The other man was a BBC correspondent called Godfrey Wardlaw. He'd arrived here the night before as I'd done, and had struck up a conversation with Langford and me in the bar of the Hotel le Royal: the unofficial club for correspondents, where I'd taken a room. Langford was generous with both lifts and information; he often helped newcomers like Wardlaw with a story, and he'd invited him along today.

"Got a cigarette for an old Digger?" Mike turned to Bill Wall, beggar's palm outstretched.

Wall shook a cigarette from his pack and held it across the seat back. He was a thin, wiry man of around forty, his sandy hair crew-cut like a Marine's. His large, slightly protuberant brown eyes had a humorous gleam, as though permanently alert for the punch line of a joke. Leaning forward, he spoke in my ear.

"This compat-riot of yours just gave up smoking," he said. He came from Kentucky, and elongated his words in the musical Southern way. "Will you ask him to take it *up* again, Harvey, for God's sake? It's bankrupting me keeping him in cigarettes."

"I had no choice, Bill," Langford said. "Vora's have run out."

Vora took one hand from the wheel to hold a lighter to Mike's smoke, his face composed and tolerant, like a wise father's. "He has taken my last one," he said. "I wanted to buy a special begging pack for him, and keep it in the glove box. But he will not allow: he said it would make him smoke more."

Only Godfrey Wardlaw didn't laugh. He was lanky, pale and serious, with dark, bushy sideburns and a handsome Che Guevara mustache. He'd not been in Southeast Asia before, and he seemed unusually quiet, staring out the window; I assumed he was simply taking things in.

Highway 5 ran towards Thailand, through a wide, flat country of low horizons: a blue line of mountains far off in the west; tall white clouds in the east. It was known as the Rice Road, since much of the rice that fed Phnom Penh came down it from the western province of Battambang. Now, it seemed, the Khmer Rouge were constantly attempting to cut it, and battles took place on it almost daily. But the war was hard to believe in, and nowhere to be seen. January's a delightful month in Cambodia: the dry season, and not yet too sticky; the time of the rice harvest, with the landscape not yet bleached out. A gentle breeze was blowing, and the high, spiky heads of the sugar palms waved and glittered above the paddy dykes. When you see the sugar palms, they say, you know you're in Cambodia. Black-clad young women in checked turbans moved in the rice fields wielding sickles; brown-faced grandmothers held infants and baskets beside the road, smiling as though all was well.

And of course, all was not well. We were now some fifty kilometers or so out from Phnom Penh—just past the old ruined city of Oudong—and here, Mike told us, Highway 5 stopped being officially secure. Yet knowing this made no difference to my morning joy.

Highways! How they lead us on: we for whom the present is everything, yet never enough! Highways have always brought me joy: highways on which we move at speed, and which go out across flatness to some edge that's beyond the possible, as this one was doing. A line of very distant treetops could be seen there against the sky, and the complex cone of an old Buddhist stupa sitting quietly on a rise, like a power plant from some alien technology. Only out there, on that edge to which we were speeding, was I promised all the answers I never seem to find: out there, where the world would at last change. It's an edge I often see in dreams: the only place where we ever actually reach it. Langford has appeared in a number of these dreams, since he disappeared. The highway runs at night then, with far, tiny lamps strung along its utmost edge. I see Mike going there on foot, to a final windy rim: a place where he belongs. I know he has his being there, in the dream: he's one of those people who do. Then he disappears.

"When's Volkov getting back from Saigon?"

Bill Wall was still leaning forward, speaking to Mike. "You can bum *his* cigarettes, then," he said.

"He'll be back next week," Mike said. "Then Jim Feng will have to worry about being scooped again."

"The Count's real manic lately—a lot more manic than usual. That fouled-up marriage, I guess: I think it hit him hard. He still does a great job, but I worry about the number of pipes he smokes at Madame Delphine's." He turned to me. "One evening recently, the Count smoked thirty pipes. *Thirty:* that's the truth, I swear. Trevor Griffiths and I had to carry him to his room in the Royal, and he didn't surface for two days. He was *out* of it, boy." He began to laugh. "On the second day we got concerned, and I went up and called through the door. I asked did he want to be told if anything big broke. Never let it be said I'm not charitable." Wall lay back in his seat, trying to stop laughing; finally he went on. "And this dying little voice came back through the door: *'Go away. I have no laundry.'* Dmitri thought I was the goddamn *room boy.*" His laughter now was ecstatic; he wiped away tears. But Godfrey Wardlaw still wasn't laughing; he frowned faintly, as though in disapproval of our frivolity.

The road ahead was now absolutely empty. It was raised above the level of the dried-out rice fields here, running high and straight across the flat yellow circle of the land like a roller coaster track at a fairground, and I suddenly realized how exposed we were. The fields here had been harvested, and were faded and empty; clumps of ragged palms and bananas and a few thatched huts were the only features visible for miles. Behind us, churning up pale brown dust at the road's edge, were a Cambodian Army truck and a motorcyclo carrying two fully armed Government soldiers in helmets, seated side by side, like a comic war toy. Even some of the Cambodian troops went to war by taxi, it seemed; it was that sort of crazy army. Close behind them, following us as it had done since Phnom Penh, came an ancient Peugeot taxi carrying a number of our fellow correspondents. It seemed they often followed Langford's Mercedes; knowing how good his contacts were, they counted on his leading them to the action.

Vora spoke suddenly. "Contested area," he said. His face had grown serious, and he kept his eyes on the road.

Wardlaw's frown deepened, and he leaned forward to Mike. "What does he mean?"

"The road up ahead," Mike said. "It's empty. And see those village houses? They're closed up, and even the dogs are gone. The Khmer Rouge are here. You'll get to know signs like those, mate, if you come out often."

"So how much farther do you intend to go? I'm not particularly anxious to become a statistic," Wardlaw said.

The familiar sinking feeling I'd known in Vietnam was entering my gut: Wardlaw's nervousness was making me nervous. Langford had turned around to look at him.

"You said you wanted to get close to the action," he said. His voice was neutral, and for a moment his gaze became empty and almost cold. His eyes seemed a paler blue than I remembered, and I noticed as well that the look of boyishness I thought I'd seen the night before had been a superficial impression: his face had grown older and harder, especially around the mouth.

"Of course," Wardlaw said. "But it's a matter of how close, isn't it? Whether we have reasonable protection."

Langford raised his eyebrows. "Protection? There isn't any," he said. "It's a movable front here, and the Government troops aren't very good at protecting themselves. They still tend to operate as though it's the Middle Ages: they haven't had a serious war since then. The troops are brave—they'll fight to the last man. But they're not properly trained or equipped, and the North Vietnamese and the VC have been slaughtering them. Now the

Khmer Rouge are doing the same. And the Yanks have left them to flounder, as you know. All they give them is air support, and that's not enough."

His expression had taken on the remote, almost fervent seriousness that I remembered from Vietnam days, and I wondered whether the Khmer Republic's army had replaced the Army of South Vietnam as the underdog whose cause he championed. But then his seriousness vanished. He grinned, and extended a hand across the seat to touch Wardlaw's shoulder, and his voice became soothing: the voice of the sympathetic Langford of our younger days. "Relax, old fellow," he said. "I've got word that the commander out here has the Khmer Rouge pinned down. He's a friend of mine. And he's not the type who gets his people killed through stupidity."

"Not like some," Bill Wall put in. "Hell, sometimes we know more than the *troops* do. Once we went down the road ahead of them, and took a village. They followed us in. Not a shot fired."

We all laughed again; but Wardlaw still looked tense. He was conscious of his dignity, and was trying to mask his feelings to preserve it. He took out a handkerchief, and wiped his face. He'd told me the night before that he'd never been in a war zone, and I began to be sorry for him: the situation he now found himself in clearly wasn't what he'd bargained for.

It wasn't what I'd bargained for either, and with every kilometer the car covered, it was getting worse.

No sound of gunfire yet; no sign of battle: but the emptiness of that raised, exposed highway was eerie. It had now become a very frightening ride, and chills began to run through me.

This wasn't at all like Vietnam. There was no U.S. Army here, with its friendly amenities for correspondents and its carefully defined limits within which we could operate. I'd begun to understand that no one was in charge here. The war in Cambodia had a nightmare vagueness, and this dry, huge, empty, yellow-and-green dish of land, under these towering clouds, was the axis of that vagueness, hiding the black-clad Others. I'd done my homework, of course, and Mike had briefed me the night before. I knew that a lot of journalists were dying on the highways, and that those who'd been taken prisoner hadn't been seen again, since the Khmer Rouge apparently executed anyone they seized. But the reality hadn't crept up on me until now. I always face reality too late: a fact which Lisa had pointed out to me before I left London. Thinking about her now only added to my ruefulness, so I stopped.

The others in the car had gone quiet, and I suspected that Wardlaw and I weren't alone in being nervous. And yet to have said anything would have been absurd, since absolutely nothing was happening. This was the sort of war that only Langford was used to, I thought: he'd virtually trained for it in his patrols with the ARVN in the Delta. No wonder he was happy here, and no wonder he got such great pictures: Cambodia was made for him. Bill Wall was looking frequently at the countryside: glances which were intended to appear casual. "Cheer up, buddy," he told Wardlaw. "This'll be a good bang-bang. You'll probably get a hell of a story. Snow will get us in and out. That's his specialty."

On the tape deck, Jerry Lee Lewis was singing "Shake, Rattle and Roll"; Mike was devoted to old Jerry Lee, and he suddenly turned the volume up to full, grinning as though he'd made us a present. We all began to rock to and fro and feel more cheerful; all except Wardlaw, that is. The noise was tremendous. Vora was smiling and nodding as he drove, and he and Bill Wall and I began to sing along. But Wardlaw sat rigid, his face sweating. "This is insane," he said.

We came to a checkpoint, and Mike turned the music off. Four Government soldiers in khaki caps and baggy fatigues, holding M-2 carbines, stood by a bamboo hut at the roadside. More soldiers squatted in the shade of a flame tree; there were women with them, in the dark cotton sarongs and blouses of the countryside, some holding infants: wives who followed their husbands to the front. A Chinese noodle seller in a straw hat was doing business with soldiers and a small group of peasants at his tricycle stall, and a number of motorcyclos were parked nearby: all of them here to serve the press. When the Peugeot pulled up behind us and disgorged its load of correspondents, the cyclo boys began immediately to negotiate.

"My God," Wardlaw muttered. "It's like bloody Waterloo. Do these battles have *spectators*?"

"The motorcyclos will take the press the rest of the way, for the right money," Langford said. "The taxi won't go any further."

"But we will?"

Langford looked at him again. "That's what we're here for," he said. "I want pictures. But you can wait here, if you like." His voice was polite, and more or less neutral.

Wardlaw's mouth tightened. "I'll come."

Vora had been speaking in Khmer with the road guards. Now he came over and told us that the command post here was two kilometers down the road. "They expect an attack soon," he told Mike. "Captain Samphan is there. We can go."

The temporary command post, when we reached it, proved to be a thatch-roofed peasant hut flying the Cambodian flag. A little grove of coconut palms extended behind it; a few fowls picked among discarded water jars. There were no local people here except for a single small boy in black shorts, seated on a buffalo at the roadside: he chewed a blade of grass, and watched proceedings. A number of Jeeps were parked on the road, which still ran straight and high here, with a ditch on each side. Armored personnel carriers stood in a field off the highway, and groups of soldiers with mortars were digging foxholes there, in the brown earth. The country continued to be open and exposed, but some two hundred yards away the road went up a low rise, and entered a copse of trees. I didn't like those trees. The deceitfully beautiful blue hills were still on our left, but closer now.

We all got out of the car except Vora. It was still only about eight-thirty, and not yet hot. The quiet was broken by the murmuring of the troops here, and by the static on a field radio in one of the Jeeps; Khmer voices came over it in sudden chattering surges. Two motorcyclos arrived, carrying our fellow correspondents. Only three of them had made the trip: two American stills photographers in one motorcyclo, and a very fat, fair-bearded English correspondent in a bent and broken panama hat, riding in another. They shouted and laughed like tourists, and called out greetings to Langford and Wall.

The Cambodian troops were squatting in what shade they could find: most of them near the coconut grove. There were perhaps a hundred of them: company strength. The officers stood beside the Jeeps and the fortress-like APCs. I'd never seen an army quite like it: in other circumstances I might have laughed. They were all essentially cheerful, smiling and laughing as Cambodians generally do. Their motley uniforms were fantastic, almost festive, and I saw what Langford had meant about their equipment. Only a few had helmets and combat boots; most wore berets or cotton bush hats. For footgear, they had rubber shower sandals or tattered gym shoes; some were barefoot. They wore American fatigues many sizes too big; old French uniforms; even jeans. Some combined a fatigue shirt with black pajama trousers rolled up to the knees. All wore the *krama,* the checked Cambodian peasant scarf that can double as a turban, and all had sacred Buddha amulets hung in pouches around their necks. These, I'd learn eventually, would render them invulnerable in battle if their thoughts were pure. They were going to need them. Their weapons were just as fantastically varied: M-2 carbines; M-16 and AK-47 automatic rifles; French rifles from World War Two; pistols; submachine guns. Some of the combat troops were women: girls in their teens. And there were also boy soldiers.

I'd heard that young boys were being recruited now, as the situation worsened, but I'd assumed that this meant teenagers: I couldn't believe that the children in front of me would be sent into combat. Many of them were no older than ten, and their old French rifles looked bigger than they were. They wore floppy olive fatigues and green berets, and all their large dark eyes shone with bright expectancy, like those of a team of little boys waiting for the start of a football game. Some were playing, climbing up the palm trees, shouting and throwing down coconuts; but most were grouped around a stocky old sergeant in a cotton bush hat, faded green fatigue shirt, pajama trousers and sandals, who appeared to be in charge of them. Weathered face dark brown and rock-like, gold teeth clenched on one of the local cheroots of hand-rolled tobacco, he smiled down on his troop with fatherly affection.

An officer in a green beret and sunglasses now came out of the house and walked slowly across to the Mercedes, his eyes on Langford. This was Captain Samphan, the company commander. He was young, tall, and stylish in well-cut American fatigues, a yellow scarf at his throat. Like his men, he was protected by magical Buddhist amulets that were knotted into the scarf. On his hip was a pistol I recognized as a .38 Magnum: he must have had very good connections to have got hold of it. Captain Samphan was something of a dandy, I thought: one of those officers common both here and in Vietnam, who played it like film stars, posing for the press and leading their men into battle only when the cameras were rolling. The other correspondents hurried to intercept him, the bearded man in the broken panama in the lead; but he waved them away, coming up to Langford with his hand extended, speaking in English with a French accent.

"Hello, Mike. You are just in time," he said. "We are expecting a little action very soon. We have had trouble at first light with the Khmer Rouge. We now think they are in those trees."

He pointed to the rise up ahead, and the sinking feeling began in my guts again.

Wardlaw, notebook out, abruptly asked the captain why he took such small boys into battle. His voice had a note of reproof, but Captain Samphan answered him courteously.

"We have not enough men, as you perhaps know," he said. "And these boys are so very keen. If we don't take them with us, they will only cry."

Wardlaw stared at him, wordless. The three other correspondents had come up to stand behind us, listening, and the bearded man in the panama was scribbling in his notebook, breathing heavily. He must have been feeling the heat with all that weight to carry about, but he looked quite cheerful and relaxed. Catching my eye, he winked.

"Any casualties yet?" Langford asked.

"Fortunately, no," Captain Samphan said. "We were not within range when they fired on us. Now we intend to advance.

I advise that you keep back, and look for cover if necessary." He turned away, and called an order to a group of young officers standing by a Jeep.

Now the warm air was full of shouts and movement. The officers were getting some of the troops into formation, ready to march up the road. Everything became very distinct, in a way I remembered all too well. Langford, Wall, Wardlaw and I still stood by the Mercedes, and Vora remained at the wheel. Captain Samphan was walking fast across the road in the middle distance, ordering some of the troops into the paddy field. The boy soldiers, shouldering their huge French rifles, were assembling near the rear of the line, their sergeant beside them. But one of them, who appeared to be about twelve, was standing at the head of all the troops, holding the Cambodian flag. Its device was the towers of Angkor Wat—emblem of Cambodia's days of ancient glory—and it fluttered in the light breeze. The boy's beret was at a jaunty angle, and his face had a cocky expression: teacher's pet, chosen for the most privileged of all duties. Another order was shouted, and the troops marched directly up the road behind the boy with the flag.

Except for the marching feet and the static on the field radio, there was a large quiet. I was wet from perspiration now as though I'd jumped into a pool. I looked around for Langford, who'd been at my elbow, and found that he'd gone. Then I saw him. Following his usual practice, he was going forward with the troops instead of seeking cover, walking fast beside the ditch that ran along the edge of the highway. He was dressed in a dark shirt and olive fatigue trousers, but was bare-headed; as usual, he carried a Leica and a backup Nikon. The two American photographers moved not far behind him, getting off some quick shots. As I watched them, they took cover behind one of the APCs in the paddy field; and at that moment, the firing began.

The noise was shattering: the hidden Khmer Rouge had opened up with mortars from the trees, and the Cambodian mortar platoons in the paddy field began to open up in response. Bill Wall and I looked at each other; there was too much noise to speak. He pointed to the ditch and I nodded and tapped Wardlaw on the shoulder. His face was white and oily: he looked dazed. I beckoned for him to follow, and then ran for it.

When we got to the ditch and rolled in, we found the bearded man already in occupancy, lying on his side. He grinned at me, still with a remarkably sanguine expression, and I wondered if he knew that some of his bulk rose like a whale's above the level of the ditch. Behind me I could hear a squeezed voice saying: "Christ almighty," and knew that it was Wardlaw. I looked at a slight cut on my thumb and remembered I'd done it in the kitchen of our flat in South Kensington, opening a can two days ago: a harmless wound of peace, in a now-unreal country, filling me with nostalgia. After a time, although the noise continued, I raised my face just above the ditch to see what was happening.

In the tropics, the pane through which we view reality is very thin. The colors are so unnaturally bright; they can suddenly cause the pane to seem to dissolve. The world becomes two-dimensional; a tapestry behind which something else waits to announce itself. This was happening now, and I fought against vertigo, knowing I might never get out of here. On the road, in a blue screen of gunsmoke, the troops were marching on with suicidal directness, firing towards the tree line as they went. They seemed to have no notion of taking cover in the paddy field; Langford was right, they were fighting a medieval battle. A man not far from me was crawling towards the ditch, dragging a shattered leg. Already the brown road was littered with bodies; but the boy carrying the flag was still marching at the head of the line: a gallant little page who bore a charmed life.

But then he fell, and it would have been like a child pretending to be killed in a schoolyard game except for his limp, small stillness, and the blood that spread from under him. The troops marched around him, firing their automatic weapons. His green beret had come off in the dust, and one half of my mind expected his mother to come and gather him up. Instantly, another little page raced forward to pick up the standard, raising it high and proudly marching as the other had done: an image repeating itself. I found myself stupidly cursing under my breath.

There were wild shouts of command; I saw Captain Samphan

waving his pistol, and the troops at last began to turn into the paddy field and take cover behind the dykes. The mortar fire went on relentlessly, and showers of earth went up. Then I heard Langford's voice, and looked up to see him crouched at the edge of the ditch.

"Get to the car," he said. "We're in a bit of trouble."

Now we were all in Black Bessie, where Vora appeared to have been sitting all the time. The cabin was full of heavy breathing and the stink of our sweat. The other correspondents had followed our example, and were already making off in their motorcyclos, but the boy on the buffalo was still here at the roadside, staring as though at a passing circus.

Vora turned on the ignition, but the motor didn't start. We waited in terrible patience, and he tried again. It started, but he didn't put the car into gear; he watched Langford inquiringly, apparently awaiting orders. I sat between them; Langford still had the passenger door open. "Not yet," he said. He was squinting, watching the two motorcyclos disappear.

"Let's go, man," Bill Wall said to him. "This ain't a healthy scene. They're being overrun." His voice was calm but urgent.

"What are we *waiting* for?" Wardlaw shouted. His voice was on the edge of hysteria. "For Christ's sake will you fucking go?"

Langford ignored him, and spoke to Vora. "Okay, go," he said. "Wait for me at the checkpoint. Give it an hour." He slid out and slammed the door, and Vora accelerated away.

Bill Wall leaned forward from the back and spoke to Vora. "He's *staying?*"

Vora smiled. "Good trick. The other photographers think he goes—they go. Then Mr. Mike gets a scoop."

"Jesus," Wall said. "Good trick? Can he also do the trick of getting out of here? These people are history."

As we drove off, I looked back to see that the troops that were left had regrouped in the paddy field behind the APCs. Captain Samphan was there, standing by one of the armored cars, and I watched Langford walk up to him. Explosions were continuing in the paddy field, but they began a conversation as though on a quiet street.

I fully believed that the two of them would die there.

When we got back to the checkpoint, it was like returning to a haven of changelessness, last seen a long time ago.

The four road guards, the flame tree, the bamboo hut, the Chinese noodle seller: all in place, in a whirring, strengthening sunlight that was innocent of gunfire. But the motorcyclos had gone, and so had the two Peugeot taxis—no doubt carrying our colleagues back to Phnom Penh.

We walked to a palm-thatch farmhouse a little way down the road. It was built on stilts, like most Cambodian farmhouses, and we went up steps onto a simple front verandah. The peasants were either in hiding or had run away, and we settled down here to wait for Langford. Vora the driver seemed not to be worried about him: he had a confidence in Langford's skills as though they were supernatural. Murmuring to me softly, his confiding smile and the concerned wrinkles on his brow creating gentle reassurance, Vora explained. Mike had been given a nickname by the troops: did I know this? He was called *Mean Samnang,* the Lucky One. This was because he always came away untouched from the heaviest firefights; he always survived, and he'd survive again today. He was not like other photographers: he was *Mean Samnang.* And Vora nodded at me happily, as though no more need be said. But although I refrained from voicing the fact, I didn't share his certainty.

The verandah had reed mats spread about, which the others lay on, and a sacking hammock was slung in one corner; I tossed a coin with Bill Wall for this, and won. Lying in it was very welcome; I was unnaturally tired, and floated off. There was a smell like hot straw, and the voices of the others came from a distance. When I closed my eyes I saw the little boy with the flag again, his death rerun like a film clip. I'd write about it, of course, for the voice-piece I'd be doing for ABS by radio-telephone circuit this afternoon; but thinking about framing it in words filled me with disgust.

An hour or so later, the humming of a Jeep sounded on the road, and I heard the others say that it was Langford. Filled with relief, I got out of the hammock to greet him.

The Jeep, driven by the old sergeant in the bush hat, stopped just long enough to let Mike out, and then swung around to go back up the highway. Mike climbed the steps without speaking, and unloaded his cameras and camera bag on a mat. Vora smiled broadly at him, and Mike put a hand on his shoulder, keeping it there while he greeted the rest of us, being just as friendly to Godfrey Wardlaw as to everyone else. Then he looked at Bill Wall, extending his hand with finger and thumb crooked.

Bill sighed, and shook out a cigarette and lit it for him. "Jesus, Snow," he said. "You have to be very lucky."

"They lost about half the company," Langford said. "But the Khmer Rouge pulled out, in the end. Samphan's a good commander."

His face had an expression of meditative peacefulness I can only describe as dreamy. He didn't speak again, and no one attempted to make him do so. He lay in the hammock, smoking, and I had little doubt that he was coming down from some enormous height: from that escarpment near death where he'd lingered with Captain Samphan.

I also began to suspect that it was a place where he needed to be.

4.

HARVEY DRUMMOND

Couscous night at the Jade Pagoda.

A mutual therapy session for emotionally dislocated correspondents. A station for the dressing of psychic wounds. A trapdoor into trance.

Only the special sadness of the war in Cambodia could have produced couscous night. There was nothing like it in Vietnam.

The Pagoda was on Monivong Boulevard: the city's main thoroughfare. You had to knock to be admitted, as you did at most Phnom Penh restaurants, and you were then frisked for weapons by a Government soldier. Langford, Feng, Volkov and a number of other correspondents and photographers met there each Saturday, hiring a private room.

The room's an odd one, like something out of another century. We sit in semidarkness around a huge circular table which fills the compartment almost completely. This, combined with dark, wood-paneled walls and weak lamps on brackets, gives the place an atmosphere that's claustrophobic, privileged and illicit: a London club crossed with a Triad headquarters. Unsmiling Chinese waiters in white shirts and black trousers stand like sentinels around the walls, watching us. Later, when my mind is rearranged, their expressions will come to seem contemptuous; even malevolent.

Things are quiet just yet, around the table. Everyone's more or less sober, and the couscous stew hasn't come in. The Nurseryman, I'm told, is in charge of the couscous, and is still out in the kitchen supervising its preparation. Who the Nurseryman is and why he's involved with the cooking is information that's being held back from me; my colleagues are getting a childish pleasure out of being mystifying.

Opposite me, Mike Langford, Jim Feng and Dmitri Volkov are drinking cognac and soda and playing the Match Game. On my left, Trevor Griffiths and Bill Wall are deep in conversation about the Paris peace accords, and the cunning of Henry Kissinger. On my right is Roger Clayton, a young Australian correspondent whom I met in the bar at the Royal tonight and took pity on; he's been sent here by a Sydney paper on his first overseas assignment, and has the youthful novice's longing to make contact with the inner circle of the press here. He treats me with gratifying deference; he's still romantic about meeting the veterans, which reminds me of my own early days, and makes me sentimental. I hope he won't prove an embarrassment like Wardlaw; but his square face appears both reliable and inoffensive, framed by mouse brown hair worn at the new near-shoulder length and nicely barbered, making him look like a well-groomed hippy.

He's been especially impressed to discover that I'm a friend of Langford's, whom he holds in some awe. This week, Langford has once again made the cover of his international news magazine, with a picture of the little boy with the flag, taken seconds after he fell; the other small boy is seen stooping to pick it up. It's caused anger and pity around the world, with quite a bit of press comment, and this adds to Clayton's professional reverence. On the way here from the Royal, he kept asking me questions about Langford. How many times had he been wounded? What was his secret of survival? Were his pictures really intended as an indictment of the war?

He now wants to ask Mike these things, and to get his views on the American bombing, and the current state of the conflict in the countryside—but an attempt at this sort of interview has met with a discouraging response from all three cameramen. The Match Game, it's made clear, is more important: in fact, paramount. I can see that Clayton's disconcerted by this; like many of the younger journalists now, he's a moral crusader, and has expected that the cameramen will immediately want to discuss the big issues. He's also the sort who looks for heroes, and the three are not behaving as he expected.

Soiled Cambodian banknotes lie on the table: the game is played for money, as all their games are.

"Eight," Volkov says. "I say eight."

He and Feng and Langford raise fists in which they've concealed their chosen number of matches, staring at each other like poker players. The Match Game, which I find boring, and which for them has the seriousness of ritual, involves each player starting with the same number of matches, and each displaying a number of them in every round; the aim is to guess the total number of matches still in play.

"Seven," Langford says.

He and Volkov look blankly at each other, and I'm struck by a vague yet perceptible physical resemblance that's developed between them in their maturity, and which wasn't there in their youth. It isn't that they're both blond; nothing so obvious. It's like a family resemblance, and I wonder whether their common occupation over the years could have produced it.

"Ten," says Jim Feng, and then the matches are counted. Noisy laughter; Jim gathers in the banknotes.

"He wins every time. He plays good mind games, the Crazy Jim," Volkov says. He grins: the stretched grin that I remember. Like Langford, he carries no extra weight, and still looks fit; but he's slighter than I remember, and unlike Mike, he's begun to age a little. There are lines that look like strain around the mouth, only half hidden by his mustache, and the blue Tartar eyes have faint, bruise-like shadows under them. Remembering Bill Wall's anecdote, I wonder if Dmitri has an opium problem. By contrast, Jim Feng seems almost unchanged. Perhaps his face has a new seriousness; perhaps his almond eyes are a little narrower; but that's all. I'm the one who's changed most, in the comfort of Europe: they're all making jokes about my baldness.

So here they are again: the Soldiers Three. I wonder if that silly name's still used, or forgotten. Looking at them across the table, it's possible to see them through young Clayton's eyes, and to understand his awe of them. They've survived covering combat for such a long time. Volkov has had two years out of it during the period of his marriage, but has otherwise filmed battle continuously since the early sixties; and Langford and Feng have survived over seven years of continuous coverage in Indochina. This is more action than most soldiers ever see. The American troops in Vietnam did only one-year tours, and most of the war photographers there didn't tempt fate for much longer than that: they got out because they were burned out, or on the edge of breakdown, or believed they'd soon die. Or else they did die. If you wanted to be superstitious, I tell myself, you could say that the odds against the three must have run out long ago. They're still quite young, of course, by normal standards; but like athletes they live by their reflexes, and their age, like that of athletes, is measured on a scale that's more pitiless than the one that applies to the rest of us.

They still have their talismans, I notice. It's stuffy in here, despite the overhead fan, and Volkov has his shirt open over his chest: I can see that he still wears his Saint Nicholas medal, and it touches and somehow saddens me.

They've finally taken pity on Clayton, and begun to talk shop to him.

"Do you know what some of these freelance stills guys get for a picture now? Fifteen U.S. dollars," Jim Feng tells him. He smiles, and shakes his head.

"Right," Volkov says. "So on a bad day, that might be all they'd make. They risk their asses for fifteen dollars. War-nuts, definitely. Not professional. For that money, you have to really *want* to be at a bang-bang."

"Are many being killed?" Clayton asks.

Volkov stares at him. "Every other week," he says. "Haven't you heard?"

"But *you* keep on covering," Clayton says.

"You show me a better war," Volkov says, and the others laugh.

"You attend by taxi," Volkov says, "and you're back around Hotel Royal swimming pool in the afternoon, eating shrimp salad and drinking French wine. That's my kind of war. The only trouble is, some don't come back through gates at sunset." He pauses, staring. "We sit by nice swimming pool and watch," he says. "As shadows get long, people go quiet. Anyone who doesn't walk up drive of the Royal by then is usually dead. Being press doesn't help you here. Khmer Rouge don't have rules."

Mike is pouring us all more cognac. "We've lost a lot of mates," he says. "We lost a terrific lady two months ago: a correspondent for the London *Telegraph*. Helen used to ride the roads wherever they'd take her, and she was in Khmer Rouge country. She and her Cambodian driver haven't been seen since."

Volkov is grinning at me. "Hey, Harvey," he says. "It's great to have you back, bald one."

"Which reminds me," Jim Feng says suddenly. "Pheng died today, out on Highway 4. Mortar shell."

"Mon Dieu," Volkov says, and looks into his cognac.

Langford frowns. "Pheng? That Cambodian stringer? Oh, shit. Not Pheng. He was such a nice bloke."

"They are all nice blokes," Volkov says.

"I liked Pheng," Jim says. "May he be in peace."

The three sit silent for a moment, hands clasped in identical attitudes, staring at the table.

At this point the Nurseryman comes in, followed by Chinese waiters carrying covered dishes, and everything becomes noisy. Inside the noise, Trevor Griffiths is muttering like a conspirator in my ear—revealing to me at last the secret of the couscous: this un-Chinese dish of meat stew and semolina that's the centerpoint of the evening. The Nurseryman laces it with marijuana, he says: grass of the highest quality, grown on the balcony of his apartment. Hence his nickname.

Cambodia's always been a paradise for potheads, since its use is legal here: middle-class Cambodians often employ it in cooking, and are said to be mildly stoned a good deal of the time. But this will be the first time I've ingested it in food, and I have some misgivings; I haven't even smoked the stuff since I left Indochina. The waiters are setting out the dishes on the wheel that revolves in the center of the table, while the Nurseryman gestures and supervises. His name is Hubert Whatley, and he turns out to be the bearded English correspondent I shared the ditch with on Highway 5 three days ago. In our confined chamber he seems larger than life, especially standing up. His sandy hair and beard are overabundant; he's tall, and his curving belly is impressive: he must weigh nearly twenty stone. His voice is a fine, penetrating bass, the accent Yorkshire crossed with BBC.

"Couscous!" he cries. "Gentlemen! Your dish of dreams is here! *Bon appetit!*"

He shakes my hand and young Clayton's, bending over us while voices and laughter rise in a sudden wave, and spoons clatter. "We met in busier circumstances, Harvey—I hope I didn't crowd you in that drain. But let me explain to you both, since this is your baptism at the Pagoda. Only *one* of these dishes is garnished with my lovely herb. You must therefore partake of *every* dish before the fairy visits you. Understood? Splendid." He straightens up, and raises a hand in blessing over the table, his bass filling the compartment. "Go to, gentlemen, and may all your dreams be weird ones."

We spoon the stew into our bowls; the wheel revolves and delivers fresh dishes; our laughter and talk rise explosively, and the Chinese waiters watch us from their places around the walls.

Griffiths jerks his head at them, muttering. "They're agents of the bloody Lon Nol Government: I have that from a very good source. So watch what you say, mate." He takes a giant mouthful of couscous. Chewing, waiting to get his hit, he seems to be listening for some distant sound. Like me, Trevor's now balding, and he's compensated by growing a curling black Welsh beard that tickles my left ear as he delivers his confidences. "All our talk goes back to the Government," he says. "Don't doubt it. And our beloved President Lon Nol would be glad to find an excuse to expel me, Harvey, since my reports show up his incompetence and corruption."

"I see you still have your conspiracy theories, Trevor."

He frowns, the beard giving him the somber, worrying authority of a biblical prophet. "So will you, after a few weeks here, Drummond. Let me give you one example. The spokesman at the Government's military briefings is a happy incompetent with no regard for reality. Every area he tells us is secure turns out to be a death trap. The man's directly responsible for the killing of journalists." His beard opens in a bitter black-and-white smile. "His name is Colonel Am Rong."

I start laughing, and find I can't stop. Clearly, I've now eaten of the magic dish; and I enter a vacuum. The vacuum is very dark, lit only by the lamps around the walls, and inside it, the talk I hear is sometimes muffled and sometimes of huge, ringing significance.

Young Clayton is giggling helplessly. "What's *in* this?" He peers into his bowl, and leans back, giggling again.

"Cambodia's already lost," Griffiths is saying. "Lost, and we all know it. We're here to watch the end. That's why they posted *you* here, isn't it, comrade? To join us around the corpse. Don't look for the Cambodia you used to know, Harvey—it's gone. The war criminals Nixon and Kissinger have destroyed it. In order to keep it safe from Communism, the B-52s bombed this country's heart out last year, killing any number of innocent villagers. Thirty-seven thousand tons of bombs. Nice clean work, flying at a great height; then they went back to their bases in Thailand and Guam."

The years haven't put out Trevor's fire, I see: his dark eyes shine and insist in the old way, and his paper-white face works with the old inner fury. But as I watch, his face becomes a huge Assyrian mask, with glossy black beard and ringlets, filling my vision. I resent this effect of the couscous, which is potentially terrifying, and I try to resist it. But the merciless Assyrian king who is Griffiths continues to sit in the darkness in front of me, his eyes flashing anger and death and pillage: he seems to wear a high, cone-shaped cap. And the king seizes a glass, and raises it to the table at large.

"Gentlemen! I give you the Stratofortress: the majestic B-52!" His voice blares like a trumpet, and his speech has bardic rhythms. "Imperial America's answer to Nelson's ships of the line! The supreme vehicle of death! Flies as high as fifty thousand feet, with a range of twelve thousand miles. Bombs inside; bombs under the wings. Beautiful as an eagle. At that height, it can't even be seen: you know nothing until the bombs arrive. The crew of a B-52 are innocent: they see not what they do. But down here, villages disappear into chasms, trees go down like grass, and the noise can make you lose your mind. Terrible beauty, brothers!"

He drinks and then turns to me, slumping back in his chair. He seems to have become Trevor again: the high cap is gone and his voice is quieter, sad. "They did their work well here, mate: they destroyed the countryside. So now we have a million refugees in Phnom Penh."

"But these are also refugees from the NVA and the Khmer Rouge. And the bombing has saved the city. You know this, Griffiths."

It's his old opponent Volkov speaking. Dmitri's voice seems to come from a great distance, and his face—like others around the table in the dark—is just a disc. "I too have hated the bombing," he says. "Yes, I hated it. But it kept the Mekong open, didn't it? It has kept Cambodia from going under to North Vietnam. It has saved the people from being collectivized, and religion destroyed and Buddhist monks butchered—which Khmer Rouge have promised to do. Already they occupy the temples in regions they take over. Already they torch the villages."

But Griffiths ignores him: he won't be diverted from giving me my briefing. "This is the Nixon Doctrine at work, Harvey. It's called Leave Them in the Shit. First they invade—to clear out the sanctuaries, they say. So the North Vietnamese are pushed in from the border to the heart of the country. Then the Yanks pull out again and tell the Cambodians: Carry on, fellers, it's your war now. We'll just bomb. And the result? All that's left now is Phnom Penh and the big towns: the Communists have the countryside. But Lon Nol and his generals are still getting rich on *bonjour*—so they like to have the Mekong and the highways open. The supply of cars and brandy must be kept flowing—eh, chaps?"

Under his oratory, and under Volkov's as well, there's a note I hear now that I didn't hear in Saigon: a sound of genuine pain. He turns to Bill Wall, and speaks in a quick aside. "Sorry, Bill; sorry to have spoken ill of your nation and your president, but you know it's all true."

Bill Wall sighs, toying with a glass of the cognac that we're recklessly continuing to drink with the couscous. "Sing your song, Trevor, don't mind me. You know I got no time for Tricky Dick. And *some* of what you're saying is right. But when anyone asks for peace, those Khmer Rouge won't even negotiate. So who are the war-lovers around here?"

Langford speaks, his soft voice only just reaching me. "The Cambodians need help on the ground, Harvey, and they're not getting it. It's true that some of their generals are on the take, and living it up in Phnom Penh. But there are some good commanders."

"Just like Vietnam," I say.

"Just like Vietnam," he says. "And the ARVN have done all right there, lately. Now that the American troops are pulling out,

I believe the ARVN will hold the line—and it could be like that here. These troops are fighting for their lives: there'll be no mercy if they lose. They know that. But a lot of them are in despair." He's addressing Griffiths now, pointing a finger at him. "Their confidence got worn down in that first year of the war, when the Americans pulled out. They're very simple people; they're not tricky. They thought the Americans would back them to the hilt; they thought they'd stay, and they don't understand why they didn't. Nor do I. But they still have real patriots here."

"Oh shit," Griffiths says. "Patriots. Those Lon Nol Army officers of yours? Is that it, Snow?"

"No," Langford says. "Not the officers. The ordinary troops: the men and the women. They're what matter. They're what always matter."

He says no more, and there's a silence. What he's said has been obvious; even innocuous; yet something is causing everyone at the table to look at him. Was it something in his voice? Time's projector has jammed; we're all fixed in stillness. I look down at my hand on the table and can't move it, and look back again at Langford. His face, in the light of one of the wall lamps, seems suddenly like a fanatic's: stony and angelic. Or is it the effect of the couscous?

The silence, which has set around us like jelly, is finally broken by Jim Feng. "Well, whichever way it goes, the people pay."

The Nurseryman nods in agreement, his vast face setting into lines of sorrow. "You speak true, squire. You speak true. The people pay. And we have to look at it, and send our little stories."

Another silence, whose length has no measurement: faces nod and nod around the table, and young Clayton is out of it, his head buried in his folded arms. Then Volkov speaks.

"Yes, Hubert, we have to look at it. This afternoon I shot film on Highway 1, in a village south of Neak Luong. Khmer Rouge are hitting Government forces there. I took pictures of a farmer with his small daughter in his lap—dead from a stray bullet. I talked with him: my driver translated. This is the last child the man has. There have been two sons and another daughter killed, and his wife as well. Now he is all alone, and what he is saying, over and over, is: 'What will I do? What will I do? Now I have no one.' "

Dmitri sniffs. He raises a hand to his eyes in ugly dismay, and I see that he's weeping. Silence resumes around the table, but it isn't the silence of embarrassment: it's the silence of communion. The waiters have vanished like spirits, and all the figures at the table are now individually distinct to me. The Nurseryman has tears glistening on his cheeks; he blows his nose into a white handkerchief. He saw the little boy with the flag die the other morning; is he weeping for him?

To round out that story, I had followed truckloads of wounded boy soldiers to the city's Russian hospital: little boys with red stumps where legs had been; boys with shrapnel inside them; boys with head wounds. They'd been dumped in the corridors because all the beds were full, and there were only two doctors there—one Cambodian, the other French—working like laborers to patch up the hundreds of wounded from the battlefields around the city. Parents sat with the wounded boys in corridors where puddles of blood and urine stood, feeding them bowls of gruel: a grisly children's party. And thinking of this, I find that I'm weeping too, not knowing when it began.

The Nurseryman's pink mask looms close, and speaks to me.

"Don't worry, my dear," he says. "We all shed a few tears on couscous night."

It was still only nine o'clock, with curfew in an hour, when we all emerged onto Monivong Boulevard. I was beginning to come down from the couscous, and the street looked almost normal. A circle of laughing Khmer prostitutes in many-colored sarongs surrounded us; but the Nurseryman waved them away.

"Not tonight, ladies. We're off to Madame Delphine's, the woman I love best."

Cyclo boys wheeled towards us in a flock, and the party began to climb into the black-hooded machines with shouts and laughter—including young Clayton, who now wore a permanent dazed smile, and had ceased to speak. I doubt that he knew where he was. Langford and Volkov hung back; Mike was trying to persuade me to come with them to Madame Delphine's opium den: the next appointed phase of couscous night.

"Come and have a pipe or two, Harvey. It won't destroy your brain. And Madame Delphine's is a great place for meeting people. Everyone goes."

No, I told him, a thousand times no. I'd avoided opium until now, and had no intention of being introduced to it on top of the couscous.

Dmitri took my arm, speaking to Mike. "Still a sensible man, the Harvey. Moderate; always was moderate, the bald one! He and I will go for coffee, and straighten out our heads."

Langford looked at him in surprise. "You're not smoking either, Count?"

"I smoke too much lately," Volkov said. "Tonight I'm being sensible, as a matter of fact. Sensible with Harvey."

Mike raised a resigned hand in farewell, and turned towards an expectant cyclo boy.

I was tired, and wanted to recover from the stew; I now told Dmitri that I'd prefer to skip coffee and go back to my room at the Royal. But the fingers still gripping my arm tightened urgently.

"Harvey, Harvey! We haven't seen each other in seven years! Don't be so goddamn middle-aged: do me a favor man, *come* with me! I need to talk to you."

The dope was making his face transparent to me in the way dope tends to do, and I detected a hungry appeal there. From a Saigon brother, this wasn't to be refused. We summoned two cyclo boys, and they pedaled us towards the river.

Under the cyclo's little hood I relaxed, soothed by the hiss of the tires and the creak of the pedals in the quiet night. Watching Volkov's machine run on in front, glimpsing his rope-yellow head and dark blue shirt when the vehicle turned, I was suddenly content to be carried wherever he chose to lead us. The alchemy of the Nurseryman's stew made the city into a theater, the shop signs in Chinese, Khmer and French becoming tantalizing, cryptic and profound, the latticework on upstairs balconies screening airy and seductive secrets. My cyclo boy pedaled, my cyclo ran on, and I blessed it all, this theater of Phnom Penh, whose sounds were fading as curfew drew near. Here were the actors, just as I remembered them: monkey peddlers, curbside dentists, soothsayers, cigarette makers, dark-faced Khmer hawkers squatting beside braziers, pale-faced Chinese shopkeepers in their doorways, and the beautiful, full-bodied women with their warm, Sino-Indian faces. Radios sounded from glowing caves along the pavement; families reclined on cane chairs there, looking out at the night. Phnom Penh wasn't changed by the war, I said; it was all as it used to be, and the thing that was gathering in the countryside could perhaps be ignored.

But as we neared the river, this illusion faded, together with the effects of the couscous. I couldn't block out the sandbags in front of the public buildings, or the Government propaganda posters showing Communist soldiers beheading and raping civilians, or the crowds of refugees on the pavements and in doorways. They crouched by cardboard-and-thatch huts erected against walls, wearing the dark, funereal pajamas and sarongs of the countryside, and they begged from passersby, here where begging had once been rare. Their brown, half-naked children dodged about under the streetlamps, black hair flying, and I thought they were playing games.

Then I saw that they were catching insects that swarmed in the light, and putting them into jars for food.

"No proper water festival now, Harvey. No Prince Sihanouk to cut the string," Volkov said.

His voice, in deference to the large, dark quiet, was low, husky and drawling. His accent sounded less American now, and more Russian. He sat holding his coffee cup in both hands, looking out over the Mekong.

In the time of the monsoon rains, when the Mekong overflows, its tributary the Tonle Sap performs its annual miracle: it turns around to run backwards. Carrying the Mekong's torrents to the lake from which it takes its name, the river enlarges the lake from a thousand to four thousand square miles. Whole forests are submerged at the country's heart; fish swim among the trees. Then, at the beginning of the dry season, Tonle Sap river flows back to the Mekong. It siphons off the water from the Great Lake and the drowned heartland; it uncovers the underwater forests, leaving fish trapped there by the thousands; it exposes silt-rich acres for rice planting. The river is the engine of Cambodia's bounty, deliverer of fish and rice to the people, and every November, back in the happy sixties, surrounded by dragon boats and fireworks and xylophone music for the river gods, the little Prince would honor Tonle Sap, cutting the magic string that caused it to come back again to the Mekong.

But tonight this seemed a memory of play; a time of Cambodian childishness that would never come again. Reality now was the children catching insects for food, and wartime silence under a high, full moon.

Volkov had brought me to a floating restaurant for our coffee: a gabled houseboat near to the point where the two rivers met. Its verandah was lined with potted shrubs, and connected to the bank by a gangway. The long room was half dark, and half empty. At distant tables were a few other Europeans—probably embassy people—and some middle-class Cambodians: Government officials and their mistresses. We were sitting by a window with open glass louvers; out through the horizontal vents, the brown spaces of the Mekong gleamed in the moonlight. The river was so wide at this point that we could only just make out the opposite shore, with tiny black heads of palms rising miles off against silver sky. Dimly, just for a moment, tracer rounds made soundless green arcs there on the darkness; then stopped.

"Khmer Rouge," Volkov said. "Scaring off ghosts from their camp. Even those bastards believe in ghosts."

By day, the convoys that brought American supplies from Saigon up the Mekong and into the Tonle Sap ran a gauntlet of Khmer Rouge fire from the banks. But tonight everything seemed peaceful: even the tracer fire had looked peaceful. Nearby on the water was the shape of a fishing sampan, its big net hung from a bamboo pole, like a dragonfly's wing. Farther out were the lights of the small, moored ships that were keeping the city alive: battered freighters and South Vietnamese patrol boats, waiting to come in.

"A beautiful night," Volkov said. "In spite of war. Even now, Cambodia is such a beautiful country." He put down his cup, looking out the window. "But why does beauty always bring pain?"

He turned back to me abruptly, as though expecting an answer, and I saw that despite his quietness, he was in one of his frantic states. His eyes had what I thought of as their white look, in the dimness, and I wondered how high he still was from the couscous. "Maybe it doesn't bring you pain at all," he said. "Is that so? You are always so *together,* Harvey."

Suddenly he leaned forward across the table and grasped my wrist. He was wearing his sternly challenging expression, and his eyes searched my face; but his words were incongruously friendly.

"It's good to see you back, brother. Any help you need, you only have to say. Any story that breaks, I will tell you about. You understand? Can I do anything right now?"

I thanked him and told him I needed nothing, and he nodded. He was still holding my wrist, still leaning forward to examine my face as though for clues to something, and despite the space left in my brain by the couscous, I began to feel uncomfortable. We sat frozen in melodramatic tableau: captor and prisoner.

"Tonight I have to talk to you," he said. "Do you understand, Harvey?"

I nodded and waited, and he finally let go of my wrist; but his eyes remained fixed on my face. "You think I am simply stoned," he said. "But I am not; grass doesn't do anything for me now, as a matter of fact. Only opium. Tell me what you've been doing, Harvey, all these years. Tell me how it is in Europe now. I have not been back to Paris for a long time."

I talked to him of my life and coverage in the UK and on the Continent; I suspect that the couscous made me ramble, but he listened with absolute intentness, interrupting only to ask questions. He gave the same intensity to listening as he did to speaking, and seemed to find my affairs more absorbing than I did myself—as though there were other meanings there than I'd realized. He'd always been like that. When I tailed off he sat nodding, like a doctor considering a diagnosis. Then he said: "There are things I want to tell you, Harvey. Tonight is the time to talk in this way, and perhaps not again. These are things I cannot speak of to the others—not even to Mike. And I know you will offer wise opinion—or at least you will hear me with understanding. You are a man of special sympathy and intelligence, and I greatly respect you for it. Yes! Don't deny it. You wriggle with Anglo-Saxon embarrassment, but it's true."

He laughed under his breath, his pale blue stare widening, his pupils hectic dots. "You have always been sane, Harvey," he said. "I knew this in Saigon days. The rest of us are not, as a matter of fact. Only you are sane, with solid marriage. You are a good man, I know this." He leaned towards me again, waving away possible objections. "You *wept* tonight, in Pagoda! You wept for Cambodian people. And you will weep a lot more, before things are over."

His voice had become increasingly resonant: unlike the rest of us, he didn't need stimulants to get to this exalted level of his, and maybe he told the truth when he said that the couscous wasn't its cause. But the agitation that I now saw accompanying it seemed unusual even for Dmitri; I could almost sense him trembling. I couldn't read the agitation's cause; couldn't even decide whether it sprang from elation or distress. I only knew that he needed my company.

"We spoke of beauty," he said, and waved a hand at the louvers. "Beauty is what we all secretly want, you agree? Beauty leads us on, Harvey, and for some of us presumably it brings satisfaction; peace. But for others, like me—" He broke off and sat back, still staring at me, his stretched mouth open in a smile that mingled cold amusement and outrage; then he went on more quietly. "Beauty mainly torments us, as a matter of fact. Beauty is very small point of light on horizon we can never reach; beauty is the sound we can never hear. And yet we go on pining for it, and can never stop. Yes, Harvey: beauty! Unfashionable concept, now. Even *word* has gone out of fashion among current fuckwit intellectuals. But beauty is all that matters, under everything. Beauty is opening to that world we can never see, but know is there—always nearby, like something through a screen—if we have a soul. But how many have souls? Do you know there are people *without* them, Harvey? Or with souls that have dried up, like corpses of insects?"

It seemed to be my night for being subjected to passionate dissertations. There were so many things that my friends wanted me to know, now that I'd reappeared: perhaps it sprang from the nature of the war here, and the nature of their existence in a beleaguered city. They needed a fresh slate to write on, in order to explain things to themselves—and just now, I was the slate. It was flattering but somewhat demanding, in my present dysfunctional state; even when Volkov's fury was merely a fury of the spirit, it was somehow more intense than the emotions of others —even Trevor Griffiths. And yet I liked him, even when I half despaired of him.

He was looking at the table now, and his voice had suddenly dropped, becoming flat and sober. "But there are those who love beauty too much," he said. "Bad mistake."

Only if beauty's an illusion, I suggested.

He looked up, clenching and unclenching one fist on the table in front of him. "You think? Possibly you are right. Anyway, for this illusion I would have been prepared to do anything. Anything. I am speaking of my recent marriage."

There was now not long until curfew. I'd been told that unpredictable Government soldiers were liable to shoot at you in the streets after that, but I knew better than to suggest that we should go at this stage. "I heard about your marriage, Count," I said. "I'm sorry."

He lit one of his Gauloise cigarettes, sat back in his chair, and stared at the river in silence. When he resumed speaking, he went on looking out through the louvers, one elbow propped on the table, cigarette poised, his voice taking on the throaty, gliding sound I thought of as Russian.

"Always I have chased after beauty. Beauty of women; beauty of action. But I do not picture myself as noble and spiritual person,

Harvey. I am a sensual man; I live and die by the senses. All my life I have been an asshole; woman-chaser; bully. Well, you know that, from Saigon—you know about my sex life and my fights. When I was young, I let down my parents by quitting Sorbonne. They had seen me as scholar and intellectual: ornament to the family. Bad investment, that." He drew on the cigarette. "My first marriage when I was young I also blew. She was good French girl, but I wasn't in love with her—and she has not really liked me, as things turned out. It lasted one year: then I went off to United States. I am not proud of this. But nothing, no one, satisfied me." He widened his mouth, released smoke and squinted at me. "Does it come from God, the hunger for beauty—or some bloody demon? I am Russian Orthodox—still a believer, as a matter of fact, although not going to church. When I was young, I knew all the time that God was there. I looked always for goodness—because it was so hard to find in myself. And *I wanted to fly*—but not in any dimension of reality: can you understand? I would see below me a landscape of lights, and a wind would rush past my ears. I would remember the poem by Alexander Blok—a revolutionary, but nevertheless great Russian poet:

> *The wind, the wind!*
> *It will not let you go.*
> *The wind, the wind!*
> *Through God's whole world it blows.*

"What I am saying is: *I always wanted life to be like that.* I wanted to smash down door; to dive through space of air that separates us from that other life. Now I am forty, and I still feel that way: that is my problem. Bloody silly bastard, you will say. Yes: silly bastard. But sometimes, filming combat still gives me that. And music always gives me that: Beethoven, Rimsky-Korsakov, Beatles—it doesn't matter; there are only two kinds of music, good and bad, as the great Duke Ellington has said. In both music and action is something eternal, Harvey—and we want what is eternal."

He poured the last of the pot of coffee slowly into our cups.

"For a time," he said, "with this woman that I married, whose name I still can't say, and who was beautiful in way very few are—for a time love gave me that. It was first time in my life I had truly been in love. Came to me after some delay—at age thirty-eight." He glanced at me sideways, perhaps suspecting he'd find amusement in my face; reassured when he didn't, he went on. "I had found at last the woman I had always searched for without knowing it—or so I thought. Everything exquisite—even her hands and feet. I have read that in poetry, and not understood it: who cares for hands and feet? When you love like that, you understand. But what I had also found was ice: the beauty of ice."

He drew on his cigarette again and was silent, closing his eyes; then he leaned forward. "Listen to me, Harvey. To die here in Cambodia is now very easy; can happen any time. Maybe it happens to me soon; maybe not. This is just a fact, and no big deal —I think you know that. And because it is the fact we live with, I want to tell you these things tonight." He paused, looking into his coffee. "You guys take the mickey, and call me Count. I am not one, of course, but as a matter of fact my grandfather Alexis was. Small-time nobility in czarist days—it didn't mean much, even then. The family wasn't rich; had no big estates: he was government official. When he fled with his family to Paris from the Revolution, my father Peter was fifteen: old enough to know what he was losing, and to remember it for rest of his life. He made me remember it too—so I have always lived with memory of Holy Russia. Memory that is not my own: a dream. This is incurable, Harvey: it was introduced from birth! Dreams are what White Russians feed on, along with their goddamn borscht and piroshkis. French citizens but never French, they waited always to go back—for Communists to fall. Can you imagine that? Imagine it! Russian cathedral in Paris on Sundays: Orthodox service, with male choir singing music from heaven. And opposite, a Russian tea shop where we would go afterwards to eat pastries, all in our best clothes. The women looking beautiful. There were all the faces: the Russian faces. The poor lost bloody nobility, and the ones who were pretending to be."

He drank down the last of his coffee.

"Holy Russia itself is a dream; yes. It never existed," he said. "And this dream made my father unable to be happy. He was low-grade clerk in French civil service; the goddamn Frogs were never going to promote him. To them, we were never French. His life in spare time was given to politics: sad fairy-story politics of White Russian groups, having secret meetings about what could never happen: overthrow of goddamn Soviets! *Mon Dieu.* It will last a hundred years, that bloody system. He wasn't a strong man; he died young—starved of his dreams. I am angry about my father. Don't misunderstand: I hate all tyrannies—not just Soviet. Nazis were in Paris when I was a boy, and I hated them. But Nazis are gone now: gone since Hitler died in the bunker. So why do so many goddamn Western intellectuals not hate this other tyranny as much, which goes on liquidating millions? Why don't they weep for those who are rotting right now in Soviet's Arctic camps? I will tell you: because they only *pretend* to hate tyranny. In their hearts, they love tyrannies that suit them. The bastards love power, and want some of it to rub off on them."

He stubbed out his cigarette, looking through the louvers.

"Despite all this, I would not play political dream games my father played. No politics. When I learned to use a camera, I had found a way to run on the edge of such things: on the edge of what was happening in the world, and not fall in. I merely put *consequences* of politics on film: a cameraman is not involved, right? But he is inconvenient witness."

It was some moments before he spoke again. When he did, it was so softly I could only just hear.

"Linda told me I could not be employed any other way: useless for anything else. I had found a way to be paid for living life of a madman, she said. She put it charmingly, wouldn't you say, Harvey?"

"So that was her name," I said. "Linda."

He made no answer, but continued to look out at the river under the moon. The net on the sampan was swinging a little, in a light wind. It was five minutes past curfew now, and the other tables had emptied; only one white-coated Cambodian waiter was left here, looking at us nervously from the shadows by the cash desk and no doubt hoping we'd go. But Dmitri had begun to speak again, lighting another Gauloise, still not looking at me.

"A beautiful American," he said; and now I could only just catch his words. "A Minnesota Swede. Worked with embassy in Saigon when we met. Perfectly groomed, perfect clothes—even her apartment perfect. Thirty-five: divorced, no children, ambitious and fastidious. Right? Wanted nothing in life to be messy. Yes, I know, all wrong for me. Jim Feng knew; Mike knew; *I* knew. Why does love choose wrong person for us? How can we ever know that? Maybe who we love is the ghost of someone else, loved in some other existence, in body of wrong man, wrong woman. Have you ever thought of that?"

I waited, and he studied the coal of his cigarette. "I never loved anyone like this," he said. "Loved even her clothes, hanging on a chair."

And you married her, I said.

"We married, we went to Washington because she wanted. She had been appointed to big post in State Department there. She asked that I come and get a nice television job in Washington: she would not be married to a man who could die any morning, any afternoon. This was reasonable. I too wanted a safe life now, with her. Wanted everything: security; a child. So I did all she wanted: gave up covering combat, gave up Vietnam." He laughed under his breath. "None of it worked, Harvey—and I was not safe at all, as a matter of fact. I was in far more dangerous and destructive life than before, which in less than two years made me almost wipe out what is left of my brain."

He broke off and leaned back in his chair, narrowing his eyes at Tonle Sap's far shore. Another green arc of tracer went up, but neither of us commented. When he spoke again, his voice was matter-of-fact and toneless.

"You can have a woman and not have her," he said. "I had not experienced this before. Only her body is there—and you have not really possessed that either. I have asked myself: why did she marry me? Still I'm not sure; but perhaps for some reason she has seen me as someone she can change and fit into her life, to be there when it suits her—and only when it suits. We were going to have child when it suited—but this didn't happen. I would come back to the apartment many nights, and she would be out at meeting or function, and I would go out into fucking Washington and get drunk. I became a very big drunk, Harvey. My performances in Saigon were not in same league as this. Some of these performances were given at formal dinners she took me to: at goddamn diplomatic receptions. I did not fit in; made some bad scenes, I'm afraid. She kept saying I was of impossible temperament: that I was exaggerated; *too much*. Am I too much, Harvey?" He gave me his open-mouthed smile.

"Your friends wouldn't say so, Dmitri."

"Diplomatic answer, bald one," he said. "I ask myself, why did she ever marry me? Answer: because when we met, I was combat cameraman for CBS, my stuff on American prime-time news every week—and that had glamour for her. She liked what was glamorous. But now I was just a lousy news cinecameraman in Washington, shooting fires and police drug busts: not so impressive."

She didn't like what she'd turned you into, I suggested.

But he stared past me, his face blank, appearing not to hear. "We had a little Persian cat," he said. "Our quarreling frightened it, and it ran away. When it went, I knew love was gone. And so I came back to Indochina to do all I am good for: covering battle." He looked at me. "*Why*, Harvey? Why do men and women quarrel? When to love each other is greatest thing in life? I have worked it out; I'll tell you for nothing. Because each wants the other to be *someone else*."

He stood abruptly, smiling as though he'd concluded a successful meeting; then he put a hand on my shoulder. "I'm sorry, brother—you are very patient, but you are stoned courtesy of Nurseryman, and I have selfishly kept you from bed and in danger of military patrols. You are looking at your watch: yes, it's past curfew, I know. Don't worry. We'll go back to Royal up middle of the road, talking loudly: that way, troops know we are press."

We walked along the path above the river: deserted, because of the curfew. The fronds of a line of tall coconut palms hissed in a little breeze above our heads; dim lights showed in the small wooden houses on stilts on the banks. Somewhere a radio was playing Cambodian pop music, carrying across the great expanse of water.

Volkov opened his arms wide, as though embracing the darkness and the river odors, sweet and sour. "Aren't you glad you stayed awake, man, even if we get shot at? Look at this old Khmer night: full of flower smells, full of sex, full of trouble!"

He was now swinging back towards joy. Joy was Dmitri's for the asking, I thought: but never peace.

TWO
THE NOON HUSH

1.

Jim Feng pushes aside a bottle of soy sauce and slides a black-and-white photograph across the table. It's the usual news-style print, six by eight inches.

"I found this last night at the bottom of a carton," he tells me. "I took it at the Phnom Penh Press Center one morning in February, in 1973. It's probably the last picture taken of Mike and Dmitri together. And certainly the only one of the two of them with Ly Keang. I have not said this to you before, Ray: but I believe that she is the real reason that Mike has gone across the border."

He glances at Harvey, who sits beside him. But Harvey's expression remains noncommittal: he plays with the soy sauce bottle, examining it as though for flaws.

In the picture, Langford and Volkov are standing on either side of a young Cambodian woman. I know of her from the audio diary, of course, but have not seen a picture of her until now: there were none among Mike's effects. I examine the photograph with interest. The three are posed in front of formal stone gate-posts, through which a nineteenth-century French colonial villa can be seen. Ly Keang proves to be as attractive as I've expected. She wears traditional dress: a white, high-necked blouse and a dark ankle-length sarong with an embroidered band around the hem. Her thick, loosely waving hair is pulled back from the forehead and temples to expose her ears; held by a comb on top and then falling below her shoulders, it combines with her slender, hour-glass figure to recall an *apsaras* in a temple carving. The men, who are dressed in well-pressed sports shirts and slacks, are both in half-profile, turning to smile at her as though someone has just told a good joke. But she isn't laughing at the joke; instead, she looks directly at the camera, her expression enigmatically solemn: even sad.

While I study the picture, Jim and Harvey watch me from the other side of the table. Although Jim doesn't get in here to talk to me as often as Harvey does, both faces have grown very familiar, in these long afternoons in the Newsroom; I've only been in Bangkok for a week, but I feel I've known them both for much longer.

"So you think she's still alive," I say. "Somewhere inside Cambodia."

Jim nods slowly a number of times. "She and Mike had only two years together," he says. "Mike has never believed she's gone; has never given up. Yes: I feel sure this is why he is in there, Ray—even though I have nothing to prove it."

Jim's use of the present tense when he speaks of Mike always makes me uneasy. I'm not sure whether he does it out of conviction, or with the stubborn, irrational idea that even to concede that Mike might be dead would finally end all hope.

The lunchtime crowd has thinned. It's around three o'clock: quiet, except for the buzz of traffic beyond the sunblinds, out on the road by the *klong*. The little fans whirr more distinctly in the ceiling, now that most of the voices have gone. Harvey looks at the photograph, straightening it on the white Formica with a big, careful thumb.

"What a lot of loss Mike had, over a lifetime," he says. "And finally Ly Keang lost as well. Swallowed by Year Zero."

"Yes," I say. "But I wonder did loss choose him, or did he choose loss?"

My question is semi-rhetorical—out of habit. Harvey and I, in our sessions here alone, have both fallen into this mode when we analyze Langford and his fate. But now I see Jim studying us—first Harvey, then me—with an unwinking Chinese steadiness that makes me a little uncomfortable. Anything that sounds like criticism of Mike makes him uneasy: his loyalty is total. He has the sort of decency and old-fashioned devotion that causes you to be careful of your words, and to guard against gossip. But Harvey and I, being story-lovers, are both inclined to wander into gossip's territories. Despite our respective professions—or is it because of them?—both of us are subscribers to the notion that falsehood and truth, triviality and tragedy, all have their roots there.

"I think loss chose *him*," Harvey says. "So maybe he was right to run away from it."

"Bloody nonsense," Jim says, and frowns. "Mike met the right woman late in his life, and then lost her. That's all. In my case, I also have met the right woman late—but I have married Lu Ying, and not lost her. I have been more fortunate."

Harvey and I are silent for a moment, rebuked, looking into our beers. He and I still grieve for Langford, but our search for him has changed. Seeing him as almost certainly dead, what we want is to solve his mystery. But Jim's determination not to give him up to death has made this indecent; premature.

The phone rings on the counter by the cash register, and the Chinese proprietress picks it up.

"You're right of course, Jim," Harvey says. His voice has taken on its mollifying tone. "Ly Keang could still be alive, and so could Mike. No one hopes so more than I do."

The Chinese proprietress is holding the telephone receiver aloft, and calling to our table. Her upswept glasses flash. "For you, Mr. Feng. London on."

Jim Feng has gone; the phone call has caused him to limp back across the square to the Telenews office. But Harvey and I sit on.

I suppose we've grown a little self-enclosed in the Newsroom, after a week of talk-filled afternoons: a little obsessive. Tented by

the glowing orange sunblinds, the fervid glare from outside filtered and softened for us as time softens memory, we're absorbed
in a sort of theater, with Langford as our leading player: a player
whose physical actuality we accept as being less and less likely.
Because of this, our talk has taken on the coloring of postmortem;
of valedictory. Now, uninhibited by Jim's presence, we're free to
let it flow into these channels again.

"Mike was always trying to *replace* things," Harvey says. "I
can see why, can't you? Loss kept dogging his footsteps. The
favorite brother and the mother dying when he was young; the
girl he wanted to marry as a boy disappearing. And then he lost
Kim Anh, when he first came to Vietnam. So he probably decided
after that to take no more chances: no more serious involvements
meant no more loss. Bar girls were safe; they were transient; not
serious. His one serious anchor was the friendship with Madame
Phan. He was still visiting her in Saigon until the end. A sort of
wise aunt, I suppose."

We've ordered fresh beers, and he takes a long draught.

"I used to think that Mike really only knew where he was
with other men," he says. "With battle companions. And he could
always deal easily with Asian children: with his orphans and street
kids. Involved yet uninvolved. He was still like that in the year
that I arrived in Phnom Penh. And he was leading a secret life
there rather like the one he'd led in Saigon. At least, I thought
of it as secret. But there was nothing particularly furtive about
it—he just didn't talk about it much. It was simply that he lived
an off-hours existence that was separate from his professional
one—and separate as well from the one he spent carousing with
us. It was a life that brought him close to the local people, revolving around that apartment he rented from his driver Lay
Vora, in the house near the Old Market.

"If you called on him—which I sometimes did—he'd be perfectly affable: he wasn't inhospitable or evasive. But somehow you
didn't feel encouraged to seek him out there, even though it was
only five minutes from the Hotel le Royal. Not many of his colleagues could understand his choosing to live in a place like that,
when he could have afforded much better. The plumbing was

pretty primitive in those old Chinese houses; we preferred the comforts of places like the Royal.

"The house was one of a series in a terrace, with the usual upstairs balconies and shutters. Vora and his wife, Bopha, ran a small photographic business in the ground floor, open to the street: I remember portraits on a board, and cane chairs for customers. Eventually I discovered that Langford had given them the capital to start the business. They had two teenage sons and a small daughter, and Langford was also paying for the boys to be educated at the best *lycée* in Phnom Penh. It was Vora who told me all this, when I got to know him: Mike never mentioned it. Vora doted on him, of course; and he and Bopha and their children had become Mike's surrogate family. Langford ate most of his meals with them, and I suspect spent as much time in their apartment as he did in his own.

"And I began to discover that his philanthropy was no longer casual now, but constant and systematic. He was looking after a large number of street kids: successors to his tribe on Tu Do Street. These were the children of the refugees who were pouring into the city from the countryside, and he was paying some Buddhist monks to give them refuge in a pagoda. He was making a lot of money with his pictures at that time, but I don't believe he ever saved anything. Certainly there was no evidence of it, except for Black Bessie.

"That apartment was the only home of his own Langford ever had. The house here in Bangkok doesn't count; he was hardly ever there. In a way I can understand his attachment to Vora's place: the Old Market was an attractive locality. It was between Norodom Boulevard and Post Office Square: a district that was a sort of axis. When you came onto Norodom, you could pick out at its far-off end the little green cone from which the city took its name: the Phnom of Penh, or Madame Penh's Hill, with the worn old Buddhist stupa on top of it, like a memory. Norodom and Monivong Boulevards stretched away together, reaching towards riverine distances that ached in the brain. Metropolitan boulevards in a country town! Parisian in their scale yet always half-empty, punctuated by flame trees, cyclos pedaling at their edges, Norodom and Monivong waited for grandeur to arrive. What they'd get in the end would be terror.

"The Old Market itself was a complex of iron-roofed buildings and little green kiosks behind railings, selling everything from flowers and fruit to notebooks, pencils and clothing. Chinese shops dealt in tea, dried meats and pastries. The combined scents made you tipsy; the colored mountains of produce hurt your eyes. Rambutans, durians, mangoes, oranges, bunches of lotus buds: Cambodia's horn of plenty, not yet run dry. Market officials collected the rents, and most of the stalls were run by Chinese or Sino-Khmers. They sat looking out from their kiosks with their faces whitened by sun screen paste: Langford used to say that this was intended to distinguish them from the dark brown Khmer peasants who traded outside the railings. The Khmers were trading there illegally, setting up tiny pavement stalls that held offerings of fruit and fish, their lamps burning there at evening like those on obscure shrines. When the military police appeared, they'd gather up their goods and run, and Langford used to like watching this comedy from his balcony.

"He'd sit there for hours on that balcony, surveying the whole life of the district. He clearly loved the apartment, and his life with Vora's family. And when people pointed out to him that he could lose it all at any time, he showed an odd blind spot. Cambodia wouldn't fall, he'd say; and even if it did, he'd never leave. He'd become like a lover: unable to accept that some final disaster could happen to deprive him of the loved one.

"The apartment was a statement; a confirmation. He'd furnished it himself, and a good many personal effects had been shipped up the Mekong from Saigon—including a collection of wood carvings, bronzes and paintings, selected with the help of Madame Phan. In his spare hours there, I see him as rather solitary; almost domestic. That's the last way most people see a war photographer like Langford, of course; but it was true. The place was so incredibly neat. Cage birds out on the balcony; his Vietnamese and Cambodian artifacts arranged to advantage. Even a Burmese cat, called Sary. His papers, his photographs, his customs declarations and work diaries—all organized as though by a neat secretary. Well, Ly Keang changed all that."

Harvey looks down at the photograph again, which still lies between us: at the laughing, black-and-white faces of Langford and Volkov; at the solemn face of the young woman.

"The Battambang Stringer," he says, and lets out a soft breath of laughter, affectionate and regretful. "She was a one-off. I can understand how Mike felt about her." He points with his big finger. "Look at that face," he says. "It's all there."

It's a shrewd, compelling face, as well as being attractive: strong yet delicate, with a wide, humorous mouth. Her exposed, well-shaped ears create a schoolgirlish touch: I would have thought her a girl of seventeen or eighteen, rather than a young woman of twenty-four. She's typically Sino-Khmer, I'll discover; it's my ignorance of Cambodian characteristics that have made me see her as Indian. Probably the large, expressive eyes—which stare at me directly—do most to create the impression of Indian ancestry, despite their Chinese almond shape. She's let her eyelids droop a little, and looks up under them with what seems a hint of mockery as well as sadness, leaving white half-moons exposed under the irises. Her long upper lip is drawn down taut. It's a curious expression: is she actually sad, or just serious?

"She doesn't look happy," I say.

"Look again," Harvey says. "There's a joke behind this picture: Jim told me. Ly Keang was hardly ever serious. Mike always said that she laughed and fooled so much that she wouldn't be able to stop laughing while this photograph was taken. He made a bet with her that she couldn't. So this is her attempt at a hang-dog look: but you can still see her fighting back a giggle."

He puts down his beer, and stares through the iron grille.

"She was a friend of Volkov's at first," he says. "But only a friend. I think both he and Langford had the idea that through Ly Keang, they could tune in to Cambodia at some special level. And she'd probably have encouraged the notion—like a game. Most things were a game, with the Stringer."

2.

HARVEY DRUMMOND

For some weeks after I arrived in Phnom Penh, she was just a nickname I kept hearing at the Press Center: the Battambang Stringer.

It was a title that began as a joke, and that was how I pictured her, at first: as a joker; a tearaway. But that was because I hadn't yet met her. By February, coverage had become very demanding: the B-52 bombing by the U.S. Seventh Air Force, flying out of Thailand, had begun again on a massive scale, and few of us had much time for social life.

She was a young local journalist, working on a Cambodian-language paper—but she had a yen to be a foreign correspondent. She came from the Cambodian middle class: her father had been an army officer up in Battambang. I gathered that he'd been killed in action, and that she now lived with relatives in Phnom Penh. She'd finished her education at a good *lycée* here, and both her French and her English were fluent. She hung about Western correspondents and photographers at the Press Center; I don't think she spent much time at her paper. The words most used about her among my colleagues were "crazy" and "zany"—but a lot of Cambodian girls had that kind of sense of humor, and I'd eventually find that this didn't really sum her up.

For some reason—mainly as a joke, I think—she took it into her head that although she was a print journalist, she wanted to learn to use cameras; even cinecameras. And Volkov was the one who enabled her to do it.

Until then, she'd just been nicknamed "Battambang." The crowd at the Press Center had called her this because of her pride in her native province, which is up in the western tip of Cambodia, near the Thai border: the richest region in the country for rice growing. Highway 5, the Rice Road, was now cut so often by the Khmer Rouge that she could rarely visit her mother and her childhood home, and this made her even more nostalgic. She was always saying how beautiful Battambang was, and how much better than Phnom Penh; we used to make fun of her about it. It was only when Volkov decided to take her with him into the field a few times—and on one famous occasion actually sent her out to get film on her own—that the "Stringer" component was added to her nickname.

This was a fairly extraordinary thing for Volkov to have done. He was risking her life, of course, but he claimed she was always pestering him to let her use a camera, and was very persuasive. CBS had ordered him on a trip to Saigon in a week when Khmer Rouge attacks were happening closer and closer to Phnom Penh; big stories were possible here, and he was going to miss them. So he asked Ly Keang to try and get him film while he was out of town. He didn't expect her to haul his big sound camera to the front; he showed her how to work the little Bell and Howell. Well, we often hired male Cambodian photographers as stringers, but never women, in those days; so sending Ly Keang out was seen as extraordinary or outrageous, depending on your point of view.

But she pulled it off. Action broke out on Highway 1, and she rode out in a taxi and got good footage, which CBS used. The Count claimed payment for her as a stringer, and it made her something of a celebrity around the Press Center.

That was where I first saw her.

The Phnom Penh Press Center was located in the courtyard of an old French villa off a side street in the middle of town. You can see the villa in Jim's photograph: it was the Cambodian Government's Military Information Office, and the Press Center itself was a long shed of woven bamboo featuring a bulletin board for military communiqués. It's hidden in the picture by those trees. We'd assemble there in the mornings; in the evenings, we'd sometimes go back there to hear Colonel Am Rong give one of his notorious briefings.

I can't remember all the jokes that were made about that name. Am Rong's plump face was always inappropriately smiling;

he was an ex–film director for Prince Sihanouk, and spoke in French of battles of the imagination rather than those that had really taken place. His were medieval encounters, like those that had been fought in his films about the kings of ancient Angkor, and in these accounts, the Republic's army was ever-victorious. With one of the most formidable guerrilla forces in history closing its circle around the capital tighter every month, this would have been funny if it hadn't been desperate—and if journalists hadn't been dying because of Am Rong's confident assertions that the Government held territory it had already lost. The translations of the briefings into English were made by a sensitive-looking young Cambodian with curly hair who we discovered was a noted poet; he had an air of quiet desperation, and his glances told us to believe nothing of what he was being made to say.

The Press Center sold breakfast, and we sat at rough wooden tables spangled with leaf-shade, over *croque monsieur* and bacon and eggs and coffee. Now that the Khmer Rouge had rejected the Paris peace overtures, and the B-52 bombing had begun again, a fresh wave from the international press was pouring into Phnom Penh, and many famous names could be seen here at breakfast: heavies from the New York and London dailies and the television networks. Some of these new arrivals were a little impatient and self-important, and my first sight of Ly Keang is associated with one of them.

I was sitting with Bill Wall, who suddenly put his coffee down, and jerked his head.

"There's the Stringer. God, that gal's attractive. If the Count wasn't so interested in her, and I wasn't married, I'd be trying to cut him out."

She'd just come up the drive and was moving among the tables, greeting first one acquaintance and then another. All the journalists she spoke to, male and female, were laughing by the time she moved on. She wore green combat fatigues and jungle boots: she would have looked like a Cambodian female soldier, except that the fatigues were a little too well cut. She was bare-headed, and the long, cascading hair shone blue black in the sun, swinging as she turned her head from side to side, no doubt looking for Volkov. All her movements were quick and energetic.

Then there was a shout from the driveway. Dmitri had appeared and was urgently gesturing to her: he seemed to be in a hurry to get off, and I guessed that he had a car or taxi waiting, and was taking Ly Keang to the action. She waved and began to move towards him between the tables, still speaking to people she knew. At the last table sat a *New York Times* correspondent who was fairly new here, and whom I found somewhat pompous: Broinowski, his name was. He had a brown Vandyke beard and the air of a noted intellectual forced to analyze tragedies whose implications could scarcely be comprehended by gross lesser mortals: which meant most of us. He wore a panama hat. Unlike the ruined specimen worn by Hubert Whatley, this panama was new and shining and stylishly slanted, and it attracted the Stringer's attention. She snatched it from Broinowski's head and put it on and posed for him, smiling. It looked very good on her.

He managed a pained smile, looking up at her. We were too far away for me to hear anything, but from the gesture she made, I guessed that Ly Keang was asking him to let her keep the hat. He shook his head and half rose, reaching for it, his face growing uneasy. But Ly Keang also shook her head, turned, and ran down the drive, holding the panama on with one hand.

Clapping and laughter rose from the tables: people were amused by Broinowski's evident annoyance. The waiting Volkov also looked amused, and it was evident that Broinowski's panama was in danger of going to the front.

The man had no sense of humor. His desire to get his hat back far outweighed his sense of dignity, and he shouted and ran down the drive after the Stringer. Cheers and more laughter greeted this. I imagined Ly Keang would relent, as she looked over her shoulder; but instead she increased her pace. Reaching Volkov, she took his hand and dragged him along with her. They both ran through the gates, and Broinowski disappeared after them. A few minutes later he was seen returning, red in the face and hatless, and was greeted by a round of clapping. I heard later that his hat reappeared the next day in his room at the Royal, unmarked, accompanied by a bunch of flowers.

That was my first sight of Ly Keang. There could be no doubt that she was different.

"She makes me go on hoping for Cambodia," Volkov said. "Even now, with Khmer Rouge all around the city. If there were more like Ly Keang, they would never win. A crazy optimist—and a genuine patriot. This is a remarkable girl, Harvey. Intelligent. Fearless. Full of electricity. And she makes me laugh."

We were eating breakfast together in the bistro of the Hotel le Royal. The bistro was a reassuring place, with its fragrances of croissants and coffee and its white-jacketed Chinese waiters. They spoke only French, but were friendly and attentive, creating the illusion for me each morning that I was back in the sixties or earlier; that the war didn't seriously exist. The bistro opened onto a terrace that overlooked the garden and the swimming pool— whose reclining chairs, tables and umbrellas had once been the undisputed preserve of Phnom Penh's French community. Now, most of the chairs and the pool had been commandeered by the hordes of invading correspondents, and the few remaining French had retreated to one end, where they pointedly ignored the barbarians.

I asked Dmitri the obvious question. Was he romantically interested in Ly Keang?

He looked at me, chewing, his eyes gone blank as metal. "No. That bank account is spent," he said. His tone warned me against pursuing the subject, and we both went on eating in silence.

When he'd finished his croissant, he brushed away crumbs with his napkin, picked up his coffee and addressed me again.

"Anyway, she is too young. And this is a respectable girl, Harvey. You know what Cambodian middle class are like: if a woman sleeps with men before marriage—especially Westerners —she is ruined. It's the nineteenth century here. She is watched. She lives with aunt and uncle, and is in contact with friends of her father's high up in Army circles, who seem to take paternal interest in her. Ly Keang is a young woman of spirit, who will do anything—but I would say she is quite possibly virgin." His stare forbade me to disagree. "First woman I have ever been friends with—not a lover. For me she is simply a comrade; a daughter; a battle companion."

"*Battle* companion? Jesus, brother, be careful with her," I said.

He shrugged. "What she wants to do, she does. Try and stop her."

He looked out over the pool, where the Nurseryman could be seen swimming on his back, belly curving majestically towards the sky. He followed the Nurseryman's progress as he spoke.

"She is always asking me questions about Mike Langford," he said. "Wants to know about his work, his views, everything. Always looking out for him at the Press Center. Admires him. She sees his pictures as big propaganda influence, to help the world notice what is happening here, and to cause Americans to send back their troops. She is serious about this. Well, she is young idealist." He looked back at me. "She has already been to visit him, in that shophouse apartment of his. Her interest is professional, I know this—but I am hoping it remains that way. That apartment is goddamn love nest, right? Langford has whole life there he keeps hidden. Ly Keang is special, and Snow never stays with any woman. Don't want to see her hurt."

3.

A color photograph of Langford sitting on the balcony of his apartment. Taken by someone unknown: Vora, perhaps. The latticework at the end of the balcony and the fronds of a palm tree that reach up here from the street cast a dream-grid of shadows. The calligraphy of eternal Holiday; of old Cambodia.

Mike is enthroned in an outsize rattan rocking chair the back of which is like a fan: a Manila chair, as they used to be called. Dressed in a loud red shirt and blue cotton trousers, he smiles at something out of sight, his expression sleepy and content.

The voice on the tapes has altered a little now, as voices do when first youth is gone. It's deeper, slower, a little less eager; but the chords of expectancy are still there. He'd always be expectant.

TAPE 42, MARCH 19TH, 1973

 —Ly Keang came here last night, at about seven o'clock.

 —I was sitting in the rocking chair, just outside the doors that open onto the balcony. Dusk. The Khmer traders were lighting their petrol lamps, across by the railings of the Old Market. Couldn't see around the high back of the chair, so I didn't see her come into the room behind me.

 —I knocked but you didn't hear, she said. Excuse me.

 —That was the first thing I heard: the voice. It's a voice you wouldn't mistake: drawling, and perhaps you'd call it flat. But attractive: a special energy underneath.

 —She was standing just inside the doorway to the balcony. I got up and came into the room and we stood facing each other.

 —Dmitri gave me your address. And Lay Vora said I could come up, she said. Your front door was open.

 —It's usually open, I said.

 —It was half dark in the room, and in this light the irises of her eyes were very black, the whites very white. She was half-smiling, with a little twist to her mouth. She wore a white blouse, and one of those tailored Cambodian sarongs that outline the hips: indigo blue, and held by a heavy silver belt. She has beautiful hips: it was hard not to look at them. Instead of telling me why she'd come, she said: I have interrupted your thinking, Mike.

 —No, I wasn't thinking at all, I told her. Just watching the street traders light their lamps. The police chase them off, but they always come back. They steal aviation fuel for their lamps, and sometimes the lamps explode. They get scars on their faces like napalm burns—but they never learn.

 —She laughed. I thought she might tell me now why she'd come; but she didn't. She looked out the door at the lights.

 —I like this time of day, she said, when everyone is getting ready for the night. It was once a beautiful city at all times of day—but now it gets sad, with the refugee huts everywhere. I'd like to leave: I get more and more homesick lately.

 —For Battambang? I said. Isn't that in the Wild West?

 —I was taking the mickey, but she didn't mind: she smiled. You should go at rice harvest, she said. The plains are gold, and you can see for miles.

Everyone is working together, all carrying bundles of rice, even the small children. And always the mountains in the distance. When I was a child my father told me that *neak taa* lived in those mountains: the forest spirits the farmers believe in.

—I was about to offer her a chair; but now she started to walk about the room, looking at things. Every so often, light glinted on the silver belt. I waited to see what she wanted. It was quiet, and a few cyclo bells and the shouts of kids came up from below in the street. She stopped and turned to me, and said: Don't you also miss your home?

—Sometimes I do, I said. Sometimes I miss the coolness, and the peace. But Cambodia's my home now. I love it here.

—She frowned and cocked her head, and her tone got serious and sharp. You love Cambodia? Why do you love Cambodia? How can you love Cambodia? A country not your own. Is that possible?

—I told her that I'd felt like this from the first time I'd come here. It wasn't easy to say why: I felt I'd always been meant to come to Cambodia. I liked the countryside; I liked the Khmer people; I liked the army troops I spent my days with. We understand each other, I said.

—That's because you're from a farm, she said. Here we'd call you a buffalo boy.

—I laughed, and so did she. For a moment we stood looking at each other, saying nothing. I had a sudden hollowing in the stomach: something that only happens to me nowadays in a firefight. Still she didn't say what she wanted. She'd stopped in front of my big Khmer sandstone sculpture of the Goddess of Fortune: the best piece I have. This is a nice Lakshmi, she said, and looked at me over her shoulder.

—Again there was a silence that neither of us broke. She was looking at me as though seeing me for the first time; as though she was digesting some surprise. But perhaps I imagined it—or wanted to imagine it. From down in the street, the voices of kids, car engines and cyclo bells still floated up. I reminded myself that this was the Stringer: a girl of only twenty-four, inclined to act the clown: Dmitri's friend, and much too young for either of us. In all the months that she and I had been running into each other at the Press Center—usually with Dmitri there too—there'd been no warning of what was happening now. In the half-dark, I was looking at a woman I'd never seen before. Beautiful: so beautiful. She'd changed everything around her, making the air in the room seem to sing. A strand of hair had come away from the comb on top of her head and hung down her cheek; I wanted to push it back.

—She cleared her throat, and looked at the Lakshmi again. A pity she's lost an arm, she said, and her voice sounded smaller, as if it came from a distance. Does she bring you luck?

—I believe so, I said. I touch her every time I leave to go into the field.

—You're superstitious. But perhaps Lakshmi does look after you, she said. That's why you're *Mean Samnang*. Isn't that what the soldiers call you?

—She went on moving about the room, still not saying why she'd called. I had prints of some of my recent pictures pinned to a board in a corner: some fairly heavy action against the Khmer Rouge at Neak Luong, and shots of peasants in the region leaving their farms, marching away in line across a paddy field in pajamas and sarongs and checked *kramas*, carrying their bundles and their children. She stopped in front of these and looked at them for a long time; then she turned and said: No one else takes pictures like these. I remember your cover on the American news-weekly: the little boy with the flag being killed. Everyone talks about that picture.

—There are plenty of photographers as good, I told her.

—No, you're the best, she said. I like the way you show the Khmer people.

—They've lost their farms, I said, and I pointed to the peasants in the picture. They don't know where they're going. Fishing and the rice harvest, their own plot of land and the pagoda: that's their life, that's what matters to them—not money or politics. And there they go, I said: now they've got nothing. The Americans and the Cambodian Air Force bomb them; the rich generals and politicians in Phnom Penh take it for granted that their sons will do the fighting. Now the Khmer Rouge take their land and smash their pagodas. I want to show what's happening to them, I said. They have to pick up and keep on, no matter what comes. It's always been like that for farmers. Nothing shows them much mercy; nothing ever has. But in my country, it's only the weather and the market and the banks that farming people have to worry about—not the North Vietnamese Army or the Khmer Rouge or American bombing.

—She sat down in one of the cane chairs without speaking: straight-backed, hands folded. I sat down opposite, and waited. Then she said: This is why I've come to see you: because you talk like this. Everyone says

280

Mike Langford never gets angry, never gets involved. But I think you're full of anger, and many other feelings. I hear many things about you.

—I asked her what things.

—She laughed. Don't look worried—nothing bad, she said. People in the Army tell me about you. My father was a battalion commander: a good and honest commander, and he had good friends. They still visit me and watch out for me, and some of them are officers who know you. They say that you care about our struggle. They say that in the field you carry two canteens—one for yourself, one to give water to our wounded and dying. And they say that often you help carry away our wounded, instead of taking pictures. Other foreign photographers just take their pictures and go back to Hotel Royal and the bars; that's all they care about. You are different.

—I'm there to get the pictures like they are, I told her. I help with the wounded if there's no backup: that's all. Can I offer you a drink? A brandy?

—She shook her head, smiling as though I was trying to take her mind off some purpose: a purpose we both knew about.

—Most correspondents have no respect for our Government at all, she said. Have they? They say that Lon Nol's forces will lose the war because they are too corrupt: I know. And of course that's mostly right. Lon Nol is a criminal and a cretin.

—She looked down into her lap; then she looked up again quickly. Her eyes gleamed, and I saw that she was suddenly angry. It was the sort of anger that could make you nervous: it had that special intensity that suddenly flares up in Cambodians.

—He lies and says we're winning, she said, and tells the Americans what they want to hear. And all the time his palace generals steal the pay of our troops. Those bastards will never save us.

—Maybe not, I said. Maybe it's too late. Is that what you think?

—But she shook her head many times, making her hair swing. No, she said. No. It must *not* be too late. People here in Phnom Penh don't understand what the Khmer Rouge will be like. They never see them, so they pretend they will not be so bad: maybe that they don't even exist. Like the *neak taa*, perhaps: just ghosts. The Others! They're not like the North Vietnamese. Do you know what things those Others are doing in the villages, if the people oppose them?

—I've been in a village where that had happened, I said. Yes, I know.

—There are still good commanders like my father, she said. I think you know this too. I tell you: they can still beat the Khmer Rouge, men like that. I'd like you to meet one of them. He is one of the best, and he was my father's great friend. That's why I've come here to see you. I hope you don't mind: I think you'd like him. Will you do that? Will you meet him?

—I said I'd be happy to.

—He's a commandant—a battalion commander. Ung Chandara is honest; he believes in our country. You could visit his battalion down in Takeo. I've spoken about it to him: he wants to get to know you.

—That's good of you, I said. But you haven't said why.

—Major Chandara will tell you himself, she said. And now I should go.

—She stood up, and began to walk off towards the door. I switched on a table lamp, and followed her to see her out. She paused by my desk, smiling as though at her own thoughts. It was very hot and still, and I could feel the sweat breaking out on my face; I wiped it away.

—So neat, she said. It's all so neat in here. Do you have a good servant?

—No, I told her, I look after myself.

—And you live all alone, she said. She shook her head, pursing her lips: mocking. Not so Lucky One.

—I reached out and pushed back the strand of hair from her cheek. Her eyes widened, she lowered her lids for a moment, then smiled as though nothing had happened. You need a wife to manage things, she said. But maybe you already have one.

—She picked up the framed photograph of Claudine I keep on the desk. I think this is your Saigon wife, she said. The one Dmitri's told me about.

—We're not married, I told her. She's an old friend.

—I know that, she said, and she shook her head, studying the picture. Just as well—I think she looks too old for you.

—I said nothing to this, and she put the picture down and turned quickly. Most of her movements were quick, causing a fragrance to float up from the neck of her blouse: sandalwood, making me giddy. Her skin dark honey against the clean white.

—Goodbye, she said, and gave me her hand: formal and French. I'm sorry for coming here without warning you. But you'll like Major Chandara, I know it.

—She disappeared down the stairs very quickly, the way she does everything. I stood there, feeling the heavy heat suddenly press down on me in a wave. I walked about the room for a bit, sweating, not able to sit still. Then I went out and headed for one of the bars by the river.

—I can still smell her scent. Maybe not sandalwood at all, but her body's real odor.

4.

Harvey pushes another photograph across the table.

"Here we are, Ray," he says. "Major Ung Chandara, with Mike. Jim took this, somewhere in Takeo Province. That was Chandara's patch, down there in Takeo, near the Vietnam border. His division was the Seventh. Their task was to defend Highway 2—a pretty thankless one, by 1973; it was going fast."

He picks up the picture, studying it. "Chandara was a serious man," he says. "You can see that, can't you? Not a dandy—not one of your Captain Samphans. An intelligent, serious, incorruptible officer in the corrupt Lon Nol Army. A patriot. What a fate. Life dealt him a difficult hand, right?" He passes the picture back. "Now he's sitting up there on the Thai-Cambodian border, in charge of that hopeless resistance movement: the Free Khmer. Proud: never doubting they'll come back in the end. Poor bastard."

Langford and Major Chandara both look into the camera close up, a bank of trees behind them. Mike is bare-headed; Chandara wears a beret and a plain military shirt with no visible insignia. He's around forty, with features that have a strongly Chinese cast: a Sino-Khmer, like Ly Keang. He looks wiry and fit, and is almost as tall as Mike. The eyes are penetrating and wide-set, and the hard-ruled Mongolian line of the upper lids makes them severe. A warrior's eyes, yet also the eyes of a thinker. The lips, beneath a military mustache, are firm but delicately drawn. An interesting face: formidable yet sympathetic.

"Of all Mike's friendships in Indochina," Harvey is saying, "this one became the most important. I can tell you a little about Chandara: not much. He was something of a law unto himself.

Trevor Griffiths used to call him a 'warlord': exaggerated, of course, but there was something in it. Some of those battalion commanders did function rather like feudal barons in their particular regions, and their obedience to President Lon Nol and his corrupt palace generals was capricious—depending on the amount of graft allowed them, or whether they felt it tactically reasonable to obey.

"According to Langford, Chandara never took graft. Mike always spoke of him with great admiration: he used to describe him as 'the best field commander in Cambodia.' Other commanders were building luxury villas in Phnom Penh with their ill-gotten gains, but Major Chandara's family home in Phnom Penh was modest, Mike told me, and he was devoted to his wife and children. The sex parties with bar girls that other officers were addicted to were not for him. And he pursued the enemy at every opportunity, leading a Spartan life in the field; risking his life almost daily.

"It was a life that Langford began to share more and more, disappearing down in Takeo for weeks at a time. This began soon after I arrived, in the early months of seventy-three. So Mike was doing what he'd done all those years ago with Captain Trung's unit, down in the Delta.

"Do you see? Didn't I tell you he was always trying to replace things?"

AUDIO DIARY: LANGFORD

TAPE 43, MARCH 25TH, 1973

—Major Chandara's base camp was set up in a village a few kilometers southeast of Takeo city: right on the edge of Khmer Rouge territory. When I went down there yesterday, he took a company out into the flat, open country there that stretches to the Vietnam border. I went with them.

—I'd had to get to the post by Cambodian Army helicopter, since the situation on Highway 2 is changing every day. The Khmer Rouge have launched a major onslaught in Takeo Province: they're trying to get control of the whole of Highway 2 as well as Highway 1, and cut the link with Saigon.

—We ran into a group of them late in the afternoon. The engagement was successful for Chandara's troops, and the Khmer Rouge pulled out; he's a very able commander. But there were many wounded to take back, as well as the dead. Cambodian troops will never leave their dead: they carry them out no matter what the risk, since the enemy mutilate them. The Khmer Rouge do this because Buddhists believe that any mutilations and deformities will go with them into the afterlife. I'm beginning to hate the Khmer Rouge.

—The village where the base was located was very small, and the people had deserted it. Major Chandara had taken over a house next to the camp, and he offered me accommodation for the night.

—It was the usual small farmhouse on wooden piles, and I shared the evening meal with him on the verandah. Afterwards we lay back in cane chairs, drinking beer. Below us were the camp's galvanized iron lean-tos, military trucks and APCs, and the flames of the soldiers' cooking fires, pale in the last daylight. The heat had been eased by a short, unexpected downpour: one of those premature storms you sometimes get in March, and which really belong to late April. The Cambodians call them mango rains. It had swept away the dust-haze, and suddenly we could see for miles across the dry, yellow, dead-flat land to the southeast: all the way to the mountains on the Vietnam border, perhaps forty kilometers away. The mountains had been hidden by the haze, before; now their pale shapes stood straight up out of the plain like a mirage.

—The Seven Mountains were among those peaks: the ones the Cambodians say are magic mountains. There are old Buddhist shrines and pagodas there where holy men live, and caves for guerrilla groups and bandits. They're not very tall, but they're eerie: peaks of whitish rock, with green vegetation, like mountains in a vision. They're a main smuggling route into Vietnam for beef and marijuana, and I remembered how Jim and the Count and I once made a trip there in the sixties from the Vietnam side, to buy prime Cambodian weed from the frontier people.

—Major Chandara leaned to offer me a cigarette, and smiled as though reading my memories. He wasn't a man you took for granted, but I felt relaxed with him: he was quiet and courteous. I'd still to find out why Ly Keang had set up this meeting, but I was going to let him be the one to raise it. Cambodians don't like to be rushed.

—It's good to see the mountains after the rain, Chandara said. You know this border country?

—I said I did. I'd covered action against the VC here.

—He'd lit my cigarette and now he lit his own, drawing deeply. You know Mike, I once spent a lot of time in the Seven Mountains, he said. I was a member of the Khmer Serei: the Free Khmer. Back in the sixties we lived in exile there, on the other side of the border. We were working to overthrow Sihanouk: we had Vietnamese backing, and help from the Americans. Some didn't like to see us turning to such allies—but what we wanted was a republic, and freedom and democracy for our country. We could see what was going to happen: Sihanouk would deliver us to the Communists. You find allies where you can, when the danger is great enough.

—He waited for me to comment, but I didn't; then he looked out over the rail. Dusk was setting in quickly, and the shapes of the soldiers were black against the cooking fires, moving in and out of the circles of orange light.

—It's pleasant to sit on a verandah and look out, Chandara said. Don't you agree?

—Yes, I said. We like to sit on verandahs in my country too.

—But you want to make your home here in Cambodia, he said. Or so Ly Keang tells me. You are staying on a sinking ship, when I understand you are famous enough to work anywhere. Excuse me, but this seems strange. I asked Ly Keang why you would do this, and she said she thinks that in your heart you're a soldier. She should know: she's a soldier's daughter. Her father, Ly Pheang, was my best friend in the Free Khmer.

—Ly Keang's wrong, I said. She's got a strong imagination, that girl.

—He smiled; he was watching my face. It was good of you to help carry our wounded today, he said. You may not fight with us—but you help us.

—We sat quiet for a while. Then he said: My mother came from this province—from a little village not far to the north, up Highway 2. My father is an advocate in Phnom Penh, and that's where I grew up; but my happy childhood memories are of holidays in my mother's village. I'd look out from the verandah of my grandparents' house as we are doing now, at the rice fields and the forest beyond, and imagine many adventures. Well, they've come to me. Here I am in Takeo again, fighting for my native soil. Last week we nearly lost this whole province: it was very close.

—I asked him had he always wanted to be a soldier.

—He shook his head. I wanted to be an architect, as a young man. But I decided as a student that I had no wish to try and live a normal life in a country full of corruption, run by a corrupt prince and his court. I wanted better for Cambodia than that—and I didn't want the answer of Communist dictatorship. So I went across the Vietnam border and joined the Free Khmer.

—He drank some of his beer and wiped foam from his mustache, looking out into the dark. Then he said: Some used to call Prince Sihanouk a clown, with his films and his jazz band and his pleasures—but he is much more than that. Cruel, like all selfish people, with much blood on his hands. To keep power for himself, he would do anything; he would deliver this country to demons. Now he lives with his patrons in Peking—still with his personal chefs preparing his meals; still surrounded by every luxury. How does such a man live with himself?

—For a moment his face got dark and set, and I saw that he'd be capable of considerable rage. He finished his beer and sat back, pouring another from the bottle.

—When Lon Nol overthrew Sihanouk, we came in from the border and helped to form the Republic, he said. Then the Free Khmer was dissolved, since its aims were supposed to have been achieved. We believed we had an honest government now, to resist tyranny. A mistake—as I'm sure you'll agree, Mike.

—I wouldn't want to criticize your government, I told him. They're facing tough odds.

—You're very polite, he said. He leaned forward to pour me another beer, looking at me from under his brows. But I'm sure you know the truth, he said, like all Western correspondents. I tell you, I'm ashamed of my government; ashamed of most of our generals. Phnom Penh never gives us enough equipment or enough troops—to get them, we must use any means we can, legal or not. But some commanders claim salaries for ghost soldiers, and use the money to build air-conditioned villas for themselves. You know this. They even sell ammunition to the enemy—and they make their own troops pay for their rice. They take money from the pay of poor peasants who are dying for us; from men like those you helped this afternoon. I'm a fool if I ignore these things.

—I didn't know what to say, so I said nothing. It was peaceful, down in the darkened camp. Low voices, sometimes a laugh. A young soldier had begun to play a flute: a Khmer folk melody. I could see him sitting by a fire with a circle of friends around him, men and women, their faces quiet. He was a dark Khmer with a mop of curly hair; he played with great feeling, and the melody was so beautiful, climbing into the dark, it brought tears to my eyes. I loved Cambodia, just then.

—Chandara glanced at my face; then he pointed to the group by the fire, and his voice became gentle, its anger gone. A country is only as good as its ordinary people, he said. And these are good people. My young men and women are brave, and will fight to the end. If the Americans don't desert us, it's only our corrupt leaders who can cause us to lose this war.

—It was fairly extraordinary for a commander to be speaking to a Western correspondent like this on first meeting, and I decided now to be frank.

—Yes. But you know what a lot of the correspondents are saying, I told him. If that's how the Lon Nol leaders are, can the Communists be worse? At least the Communists are dedicated.

—He looked hard at me without blinking, and I wondered if I'd gone too far.

—I'll try to answer you honestly, he said. You think to choose between President Lon Nol and *les Khmers Rouges* is to choose between two evils: I know. It's a choice between the corrupt and the fanatical. But I have to say to you that it's better in my opinion to choose the corrupt—even though I detest them. The corrupt are merely weak and vicious; they want to drink their brandy and have parties with their bar girls and wear nice uniforms. They love themselves, and have no sense of duty. But they also have no ideology. That means they have no wish to control our minds or our lives; no desire to destroy our religion. They are not fanatics. Under fanatics, there are no loopholes—they close them all.

—He looked out at the dark, and at the orange sparks of the cooking fires: only the faces near to them could be made out now. We have some knowledge of the Khmer Rouge leaders, he said. They are ex-students, who studied in Paris. Marxist intellectuals: a product of the West! But they recruit young people here who have no education—boys and girls from remote regions, ignorant and suspicious of the world beyond their villages. And these Paris intellectuals are telling them that the world outside is a bad world, and has to be destroyed. They urge them to cruelties: to blood lust. Before, I was fighting the Vietnamese invader. Now I must fight my own people: simple people, infected with a virus.

—I asked him what he'd do if they won.

—If the Khmer Rouge win, he said, the Free Khmer must revive and form a Resistance. We'll fight a guerrilla war from the border, just as the Communists have done. There'll be no choice: no compromise with the Khmer Rouge will be possible—and no hope of mercy. Ly Keang knows this: she knows what they can do. They murdered her father.

—This surprised me. I thought he died in action, I said.

—No, he said. They murdered him. But Ly Keang will tell you about this herself, when she's ready. Not me. Well? Will you think about helping us?

—I stared at him, and he smiled: his expression was lighthearted now. You say you won't leave Cambodia: that this is your home, he said. Good! If the country falls, you can join us: join the Free Khmer.

—I thought he was joking; I laughed and shook my head. Then I looked down at the camp again. The flute player had stopped, and our voices were very distinct, on the verandah. The whole point about my work is to stay uninvolved, I said. A correspondent can't be involved.

—But the formula was sounding more and more feeble to me lately, and Chandara seemed to know this. He smiled now as though I were a slow child. Mike, you are coming to middle age like me, he said. And this is the time when we must find true purpose in our lives. As a Buddhist, I know it's time to start acquiring merit. Maybe you should know this too.

—Half joking, I asked him how he could be a Buddhist and a soldier at the same time.

—He laughed. Because I'm not a monk, he said. Only they can follow the Eightfold Path. I'm a man of passions, you can see that. But Buddhism's tolerant of people like me. It only asks that we live our lives as well as we can. And this is what the Khmer Rouge threaten too. They used to pretend to respect Buddhism, just for propaganda; now they mock it, and desecrate the pagodas and say there is no spirit: that human beings are only clay. That's how we know they are people of darkness, who'll destroy goodness. If the mass of the people aren't good, what hope is there for our lives?

—We talked of other things for a time. A soldier brought us some fresh bottles of beer, and we sank quite a few, in the end. I began to feel pretty happy, and I think Chandara did too. It was so dark now that, when he spoke next, lying back in his chair, I could barely make out his expression.

—Perhaps Cambodia won't fall, he said, against all the odds. But if it does, I'm hopeful that you'll be with us. No need to answer now. Battle is at the center of your life, even if you don't use a gun: I know this. And I think you may be more of a soldier than I am. I'm a soldier only because it's necessary: I hope in the end for peace. I know that my family are waiting for me, up there in Phnom Penh; I wait to see them. I long for my wife, I long to feel my children put their arms about my neck when I pick them up, and to smell their hair and skin. This is the greatest thing in life: not fighting. But what about you, Mike? Forgive me for being personal. You'll go back now to your empty apartment that Ly Keang tells me about. Maybe you should be married. Time you had children of your own, at your age.

—He sipped his beer, and watched me over the rim of the glass. He'd really become quite drunk, and so had I. If you want to become Cambodian, he said, and make this your home, you should perhaps look at Ly Keang. She greatly admires you. She's a fine girl.

—He'd surprised me again, and I answered carefully. Yes she is, I said. But I hardly know her. She's closer to my friend Dmitri Volkov.

—She sees death in your friend, he said. She sees life in you. So do I.

—He raised his glass to me and smiled, as though what he'd just said had been quite ordinary.

———

5.

Harvey looks out through the grille, hands folded.

"Kompong Cham," he says. Then he stops; staring into the white afternoon.

"Kompong Cham in that April just wasn't a place to be," he tells me. "It was expected to fall at any time. All the Government held any more was a buffer zone around it. So for Mike to urge that the three of them go up there—"

Turning back to me, he spreads his hands palms upwards. Then he expels breath through his lips so that they bubble, and drops his hands to the table. "I didn't offer to go with them," he says. "Not many correspondents would have. And I'm not gung ho, Ray—as I've told you."

He stops, staring at me for a moment, as though expecting a question.

"Oh shit," he says softly. "I'm not saying that Mike lured them up to Kompong Cham irresponsibly: of course not. But in a way, he was challenging Dmitri. There was a sort of extra rivalry between them at that time. For no good reason—they weren't in direct competition any more, now that Mike had given up film work. But they all played that game, those bloody cameramen, even when there was nothing to be gained. It was the way they were."

He raises a hand to rub his bald crown, and then takes off his glasses. Exposed, the large, fish-like eyes are sorrowful, and he sighs.

"This time it was different," Harvey says. "It'd be another two years before Phnom Penh fell—but for me everything began to be over, in that April and May. The war was coming to its climax, we all knew that: and when it reached it, nothing could be the same again. We knew that too."

He suddenly smiles. It's a benevolent smile, but not really directed at me: he's far off inside himself.

"We'd lived inside that war for so long," he says. "What the bloody hell were we going to do without it?"

HARVEY DRUMMOND

The opium lamp stood beside me, on its brass tray. It was an oil lamp, made of copper and heavy glass to focus the heat, and it gave off a warm golden glow. An antique: a lamp from the nineteenth century, still burning here in Asia, at Madame Delphine's. There was also a warm golden smell: it made my mouth water.

A little marijuana I could handle; couscous nights I now half enjoyed; but opium I'd always drawn the line at. Yet here I was, on an evening in the last week of April, naked except for a sarong (as the ceremony at Madame's required), stretched on my back on a floor which was a single huge mattress, my friends lying in the dimness around me.

The majority of journalists only had a pipe occasionally; but Langford, Dmitri Volkov, Jim Feng and Hubert Whatley now came at least once a week to Madame's. Langford seemed unaffected by it, just as he was unaffected by alcohol, and by every other physical stimulus and stress: he had the constitution of a bull, and kept his intake within bounds. So did Jim Feng. But rumor had it that Volkov and Whatley were lately coming here even in the lunch hours, and were well on their way to becoming addicts. They came to numb themselves to what was outside: the bombing, the ruined countryside, the people half crazed from grief, rocking the bodies of dead children on their laps. Tonight I wanted oblivion too, if opium would give it to me.

The atmosphere of the city had become unnerving. I would have gone anywhere, that evening, rather than stay in my room in the Hotel le Royal. The power had gone off again: the fans had stopped working and the room was stifling. The continuing artillery fire outside the city was causing the building to vibrate, and once there was a huge crash in the bathroom. I'd run in there, my heart thudding: I thought a rocket had scored a direct hit. But it was only the manhole cover in the ceiling: it had fallen down into the bath.

The Khmer Rouge blockade of the Mekong was now preventing all but a small number of supply ships and tankers from getting up the river. Most supplies were being brought in by air. The Rice Road to Battambang had been cut, petrol was running out, electricity cuts were constant, and we were told that Phnom Penh currently had enough food and fuel to get through three more weeks. Beyond the city, the bombing by the invisible B-52s went on: massive and terrifying, targeting the army of Khmer Rouge guerrillas there, but often hitting villages as well. The American aim was to stall the Khmer Rouge's dry-season offensive: an offensive directed against Phnom Penh itself, and already reaching its suburbs. The received wisdom at the Press Center was that the city would fall by August.

I was lying on the straw smoking-mat. It was my turn; time

for my first pipe. Madame Delphine squatted on her thighs beside me, the lamp putting big shadows on her fleshy, French-Chinese face, her eyes shining like black olives. Madame was like a nurse; she could almost make you believe this was good for you. She didn't smile much, she was middle-aged and stern, but she had a sort of matronly charm, and the Nurseryman claimed to be in love with her. Careful as a surgeon, she held the opium bead over the flame on its needle, and then coaxed it into the pipe. Muttering in French, she brought the stem to my mouth, urging me to draw.

"*Tirez! Tirez!*"

I inhaled, and the opium bubbled like sugar on a hot plate. Then I rolled off the mat to make way for Jim Feng, and a heavy tingling went down to my toes. It brought with it love of the world and my friends; love of the world inside me. I lay bathed in yellow delight, my head on a little leather pillow.

There were many smoking rooms in that dark family house; I found it a confusing place.

Madame Delphine's was in a lane off Monivong Boulevard, smelling of open drains: a Cambodian house on stilts, entered by a set of wooden steps, all in darkness from outside except for a single electric bulb, as a precaution against the police. The walls in our smoking room were hung with Cambodian straw mats worked in gold and chocolate, and a big, dim mosquito net hung above us like a cloud. No ceiling: through the net, from our mattress floor, we were looking up at the beams of the roof, and at fans that were slowly turning: the power supply was back. A radio was playing somewhere, turned down low. Quiet voices floated from adjoining rooms: the voices of French businessmen, Sûreté operatives, correspondents, and diplomats from the various Western missions. No Cambodians: this was a den for foreigners.

Blissful sighs came from out of the dark on all sides; the pipe bubbled. I could just make out the motionless shapes of my colleagues. They all spoke on a calm, purring note I'd not heard before: the voice of opium. No one spoke aggressively; no one sounded tense; every remark hung in the dark as something to meditate on. Time slowed to the ooze of honey, and often after someone had spoken it seemed to me that an hour went by before anyone replied, although it might have been two minutes. Sometimes the voices went away to somewhere else, and I no longer heard them. Madame Delphine came and went, her lamp creating big shadows, and after my second pipe, I found that I was in two places at once.

I was still in the smoking room, but I also saw a wide plain stretching away: an empty place of dry white grass and low bushes, going towards a green sky. I neither liked nor disliked it; it was simply there, inside me. At the same time, I could hear Hubert Whatley speaking. His voice was very distinct, entering my head as though through an amplifier.

I opened my eyes and turned towards the sound: I could just make out his face and beard, and the great white hills of his naked chest and belly, rising on the other side of Volkov. He seemed to be replying to something that Dmitri had said: a remark I hadn't heard; a gap on the tape.

"Soon, dear boy, yes. Soon they'll close the Mekong. But we still have our Cambodia for a little while longer. A country one saw in visions before one ever came here. The B-52s are dropping their bloody tonnages on Paradise."

After perhaps ten minutes, Jim Feng spoke. "True, Hubert: Paradise. Greatest supply of cheap grass ever seen, and prettiest women."

Soft laughter; but the Nurseryman wasn't to be deflected from his theme. A little while later, he resumed.

"Soon we'll be the only ones who remember the magic peace. Our crass colleagues arriving here now never knew that peace, did they, gentlemen? The French planters drinking coffee at their curbside tables. The caravans of oxcarts coming in from the country, with all the country's fruits. Upswept shafts like the prows of boats. Straw piled on their awnings; the kids and dogs trotting beside them. Was it always noon when they came?"

A long silence followed: nobody answered, and I wondered if his rumbling voice would go on. It went on; speaking to itself.

"Yes: the noon hush. No guns to break it then; no sound of

bombers. Just the oxcarts, coming into town in lines a mile long."

We all lay watching the carts, and hearing their creaking in the heat.

Madame Delphine had arrived with fresh pipes, and the Nurseryman, grunting, rolled onto the mat by the lamp.

"*Ah Madame,*" he said. "*Je t'aime. Je suis ton esclave.*"

"*Je vous en prie, Monsieur,*" she said. "*Ça suffit! Vous êtes trop galant.*" But her impassive face showed faint amusement.

"Alas," he told us. "I am in love with Madame, but she has eyes only for Snow."

Turning the opium ball on its needle, Madame Delphine glanced at Mike. "*Il est plus beau,*" she said. And for the first time she smiled faintly.

But Langford now had gone deeper into trance, unconscious of what was being said. Arms at his sides, curved blond shards of hair lying on his forehead, he was looking up into the mosquito net, dead-white face in profile. And his face had suddenly become a statue's, empty of expression and even of life: a phenomenon I remembered seeing only once before, when he was wounded in Vietnam. He was suddenly no longer himself, but someone else.

As I watched, he turned his head towards Volkov and came back again, his eyes refocusing and reflecting the flame of the lamp.

"I've got something for tomorrow, if you don't want to retire just yet, Count," he said. He spoke slowly, as though in his sleep. "I'm going up to Kompong Cham. Taking a Government chopper. You and Jim could come. There's room."

"Kompong Cham?" Volkov said. "You are serious?"

"Yes, I'm serious," Langford said. "There's a risk—but that's why it's a good story."

They peered, heads turned towards each other. Then Mike smiled, and Volkov let out a hiss of laughter. He nodded once, as though agreeing to a crime, and looked across at Jim.

"I'll come," Jim said.

Kompong Cham, fifty miles to the northeast, was an important city: a crossroads on the Mekong, strategically vital. Any action there was worth covering. But nearly all of Kompong Cham

Province had now fallen to the North Vietnamese and the Khmer Rouge, and the rest was going fast. The city itself was said to be about to fall.

Hubert, who had inhaled his pipe, raised his head from the pillow. "You have all gone mad," he said faintly, and lowered his head again.

I'd like to be able to say that this was a tense, decisive moment. But it wasn't; not for me. I'd had five pipes now, and had begun to float away: I saw my grassy plain again.

It was sinking into twilight, and the Soldiers Three were there. They were walking fast through the grass, looking as I'd seen them a hundred times before: all of them hung with cameras and camera bags, wearing their fatigues.

They were laughing and looked happy; but I knew that they were going to die, and a terrible vertigo gripped me.

Volkov was kind to me that night. He helped me through the attack of nausea which is the usual reaction to opium in a first-time user.

Like me, Dmitri continued to live at the Royal; his room was one floor down from mine. He saw me back there, when we finally emerged from Madame's, holding me by the arm all the way. The nausea got worse, and as soon as we got to my room, I rushed to the bathroom to throw up. When I came back, Volkov was sitting in the rattan chair beside the bed.

"Hit the sack, Harvey," he said. "I will sit with you for a while."

I said there was no need, but he held up his hand. "Just stretch out, man, and don't argue. A bad trip is a bad trip. Go with it; don't fight it: float. I will sit awhile."

I pulled off my boots and lay down on the lumpy double bed. Speaking was now difficult, and Dmitri seemed to understand this. The air-conditioning was still off, but the ceiling fans were working, and I blessed them: I was pouring with sweat. Dmitri turned off the bedside light, leaving one lamp lit on the writing desk; then he lay back in his chair in the half-dark, taking out his cigarettes. He didn't attempt further conversation, but I was glad he was here.

It was now about ten o'clock. For some time I was aware of Volkov a few feet away, smoking and staring in front of him, apparently deep in thought. Then I drifted into sleep, and had terrifying dreams, none of which I remember.

I woke suddenly, and thought I was still on the mattress at Madame Delphine's. I found my head was clear; but I had no idea how many hours had gone by. Volkov still sat here, smoking. He'd never been a big man, despite his physical toughness, and in those first seconds of waking he looked to me almost frail.

I peered at my watch, and found that it was nearly one in the morning. He'd been sitting here for three hours.

My God, Count, I said. You didn't have to stay all this time. Go to bed.

"That's OK," he said. "Somebody had to see you through this, *tovarich*. After all, we took you to Madame's den. Your first and last visit, I presume."

I was inclined to think so, I said.

"Probably wise," he said. "You are not the junkie type. Unlike me. I am a junkie for everything."

Including trouble, I said. Would he really go to Kompong Cham tomorrow?

"Yes, I will go," he said. "You want to come, Harvey?"

No thanks, I said, it was too much like Russian roulette to ride the roads now. More your game than mine, I said—but I think you should skip this one, brother. So should Mike and Jim. It smells bad.

He smiled. "Sensible as always. You are no doubt right, Harvey. Yes, it gets worse. Last week, two American correspondents tried to drive down Highway 1. New here. They put a notice on their windshield that says: 'Don't Shoot. Press.' Jesus. They only got as far as Neak Luong and have not been seen again, poor bastards. Khmer Rouge have executed them, for sure. Khmer Rouge are even worse than Viet Cong: they do not seem to play by any rules at all. It's bad now: it's creepy." He stretched and yawned. "You are a words man, Harvey; you can avoid some of this. But getting shot at on daily basis is my game, you know this. Bloody bureau chief in Hong Kong keeps riding me, for one thing. Last week I sent only four hundred feet, and bastard asked on phone did I take the lens cap off. So I go—and so does Jim. Mike doesn't need to—but always he wants to push his luck a little further, and I can't allow him to do this on his own. Besides, he has said the big story is at Kompong Cham, and he is generally right."

He stood up. "You should sleep, brother. Can you manage to do this now without bad dreams?"

I said I was sure I could, and got up and saw him to the door. He paused outside, standing in the deserted corridor with its dim green walls.

"I have favor to ask you," he said. He fumbled in his shirt pocket, and produced a sealed envelope. "I want you to keep this for me."

I took it doubtfully, and he said: "Duplicate key. If anything happens to me tomorrow, or any time, I want you to take charge of small wooden box under my bed."

Of course, I said. But just don't let it happen, Count. What's in the box?

He smiled again. "My life is in it," he said. "Send it to the person whose address is inside this envelope."

And that will be Linda, I said.

His smile vanished. His eyes became cold in a way that quelled me; he could still create that effect. "You are very clever bastard, Harvey," he said. He turned without speaking again, and went off down the empty, high-ceilinged corridor, raising his hand without looking back.

I was still affected by the opium. Because of the uncertain power supply, the shaded lamps along the walls gave out an ominously faint light, and Dmitri seemed to walk through this light into another dimension of time: into an indistinct region whose exit was always retreating. He walked quickly, as he always did, in the navy shirt he so often seemed to wear. He passed a lone, white-coated Cambodian room boy; his figure dwindled; then he turned a corner and disappeared.

I stood looking at his envelope with mixed feelings: compassion, and that secret irritation we have when a responsibility is thrust on us unasked.

THREE
THE COMMON POT

1.

JIM FENG

One thing I want to make clear, Ray: I don't blame Mike for what happened at Kompong Cham. We both wanted to go with him, Dmitri and I: we made a free choice, like we always did.

But as we rode up there in the Government chopper that morning, I had a bad feeling. I believe in my sixth sense; it has always got me out of tight spots in battle; yet I couldn't really justify this feeling today. I knew Mike's information was always reliable, and that he would have assessed the situation carefully. I trusted him.

But the situation wasn't good, up there. For nearly a year now there had been reports of clashes in Kompong Cham between the Khmer Rouge and the North Vietnamese, and it was beginning to be suspected that the Khmer Communists were rebelling against their allies, and wanting to push them out of Cambodia. The village people in the province were growing angry about the Vietnamese Communists sheltering in their villages to try and avoid being bombed—and a few months ago, when some villages had been destroyed, the Khmer Rouge had led the villagers in a protest. This was said to have brought on clashes between the two Communist armies.

Mike said he'd like to find out whether this friction was still going on. He even talked about going a little way on to the east bank of the Mekong—which was all in Communist hands now. This would make a very good story, but it was one for a print correspondent, I thought, rather than a photographer. And it crossed my mind that Mike might want to report on the situation to Aubrey Hardwick. He still had dinner with Aubrey, when the old man was in Phnom Penh.

All of it worried me. It looked as though the Khmer Rouge would take Kompong Cham city at any time, and to cover there now was unwise. I'd no wish to do it, in the light of day. I wanted to stay alive. I had Lu Ying to come back to now, and this had changed me.

I remember the taxi driver clearly, even though I never knew his name. I remember this man only because he got killed for the sake of a day's fare.

But he knew the chances he was taking. Some of those guys would drive you to Hell for a few dollars, and he was of that type. A young Khmer, with a lot of wavy hair and a face that was amused all the time. Western shirt and trousers, but a red-checked Cambodian *krama* hung around his neck. He drove us fast, in a battered green Peugeot, and he tried to join in our conversation, even though his English was very bad.

We'd hired him in Kompong Cham city and were headed southwest, on Highway 7. It was very hot that morning; there was no air-conditioning in the Peugeot, and our shirts were soon soaked with sweat.

April in Cambodia is the last of the dry months before the monsoon: a time of great heat, when the earth is baked hard, and the water is gone from the paddies. Not a time I like. Kompong Cham is red soil country, and the red dust blew across the bitumen of the highway in the hot wind, and came through the open windows. There was a red-brown haze over everything: banana trees and palms looked shabby in it, village huts looked withered, and the paddy fields on each side of the road were cracked and crazed like crockery, waiting for the rain. When everything has been harvested, open country like that is more exposed than usual; you can't take cover in the rice. That's a thing you think about, when you're about to film a firefight.

We'd learned that there were two Government battalions a few kilometers down the road from the city, which the Government still held. This seemed safe enough: we had a combined force of a thousand men in front of us. When we reached the rear battalion, we found nothing happening: a line of trucks, buses and APCs stood halted here. The commander told us that the other battalion was four kilometers up ahead; it had made no contact with the enemy, and we could join it if we wanted. So we got in the car and went on.

The road was empty; once a peasant on a bicycle passed, and that was all. No children about, which was always a bad sign. We came around a bend, and found the other battalion: another halted line of trucks and buses. But as soon as we got out of the taxi we saw that they'd run into trouble. Wounded soldiers were lying in two of the trucks, with medics attending them. No gunfire, though: all quiet. It was nearly noon, and the heat made you dizzy.

The battalion commander was standing by a Jeep, talking to a young sergeant in a helmet who was operating a field radio. The commander was a thin, elderly man in glasses and a cap and camouflage fatigues. He looked worried, like a schoolmaster whose school was getting out of control. Dmitri held a conversation with him in French; then he turned to us and explained.

The battalion had been hit a few minutes before. The Khmer Rouge were somewhere up ahead, and they'd attacked with B-40 rockets, machine guns and mortars. The Government troops had mortars and machine guns in the trucks, but had not had time to respond with them; they'd been forced to defend themselves with their automatic rifles, and had taken quite a few wounded.

There was a lull now, and they were setting up their mortars in the paddy field beside the road, and digging foxholes there. The sergeant was calling in air support.

Mike and Dmitri and I moved into the dry paddy field behind the troops, leaving the taxi driver to wait for us by the commander's Jeep. We got under a small clump of mangoes and banana trees that would give us some protection. With two battalions at our back and air support supposedly coming, we thought we'd be reasonably safe, and we began to concentrate on checking our cameras. It was hard to concentrate, the heat was so great now. Dmitri and I had decided to travel light, with no sound recordists; we'd brought clockwork Bell and Howells, with tape recorders on our belts for sound. Mike had his usual Leica and Nikon.

The Khmer Rouge suddenly opened up from a long line of trees on the far side of the rice field. The noise was shattering: the treetops bent as though in a high wind, and shells exploded quite close. At intervals there would be the scary *cluk-cluk-cluk* of a B-40 rocket on its way, and one of these rockets hit a bus on the road dead on. The survivors, covered in blood, came stumbling and crawling out, and I got some footage of them. The Khmer Rouge couldn't aim straight at the Lon Nol force from so close; instead they were putting the rockets into the air and dropping them.

It's not a battle I like to remember. The hot wind was still blowing, and the red haze mingled with the gunsmoke to make everything vague, like a painted battle instead of a real one. The Lon Nol troops were putting mortar fire into the trees for all they were worth; but after about an hour the Khmer Rouge hadn't budged and were still firing back, and more and more buses were retreating with the wounded. The trucks coming up with replacements seemed to make little difference. There were now many dead and wounded in the rice field and on the road, and the numbers of soldiers still fighting seemed much fewer. Cries and moans came through the red and blue haze, close and far off.

I shot some good film; we all did. But mortar shells had begun to explode closer to our clump of trees, and now we lay flat, no longer trying to film, just hugging our cameras to protect them from flying earth. We had a quick conference, and decided to get back to the taxi. Then we'd try and retreat down the highway to the other battalion.

In a lull in the firing, we ran for it. Buses and trucks were making off down the road, retreating towards Kompong Cham with the dead and wounded. There weren't many vehicles left here. Someone was shouting orders; a few voices sounded in response, but their tone was faint, like the voices of people who know they're lost.

Our taxi driver was still sitting behind the wheel of the Peugeot: seeing us, he got out, and began to hurry over. The young sergeant in the helmet was still here too, standing beside his Jeep and speaking into his field radio; but there was no sign of the battalion commander. Dmitri asked the sergeant in French where the commander was, and the man told him the commander was dead. His face was perspiring and blank; he seemed to be in a dream. A folded-up letter showed in the top pocket of his shirt, written in Khmer in blue ballpoint: I wondered if it was from his wife, and whether it would ever be answered.

The taxi driver pulled at my sleeve. His expression was like a scared boy's. We go! he said. Go! Go! Go!

As well as shell fire, I could now hear the crack of AK-47s, but I told him to wait. Mike was speaking rough French to the sergeant, asking what had happened to the air support. The sergeant said he kept asking for it, but could get no response. He was getting no response from the other battalion, either.

We all looked at each other.

Merde. In that case we are fucking well in for it, Dmitri said. His voice was very dry and quiet, and I knew he was right. We had never been in a position as bad as this.

We go, the taxi driver said. He was clasping his hands and looked pleading, as though he might weep.

Dmitri put a hand on his shoulder, while looking at Mike and me. The man is right, he said. Let's go.

We ran for the taxi.

It's difficult to explain the confusion of battle to those who haven't been in one: a lot of the time, no one's sure what's happening. The mortar shelling had stopped, but sporadic bursts of automatic rifle fire went on from both sides. The taxi driver accelerated away, Mike sitting in the front, Dmitri and I in the back, but just as we were about to turn the bend, there was a rattle of automatic fire from somewhere in the rear that seemed quite close, and bullets began to hit the car. One shattered the back window, but no one was hit.

Keep going, I heard Mike call. Step on it!

But one of our tires was punctured: the car was slewing everywhere, and the driver had slammed on the brakes. As it halted broadside across the road there was another burst of fire and we all began to come out the doors, looking for the ditch. I ran towards it in a crouch, keeping my camera high in one hand and rolling through the dust at the verge. Once in the ditch, I got my head down; Dmitri appeared quickly beside me, panting hard.

When there was a break in the firing, we peeped over the edge and saw the stalled Peugeot with its doors open. The driver still sat at the wheel, slumped forward and still. The back of his head and his red-checked *krama* were soaked with dark blood, and I knew for certain that he was dead. The firing had stopped, and now Mike appeared, crawling up the ditch to join us. We three crouched against the crumbling red earth, not daring to speak or make any sound.

I smelled the dry Cambodian dust, and buffalo dung nearby. We looked at each other, and our thoughts were exchanged quite clearly. We were together and alive and glad of it, even if we should only live for a few minutes more, or half an hour. Dmitri was next to me; Mike on the other side. I saw that Dmitri's lips were cracked, and his lips and the cracks in them seemed precious. Mike had a cut from shaving on his chin, and I wanted to laugh at this. These feelings may seem strange, and are difficult to explain; but now that Lu Ying and I have had our daughter, I can say that the same sensations are experienced when you look at your first infant: at its skin and hands and feet.

We never found out what happened to the remnants of the battalion. I imagine they made their escape down the road, and that the Khmer Rouge then withdrew, having achieved their victory. But this wasn't something we knew at the time, since we didn't put our heads up to see. We went on crouching in the ditch, not daring to show ourselves, and expecting at any moment to see Khmer Rouge troops appear above us.

After about twenty minutes, when it went on being quiet, we crawled on our bellies in an easterly direction. Then we held a conference in whispers. Because it was quiet didn't mean that the Khmer Rouge weren't still out there; they could be anywhere, we said. But we decided that we'd risk walking east to Kompong Cham when evening came. We wouldn't walk on the highway; we'd go through the fields here on the southern side, using whatever cover we could.

At sunset we set out, our shadows long in front of us. Maybe we should have waited until dark, but we'd emptied our canteens, and were very thirsty. So we took a chance. We walked for perhaps half an hour across the cracked earth of the paddies, and on dusty red cattle paths. At first we saw no sign of life except for some buffalo; it was as though the countryside had been emptied. Then, as dusk began to fall, we saw the lights of a cluster of thatch-roofed buildings, just off Highway 7.

That very thick, breathless darkness you get in April was coming on fast. But we made out that one of the buildings was a bulk store of some kind, with rice sacks and crates outside, and two wagons parked there harnessed to oxen. It was a trading post, but still we could see no people; they must all be inside. We stopped on the path in front of a stand of tall bamboos, and began to discuss the situation. We considered trying to see if we could find some sort of transport here, to take us the last few kilometers to Kompong Cham.

But then we heard a voice call an order from behind us, sharp and loud, and my heart jumped in my chest and hit like a hammer.

Oh shit, Mike said, and put his hands up without turning.

Dmitri and I did the same. As we turned, I was sure we would find Khmer Rouge. But instead, what we saw were three soldiers in the uniform of the Army of North Vietnam: light-green fatigues, belted at the waist, and floppy cotton bush hats like the one Mike wore.

They had come from behind the bamboos, and they were pointing assault rifles at us: AKs, with their banana-shaped clips. They jerked the guns upwards to tell us to raise our hands higher. We obeyed, looking at each other, and one of the soldiers moved closer, gun pointed, examining each of our faces in turn. He looked at me longest: I think he could not decide whether I was a Cambodian Chinese or a foreigner. He had to look up at us; he had the Vietnamese small stature and light-boned frame, and could not have been more than twenty-two. All three were little more than boys; but all looked battle-hardened.

Nha Bao, Mike said quickly. He was telling the soldier that we were journalists.

The soldier spoke rapidly in Vietnamese; but Mike shook his head, and so did Dmitri and I. Actually I spoke more Vietnamese than Mike and Dmitri did, and had understood that the soldier wanted to know what we were doing here—but an instinct told me to conceal my knowledge of the language.

The soldier was now pointing at Mike and Dmitri. American, he said. This was the only English word he'd ever speak: we'd soon discover that none of these soldiers knew anything but Vietnamese.

With their blond hair and U.S. Army fatigue trousers and jungle boots, Mike and Dmitri did look like Americans—or an Asian's idea of an American. And Mike had on one of his bad-taste cowboy shirts.

No, Mike said. Australian. He pointed to his chest. *Toi la nguoi Uc dai loi.*

The soldier looked puzzled; then he turned to Volkov and me.

Français, Dmitri said. *Phap,* understand?

Chinese, I said. *Tau.*

It seemed easier to say this for now than to explain that I was a British subject, and a citizen of Hong Kong.

The soldier went on staring for a moment; I don't think he believed any of us. Then he spoke again in Vietnamese. He waved his rifle to signify that we should walk towards the bulk store, and we obeyed. Here we were made to wait in the doorway while one of the other soldiers vanished inside. He came back with what looked like vine rope; we were ordered to turn our backs, and our hands were tied behind us. Another thin rope was used to link us together; then the soldier who'd been speaking to us waved his rifle again, and shouted. *Di di!*

We were being ordered to march. Two of them walked beside us, guns at the ready, another in front. They were heading south down the cattle track, away from the highway and the settlement, out across the empty rice fields. And I realized what this meant: they were taking us towards the Mekong.

As soon as you're a prisoner, your feeling about yourself changes. Being a captive wasn't real, at first; it was like a mistake, or a game. I immediately began to look for the possibility of escape: to watch for anything that would let me hope for it—or even pretend to hope for it.

I also took comfort from the fact that these soldiers were North Vietnamese and not Khmer Rouge. I told myself that this gave us some hope of survival, where otherwise there would have been none. Nevertheless, I knew that anything might happen; they might quite easily decide to shoot us. It was surprising that they were on the west bank of the Mekong, now that the North Vietnamese were said to be leaving all combat inside Cambodia to the Khmer Rouge, and I wondered what they were doing here. Later we'd discover they were negotiating purchases of rice. This went on all the time up here, like the trade between the two sides in rubber and arms.

It was strange to see these North Vietnamese at close quarters. In all my years in Indochina, I'd only ever seen them as prisoners of war; or else I'd viewed their dead after a battle, when they looked very small, like dolls. Now, here they were, in their green, baggy uniforms and Ho Chi Minh sandals made from car tires. They don't believe that we're correspondents, I thought: when they understand, perhaps they'll release us. But this idea didn't last long.

Di di mau! they kept shouting. *Di di mau!*

We couldn't seem to go fast enough to satisfy them, no matter how we tried. We were still slung with our cameras and camera bags, and the vine rope binding my wrists was very tight, and hurt. I was last in line, linked to Dmitri, who marched behind Mike—and whenever Dmitri or I stumbled on the rutted earth of the paddy field, the rope jerked and cut deeper into our wrists, and no doubt into Mike's too. Then the soldiers would shout at us again. I heard the Count curse under his breath; but when we'd tried to speak to each other, our guards had immediately ordered us to be silent, and we hadn't tried again. We plodded forward, clumsy and helpless, heads bowed, sweating in the night's heat. We seemed to march for a long time, since they allowed us no halts; but I've realized since that it can't have been far: seven kilometers or so.

I smelled the Mekong before I saw it; then its big brown spaces appeared, shining under a half moon. The black trees of the far-off east bank were hard to make out; there were no lights over there. There wasn't much sign of settlement on this side either; just a single peasant house on stilts beside the water, next to a grove of mangoes. One of the soldiers took a flashlight from his pack and put the beam on each of us; then he shone it on the house, and called out softly.

An old bent Cambodian in a limpet-shaped straw hat and black pajamas came down the steps. He led us along a path on the bank to a motorized sampan tethered in the reeds. The soldiers ordered us on board, making us crouch in the bow, one of them keeping his gun on us. Then the old man started the motor and steered us into the stream.

Out on the water, I breathed in the soft, cooler air, and looked about me. From the middle of the stream, I saw a big cluster of lights upriver on the west bank, and realized I was looking at

Kompong Cham city. I could just make out the distant shapes of the two-storied yellow French warehouses on the riverfront. I turned to Dmitri and Mike, and saw that they were looking there too.

Dmitri muttered under his breath, jerking his head at the town. Shit, he said. We could be eating pork and noodles there now. Think of it, men. Having long cold beers.

We grinned at each other, and licked our lips: all we'd eaten that day had been croissants and coffee for breakfast at the Hotel Royal, and we were hungry as well as thirsty.

You got your wish, I told Mike. We're going to the east bank.

Yes, Dmitri said. Maybe he has set all this up, the bastard.

We all started to laugh under our breath. We found we wanted to laugh; things no longer seemed so bad then.

Once on the east bank we were marching again, plodding and stumbling. Our thirst was now very bad, and we asked the soldiers a number of times for water, in Vietnamese. But they ignored us.

Nuoc, we said. *Nuoc.* We sounded like tired kids.

Finally one of them brought us a very small amount of water in a canteen, and untied our hands. Even as I drank, I hoped that the water was boiled: in all these years in the field, I had never drunk unboiled water. To catch an infection would cut our chances of survival in half. We offered the soldiers cigarettes; they each took one and nodded, lighting up with expressions of pleasure; we knew how they coveted American cigarettes. But they didn't smile, and they tied our hands again.

It was darker now, and long, ghost-white rows of rubber trees appeared, like columns in a ruined temple. We were into plantation country. The Vietnamese had little fear of enemies here, and talked quite loudly. After a time of further nonstop marching, I heard the barking of dogs, and knew we were coming to a village. Small lights appeared, and the usual thatched roofs like haystacks among groves of mango and banana trees. We were marched quickly between stilted houses, where people stood looking down at us from the verandahs. Lit from behind by oil lamps, they were just black shapes. I heard someone laugh: a woman.

Two of the soldiers disappeared into a house; the other took us on to the end of the village and a little beyond: to a small clearing among big dark tamarinds and fan palms, where a single thatch-roofed hut stood. Halting us here, he untied our hands. We shook them, trying to restore circulation, wincing at the pain. There were weals on our wrists that had begun to bleed; our clothes were dirty, and our faces swollen with mosquito bites. The soldier ordered us inside the hut.

It was very small, and had a mud floor; it was furnished rather like an office. A wooden table stood in the center with a tiny oil lamp burning on it: a simple glass bottle with a wick. There were a number of plain wooden chairs, and nothing else. The soldier ordered us to sit on the chairs in front of the table, and kept his gun trained on us.

We looked at each other and were about to speak; but two men came in immediately and seated themselves on the other side of the table. One of them wore the usual green cotton uniform, but with three ballpoint pens in his top pocket. And now I understood what was happening.

Because of the Communist doctrine of equality, the soldiers of the North Vietnamese Army displayed no rank badges or insignia; the only way you could tell a high-ranking officer was from the number of ballpoint pens in his pocket. So this man was an officer. None of the young soldiers who had brought us here had displayed pens; none of them was an officer, and they would have had to get us to someone of higher rank in order to know what was to be done with us. That was why they had brought us across the Mekong, I thought.

The other man at the table surprised me. He was very thin, quite old, and wore spectacles and civilian clothes: a white, short-sleeved sports shirt and dark trousers. He had the look of an official, and did not appear to me to be Vietnamese.

The military officer began speaking to us in Vietnamese. Mike and Dmitri shook their heads, and so did I. I think it seemed a good idea to all of us to conceal what knowledge of the language we had. The officer frowned, as though disbelieving us. Dmitri repeated the Vietnamese term for press—*bao chi*—but the officer simply stared, the light of the oil lamp putting deep shadows on his face. It was a plain, peasant face, but not a good one, I thought. His jaw was heavy, his mouth without kindness, and his eyes were small, flat as mud and resentful. I have seen men with such faces practice great cruelties.

He now looked sideways at the old man, who sat smoking a cigarette in a holder, legs crossed, studying us. The old man leaned forward, and I found he was looking at me. He spoke for the first time; and the language he used was Mandarin. This didn't surprise me; I had already guessed him to be Chinese.

You are Chinese? he asked.

Yes, I said, and I told him I was from Hong Kong: a British subject, and an accredited news cinecameraman, working for British Telenews. My friends were also accredited war photographers, I said. I put my press cards on the table, and Mike and Dmitri did the same.

The two men examined the cards slowly, and the Chinese official smiled. Yes, he said to me, and pushed the cards back. Accreditation by the puppet government of Lon Nol. His expression was amused, but not pleasant.

We are independent journalists, I said. We're here to film and report on the war, without taking sides. Why are we being held? We would like to return to Phnom Penh.

But the official drew on his cigarette holder and studied me without answering. While he did so, the NVA officer leaned forward, pushing out his jaw, and spoke suddenly in broken English. His eyes had the strong gleam of a man who is holding back anger with an effort.

You are CIA, he said. All of you. This is what we think.

He was shouting, and his voice filled the hut. If true, he shouted, you will be executed as spies. You understand?

I went cold all over. I tried to keep my face composed, but I was very tired and hungry and began to be alarmed, just as he wanted.

No, no. Mike was speaking, leaning forward and smiling. His

voice was soft as always, and he appeared almost as fresh as he'd done this morning. We're not Americans, he said. And we're not CIA. We're news photographers. It's our job to show what's happening—nothing else. We're glad of the opportunity to talk to you. We'd like to report on how the war is going from your side. The public in the West would be very interested.

But the officer still frowned; he had not understood all of this. He looked at the Chinese official for help, and the old man translated. Instead of responding, the officer grunted deep in his throat, like a boar. He widened his eyes, looking at Mike in disbelief. This grunt had conveyed great threat, and I feared that he might become violent. But now the old Chinese spoke, and this time in quite good English.

Certainly you will not take pictures, or take back information, he said. In fact, you may not go back at all. It depends on what we are able to learn about you. We want you to provide answers to some questions.

He leaned down now, coughing softly, and picked up a green canvas bag from beside his chair, drawing out papers and some ballpoint pens. He pushed one of the papers into the circle of light from the oil lamp. Huge jungle moths circled around the lamp, and their shadows crossed the paper.

You will tell us whether you know any of these names, he said.

We all craned to read them; they were handwritten. From their mixture of origins and their use of middle initials, they could be guessed to be American; but we recognized none of them, and said so.

The two men looked hard at us; I don't think they believed us. Then the Chinese official pushed some blank sheets of paper across the table to us, and some pens. You will write down here all personal details, he said. Your name, the names of your parents, your place of birth, your rank, the name of your organization. You will then state what you were doing alone on foot near Kompong Cham, and by what means you came there.

Dmitri spoke now. And when we have done this to your

satisfaction, he said, and you realize that we are members of the press—you will release us?

We will not be the ones to make that decision, the old man said. Write, please.

We wrote, while they watched us. I could hear the occasional calls of night-birds, out in the forest; mosquitoes whined in the little hut, and the old man went into another long cigarette cough. It was very hot and still; my hands sweated, and sweat dripped from my nose onto the cheap paper. The moths flitted, like bad spirits. It was like being in a schoolroom doing a test, sitting on those hard chairs.

And if we don't pass this test, I thought, we will die. I grinned at the foolishness of the thought; and looking up, I caught the officer watching me. That smile will probably be a mark against me, I thought.

When we'd completed our statements, we were ordered outside the hut, and saw no more of our interrogators. Two of our three soldiers now took charge of us again.

First they gave us water from a pannikin, which we drank greedily; then they allowed us to take a piss beside the path. After that they led us back into the village. It was now nine o'clock by my watch, the road between the houses was deserted, and I assumed that most of the villagers were asleep. But there were a number of Vietnamese soldiers squatting under the houses among the carts and chickens and storage jars. Clearly this was an NVA-controlled village.

We were led under one of these houses, and ordered to halt beside a bedstead covered with matting. Smoke rose from a clay oven nearby; two soldiers were cooking, and I could smell cinnamon and fish mixed with the wood smoke. Hunger cramps went through my stomach, and a wave of weakness came over me. But still we were offered nothing to eat. The soldiers now took away all our possessions: cameras, camera bags, tape recorders, wallets, press passes, pens, notebooks. They even took our watches, and I mourned for my Rolex, which I was sure I would never see again. But they left us our cigarettes and lighters. Then they ordered us to remove all our clothes, including our underwear and boots, and to throw them on the bedstead with our pile of possessions.

The third soldier now appeared out of the dark with a big wooden bucket of water and a bar of soap, and we took it in turns to wash on the spot. I'd been aching all over, and felt refreshed and much more cheerful when I'd had my turn; I was beginning to be grateful for little things. Then the soldiers produced some cotton Vietnamese underpants and pale green NVA fatigues like their own, which they handed to us, gesturing for us to put them on.

Pulling on trousers much too small for him, Mike grinned and winked at Dmitri and me. I think we've just joined the People's Liberation Army, he said.

Immediately, one of the soldiers told him in Vietnamese not to speak.

Mike pointed to his feet, asking politely for sandals. None of us had been issued with these. But they shook their heads. We remained barefoot, which filled me with a helpless surge of anger. Our feet would be cut to pieces, if we marched.

They had now taken everything from us: everything that linked us to our former identities, except for the lucky charms we wore on dog tag chains around our necks. They had tried to take these as well: Mike's brass Viet Cong belt buckle with the Communist star, Dmitri's Saint Nicholas medal, my Cambodian tiger claw. But Dmitri had made a loud speech in French, pleading with them, telling them that these things protected us—and Mike and I had joined in. The soldiers had no French, but they quickly understood our superstition; after all, they were peasant boys. They murmured to each other; finally they shrugged, and let us keep our charms.

It was a great relief. For all three of us, in that moment, it was very important that these objects remain around our necks. They'd been with us since the old days in Vietnam, and we saw them as part of the special luck that had helped us survive through the years, while so many of our friends were now dead. They could not be replaced. Yes, we were very superstitious, very sentimental, since so little remained constant in our lives. If you had asked us point-blank did we truly believe that our lucky charms warded off death, we probably would have said no; but in a childish corner of our minds, we believed that they did. And the childish corners of men's minds have a strange power, I think: they fill simple objects with meaning, and make the past live on in the present. Such things become remarkably important, when you find yourself a prisoner. A prisoner has nothing; he is stripped as bare as an animal, and human beings cannot tolerate being bare. Surely that's why we furnish our houses and ourselves with objects that give us comfort, in the loneliness of the universe.

Our charms were the last physical link that Mike and Dmitri and I had with what we'd been. They were part of what had made us ourselves. My boots and clothing are gone, my Rolex is gone, and my camera too, I thought; but I still have my tiger's claw. Already I was thinking like a prisoner.

Dressed in our thin, baggy uniforms, we stood waiting to see what would be done with us next. Dmitri smiled at the nearest soldier, offering him a cigarette. I'll have ham and eggs and coffee, he told him. Please ring room service, comrade.

The soldier took the cigarette, but he looked at us warningly as we laughed. It would be Dmitri's last joke for some time, because now things began to get worse.

They set about tying our hands again: this time in front of us, and without linking us.

Not so tight, fuck you. Dmitri spoke in English, squinting through the cigarette he could no longer remove from his mouth, staring hard and without fear into the face of the soldier working on his wrists. The man looked up and seemed to understand; I was afraid of what he would do. But he simply went on tying the knot, and did not seem to tighten it as viciously as before.

Then another of the soldiers came up to Dmitri, carrying a bunch of checked Cambodian scarves. He blindfolded Dmitri with one of them, and then did the same to Mike. Dmitri and

Mike were red-faced from the heat in the way that fair Europeans become; their yellow hair stuck out like straw over the scarves, and their light green uniforms had dark patches of sweat. They looked like boys in pajamas too small for them, ready for a game of blindman's bluff. In other circumstances, it would have been comical.

What *is* this? Goddamn it, what for? I heard Dmitri shout.

But the soldiers didn't answer him. It was my turn to be blindfolded now, and a cold wave went through my bowels and scrotum. As I lost sight of the world, I didn't doubt that they were going to execute us. Listening, my face running with sweat under the scarf, I heard other voices speaking Vietnamese, and guessed that some more soldiers had arrived. Both my elbows were gripped by hands, and I was ordered to march.

I walked inside darkness, feeling only the soft dust under my feet. I wasn't ready to die; I loved my life, and I loved Lu Ying, and I could not bear the thought that I would not get back to her. I began to pray. At the Church of England school I was sent to in Hong Kong, I had received Christian instruction, even though my father was a nonbeliever, his only values based on Confucianism. He wanted me to fit in, and he was tolerant of all religions: he said being C of E would help me to get on. So that is what I put on forms when asked my religion; but I had never really taken it seriously. Now I found to my surprise that I believed in God, although I didn't imagine him as being very much like the Church of England God we'd been taught about. I had no idea what God was like, but it somehow helped me to pray to him.

We marched for some time through dust, but then I felt it give way to a much harder surface—an oxcart path probably—filled with sharp stones. I had not often gone barefoot, and I found this very painful. Both my feet were soon cut in a number of places, and I could scarcely hobble along; but the hands gripping my arms forced me to do so. This went on for perhaps a quarter of an hour.

Then I heard one of the soldiers order us to halt, and at the same time I heard a motor running. The hands under my arms were half lifting me now, and I was helped into what I knew was the back of a truck, and pushed down onto what felt like a sack of rice. Then I heard Mike say: Jim? Is that you, mate? Dmitri?

We both answered him to say that we were here, and my heart lifted when I found that my brothers were with me still. If we were going to die, we would die together. The truck roared into gear, and we were moving off through the night.

I guessed that we were running on an old rubber plantation road, and I began to hope that we were simply being taken to another location, and would not be shot. After all, they could have done it anywhere on the path, if that was the intention.

We rode for perhaps an hour. I had no way of knowing in which direction we were going, but I guessed it to be further east, towards the border. When the truck pulled up, I was helped down to the ground, which I was glad to find was dusty, not stony. I hobbled on my cut feet, blindfolded still. I could hear frogs croaking, and the soldiers murmuring in Vietnamese; then my blindfold was removed.

We were in another village, with just one or two sluggish lights showing in the stilted houses. Mike and Dmitri were in front of me, looking back and grinning. The truck had gone, and our original three soldiers were with us: no one else.

We were led up the steps of one of the houses, about ten feet above the ground, and came into a large, dark room where one of the soldiers lit an oil lamp on a table. There were straw mats on the floor, some wooden chests, and sacks of rice stacked against one wall. There were also four beds here, with mosquito nets. We sat in a row on one of the beds, while a soldier stayed at the door, gun trained. A short time later, a very old and bent Cambodian woman in black pajamas came in with bowls and cups and baskets of steaming rice on a tray. She smiled in a friendly way and spoke in Khmer, urging us to eat. We found we had not only rice, but eggs with soy sauce, and tea.

We devoured it very fast, while the soldier stood in the doorway with his AK-47, ignoring us. We seemed to be allowed to talk now, and we began to discuss our position in low voices, and to speculate on what they would do with us. But we didn't have time to talk for very long.

Another NVA soldier came into the room. He was dressed in the same green fatigues as the others; but instead of a cotton hat, he wore the old-fashioned, colonial-style NVA sun helmet, with the red star of Communism on the front. Even without the pens in his top pocket, his bearing and the authority in his expression would have made me certain that he was an officer. He took off his sun helmet and stood in the center of the room, looking at us. His expression was serious but not intimidating. He was light-skinned, shorter than any of us, but tall for a Vietnamese and strongly built. He was perhaps in his late thirties, and had a serious, intelligent face.

We all stood up, and waited. When he spoke, it was in English; and his English was that of a well-educated man, if a little stiff.

I am commanding officer here, he said. My name is Captain Nguyen Van Danh. I hope that you have eaten sufficiently?

We said that we had.

Have you any complaints of your treatment?

We hesitated. Then Mike said: No complaints. But we'd be glad of some sandals. And some shaving gear.

I will do my best, the captain said. Sandals are in short supply: so are razors. But you must certainly have some.

He frowned at our cut feet. A medical attendant will deal with your feet, he said. Then, without turning around, he called a command in Vietnamese.

A second soldier appeared at the door carrying two rucksacks, which he brought over to a chest in a corner and emptied out. All our belongings lay in front of us: cameras, tape recorders, clothing, boots, wallets, personal papers and documents. Even my Rolex was there.

I believe these are your possessions, the captain said. He produced a notebook and a pen. I want you to examine these things, and be sure that nothing is missing.

We went through the articles and he made us name them all, listing them in his notebook. When we said that everything was there, I asked him when it would be returned to us.

The captain looked at me as though considering his answer. Before he could reply, Dmitri said: What my friend means is, Captain, when will we be released?

The captain's face became blank. I cannot answer that at present, he said. The decision cannot be made yet whether to release you or not. You are accused of being in the employ of the CIA. Your position will be studied. You are prisoners of war, in the hands of the People's Liberation Army, and you will be treated correctly. Now I think you will need sleep.

He turned and left the room, giving us no opportunity to answer.

I lay stretched on the bed in the most peaceful state I'd known since our capture, which now seemed days ago. I was so tired that I floated as though in delirium; but I was comfortable. A medical orderly had painted our feet with Mercurochrome, and my cuts gently throbbed. Mike and Dmitri, already asleep, lay in beds nearby. We had the mosquito nets drawn, and it was a luxury not to be bitten.

For a short time, the three of us had talked, even though we were almost too tired to speak. Our meal had given us strength and revived our spirits; so had our interview with the captain. But our most likely fate now, we decided, was to end in a prison camp on the other side of the border: and that wouldn't be something we'd survive very easily, from what we'd heard of those camps. We had to convince the Vietnamese that as war photographers, we were neutral. And we had to somehow prove that we weren't CIA.

Mike was snoring; Dmitri scarcely seemed to breathe. In my heart, I spoke to them both as though they were my blood brothers. *Sleep,* I said. *Rest, brothers.*

I was kept awake for a little longer by the sound of military trucks passing somewhere outside the village, the whining of their motors telling me they were old, and heavily loaded. Even when I slept, they got into my dreams: they seemed to be moving by at intervals all through the night.

By blindfolding us, the Vietnamese had taken great trouble to conceal from us where we were. But I felt certain we were in country near the Vietnamese border, since this was probably the only region where the North Vietnamese Army would still be coming inside Cambodia in any numbers. All their forces were pulling back over the border now, in accordance with the Paris peace agreements. I would prove to be right: what I was hearing was the NVA's supply trucks, moving down a section of the Ho Chi Minh Trail.

I hear it still, in my head: a sound that's now part of history.

2.

JIM FENG

We were held in the village for only one night. The next morning, we were taken away with Captain Van Danh's patrol.

There were only seven soldiers in the unit, and we marched with them on a track whose surface was sealed with crushed stones, its bed of packed red earth. It looked not much better than an oxcart path: but we were walking on the Ho Chi Minh Trail.

So few people ever saw the Trail, except from the air. It was a fact and yet not a fact: a rumor. And it wasn't one trail, but many: a network of roads and tracks that ran for thousands of miles. It came over razorback ridges; through mountain corridors and jungle; across flooded rivers. Thousands died to build it: of malaria, dysentery and exhaustion, as well as from air attacks. Its flimsy pontoon bridges were all the time bombed and all the time remade, and its convoys of trucks and bicycles never stopped coming, bringing their troops and their arms in an endless flow from the North. The Trail was what won the war; and now that the war's over, I suppose it will exist soon only in memories, and in North Vietnamese soldiers' songs. So it's sometimes difficult to believe that we marched on it, Mike, Dmitri and I. But we did; and for me it's a great thing to have done, despite all the sadness of what happened.

As I'd guessed, the village where we'd slept had been close to a point where a branch of the Trail came through Cambodia. A hundred kilometers or so to the southeast, it would pass into South Vietnam through the Parrot's Beak: the section of the border that points at Saigon. This was where the patrol was headed: they'd been posted back to Vietnam, they said, and were taking us there with them. Captain Danh told us that we'd cross the border somewhere near Highway 1, but he wouldn't say what they planned to do with us then: only that he was joining a larger unit.

Along the Trail at intervals, we passed way stations guarded by a few NVA soldiers: groups of little huts whose roofs were camouflaged with palm fronds. Arms and food were stored there; trucks could be hidden from air attack, and sometimes there were vegetable plots to supply the convoys. I've learned since then that further north, where the Trail went through the jungles and mountains of eastern Cambodia and Laos, it was far more impressive than in this section. It had become a two-lane highway, and some of the main control points were as big as villages, with barracks, fueling stations, dispensaries, shop facilities and comfortable rest houses. Hidden from the air by the jungle canopy, the convoys of trucks moved bumper to bumper, like traffic in a city at peak hour, their headlights at night making glimmering chains in the blackness.

But there wasn't much traffic on our branch of the Trail, since the Delta provinces it led to weren't where Hanoi's troops and supplies could yet be concentrated. Also, the border region here was an open country of paddy fields and light forest—so that trucks would easily have been seen from the air. Traveling by day, it was safer to go on foot, as we were doing. Trucks moved at night, and even then their numbers here were few.

At first we kept hoping that we'd ride in one, instead of walking. But Captain Danh told us that the trucks were heavily loaded, and our patrol would go all the way on foot: it was less than ten days' march, he said. He didn't talk much about the unit's function, except to say that it was part of a liaison team that helped to secure the Trail, working in cooperation with the local villagers.

A liaison team could be doing a lot of things; we all knew that. When we talked it over, Mike said he believed that Captain Danh's unit was connected with COSVN: the secret Central Office for South Vietnam the Americans were always looking for, which was supposed to be directing the war. He'd heard that COSVN was located just a few kilometers north of here, in the rubber plantation area called the Fish Hook. And he thought that the team's real function would very likely have been to negotiate purchases of arms from corrupt Lon Nol commanders on the west bank. It might also have been involved in the rubber trade, he said. The Communists sold rubber to the Lon Nol forces, and the Lon Nol Government sold it abroad: they added a lot to their treasury that way. Mike had a lot of information like that. Some of it probably came from Aubrey Hardwick; and I would guess that Aubrey's sources were his friends in the CIA.

We were dressed and equipped just as the soldiers were, except that we carried no weapons. We wore our green cotton uniforms and cotton bush hats, and carried our packs and our cotton tubes of rice as they did. And Captain Danh had kept his word: we had Ho Chi Minh sandals on our feet. When we'd first put these on, we'd felt as though we were flying. But with our feet half-bare, we constantly feared a bite from the small brown krait which the soldiers called *cham quap*. It looks just like a dried branch, and the men were always watching the ground. Many North Vietnamese soldiers died from the krait's bite, they said. The medic carried snakebite capsules—but this didn't reassure us very much.

The team's diet was extremely basic: small portions of rice, shreds of dried meat and fish; a few vegetables. Most of their provisions they got from the way stations; but sometimes they got supplies from the villages we passed through. They always paid for the food; they never plundered. They ate only twice a day, morning and evening, and marched for very long periods without breaking to rest. By carrying such light gear, they covered many more kilometers a day than Western soldiers could have done. But the weather was still very hot and humid, with little rain, and this made the march tiring. The gear we carried consisted of one canteen, a rolled-up hammock, a light nylon poncho, a mosquito net, a single change of fatigues and underpants, a metal dish, a small towel, and a fragment of soap. To clean our teeth we used splinters of bamboo. We washed in streams off the track, and filled our canteens there or from springs, adding purification tablets.

Captain Danh didn't say much to us at first, but he was always courteous and considerate. He gave us a small ration of Vietnamese cigarettes each day which I suspected were from his own store, and he lent us his own cut-throat razor to shave with, since no other was available. It was very blunt.

There isn't much to tell about the first four days of the march. We walked a little apart, always with one or two of the soldiers behind us. We were with these men, yet not of them: we were even made to eat our meals separately, sitting at a distance. It was only on the fifth night that we began to know them better.

That was when we were allowed to sit with them around the rice pot. The story of our march really begins there.

The woodland areas we passed through now were full of splintered trees and bomb craters—some new, some dating from the B-52 bombing of three years before. The craters were enormous: thirty feet or more across. Some of the craters had filled with water, and had turned into ponds where villagers kept ducks. Sometimes we passed ruined, deserted villages with smashed and burned-out houses that had never been reoccupied, where half-wild dogs snarled at us.

Here in this Vietnam border country was where the war in Cambodia had begun. The Americans had carried out their secret bombing raids here, trying to hit the Viet Cong sanctuaries; and this was where the American and ARVN forces had invaded in 1970. Now the B-52s were bombing here again; but during those first few days, no bombs fell in our vicinity. The important convoys they were seeking weren't here but further north, behind us. Once we heard low thunder from the north and felt a faint trembling in the earth, and we guessed that it came from the Fish Hook.

Then, on the fifth afternoon, at about four o'clock, they came.

There was a low, white gray sky, and we didn't see them. But you never do; they fly too high. The Trail was taking us out of the open into a small forest when we heard the explosions. They must have been many kilometers away, but they shook the earth under our feet, and I knew instantly what they were. I'd heard that *whump-whump-whump* coming from around Phnom Penh, as the Americans carpeted the Khmer Rouge forces: but always a good way off. This was closer, and its volume was frightening.

Captain Danh shouted an order, and the unit moved quickly into the shadow of some palm trees. They threw themselves flat, and Mike, Dmitri and I did the same. The earth here was pinkish and bare and dry as biscuits, and covered with dead leaves. I will never forget that earth, because a few moments later it heaved under us.

It heaved in a huge spasm, and I found myself hugging it as though I were clinging to an upturned boat; then a roar engulfed us unlike anything I'd ever known. I'd never imagined such a sound. It was not a sound, it was something beyond sound; it opened up a gaping hole in the world and in my head, making my mind cry out in terror, making the whole world rock and sway. The palms and bigger trees nearby were bending like grass. This is not right, this is not war, nobody should be doing a thing like this, I said, and I pissed my pants. I was very ashamed: in all my years of covering action I'd never done such a thing. So I felt better when I learned later that many of the NVA soldiers did the same, in their first B-52 raid.

Now, as the sound died away, we were all staring at each other, serious and amazed. There were no more explosions; the bombers had passed on. I found that I was shaking uncontrollably, and saw that Mike and Dmitri were shaking in the same way. Captain Danh, lying close by, was looking across at us with an expression of cheerful sympathy; he saw our condition, but made no comment. He pushed back his old-fashioned sun helmet with its red star; then he smiled, and sat up.

We are lucky, Mr. Jim, he said. That was not really very close. One kilometer closer, and maybe we would have no eardrums.

The pot was big, and of black iron. The soldiers cooked their rice in it every morning and evening, and they sat around it in a circle with their metal dishes and ate from it together: Captain Danh included. In the mornings, there wouldn't be much talk, but in the evenings they'd talk and laugh quite a lot, lingering over their canteens of hot tea. They were doing this now.

Darkness was falling, and their faces reflected the flames from the low fire on which the rice was cooking. Most of them, including Captain Danh, had taken off their bush hats and sun helmets. Their assault rifles were beside them; they were always alert; but they seemed unconcerned about the bombers. They were in constant radio contact with other groups, and seemed to know when raids were happening; apparently everything was quiet this evening, and they were listening to a newscast from Radio Hanoi on a shortwave transistor radio.

We were camped in a clearing, in the sort of forest that was common here: almost like parkland, with spindly, white-trunked trees that looked like birches, palms and stands of bamboo, and spaces of the pinkish dry earth. As usual at mealtimes, Mike and Dmitri and I were sitting apart from the group. We squatted against a clump of tall bamboo that rose like a wall behind us, watching the little circle around the fire. Soon, we knew, a soldier would bring over our helpings in metal dishes. Our hands were never tied now, on the condition that we stood and sat exactly where we were supposed to, and made no unexpected moves. But we always felt a little sad to be segregated from these men we marched with all day.

This evening, the feeling grew much stronger. We spoke about it together; we all felt it. Why could we not eat with them?

This will no doubt seem strange and absurd to you; after all, we were prisoners, and regarded as enemies. But the feeling had partly been strengthened by the B-52 raid. No doubt prisoners begin to grow childish; but the fact is, with the raid still fresh as a thing we'd all shared, we felt that we were no longer simply prisoners, but temporary members of Captain Danh's unit. And waiting for our rice, exiled from the cheerful ring around the fire, we grew more and more sad and resentful. We should be able to eat around the pot, we said.

Until now, North Vietnamese and Viet Cong soldiers had not been real to us: they had simply been the People Over There. We had seen them only as prisoners, or the dead. Once, after covering a battle in the Vietnamese Highlands with the Americans, I had watched U.S. officers examine the body of an NVA soldier and go through his effects. It was the first time I had covered action against the North Vietnamese, so he was the first NVA soldier I'd seen at close quarters, and he had stayed in my mind. He'd looked so very small. All he had was his pack, and there was nothing inside it but a change of underwear, some letters from home, and a sad little plastic packet of rice. Such a small amount of rice, I thought, how could it sustain him? Now, I saw that these soldiers of Captain Danh's liaison team were the same. He and his men had very little of anything; they managed on the bare essentials, and although we didn't forget what sort of regime they fought for, we couldn't help admiring their hardiness, and being touched by their poverty and simplicity, now that we saw it for ourselves.

We'd already begun to be familiar with all the members of the team. Except for Captain Danh, they were all a lot younger than us. They didn't tell us their names, so we made some up. The medic, with his open boy's face and a big cap of hair cut straight across the forehead, was of course called Doc. A tough-looking man with slit eyes, who carried the field radio, was called Lenin. One with glasses and a sensitive face was the Professor; another, with heavy eyelids, prone to malaria, was called Weary; and there was a quiet, handsome one with a broad face, whom Mike called Prince. A stocky, cheerful man who always carried the rice pot on his back we called Turtle, because the pot looked like his shell.

And we were getting to know the small habits of these men whom we'd never truly know. Turtle joked a lot, nudging his comrades in the ribs; Prince stared into space, as though remembering lost love; Lenin squinted and watched people, and sometimes picked his nose; Doc repeatedly pushed back his fringe of hair from his forehead; the Professor bit his nails and reread letters from home. They marched always in groups of three: Doc, Weary and Lenin; Prince, Professor and Turtle. Captain Danh told us eventually that this was the NVA practice: three-man teams, who supported each other as comrades. Strange, I thought, they are like us: Mike, Dmitri and me.

Some of them had begun to show small signs of being friendly. Doc and Turtle would now and then smile at us as we marched, and it's hard to convey what a smile means when you are in the hands of the enemy. They had begun to try and communicate with us in Vietnamese, telling us the names of objects and laughing when we pronounced them. When Mike spoke whole sentences—which he did quite well—most of the team clapped and laughed; and when I revealed that I knew more Vietnamese than they'd thought I did, many of them grew quite warm to me. They knew very little of the world we came from: when I tried to explain to them that I shot film for television, they couldn't understand, although they pretended to, and I guessed that none of them had ever seen television.

Tonight they were cooking pork soup and cabbage leaves to add to the rice: ingredients they'd got from a friendly village nearby, together with some bunches of bananas and palm-sugar juice. This was considered an unusually good meal, and the faces in the firelight were especially cheerful as they waited for it to cook. Our mouths watered. Hunger was gnawing at our guts as usual: we thought about food nearly all the time.

Suddenly Mike stood up. He walked away from the wall of bamboos and approached Captain Danh, while we watched in surprise: he was breaking the rules.

The captain turned and looked at him. He was standing by the pot while the men squatted, his face reflecting the flames of the fire. Mike smiled at him, but the captain kept a stern expression, and the men looked up in surprise. Lenin, who had been stirring the soup with a wooden spoon, stopped stirring.

Excuse me, Captain, Mike said. We'd like to eat with you. Can we do that?

You will be brought food in a moment, Captain Danh said. You should wait where you are.

No, no, Mike said. I mean we'd like to sit here around the pot. We don't feel good about being separate. It seems unfriendly.

For a moment, his eyes getting wide, the captain said nothing, and stared.

Stooped a little, standing there in the too-small green uniform that left his shins bare, Mike looked a bit like an overgrown boy asking for a treat. All of us feel this way, he said. We're sharing everything else. We even got bombed with you. Can't we share the meal from the pot with you?

His glance was both joking and confidential: a look that I'd seen other Australians use. He gestured with his hands, holding them palms upward, seeming to welcome whatever life might put in them. I'd seen Mike charm so many people like this, from customs people who would help get his film out to officials who would give him information. Would it work with an NVA officer?

Captain Danh stared at him a little longer. So you want to eat rice with us, he said. He was still serious, and I thought he would now order Mike back. But suddenly he smiled too; and instead of answering, he held out his arm at full length towards the circle of men around the pot, his hand open, all the time looking at Mike. He nodded, still smiling; then he said: Please.

Dmitri and I stood up, looking at each other. As we walked towards the pot, I had a surge of gladness; and when I found the captain smiling at us too, this gladness made my throat swell.

How can I explain to you the feeling that night, as we sat in the circle around the rice pot? You will find it strange. You'll also perhaps think it false, remembering all the stories about prisoners and hostages who in their fear and weakness begin to love their captors. But it wasn't like that. We weren't afraid of Captain Danh and his men; we weren't kissing arse in the hope of release; we had simply begun to like them. And since we were officially neutral, these feelings didn't make us feel compromised.

Squatting down together, we filled our dishes, and for a time, everyone just ate. The heat was still heavy, but the sky was clear; looking towards the north above the dark tops of the trees, I could pick out the star we call in China the Herd-boy. *Far away twinkles the Herd-boy star,* I thought: a line from one of the old poems my father used to read to me. For some reason I'd begun to think in Mandarin again; usually I think in English. From somewhere in the bamboos, a night-bird kept making the same call; now and then a group of monkeys chattered in alarm. There were no other sounds.

Turtle belched, and everyone laughed except Captain Danh, who ate without expression. He was sitting directly opposite me, and I stealthily watched him: it was like trying to understand a strict schoolmaster. I'd begun to suspect that our fate was in his hands: that he could turn us over to his superiors, or else set us free at the border. When I thought of being in some prison camp in Hanoi it made me sick with dread, and I would study Captain Danh's face for clues to his likely intentions. He had taken his helmet off, and a lock of his thick hair fell across his forehead. In the firelight, his face had a bronze tinge, and was deeply shadowed—which could have made it threatening, but didn't. He had a habit when he smiled of raising his eyebrows and wrinkling up his forehead: his face then became very warm. His eyes were set wide apart, and he had the sort of gaze that did not shift from your face when he spoke to you. Two kinds of men do this, in my experience: those who are dishonest and unusually calculating, and those who have the sort of honesty that will not allow them to compromise. Captain Danh seemed to be of the second kind; but how could I be sure?

He had spoken to us very little until now, except about practical things. And I had to remind myself that like all NVA officers, he would also be a dedicated Marxist cadre, no doubt with a fanatical devotion to his cause, and a fanatical hatred of the West. The evening before, he had sat down with his men and conducted some sort of political session, obviously aimed at boosting their morale; it had ended with the singing of a patriotic song. But he had not been very authoritarian about it: the six young soldiers had been relaxed and casual: laughing, exchanging jokes and cigarettes and even clowning with each other like schoolboys. They obviously respected him without fearing him. Captain Danh didn't seem like a fanatic; but his reserve could be hiding it.

Mike rubbed his belly, grinning at Turtle across the fire, and spoke in his rough Vietnamese. This is good, he said. Then, in English: Bloody good pork, mate.

All the soldiers laughed; they always laughed when Mike spoke Vietnamese, and Turtle repeated his phrase with amusement: Bluddy good pok!

Captain Danh spoke to Mike in English. I think this is not as good as the food you are used to, he said.

Mike said that he was quite used to this food; that he had often eaten similar army rations in Vietnam.

But those would have been American rations, Captain Danh said.

No, Mike said. They were South Vietnamese rations.

Captain Danh raised his eyebrows. And what did you think of the Army of South Vietnam? We hear the Americans have a low opinion of them.

The Americans are wrong, Mike said. The ARVN stay in the field as long as your troops do, and mostly they fight just as hard. Now that the American troops have gone, they're fighting even harder. They stopped your army at Hue last year, didn't they? And now they seem to be stopping you at An Loc.

He said this with a pleasant expression, sitting quite still as he spoke, his eyes not moving from Captain Danh's. Danh studied him for a moment, and the circle of firelit faces watched Mike too, not understanding what he'd said.

For this they needed help from American bombing. And I don't think they will win the war, Danh said. His voice wasn't argumentative: it was low and thoughtful. They will not win because they have nothing to believe in, he said.

And what do your troops believe in, Captain?

Dmitri Volkov had spoken up, and my stomach was clutched at by unease. The Count was so likely to say unwise things, even in our present situation.

My troops?

Captain Danh looked around the circle of listening young men, whose frames were so delicately made that they scarcely appeared capable of bearing any sort of hardship at all. They know very little about politics, he said. Often they have marched for hundreds of kilometers; they have been bombed until they feel crazy; they are half starved, and homesick for their villages and their families. But they believe in their country.

And you think in the end that this will be enough? Against B-52s?

Dmitri sat hugging his knees, grinning at Captain Danh across the fire. Please, Count, I thought, don't make trouble.

All the bombs the Americans drop will make no difference, Danh said. His voice stayed quiet, and he didn't seem annoyed. You know, they don't kill many of us, these bombs. We have learned how to avoid them. Malaria kills more of us on the Trail than the B-52s do: we call it the jungle tax. So the Americans are deluded. They sit in the sky like gods, pressing buttons. But when we shoot them down over Hanoi, they don't look like gods. Wars are won on the earth, in the end—and this is our earth.

He smiled. But I think you will not like hearing this, he said.

I spoke up now, before the Count could. As news photographers, I said, it wasn't our business to like or dislike the war: we just recorded it.

The captain frowned. But Mr. Mike and Mr. Dmitri represent the American press and television, he said. He seemed to mistake our given names for family names, as Vietnamese often do. Or perhaps—being an educated man—he was aware of our custom, but still chose to address us in this way. It may have amused him.

So they also represent the American government, he went on.

And you, Mr. Jim: you represent the British government in the same way. Isn't that true?

No, I said. And I tried to explain that the American and British television networks and magazines we worked for were independent, and not owned by governments. We showed what was happening in our pictures and film stories whether it was good news for the Americans or bad, I said.

You risk your lives, Danh said, and narrowed his eyes. Why would you do that if you are on no side?

It's our living, I said.

You do it just for money? Danh looked from one to the other of us.

Money and fun, Dmitri said.

And you have no beliefs?

Beliefs? Sure, I have plenty of beliefs, Dmitri said. Too many. My friends will tell you that. But beliefs have nothing to do with the job. Beliefs are private, Captain.

I found that I was gripping my elbows tightly as I sat; I had become very tense. This discussion surely had a purpose, and if Dmitri went too far, he could lose us whatever chance we had of freedom. A spark snapped in the fire, and we all turned our heads; it was that quiet.

Please explain to me, Danh said. Are you saying that you would report the truth about battles won by our forces?

We do it all the time, I said.

Not like Radio Hanoi, Dmitri said.

Danh appeared not to hear this; or perhaps didn't wish to. He turned to Doc, who sat beside him, and whom I guessed to hold a higher rank than the other soldiers. He spoke quietly to him in Vietnamese, while Doc nodded; I could understand almost nothing, but I gathered that Danh was repeating what we'd just said. Lenin was listening intently, his eyes glinting and fixed. Then the monkeys chattered again, in the dark wall of trees and bamboos, and Danh glanced towards the sound and smiled. He had the sort of smile that stopped things from being too serious.

They too have an opinion to express, he said, and we all laughed.

The next night, we sat around the pot in the open again. As we were finishing off our rice, Captain Danh picked up the conversation of the night before as though we'd only just dropped it, pointing a finger at us and smiling.

I believe I understand your outlook, he said. You are individualists. I have once believed in this sort of individualism myself. But when I thought and studied, I realized we could not afford it in Vietnam. Perhaps no one can afford it, since it leads to anarchy and immorality.

How does that follow? Mike asked.

Have you read Hegel? I believe Hegel to be right, Danh said. We can only be truly moral and free if we subordinate ourselves to the State. This is a paradox—but true.

And the Hegel gave us Marx, who used the same argument, Dmitri put in. And Marx gave us Stalin and Mao Tse-tung, and so people didn't gain freedom, but lost it. And millions were liquidated.

His voice had that purring sound it sometimes got, which meant that he was liable to say anything. The danger had been averted last night; but now I grew cold inside. I caught Mike's eye, but his expression told me nothing. Dmitri had been to university; Mike and I hadn't. If the Count chose to pursue an argument in political philosophy, there wasn't much we could do to come in and head him off.

You are a French citizen, Mr. Dmitri, Captain Danh said suddenly. But your name is Russian. Are you Russian?

I am of Russian family—but as you say, I am French citizen, Dmitri said. I have never been in Russia. Why do you ask?

I thought that you might have firsthand knowledge of the Soviet system, Danh said. That is all. And I want to say to you: please don't think that the Vietnamese Communist Party follows the Soviet model in all things. I want also to say that what you have said is not necessarily logical.

He leaned forward a little, drawing his packet of Vietnamese cigarettes from his shirt pocket; but still his tone was pleasant, not

333

angry. He offered a cigarette to Dmitri, who took it and thanked him; then he held the packet out to Mike and me. I saw that he was a man who liked to debate.

If we accept the State as the main source of justice and security, this should not necessarily lead to tyranny, Danh said.

He was looking at Volkov again.

The State is the community, he said. And human beings cannot be civilized without a lawful community. You agree? Unless we are protected from want and exploitation and criminal attack, we cannot fulfill ourselves. There can be no science; no poetry; no art; no philosophy. And this protection is what the State gives us. So in making the State paramount, we are liberated.

Weary slurped loudly on his tea, and Danh glanced towards him with no expression. All the soldiers appeared to be listening, watching our faces like students, and I wondered if some of them actually understood a little English. Lenin was especially intent, his canteen of tea clasped in both hands, his eyes narrow, examining Dmitri's face. And suddenly I saw that the light in Lenin's eyes was one of deep dislike—perhaps even hatred. It gave me a little shock, and I feared for Dmitri. None of the others looked at Dmitri or any of us like that, and I began to suspect that Lenin did have some English—and also that he was not an ordinary soldier. I had heard that there was always a second Communist Party cadre in even the smallest of these units, whose job was to report on the leader. Maybe this was Lenin's function; and I wondered how politically orthodox Captain Danh was being when he spoke.

This is an elegant argument of the Hegel's, Captain, Dmitri was saying. I sympathize with your reasons for accepting it. Unfortunately it went further, you might remember. The monarch is the embodiment of the state, so his power is not to be questioned. And Marxism substitutes for this the Party and its bosses —with absolute power, also not to be questioned. In other words, dictatorship, pretending to represent the people. Correct?

The captain said nothing for a moment. Then he looked at each of us in turn. When we have won this war, he said, it will not be like that in Vietnam. We will liberate the people, not enslave them. He drew on his cigarette, releasing the smoke slowly through his nostrils. I am a patriot, he said, and so are my comrades. I am first of all a patriot and only secondly a Marxist. Do you understand that? Shall I tell you why I am a patriot?

We waited, and he pointed into the darkness towards the west. Out there are the old French rubber plantations, he said. You have seen them. In the colonial days, Vietnamese were brought here to work. My mother's father was one of them. He was beaten constantly; he was fed barely enough to live. He was a slave to the soil. There is no worse slavery.

You're right about that, Captain.

I looked up in surprise; Mike had said this.

Danh glanced at him. You agree? Then you will understand, Mr. Mike, when I say that this was why the Viet Minh fought; and why we go on fighting as sons of the Viet Minh. No one else will own our soil! You come from countries where patriotism no longer matters—but that is because you do not have to fight for your soil.

He turned back to Dmitri. I know the dangers you are speaking of, he said. It is the passions of the mind that are most dangerous, I think—not the passions of the body. Europeans have been very prone to those passions. So are we.

Dmitri regarded him with a delighted expression. He had begun to look like some sort of bandit, in the last week: his blond hair tangled, his face red from the sun, his blue eyes faded and staring. Now he gave the captain the sort of open-mouthed smile he usually reserved for his friends. "The passions of the mind": good, Captain, what you say is true. Did you study history, in your youth?

I wondered whether Captain Danh would react badly to this familiarity: but he still answered courteously. Yes, he said, I studied in Paris, in the fifties—like many of my comrades. I wanted to be a teacher. I studied European history and political philosophy.

His frankness and pleasantness were reassuring; but I knew that we would be foolish to trust him. He's probably playing a game with us, I thought: he's encouraging this discussion in order to report what we say to his superiors.

My friends and I would read everything we could, in those

days, Danh said. We wanted to know everything. We read Tom Paine, Montesquieu, Voltaire, Marx, Sartre. We were drunk on ideas; drunk on revolution: we would talk all night, in Paris. And I have to admit, Mr. Dmitri, it was European history and European thinkers that we learned our lessons from. Mostly French. The French didn't want to give us liberty, but they have certainly taught us about it.

I too was a student in French hands, Dmitri said. For a very brief time: one year, before failure and forcible removal from Sorbonne. I was not scholarly type. But my reading was much the same as yours. Tom Paine gave me a big buzz.

Danh frowned, not understanding this term; but Dmitri was going on.

"To begin the world over again": yes. That is very exciting idea when you are young. But I put it to you, Captain: we cannot begin over again. To begin again is impossible: what results is destruction; murder. Tyranny by the worst: those for whom destruction is their food, and who in fact want nothing but power. We still have to learn from French Revolution, in my opinion. French Revolution is not over, any more than Russian. The trouble is, with revolution: first comes romantic frenzy—then comes sickness. First comes lovely idealism and love of mankind—then comes power-lust and Terror.

Danh had no expression as he listened to this. His eyes never moved from the Count's face, and his cigarette stayed still in his hand.

Do you not credit the French revolutionaries with love of liberty? he asked.

Please, Count, I thought, no more. This was far worse than the night before, and it's hard for me to explain to you how scary Dmitri's talk was in that situation. Speaking like this to a Communist cadre who was our jailer must surely be jeopardizing any chances of release we might have: I felt sure of it.

But Dmitri went on.

Of course, he said. They have all loved liberty: Marat; Robespierre; Saint-Just. They were all Inquisitors defending liberty—and seeing heretics against it everywhere. Robespierre was very religious man, as a matter of fact: high priest of a new religion —right, Captain? Young Saint-Just the same: you will remember he has said that the fire of liberty would purify society. So he drew up lists for his secret police to carry this out, sending thousands to guillotine. *Mon Dieu,* it's mind-blowing! Faster and faster goes Madame Guillotine, and the prisons are jammed— until people can bear no more, and rise against these men of liberty. One of the Great Committee said that their eyes were fixed too high to see that the ground was covered in blood—and he was proud of this!

He drew quickly on his Vietnamese cigarette, then wrenched it from his lips and exhaled, looking around the silent circle of faces with his pale eyes. His face wasn't smiling now: it was fervent; severe. Captain Danh and Lenin were watching him as though seeing him for the first time—as though wondering what trick he would perform next. As for me, I was in despair, a knot in my belly; I had just about given up hope for us. I half hated Dmitri for what he was doing, while a part of me admired his daring—if daring was what it was, rather than foolishness.

He now threw his cigarette into the fire, and looked at Captain Danh again.

They always come with revolution, guys like that, he said. They are special. Robespierre; Saint-Just; Lenin; Stalin. Lenin has a lot in common with Saint-Just: he too has established secret police immediately on arrival. These are educated men, you remember. Full of crazy enthusiasm; full of hate for what doesn't fit their plan! "The passions of the mind," Captain! And the people, the peasants, finally try to rise against them. They tried to rise against Jacobins; against Lenin and Stalin too. With very shitty results for themselves in both cases, poor bastards.

He went on and said more, but I've forgotten it now; perhaps I blocked it out. When he concluded, Danh cleared his throat and spoke as quietly as before.

We are not like this, he said. Our land reforms have freed the peasants from landlords who were squeezing them to death.

And then he turned to me.

You will know about such land reforms in China, Mr. Jim. I

understand you came to Hong Kong from the mainland: that your family lived in Peking. You must have been a boy there before the Liberation.

A chill went through me. Now I understood, or thought I did. This was an interrogation. Everything we said was helping to fill out a dossier that would affect our fate. The statements we'd been made to write out in the hut on the evening of our capture had clearly been passed on to Captain Danh; and he and his superiors had deduced what I was: a class enemy, to use their language. I felt despair. As a Chinese, I would be looked at differently by the North Vietnamese authorities from the way in which they would regard Mike and Dmitri. My accreditation as a correspondent and my Hong Kong passport would mean very little. But there was no point in lying.

Yes, I said. My father was a scholar.

Captain Danh nodded. So you were of the *shen-shih,* he said. The gentry class. Many were landlords, and treated the people very badly. Is that not true?

Yes, I said. But not all. My father was a public official, not a landlord, and he believed in reform himself. His chief love has always been T'ang poetry, not money making.

Danh looked at me for a few seconds more, but said nothing. Then he turned to Mike, who was sitting beside me. And you, Mr. Mike, he said. What do you think? You say very little.

Mike rubbed the back of his neck, not answering at first. Then he threw the last of his tea onto the ground.

I think we have to care about each other, he said.

Danh pursed his lips, and looked amused. That is all? And this includes all enemies?

As long as they don't try to shoot us, Mike said. And then he winked at the captain, keeping a straight face.

I could tell now from the captain's expression that he didn't know what to make of Mike, and didn't know whether Mike was kidding him or not. But you often didn't know, with Snow. After the discussion between Captain Danh and Volkov, his words sounded quite naive. Well, Snow was no big thinker, any more than I am. But it was strange: these unimportant words and his wink had eased my anxiety, and had somehow taken tension from the air. Perhaps it had something to do with the power of his silence, and the calm in his face. Even the faces of the young soldiers—all except Lenin, that is—seemed to soften and grow happy as they looked at him. Nothing ever changed Mike, I thought; nothing ever could, it seemed. And I found myself looking at him as a child looks at a certain kind of adult, believing that such an adult has the ability to solve any problem, and to remove all fear from the world.

Captain Danh turned back to Dmitri. I would just like to say this to you, Mr. Dmitri, he said. Marxism is not a religion for us that cannot be changed: Marxism is a tool to help us free our country. Do you understand?

Dmitri raised his eyebrows; then he lifted his canteen of tea in a toast. I understand, he said. *Bonne chance,* Captain.

In one way this surprised me from Dmitri; his hatred of Marxism was so great. But in another way it didn't. Captain Nguyen Van Danh was a likable man, and for Volkov, the person always came first, not the beliefs. And I saw too that despite all Dmitri's talk, he didn't seem to have antagonized Danh—which wasn't to say that he hadn't done us great damage in regard to the report on us. But whatever the outcome of his behavior, there was some kind of spark of interest between himself and Danh that I believe was genuine. Of course, Danh might be a very good actor, and his interest might be secretly hostile; but somehow I didn't think so. Sometimes an atmosphere springs up between two people that cannot be manufactured or faked.

I raised my canteen. So did Mike, and Captain Danh laughed. A pity we have no wine, he said.

The spindly trees with the white trunks grew close together here, and we slung our hammocks between them: close enough to talk to each other in whispers, and a little way off from the nearest hammocks of the soldiers. Across by the dead fire, Prince sat on watch, his rifle across his knees. The team took turns on watch throughout the night.

I wanted only to sleep, but Mike and Dmitri went on whispering to each other.

I like this Danh, Mike said. I think he has good feelings.

I also like him, Dmitri said. But remember what he is. Don't fool yourself he's our good old buddy.

I think there's a chance he'll set us free, Mike said. But listen, Count, go easy on the political speeches. Don't fight the Cold War here, mate, or he'll never let us go.

Dmitri chuckled. They are very unlikely to do that anyway, haven't you realized? You think I am being unwise, but I tell you, Snow: it doesn't matter. Everything is down against us already—opinions will make no difference. They think we are CIA—and the Danh just likes to talk. He has his duty, which is to hand us over to much tougher bastards on Vietnam side—where we will go to goddamn prison camp.

Maybe, Mike said. But I'm going to keep on hoping that's not so. You should do the same, Count.

Dmitri's voice rose slightly above a whisper: it was weary and small, and suddenly drained of its life.

I try, Snow—but I am getting very tired. I think I am in for one of my malaria attacks.

We'll get you through, mate. Right, Jim?

Mike's pale face had turned towards me under its mosquito net, and I roused myself. Right, I said. Don't worry, Count. Hang in there.

There was silence for a time: nothing to be heard but the rustling of leaves in a breeze, the whine of mosquitoes, and the sounds of other insects. Then I heard Dmitri again, very soft, like a child.

Hey, Jim: where would you like to be now?

It was a game we often played, to help ourselves along.

Sitting in the York in Singapore, I said. With a long cool beer, and Old Charlie breaking up the ice.

Old York is gone now, Dmitri said.

So is Old Charlie, Mike said. A lot of things are gone.

Whatever happens, Dmitri said, we had some good times— right?

Right, we both said, and were quiet again. We had meant what we said, and it was important to us. I drifted into sleep, feeling comforted.

The next day, the march got much harder.

We'd now been moving down the Trail for seven days, and were into the first week of May. The monsoon was arriving, and the afternoon downpours were turning the surface of the Trail to a thick red mud: mud that sucked at our sandals, making it difficult to walk. Soon these rains would get heavier and more frequent, and I dreaded what this would mean. Never dry, we would get foot sores and fungus, and there would be mud, mud, mud.

Turning, I found that Dmitri had lagged far behind, and I stopped to wait for him. So did Mike; and Weary halted to watch all three of us, while the rest of the patrol went ahead. We were always watched.

Dmitri trudged up to us slowly, looking very pale and tired. I remembered what he'd said the night before about his malaria coming on, and Mike obviously remembered this too: he asked him whether he was sick. But Dmitri shook his head.

I'm OK, he said. He is the one with malaria.

And he jerked a thumb at Weary, who stood with his rifle drooping to the ground. Weary's eyelids were half closed now; he was a bad yellow color, his face shining with sweat, and he was shivering in regular spasms. We all knew the symptoms, and looked at him with concern: that he walked at all was remarkable. Mike spoke to him in Vietnamese, pointing to his rucksack. He was asking to take it.

Weary looked baffled and uneasy, shaking his head. But Mike took the pack from him; he tried to take his Kalashnikov too, but Weary looked so alarmed that Mike grinned and gave this up. He slung Weary's rucksack from one shoulder, and was now marching with two packs.

After a few minutes, Captain Danh turned and saw what had happened; he stopped, frowning, waiting for Mike to come up to him. What are you doing? he asked.

He's sick, Mike said. Malaria. He should lie down.

We cannot stop. Our medical officer will give him tablets, Danh said. But you cannot carry two packs.

It's no trouble, Mike said. Let me do it.

Captain Danh hesitated. Then he said: If you wish. Thank you for telling me: he is a man who does not complain.

As soon as Doc had given Weary some tablets, we moved off again on the muddy red track through a swampy country. There were thick clumps of palm trees here; the rain had stopped, but the shining green palm fronds dripped like leaky taps. We were all in single file except for Captain Danh and Mike, who walked together at the head of the line. I watched through the gloomy green light as Mike bent to speak in Danh's ear, gesturing in that way he had, but only with one hand, since the extra pack impeded him. Once, Danh turned and looked at him and laughed.

I began to find Mike's powers of endurance awesome. Like Dmitri, I was getting more and more fatigued and weak. I'm generally pretty strong, but I wasn't used to functioning on starvation rations like these, or to marching for such long periods without rest. I'd begun to develop a blister on my right foot— and this is one of the worst things that can happen on such a march. And I too feared malaria: bouts of it came to me occasionally, as they did to Dmitri. In normal circumstances, with the right drugs available, this would have meant a few days' inconvenience; but going down with malaria here would mean being left behind at an NVA rest station, since the unit would certainly not stop. And under such conditions, this could mean getting very ill indeed—or even death.

These were things I tried not to think about. No such fears worried Mike, apparently; his years with the ARVN had made him as tough as these North Vietnamese. And even some of the soldiers had a strained look now, their faces pallid and yellowish. They made jokes all the time about being hungry.

That evening, we had our first encounter with the Khmer Rouge.

We had come out of the swampy country, and the red road widened: it was coming on dark, and although there were paddy fields here, there was no sign of life nearby: no lights. Turning a bend, we found a halted North Vietnamese convoy: a row of four military trucks, Soviet-built, solid and old-fashioned, with bicycles tied to their radiators. They were filled with NVA troops in their baggy green cotton uniforms and sun helmets—at least a third of whom were young women.

The lead truck had its headlights on and its engine running. Near it, like shadows, stood a dozen or more figures in black pajamas. They were slung with AK-47s, and one of them was talking to an NVA officer in a sun helmet. They turned to stare at our unit, examining Mike, Dmitri and me with great curiosity.

I had not seen Khmer Rouge at close quarters before. They were all very young, except for the man talking to the officer: brown-skinned Khmer peasants, with long wavy hair. All of them wore the red-and-white checked *krama:* either as a scarf or as a turban. From their looks, I suspected that they came from forest and mountain regions which had very little contact with the outside world; and what was most noticeable about them was a look they had in their faces. How can I explain this look? All of them had it. In the lights of the truck, which put strong shadows on their faces, their eyes seemed to shine with anger at something: something they didn't understand; something which made them all the more hostile because they didn't understand it. It was as though something larger than themselves had taken possession of their spirits, filling them with malice. I don't say this because of what they have done since; I saw it then. More than anything else, they reminded me of a street gang: the sort of street gang you have to fear.

We halted at the edge of the road, and I noticed that all our soldiers were fingering their rifles. Captain Danh had walked over to the NVA officer and the Khmer Rouge leader, accompanied by Doc and Lenin. He produced a document from a pocket of his uniform, and the Khmer Rouge leader examined it in the headlights, while Captain Danh spoke to him in Khmer, smiling pleasantly. Danh was obviously accustomed to this situation.

Next to me, Weary suddenly muttered in my ear in Vietnamese, looking all the while at the Khmer Rouge.

They say they have a right to some of these arms, he said.

They say that the Chinese send the arms for them. They are thieves.

After a prolonged conversation, Danh and Doc and Lenin began to walk back to us, and the NVA officer attached to the convoy called an order.

A stack of automatic rifles and some Chinese B-40 rocket launchers were unloaded from some of the trucks, and the Khmer Rouge began to gather these up. Then, without looking back, they made off into the darkness among the palm trees and turned into shadows again.

I was hoping against hope that we would now ride down the Trail in the convoy. But the trucks were pretty obviously full, and we weren't taken aboard. They began to pull out, the young male and female soldiers staring at us curiously as they went. One or two women smiled, and a group of young men waved to us.

As they jolted off down the Trail, I watched them go with a growing despair. I should not be giving way like this, I thought; and I resolved to harden myself. But I was worried about the blister, which had now begun to throb.

There had not been much food available at the last relay station, and that night we had nothing to eat but rice and some dried fish. But we were camped near a village, whose lights we could see through trees, and Prince and Turtle went off to see whether food was to be had there.

Weary didn't want to eat. While the rest of us sat around the pot, he lay sweating on his poncho in the full grip of malaria. The first stage of it had also come to Dmitri; he sat shivering in spasms, his face sweating, hugging his knees and looking ahead of him with a fixed stare.

Captain Danh had ordered Doc to give both Weary and Dmitri some malaria and vitamin tablets. Now he frowned at Volkov across the fire, and then looked at Mike and me. I am concerned that Mr. Dmitri is not fit to walk tomorrow, he said. We must get to the border in the next three days, to make connection with my superiors. I am under orders: I cannot stop. We may have to leave him at a rest station.

The Count gave him a sickly grin, and spoke with an effort. You can leave our whole three-man team behind, if you like, Captain. We don't want to be separated.

I cannot do that without leaving three of my men with you —and I cannot really afford this, Danh said. Also, I would not like you to fall into the hands of Khmer Rouge, which is possible. He paused, looking at us without expression. Some of them are not civilized, he said.

Prince and Turtle appeared out of the darkness, walking into the light of the low fire. Each of them carried a live chicken by the legs, and the soldiers set up a cheer, talking and laughing excitedly: this was a feast. The chickens flapped their wings and faintly squawked.

But Captain Danh held up his hand, speaking to Prince and Turtle in Vietnamese. He spoke clearly, and I was able to follow. Where did you get these chickens, he asked. Did you pay the villagers?

Prince's handsome face went sullen. No, he said. They are bad people in that village. They would sell us nothing. They say they have not enough. So we took these. All of us are very hungry, and getting weak.

No. You will take the chickens back, Danh said. His face was stern; his lips tight.

The soldiers around the fire went quiet; and Prince and Turtle stood holding their chickens, staring at Captain Danh. Turtle's round face had a comical, puzzled look, like that of a dog refused a walk he has been promised. But it was not amusing; we all wanted the chickens too badly.

Do what I tell you, Danh said. This is not the way we deal with the people; you know this. We do not come to rob them; we come to free them.

The two men turned away without a word, and trudged off into the darkness. I waited for some mutter of protest from around the fire; even perhaps for anger. But there was none; only silence.

It was then that I knew that the North would win the war.

. .

Dmitri was in his hammock before Mike and I were, and we stood beside him. His malaria was coming on fast now; he shook violently, and sweat streamed down his face and soaked his shirt. His half-open eyes were pale and blind, staring up at us, and I saw that he was only half conscious.

Mike wiped Dmitri's forehead with a handkerchief, bending over him. Ride it out, Count, he said. It'll pass by morning.

Dmitri answered in a small voice, and we both bent nearer to hear. Just don't leave me to those fucking Khmer Rouge, he said. You saw their goddamn faces.

We won't leave you, mate, Mike said. You're too valuable. We might be able to trade you for something at the border.

We both tried to joke and reassure him, but I don't think he heard us any more; he was looking straight up into the overcast sky, his eyes rolling back in his head.

Lying in my hammock, I hoped that the rain wouldn't come back during the night. I had found that the blister on my foot was turning into an open sore, and it was throbbing badly now. Doc had put Mercurochrome on it; he had no adhesive bandages, and he'd wrapped a cotton bandage around it, but I doubted that this would stay on. He had frowned and clicked his tongue, and he spoke to me in Vietnamese. This could stop you walking, he said. It could spread and turn into jungle fungus—especially if the rain sets in.

I knew this was true; I had seen what happened to soldiers in the rainy season: to both Vietnamese and American GIs. It was the time of skin fungus; of ulcers that didn't heal because they were never dry. But I also knew as Dmitri did that I must keep on; and I didn't speak about it to Mike. In my head, I kept seeing the black shadows of the Khmer Rouge.

For a time, Mike and I lay in our hammocks without speaking. The Professor sat on guard a few yards away, leaning against a palm, his head on his chest, rifle across his knees. There was a moon showing through a break in the cloud, and we could see Dmitri's white, streaming face under the mosquito net, his eyes closed. He was delirious, tossing his head and muttering.

I'm afraid he may not make it tomorrow, I said.

He'll make it, Mike said. Even if I have to carry him.

I saw from his face that he meant this literally. We'll both carry him, I said. But I'm getting a little worried, Snow.

So am I, he said.

This surprised me. He hadn't admitted it before; it wasn't like him. He pushed his net aside and lit a cigarette.

Sometimes I think we may never get back to Phnom Penh, I said.

I hadn't meant to say it: if I hadn't been low from hunger and fear about my foot, I wouldn't have, and I expected Mike to dismiss it.

But all he said was: You could be right, mate. But don't think about it.

Then I asked him if he ever prayed. I'd never asked such a thing before, but it seemed natural just then, and not embarrassing.

Now and then, he said. When I'm tired. I'm not quite sure who I'm praying to. But whoever it is, I imagine they're marching with us. It helps.

Then I asked him did he ever think about home.

Sometimes. Mainly I think about the coolness, he said, and I saw a small longing come into his face. Just for a while I'd like to be back in our valley, he said. In the hop fields. It was always cool there.

I find I'm also thinking a lot about my childhood these last few days, I said. I think about our family home in Peking.

And I talked of the things I missed about our lost home, which I hadn't thought of for years. I spoke these things aloud because it gave me a sort of peace. The past is a story, and we cannot get back into it, so our yearning for it is sweet and not too sharp. I wouldn't let myself think about Lu Ying now, because she belonged to the present, and I found this too painful: I might be years in some camp, and I didn't know whether she'd wait for me. Now I know she would have.

I told Mike about our family house, with its high walls and red lacquer gates and its many apartments that accommodated our large family. I told how my brothers and sisters and I would play among the stone lions in the courtyard, under a big magnolia tree. And I recalled especially the moon gate, which always looked to me then like the entrance to some magic country: a country in a story. It always seemed to be summer in this memory, when Peking was hot and dusty, and everything smelled dry like pepper. But the locust and plane trees in the streets would be in leaf: a light, tingling green. I recalled the dim, airy rooms in the old house, with the many ancient things passed down through the family, most of which were left behind when we fled: the painted scrolls and vases; the lacquer beds; the pearl blinds. Old China. And I talked of my mother, who died soon after we came to Hong Kong, who was small and neat and always indulgent of us children, and who would let us come into the big kitchen where she supervised everything. The kitchen was full of the smells of preserves and spices, and I recalled the rows of brown ceramic storage jars: for some reason those jars were good to think of, just now.

Mike was a good listener. He seemed truly interested, and I began to talk about my father, whom I'd told him of before. I'm glad he read us those old poets, I said. Tu Fu. Po Chü-I. Some of it still stays in my head, even though I was never a scholar.

That must be good to remember, Mike said. His voice sounded sad, I thought, and it was very low; we were both near sleep.

There seemed often to be barbarians in those poems, I told him, waiting beyond the Great Wall. This was during the War, and I imagined the barbarians to be like the arrogant Japanese officers we passed on the streets of Peking. I still half remember a poem about the Tartars, and the sound of their horns on the north wind, and moonlight on the Wall. And one about the Herd-boy star.

I looked across at Mike. He had gone to sleep.

The next two days were the worst of our march. They would pass in a blur of silver, because of the rain. The rain set in early, just as Doc had feared.

We were wakened in our hammocks in the morning by thunder and a cloudburst. It was brief, but we were immediately wet through. We struggled about in waving, solid sheets of water: ponchos over our heads, thin cotton uniforms plastered to us. The once-dry earth became a red quagmire; gleaming leaves and branches streamed; little waterfalls ran everywhere.

There was no breakfast; Captain Danh ordered us to take cold balls of cooked rice in our hands, and eat them as we walked. Our line began its march. For me, from the first hour, it was a march of pain.

The rain came back again in the afternoon, and this time it didn't stop. Usually the monsoon downpours in Cambodia come only in the afternoon; but sometimes it will rain for two or three days without a break. This turned out to be one of those times.

The sore on the sole of my right foot was now an ulcer. Another ulcer had begun above the ankle, and the skin on both feet was beginning to flake off. Every time I put my foot down, pain shot through me. Doc did his best, applying more ointment and bandages; but as I marched through the mud the bandage would come off, and every step meant a knife-thrust of pain. After an hour of marching I felt I could not keep on: I could scarcely put my foot down. I stopped, and Dmitri came up beside me, panting. His bout of malaria had lifted a little this morning, but he was still deathly pale.

You are a goddamn cripple, he said. Put a hand on my shoulder.

No, I said, you're too weak, Count.

We had to shout, the downpour was so loud. The Count looked at me fiercely, water dripping from the brim of his cotton bush hat. I'm better now, he shouted. Do what I goddamn tell you, Jim, or you will get left behind.

So I put my right hand on his shoulder as I went along, and took some of the weight off the foot. It was a big relief. Dmitri had always been a difficult man, but I had a great fondness for him, and knew now that this feeling would never be broken. As we stumbled forward, I heard him singing to himself: panting

and singing at the same time. It was the Elvis Presley song he'd
been so fond of years ago, when we were young in Saigon:

> *Wise men say*
> *Only fools rush in . . .*

After a time, I saw that he was shivering again; he had
stopped singing, and was very short of breath. I persuaded him
to let me walk alone: I found a strong stick beside the track, and
went on with that. He and I were last in the line except for Lenin,
who came along at the rear of us: our guard. We walked slower
and slower, through a landscape like a blurred painting, and
Lenin began to shout at us to go faster, his voice becoming
threatening.

Di di mau! Di di mau!

How weary I grew of that phrase. I had never liked Lenin,
and now I began to hate him. Up ahead, Mike had stopped and
turned to see what we were doing; he waited for us to come up
to him.

You blokes don't look too bright, he said. Let me take some
of the weight.

And while Lenin watched with a sort of sneer, he took my
pack as well as Dmitri's, distributing most of their contents into
his own. We protested, but he wouldn't listen; he even took our
tubes of rice. None of these things was very heavy in itself, but
together they were, and when you have the pain and debility that
Dmitri and I did, to be rid of any weight makes a great difference.
Then, finding that Dmitri's malaria was coming on again, Mike
made the Count walk close behind him, holding on to his shirt.
He was virtually dragging Dmitri along; and he would do this
now hour after hour.

We slept that night in the huts of a way station, and at least
were dry, and ate well: the soldiers there gave us fresh supplies.
But the next day the rain went on, and seemed even heavier. I
found that the skin on my feet was turning black and mushy, and
coming away in lumps; and Mike and Dmitri also found their
feet in this condition. There were more ulcers on my legs: one
near the groin.

We stumbled on, chewing our cold rice, and there seemed to be a sort of urgency in the march now; we were being made to move faster, and going longer and longer periods without rest. Captain Danh told us that they'd learned on the field radio that B-52s were expected soon to concentrate on this region, and he wanted to get quickly to the border.

I was still using my stick; and Mike still carried the contents of my pack and Dmitri's. Turning to look at Dmitri, who once again held on to Mike's shirt, I experienced a shock. His malaria was worse: he staggered and wove, his eyes blind, his face a corpse's. But soon I was beyond worrying about Dmitri. Griping pains went through my guts, and a wave of nausea came over me. I knew immediately why this was: I was getting dysentery.

I was soon struck with diarrhea, and had to crouch by the Trail over and over again, voiding myself until there was nothing left. The spasms in my guts becoming agonizing. But far worse was the nausea, which robbed me of my courage, and turned the world into a place from which I longed to escape. I wanted only to sink into the warm red mud and stay there.

The mud was now ankle-deep. Our trousers were rolled up to the knees, and every so often we had to stop and burn leeches off with our Zippos—which were hard to light. The red glue sucked at our sandals, making it impossible to keep them on; Mike and I carried ours in our hands, but Dmitri had lost his. I doubt that he was even aware of it. Each step in this red glue was a struggle; each was taking the last of my strength. We fought through rain so solid that we seemed to be walking under water, blinking it from our eyes, letting it run into our dry mouths. Sometimes I forgot I was Jim Feng, and became an animal, conscious only of pain in my foot and in my guts. I had no thoughts, but I kept myself going by reciting again and again some lines that came back to me from the poem about the Herd-boy star. It was my great comfort; I heard my father's voice reciting it too.

> *Far away twinkles the Herd-boy star;*
> *Brightly shines the Lady of the Han River . . .*
> *Her bitter tears fall like streaming rain.*

That evening the rain stopped, and we camped in the open again.

I could eat nothing, and continued to be ill. I drifted into a sort of delirium, in my hammock, and floated in and out of bad dreams. I seemed to be begging for something from people with masks on their faces. Then I felt Mike gently shaking my foot, and found it was early dawn.

He always did this: he was always the first up, and I would open my eyes and find him smiling at me. I saw that we were camped in a clearing: a rather gloomy place. There was white mist on the ground, and a red dirt track ran off into a belt of trees: areca palms and some big tamarinds. Red streaks were in the sky above these trees, and the noise of the birds and monkeys had begun. It seemed very loud to me.

Wakey, wakey, Mike said. Rise and shine, Jim.

He always said this; but he didn't do it in a jarring, stupid way. His voice was a half whisper, and it somehow soothed you. So did his jokes. They were silly jokes; I've forgotten most of them. Sometimes he just recalled crazy things he and Dmitri and I had done years ago, in Saigon or Singapore, and he would make a comedy out of these incidents. But it cheered us up, and we knew why he was doing it. It gave us hope: it made us believe for a moment that we would get out of this, and be who we were again, and not prisoners. Because most of the time we did not believe this would happen. We liked Captain Danh, but we knew that eventually he would deliver us to people very different from himself: people like the man who had first interrogated us. We could not really see a way out. We might never be our old selves again.

Trying to sit up, I could hear the nearby voices of the soldiers getting their gear together; and I heard it with dread. I could not march again, I thought. Every part of me ached, and I was too weak and nauseous to move. I just wanted to drift away. This sounds shameful, I know, but if you have had that kind of illness, you will perhaps know what I mean. Dysentery drains you of your will, your pride, in a way that other illnesses or hurts don't.

You want only to crawl away and die. And of course, in the situation we were in, you sometimes do die.

I told Mike I couldn't go on; that they would have to leave me. But he just smiled.

Bullshit, mate, he said. I've seen you with shrapnel in you, and you went right on filming. So what's a bit of gutache? Hit the deck or I'll boot you out.

And he began to talk me into going on as though it was a game, his voice still a whisper. I have forgotten what he said, but I still see him there in the gray green light and the mist, in his shrunken-looking NVA uniform, like a pale-faced giant smiling down at me. And it seemed to me then (perhaps because I was light-headed) that there was something supernatural about him. Nothing seemed to break him or change him; but it was not just this. He was pretending to talk harshly to get me on my feet; yet his voice was like a gentle woman's. And just then it seemed to me that his face was like a gentle woman's too, looking down at me. This of course was a trick of the light, and of my illness; Mike doesn't look like a woman. But—how can I put it?—his expression was tender, looking down. He was tender with me, and it somehow healed me, and brought back my courage. That is the truth. It made me struggle out of that hammock, and face going on.

I don't know how I marched that morning, but I did. And after taking some of Doc's tablets, and having my foot dressed, I felt a little better. But Dmitri's malaria was still with him; he was shaking, weaker than I was, and barely able to keep up.

We trudged for five hours without a break, eating on the march, and in the afternoon the rain began again. Many of the soldiers were not much better now than Dmitri and I; they were staggering and faltering too, weak from lack of proper food. They were not supermen, any more than we were. Weary was almost unconscious again, and held on to Doc's shirt as Dmitri hung on to Mike's. I watched Captain Danh's bobbing sun helmet at the head of the line, and I began to hate him for what he was doing to us. But of course, he was doing nothing but his duty.

Finally I stopped, my head swimming, feeling my legs buckle.

The pain in my foot drummed also in my brain. We were skirting an empty paddy field that shone silver with water. Ahead, on the southeastern side, more forest began, ghostly in the rain.

And then, far off, I heard the bombs again: *whump-whump-whump.*

I felt distant vibrations in the earth, and looked up into the white, raining sky—but nothing was visible. The soldiers had begun to shout, and Captain Danh waved us forward, shouting something I couldn't hear above the rain. The line waded forward towards the forest, struggling to hurry. Soon Captain Danh and those in front were well ahead of us.

I will not make it across there, I thought.

I stood clinging to my stick, swaying, knowing that I would fall into the mud at last, and not get up. My fear came through a screen: fear felt by somebody else. If the B-52s bomb me, let them, I thought. In a way, I wanted it.

The bombs sounded again, and the earth shook. But they were still at a good distance: not yet near us. Mike had turned to look for me, and halted. Even he was sickly white now, his eyes dark-shadowed and staring with fatigue, his chest heaving. Dmitri had stopped automatically, holding to Mike's shirt like a child; I doubt that he knew what was happening. Their green uniforms and cotton hats were red with mud and black with rain. Lenin stopped too, and watched us with a grin that was not a grin, tilting his rifle.

Di di mau, he shouted.

We didn't answer; we panted; and anyway, the rain was almost too loud for us to make ourselves heard. Mike was holding out his hand, and I took it. He pulled me close to him, and shouted.

Come on, Jim, grab hold of my shirt.

No, I said. Help Dmitri.

You too, he shouted. I'm not leaving you. Grab hold.

His eyes were a washed-out blue in the rain, but they gleamed and commanded me. I took hold of his shirt, and he turned and started forward with Dmitri and me both holding on. Yes, he dragged us both, like a buffalo.

But then Dmitri fell. He fell suddenly, and lay still on his side in the mud, his eyes closed, shivering. The malaria had finally taken over, and he was unconscious. We stood looking down at him while Lenin waved his Kalashnikov at us, urging us on and shouting his *Di di mau!* He yelled some more words in Vietnamese, and I understood that he was telling us to leave Dmitri behind.

But Mike stood in front of Dmitri, his legs apart, and spoke in English.

No. We're not leaving him, he called.

And Lenin answered him in English, which he'd never done before. So he did speak it. Hysterical anger was in his voice.

Go now! he shouted. *Finish,* this man! Go!

No, Mike shouted.

Head lowered, he looked at Lenin from under his dripping hat, and again he seemed to me like a buffalo: one that would charge.

Captain Danh would stop this happening, I thought, but he's too far away to see. And all the time I was expecting more bombs to fall. But none did: the bombers had been farther off than they sounded, and must have passed on.

Lenin leveled his rifle at Mike's chest. I saw that he was losing control, and would probably shoot. He was not like the others: he would do it. I believe he wanted to, and wanted to leave Volkov to die, because of the things he had heard Dmitri say around the rice pot. I began to plan how I might go for his gun, knowing that I was probably too weak to succeed, but also knowing I would try. Because of the nausea, I didn't really care if I was shot: I would have half been glad of it.

Go! Lenin shouted to Mike. Go! He jerked the gun upwards, and I saw him stiffening, ready to fire.

Mike shook his head. You'll have to shoot me first, he called.

I got ready to jump for the gun, my heart hitting in my chest; but then I saw that Mike was slowly squatting down next to Volkov, his eyes never leaving Lenin's. He picked Dmitri up and began to carry him, staggering forward.

Lenin watched him, his eyes shining with anger, but he didn't shoot. He followed, still wearing his grin of hate. I followed too, my wave of weakness lifting.

We made it to the forest, where Captain Danh was waiting for us, and Mike lowered Dmitri to the ground. He was taking in air in big gasps, and couldn't speak; he sank to the ground and sat with his head on his knees. Lenin walked away, not looking at anyone.

Captain Danh ordered Dmitri to be laid on a poncho, and told Doc and Prince to carry him. And so we went on.

People say many things about Mike: I say he was a hero.

The rain went on, and so did we. I had a fever now, and was becoming light-headed, so I scarcely felt the pain in my foot any more. I marched, still using my stick.

Then, at nightfall, everything changed. Without warning, we were led by Captain Danh through a trapdoor in the ground.

Because of my fever, I doubted that this was happening. But it was happening.

The trapdoor was located in a small grove of palm trees, and had been well hidden. It was pulled back, and we found ourselves climbing down a ladder, one by one, through a hole that went straight into the earth. And now there was no more rain: no more water.

Looking back, I'm still not sure how much of what I remember now is real or not, because my fever at the time made everything like a long, worrying dream. Strange shapes had been looming up in front of me on the Trail, mingling with my memories of other times and places—all of these images appearing together, in a jumbled stream. But I was certainly going down this ladder now, rung by rung, my wet face burning, fearful of losing my grip. Straight below me, Captain Danh had a flashlight on, which bobbed like a firefly. Above me, I saw Mike and Doc encouraging Dmitri to climb down: he seemed to be conscious again.

Then, panting and dripping, we scuttled down red-brown corridors of earth, bent under a very low roof, following Captain

Danh into a musty underworld. I began to comprehend that we were in a North Vietnamese bunker complex; but that didn't make it any more real. None of us had ever been inside one: few people from our side ever had.

Shadows leaped in the tunnel. Strange soldiers appeared to greet us: young men and women in pale green uniforms. It was wonderful to see the delicate, elf-like faces of the Vietnamese girls, and I wondered at first whether any of these people were real, or whether I was hallucinating.

But they were real. They led us into a chamber where we were able to stand upright, and now we experienced our first physical relief in days: taking off our wet fatigues, washing ourselves in buckets of warm water, changing into dry clothes. All this happened for me in flashes, with my grip on consciousness strengthening and weakening, and I saw only what was in front of me: a bucket; a cake of soap; Mike's face grinning at me as he washed. I remember Doc dressing my foot, and giving me precious aspirin: I still see his bushy head bent over my feet.

Then we were led to hammocks around the walls.

I opened my eyes. I didn't know where I was, or how much time had gone by, or whether it was day or night. I only knew I was underground. Distant voices and laughter had woken me, so distant they seemed like dreams, and it seemed to me that I'd entered some old fairy story, and had come into an underground citadel of goblins, where time and the days and the seasons had no meaning.

Looking about, I found I was in a large chamber of red-brown earth, with walls of hard-baked clay, and timber supports for the ceiling. The hammocks were slung from these. The place was lit by a pressure lamp standing on a table; there were even chairs. The dry earth smell made me feel safe. I was still weak, but my fever had gone down, and so had the griping in my stomach, and it was wonderful not to have to walk.

The soldiers in our team hung motionless in their hammocks, and so did Mike and Dmitri, who were in hammocks near to mine. I could see through a doorway into an adjoining chamber which seemed to be a kitchen, where two strange soldiers were preparing a meal in a fireplace, the smoke taken away through a pipe. The far-off voices I'd heard were coming out of tunnels that entered the chamber.

When our team ate, sitting at a table in the kitchen, we had fresh vegetables and chicken with our rice, and hot tea with condensed milk. I had little appetite, because of the weakness from my gastric attack, but just picking at such a meal was a pleasure. Dmitri's malaria had lifted, and although he was too fatigued to speak much, I saw that he ate a little too, and that his color got better.

I had never known such a feeling of luxury; and the greatest luxury of all was to be dry and safe. Captain Danh, who was eating with us, told us that these bunkers could withstand B-52 bombs from as near as one hundred meters. The only danger in here was spiders, he said; but I wasn't inclined to take this seriously.

Looking across the table at Mike, I noticed that he was more drawn-looking than I'd ever seen him; he wasn't talking much, and I feared that he might have strained himself in some way. But he gave me his wink: he could still do that.

All that day and the next night, we rested in the bunker, and nothing was asked of us. We stayed in the chamber where the hammocks were, listening to Radio Hanoi on a transistor radio, talking in our bad Vietnamese to some of the soldiers, and playing the Match Game. Dmitri's malaria was passing. So was my dysentery, and Doc had dressed my foot properly with adhesive bandages. We were better, but all of us were still weak, and we spent a good deal of time loafing in our hammocks.

The next morning, straight after breakfast, we were approached by Captain Danh. He seemed unusually serious, and asked us to follow him.

Crouching, he led us some yards down a tunnel to a smaller chamber. Lenin followed us: still our guard, his face telling nothing.

An NVA officer sat here at a wooden table. A pressure lamp stood on it, lighting the room, together with some papers, a cheap Japanese camera, and a bowl containing candy. On a bench nearby stood three bulging packs. The officer was older than Captain Danh: thin-faced, with cheekbones like knobs, and wiry, graying hair. He smoked a cigarette in a holder, his movements seeming elegant and languid: but I believe he was just fatigued.

Danh sat down beside him, and indicated that Mike and Dmitri and I should sit on benches in front of the table. Lenin stood by the door. The officer gave us each a cigarette and gestured at the candy, asking us in Vietnamese to help ourselves. It was strange; I thought of schooldays, with a small treat being given by strict masters. And my heart began to thump: I think I already knew what was coming, but didn't dare to believe it. My mouth was flooded by the unaccustomed sweetness of the candy; and it was like the taste of hope.

You walked well yesterday, Captain Danh said. He glanced quickly at Mike. You are very strong, Mr. Mike, or your friends might not be here. I am sorry it has been so hard for you all. You must be missing your families, as we do.

We have no families, Volkov said.

Danh raised his brows. That is sad, he said. You truly are individualists.

Except for Jim, Mike said. He's planning to go respectable: he's getting married, when he gets back.

I am happy for you, Danh said to me. I am hoping that you can walk again today, Mr. Jim, despite your bad feet. You will now have your excellent boots back. All of you will.

He looked at the others. Today our unit goes over the border, he said, but you will not be with us.

He picked up a piece of paper from the table, and my heart thumped harder as he began to read aloud.

It has been decided by the People's Liberation Army that the captured war photographers James Feng, Michael Langford and Dmitri Volkov are to be released. They will be given safe passage to a point where it is possible for them to make their way back to Phnom Penh. It is the hope of the People's Liberation Army that they will report fairly on their treatment, and on what they have learned of the struggle of the Vietnamese people against American imperialism and its lackeys.

Captain Danh put the paper down and looked at us. This is on my recommendation, he said, because I have come to believe you are honest, and not in the pay of the CIA. I trust you will report honestly to your press on the hardships our soldiers endure to liberate their country, now that you have shared them. My comrade asks: will you sign a paper to this effect?

We all sat very still, looking at the officer with the cigarette holder. Finally Mike answered. Yes, we will, as far as I'm concerned. You've treated us well, Captain.

When Danh looked at Dmitri and me, we simply nodded. I did not feel able to speak, in that moment: I was thinking of Lu Ying.

Danh now signaled to Lenin, and pointed to the packs. Lenin came forward and unloaded them on the table: and there were our boots, our clothing, our press passes, our watches, our wallets: everything except our cameras. It all must have come down on one of the trucks. Sitting here in our NVA fatigues and Ho Chi Minh sandals, it was strange to see these clothes; they seemed to belong to other men, and to come from another reality.

We were asked to check all the items, and then to sign a list that identified them. We also had to sign the statement that Danh had spoken of. As we did this, Volkov looked up, his pen poised, and asked a question.

Where are our cameras, Captain?

Danh's face became blank. They have been confiscated by the People's Liberation Army, he said. They are not strictly your property, but tools of the imperialist press. They will now serve the Liberation.

He and Dmitri stared at one another in silence. I had the impression that Danh had made this speech for the benefit of the other officer, and that it was not something he was comfortable with; anyway, I like to think so, because for me Danh will always be a good man, and one I will not forget.

Finally Dmitri shrugged, and signed the paper. When he had done so, Danh smiled, wrinkling up his forehead in the way he had. I will miss our debates, Mr. Dmitri, he said.

Dmitri managed a small sardonic smile of his own: the first that had appeared since his illness. Then he said: You are the first Marxist ever to say so, Captain. Also the only nice one I have met, as a matter of fact.

Danh now turned to me again. Mr. Jim, you are fond of the old poets of the T'ang, he said. I too. But you should know that our revolution also has its poetry. I have something by our best poet for you, translated into English. Take it with you, and think of us when you read it.

He handed me a piece of that cheap lined paper of theirs, like something from a child's exercise book, on which I glimpsed some lines written in ballpoint pen. I began to thank him politely, but he was already turning away and standing up. The other officer did the same, and we all got to our feet too.

We are quite near Highway 1 here, Captain Danh said. Not far from Svay Rieng, where there is a Lon Nol Army post. Three of my men will escort you there, leaving shortly. I wish you all safe passage, and *bonne chance.*

It was odd: it was all ending very quickly, and I didn't want it to be so fast. Why was this? Perhaps because we seemed to have lived with these men for months, not ten days or so, and I found I would miss them—all except Lenin—and was sad to think of what might happen to them.

At this point the officer with the cigarette holder leveled the Japanese camera at us and told us in Vietnamese to look at him; then he took a flashbulb picture. Captain Danh came and stood next to us, and we all posed for another.

For our records, Danh said, and the flash went off again. We all laughed, looking at each other. Only Lenin, standing by the door again, didn't laugh: he watched with an empty face.

Sometimes I think I would exchange some of my best still pictures for a copy of that one photograph I have never seen. Presumably it must exist somewhere—perhaps in some file in Hanoi. The last picture ever taken of Mike and Dmitri and me, together with Captain Nguyen Van Danh! I like to think that Captain Danh survived the war, and became a teacher: but they say it's the good ones who die, and I fear he will have been killed on some battlefield in South Vietnam.

There is no sadness like the sadness that fills you when you look at the faces in such a photograph. They are not older, as they would be in life, or faded, as they are in your memory. They are real—real all over again. And that pierces; pierces. No; perhaps I couldn't bear that picture. Better that I never see it.

I still have the poem Captain Danh gave me. This tattered piece of paper is the only thing that proves I was ever there, on the Ho Chi Minh Trail. Here it is, Ray: I brought it for you to read. It's about two soldiers meeting on the Trail. To tell you the truth, I didn't bother to look at it for some time; I thought it would be just propaganda. When I changed back into my own clothes, preparing to leave the bunker, I pushed it into a pocket of my shirt, and forgot it. I only found it when we got back to Phnom Penh.

It is the first time we meet—
What is your name, what is mine?
Where do you come from, where do I?
Close to each other—we are brothers.

A glance without a word is enough:
Our eyes meet and want to speak;
Our brown clothes dyed with the same root
Silently tell our affection . . .

This noon, up there on the pass,
Lulled for a few minutes,
Sharing a water pipe,
You take a puff, then I.

An instant after, we go our ways,
You to the plain, I up the hill:
Your heart and my heart
Heavy with feeling.

Oh, the fish in water.

3.

JIM FENG

Late in the morning, they sent us off towards Highway 1 in the care of Doc and Lenin. We were sorry that Lenin had to be with us: we even wondered if he might do something to prevent our getting away. But we agreed that this was unlikely: he would follow his orders, whether he liked them or not.

Before leaving, we had shaken hands with all the others, at the entrance to the bunker. To be leaving them gave me a lonely feeling. And I was surprised to see the expressions on the faces of the soldiers; they smiled, but something else showed through: a wistfulness. Weary held Mike's hand for a long time: he had not forgotten how Mike had carried his pack. He looked very weak, with his thin body and the drooping, old man's eyelids in his boy's face, and somehow it came to me that he would not live long. But perhaps not many of these young men will live long, I thought, and I said a prayer for them inwardly, asking that they be protected on the battlefield.

As we walked away, Captain Danh waved to us from the entrance of the bunker, standing straight and still in his sun helmet with its red, enemy star. It was a wave like a salute; he stayed there until we turned a bend in the track, and I said in my heart: Take care on the battlefield, Captain—and watch out for Lenin.

Now here we were, walking in our good American jungle boots and fatigue trousers again: Mike in his green cowboy shirt, Dmitri in his navy blue one: all as before, like time wound back—except that each of us had lost about ten kilos, and our clothes were very loose. I still had to use a stick to help me, and the ulcer still throbbed, but it was wonderful to have the boots, which felt at first very heavy and strange; and because I had nothing to carry, not even a camera bag, I felt light and free and irresponsible. I kept looking with affection at the Rolex on my wrist. That no one had stolen it impressed me very much.

Doc marched in front of us, Lenin behind. There had been

no rain that day, and it was clear and hot, with pools of water everywhere, the red soil moist and steaming but not sticky. We had left the Trail, and were walking along a shady cattle track in an area of occasional villages and half-flooded paddy fields—in one of which the peasants were already planting young rice shoots, as though in a country at peace. It was fairly open country, with distant blue hills in the east: the country of the Parrot's Beak.

Doc told us it would take about two hours to get to Highway 1, and that they would leave us as close as they could to the town of Svay Rieng, which was still held by the Cambodian Army. But we would have to make our own way to the Cambodian military post up the highway, hoping that we met no Khmer Rouge.

At noon, we stopped for a brief rest. Then we went on, and at around two o'clock we came to a deserted village.

Just a few of the usual houses on stilts, with banana and mango trees nearby, and a pond with lotus flowers. And nobody here; nothing. No dogs. There must have been fighting here, and the people had fled. Doc and Lenin stopped to discuss the situation, in the shade of a banana tree. As they did so, we all suddenly heard the distant boom of artillery, and lifted our heads.

Lenin frowned and spoke rapidly to Doc; I could not follow it all, but he seemed to be saying that there must be an engagement here between the Lon Nol forces and the Khmer Rouge—and that he and Doc should now leave us.

Doc seemed to argue against this, but Lenin became quite fierce, speaking even more quickly, his voice raised and hectoring. He shot quick hostile glances at us.

Finally Doc turned to me and spoke slowly in Vietnamese, his expression uneasy and ashamed. We must leave you here, he said. We cannot go further, or we may be captured by Lon Nol forces. I am sorry. If you continue west, you should soon come to Highway 1.

He pointed; then he shook hands with each of us in turn. Remember us in friendship, he said. *Bonne chance.*

We thanked him for all he had done for us, while Lenin stood on one side, fingering his Kalashnikov impatiently, his eyes narrow and contemptuous. I held out my hand to Lenin as well, but he ignored it and turned away, muttering something I didn't catch.

We watched the two of them go, and then looked at each other. We did not waste time discussing Lenin's action, or the fact that we had been left so far from the highway; we knew without speaking that we must plan our next move quickly. Over the years, we'd become accustomed to communicating with a minimum of talk, in situations like this. Finally Mike pointed towards a grove of small trees, in a westerly direction. Over there, he said. We're too exposed.

We got across to the trees and then walked between them, in the thin bars of shadow cast by their trunks. Moving into a small gully, we heard a loud buzzing of flies.

Bloody hell, Mike said, and put a hand to his nose.

Dmitri cursed softly, and did the same. I was a little behind him, hobbling along, and he turned as I came level. Don't look, James, he said; but I looked.

The upper part of a man's corpse lay on the red earth, in the bars of light and shadow, hacked in half at the waist. Just the upper half: there was no sign of the lower part or the legs. He was Cambodian, and almost certainly a Lon Nol soldier, since he wore an olive American-style military shirt, a checked *krama* about his neck. No weapon lay near; they would have taken it. His eyes were open and glaring, his lips set in a snarl of agony that made the face like an animal's. Huge gleaming brown entrails protruded from this half-body, looking not like part of a human being but like tubing in the engine of an old car: they were black with the flies whose hum seemed louder and louder here. The smell was very bad. I have seen many dead, and grown much too used to it, but this body was different: not just because of what had been done to it, but because of its mystery, in that spot. Some old shell casings lay about, but there wasn't any other sign of a firefight having taken place here; no other bodies. Why was just this one soldier here? And why was half of him missing?

We discussed this, and Mike said: Maybe dogs ate the rest of him. And maybe the Khmer Rouge ate his liver.

We looked at him, and he said: For strength. Some Cambodians do it, on both sides. A faint spasm crossed his face: the nearest thing to fear I ever saw Mike show. This is a bad place, this gully, he muttered, and pulled his bush hat over his eyes. Let's move.

We continued to walk west, in a direction we hoped would get us to Highway 1: the highway that ran straight to Phnom Penh, and back to our other life. The Khmer Rouge held many sections of it now, but if we got to the Lon Nol army post near Svay Rieng, we'd be saved: the Cambodians would contact our embassies, and put us on a chopper to the city. At present, though, we didn't even know where we were.

We wanted to find a village and ask directions; but there was no sign of life. We suspected that all the inhabitants here had fled from the B-52s, or else from the Khmer Rouge. Now and then the rumble of artillery continued to sound from the northwest, and despite the danger, we decided our best bet was to head for it, since at least this gave us a chance of contacting the Cambodian Army. So we continued in that direction along the red cattle track. And all the while, as we walked, we were glancing out of the corners of our eyes for the black figures of the Khmer Rouge. They were near; they must be near: but we didn't say so to each other.

Soon we saw a thatch-roofed farmhouse up ahead, and assumed it would be empty. But as we came up to it, two men and a woman came from behind a clump of banana trees at the side of the house.

They were peasants, the men wearing black pajamas, the woman a black sarong and blouse. The men had the red-checked *krama* hanging about their necks; the woman wore hers as a turban. She was young, with a handsome, sullen face which showed no animation at all when she looked at us. The men were young too, with shocks of long hair; they looked at us with interest, but not with friendliness, I thought. One was short and stocky—a dark-skinned, tough-looking Khmer type—while the other was taller, with a more Chinese face. They looked like Khmer Rouge, in their black clothes; but of course, the Khmer Rouge dressed like the peasants. And these men weren't armed, so that at first I wasn't worried.

I was the only one of us who spoke any Khmer, so it was up to me to deal with them. I asked them where we were, and how we could get to Highway 1.

They said nothing for a moment; then the stocky one asked some questions in return. I noticed that one of his eyes was slightly crooked, rolling outwards to the corner. Who were we? he asked. What were we doing here?

I told him we were correspondents for the Western press; that we'd wandered off the highway and lost our transport, and wanted to get back to Svay Rieng. I began to sense something I didn't like, and didn't feel inclined to tell them our true story.

The man with the crooked eye frowned, as though suspecting me of lying. The tall one was frowning too, and so was the woman. And these frowns put a cold, shivering jolt through me.

This is just peasant caution, I told myself: they have good reason to be cautious. But I knew. They were exactly what I feared they were.

The tall one spoke now. You are Americans?

No, I said, we were not Americans; and I explained what we were.

The two men continued to examine all three of us from head to foot, without saying anything. The woman stared away across the fields. Then the tall man pointed to the west, across the paddy fields. The highway is there, he said. Just across the rice field. You can walk up it to Svay Rieng: not far. But there is a battle there: it is dangerous for you to go there.

Thank you for your help, I said. We'll go on and take our chances.

I explained to Mike and Dmitri what had been said, and their faces brightened.

The highway is just across this paddy? Then let's go, Dmitri said. Our troubles are over, brothers. He laughed, and punched Mike's shoulder, and Mike smiled. Dmitri hadn't laughed for a week, and he sounded out of practice; his malaria was gone, but he still looked frail. I tried to look happy too, but my bad feeling wouldn't go away. I could feel the eyes of the three peasants examining us still, and I knew I would not be easy until they were well out of sight. If Dmitri and Mike had sensed anything, they didn't show it.

We walked away. As we did so, I knew that the peasants were watching us go, although I didn't look behind; and I felt a cold tingling in my back, and a shriveling in my scrotum. But I hobbled forward, saying nothing to the others, and praying I was mistaken.

We walked across the paddy, on top of one of the dykes. Most of the field was dry; there hadn't been enough rain here to fill it. On the other side, on top of the last dyke, was a belt of trees. In such a situation, trees on the skyline take on many meanings, and you are not sure which meaning to believe. Quiet against the sky, they are a decoration in a book, or a pleasant park to create peace; they are perhaps a refuge from danger. But then again, they are the treacherous cloak that hides danger itself. Which were these trees?

We moved among them, in their shade. Don't look back, I told the others. I didn't like the feel of those people.

I know, Mike said. But they're not coming behind us: I checked. Stay cool. Just keep moving.

Then, coming out of the trees and down a bank, we found Highway 1. Its gray bitumen ribbon ran straight and empty, with woods here on the eastern side, and more paddy fields on the other, stretching into the distances of the southwest. No traffic; but up ahead, by a bend, were some thatched roofs.

I don't remember what we said, but we all began to feel great hope. Side by side, the three of us began to walk up the highway: northwest, in the direction of the roofs, and of Svay Rieng. It was good to feel the hard bitumen under my boots. I could tell the others wanted to go fast, and I did all I could to hurry.

We passed the houses, which were silent, and turned the bend. Up ahead now, some four hundred meters away, where the road ran into blue hills on the horizon, were a group of military trucks and armored personnel carriers, with soldiers standing beside them. We stopped, and narrowed our eyes in the heat: a shimmer rose from the bitumen, and the soldiers and vehicles seemed to dissolve and re-form in the air, like a dream. They didn't seem to see us. But we could make out their helmets and their olive battle dress: no black pajamas.

Government troops, Mike said, and we looked at each other; then we all began to smile, and found we were embracing, laughing. Watching Mike hug Dmitri, the two of them laughing into each other's faces the way they did when they were young, I found myself saying, Thank God, thank God; but whether I said it aloud or to myself I'm not sure.

We needed a white flag, we decided; Dmitri had a white handkerchief, and he tied it to a stick and carried it held high. We walked on towards the soldiers, in the middle of the road. As we got nearer, we saw that one of them was watching us through field glasses. We waved, and I called out, *Kassat, kassat* —which means "press"—but I think we were still too far away to be heard.

At that moment there was the sound of an AK-47, coming from somewhere in front of us, in the trees on the eastern side of the road. *Crack-crack-crack:* there's no mistaking the sound of that damned Kalashnikov.

I did what I'd done so often in the past: threw myself flat, and crawled towards the ditch on the western side of the road. Mike did the same, and we crouched there, panting. But where was the Count? We peered through the grass above the ditch.

He lay on his side in the middle of the road, the stick with its white handkerchief beside him. He was curled up like a child preparing to sleep, his mouth open and working a little, in the way it used to do when something had just provoked him into one of his speeches, his eyes staring towards me. They seemed to ask me about something that bewildered him; and they will never stop looking at me. I have always privately found blue eyes very strange; I can't help it. In that moment, Dmitri's were not their usual color: they were stronger, more brilliant, like blue flame. I looked past him to the trees, and saw there the two peasants from the farmhouse, the tall one and the stocky one. The tall one had the AK.

He fired again: fast single shots. The bullets whined above our heads: but it was a good deep ditch, and with our heads down, he had no way of hitting us. Then I was conscious that Mike had stood up.

It was suicidal, what he did, and not typical: I had never known him to expose himself to fire in such a way before. Crouching, he ran fast into the center of the road, took Dmitri under the arms, and began to drag him back to the ditch. But this time, amazingly, there was no fire. If there had been, I believe he would have had very little chance. He pulled Dmitri fast into the ditch with us, and lowered him flat.

Why hadn't the Khmer Rouge fired?

Lenin, I thought: that bastard Lenin made contact with them. He ordered Dmitri hit; it was only Dmitri he wanted, not Mike and me. A crazy idea, I know: but at the time I believed it. How else was I to explain why the one with the AK hadn't fired at Mike?

There was no more fire after that; but this didn't surprise me. To hit us, he would have had to come across the road; but then he would have shown himself to the Government troops. Maybe he's gone, I thought, and Mike and I crouched above Dmitri, keeping our heads below the level of the ditch.

He was alive, looking up at us both, his face even paler than it had been on the Trail. Mike held his hand, panting, staring into his face and saying nothing. At first, we couldn't see a wound.

Where are you hit? I asked.

Dmitri's eyes dropped, like those of someone who looks for spilled food on his front, and I saw that there was a patch of blood below his chest, in the center of the dark blue shirt—hardly noticeable on the dark fabric, and such a small amount that I allowed myself to hope. But when I drew the shirt up to his chest, the red hole in his skin confronted me like a small ugly mouth. A bullet had entered just below the breastbone, in the solar plexus. I had learned enough about wounds over the years to know what this meant. Most of the bleeding would be internal, and if the bullet had pierced the aorta, he could not have long to live; perhaps ten minutes.

Leave me, Dmitri said. Get out of here, both of you.

His voice was faint, but distinct; he looked up at us calmly.

No way, Mike said. He continued to grip Dmitri's hand. You'll be OK, Count. Hang in there. The Government troops are coming.

I peered through the grass and saw that this was true: two APCs had begun to rumble down the highway towards us. There was still no fire from the Khmer Rouge, who had pretty surely gone.

Dmitri suddenly belched, and looked up at us with an expression of embarrassment: he seemed to be asking us not to judge him for his dying body's lapse. A spasm of pain crossed his face, and his eyes widened, as though in disbelief.

Don't try and talk, Mike said. We'll get you back. They're coming. Just hang on, mate. Hang on.

Don't let go my hand, Dmitri said. He was looking up at Mike, and his eyes had changed. Then he looked away, and said something in Russian, very low and weak. Then he said: *Mon Dieu,* and made the sign of the cross Russian Orthodox style, using his right hand and touching his left shoulder last. Mike still held his other hand. Dmitri's lips moved again, and I brought my face close to his in order to hear. But no words came, and his eyes looked at me through a film.

Mike looked at me quickly across his head, and I nodded. Yes, he was gone.

Mike frowned at me, his face bewildered, as though he'd just learned something he'd never imagined before. He sat up, his head above the level of the ditch, and took Dmitri's head on his knees, looking down at him. He pushed some hair off the forehead. The eyes were still open: still the blue of flame, but all the strong life of the flame gone.

Better stay down, I said, but Mike took no notice. I heard the sound of a motor, and saw the APC pull up almost beside us, above the bank. Two Cambodian soldiers in helmets, carrying M-16s, stood looking down at us.

Kassat, I said, and raised my arms. They smiled and nodded.

I stood up and climbed from the ditch, but Mike didn't move. He sat in the ditch with Dmitri's head on his lap, looking down into the Count's white face, his own face almost as white, with no expression at all. He began to shake his head, and to mutter to himself: I could only just hear.

Not you, Count, he said. Not you.

I put my hand on his shoulder. Come on, Snow, I said.

He looked up then, his eyes shining and sharp as though he was rejecting something: something he hated. Then he took the Saint Nicholas medal from around Dmitri's neck, and dropped it in his shirt pocket.

When we rode back to Phnom Penh from Svay Rieng in the Government helicopter, Mike still wouldn't speak. Dmitri's body was zipped into one of those plastic bags they used for the troops, and we sat on the floor beside him. I began to weep then, and the four Cambodian soldiers riding with us watched me across the cabin.

But Mike remained dry-eyed all the way, staring out the open door of the Huey. He seemed to look for answers in the sky.

FOUR
DREAM PAVILION

1.

HARVEY DRUMMOND

When Mike Langford and Jim Feng were released by the North Vietnamese Army, the news got to the press corps a little ahead of the helicopter that was bringing them back to Phnom Penh. So did the news of Dmitri Volkov's death. This was during siesta time, when many correspondents were in from the field, and a contingent of us went out to the airport.

It would have been a celebration, if it hadn't been for the fact that only the two of them had come back. But those correspondents who hadn't known Dmitri well saw it as a good story, and the departure lounge at Pochentong was crowded with press. Langford and Feng came through the glass doors, accompanied by two Cambodian Army officers, and were mobbed by journalists brandishing bottles of cognac and whiskey as gifts, who began immediately to put questions to them.

But neither of them smiled, and at first, neither responded. Both were noticeably thinner, and very drawn, and Jim Feng was limping from an infected foot. Halting, they looked at the faces around them in a manner that was sober yet dazed, as though wondering where they were, and why they were here. They gave the impression of being in a different dimension. The questioning voices died, and the lounge became almost silent.

Then people began to murmur low-voiced regrets about Dmitri, and at the same time to put questions about his death. Jim answered briefly, but Mike not at all: he stared, his eyes empty. This worried me. I badly wanted to talk to both of them alone; but that was impossible, so I hung back. They were shortly commandeered by American and Cambodian officials who took them away for a medical check, and some sort of official questioning.

At nightfall, after a bath and a long siesta in the Hotel Royal, they emerged for a press conference by the swimming pool. I was present at this too, and able to greet them; they seemed pleased to see me, but there was still little chance of a private conversation. I was thinking about the "box" that Dmitri had made me responsible for, which was still presumably up in his room. The responsibility was preying on my mind. That afternoon I'd telephoned the French embassy, and had discovered that they'd already contacted Volkov's CBS bureau chief in Hong Kong, and had informed his mother and sister in Paris of his death. His body would be flown to Paris for burial. But no one had thought about his personal effects; and the weary male voice on the phone had hinted strongly that in the present state of things in Phnom Penh, they had more urgent matters to worry about. So then I felt free to carry out Dmitri's wishes. But I wanted Mike and Jim to come with me to his room: I didn't want to open the box alone.

This too had to wait, since an emotional correspondents' dinner lay ahead at the Jade Pagoda. There was no couscous that night, only liquor; and it turned into a sort of wake for the Count. Strangely—or perhaps not—the person most visibly affected was Trevor Griffiths.

Very drunk, he stood up and called commandingly for silence, his eyes red-rimmed, black brows frowning, black beard thrusting. "Dmitri Volkov was a brother," he said. "What else is there to say but that?" Then he recited "Do not go gentle into that good night," bringing it out from his chest, using his best Welsh bass notes.

For some reason, then and afterwards, I kept seeing Volkov at the battle in the Iron Triangle, when Langford took shrapnel in the head: saw Dmitri running out of the orange screen I'd thought at first was fire. For many nights following, when I lay on the edge of sleep, I'd see this image repeated: he'd come running towards me out of flame.

Run, Count, I'd say, and it would seem to me that if he ran hard enough, he'd run back into life.

Mike, Jim and I got back to the Royal at curfew time. Mike had agreed to come to Dmitri's room, but Jim asked to be excused, pleading tiredness. He was suffering from exhaustion, in fact, and so was Langford.

The manager made no trouble about letting us have the key. He'd held Volkov's room, as he'd done Jim Feng's, in the hope of his return. The room was on the third floor at the front, and pretty much identical to mine: as large as a small restaurant, with the same expanse of red-tiled floor, a big double bed with a lumpy mattress, and a dark, groaning old French wardrobe whose doors would stick. The place was dark and stifling when we went in; we turned on the fans, and a bedside lamp. A white shirt and a pair of pale blue cotton trousers hung on a chair, dropped there carelessly; a pair of sandals was by the bed. The terrible mute voices of objects abandoned forever! They speak much more distinctly than anything else, at a death.

Oh Christ, I said; but Mike said nothing.

There was little else to show that the room was occupied. A small stack of books and papers on a desk; his big Auricon sound camera; a few film cans; a Nagra tape recorder. The shutter doors to the balcony above the drive stood closed; we opened them to let in air, and let in as well the grumbling voice of the war: artillery and rocket fire outside the city, sounding even closer than it had done a month earlier.

I looked under the bed, where Volkov had said the box would

be. It was there, near the foot, and I pulled it out: a small, varnished wooden trunk rather like an old ammunition box, with a black metal hasp secured by a padlock. I slit the envelope containing the key, while Mike watched me. As Dmitri had promised, there was a piece of paper inside with a name on it: *Linda Holmstrom,* and an address in Washington.

I pushed back the lid of the trunk, and Mike and I sat down side by side on the bed next to it. When I began to sort through the contents he made no attempt to involve himself but simply sat watching me, with heavy eyelids. His exhaustion clearly made every movement an effort, and I began to feel guilty for keeping him from bed.

My life is in the box, Volkov had said. Well, here was his life: these few things.

His will was on top: not a formal legal document, just two typed and signed sheets, dated six months earlier, and witnessed in Hong Kong by his boss at CBS. Glancing at the first page, I saw that he'd left everything to Linda Holmstrom. This meant all his savings: an amount of some $50,000. He had few possessions of any value. Not much to show, I thought, for half a lifetime of risk.

"Jesus," Mike said slowly. "To her! But this lady quit on him: she divorced him. Why would he leave it to her?"

The Count was one of those people who don't love enough, or else too much, I said.

He shot a questioning glance at me, but made no comment. I turned back to the trunk, and picked up four portrait photographs.

The first, which was framed, was a black-and-white picture of a blond woman in her late thirties. She looked directly at the camera, smiling to put us at our ease; but her well-spaced gray eyes gazed through us into some distance of which we knew nothing, and had no right to know. This, I didn't doubt, was his "Minnesota Swede": a Scandinavian-American of essentially prosaic beauty, whose face showed intelligence without imagination. She wouldn't get intense about things that weren't supposed to matter, I thought: and certainly it was a face that would have frowned on Dmitri's excesses.

The other portraits were of people who were pretty clearly Volkov's family. A rather vulnerable-looking man of middle age with a neatly trimmed blond beard, Dmitri's mouth, and an expression of melancholy dedication: his father, I decided. A handsome, big-boned woman in a formal, sleeveless gown from the thirties: no doubt his mother when young. And finally, an unframed portrait in sepia of a man in a nineteenth-century suit with a decoration on the lapel, and a cravat. He was clean-shaven, but with long side-whiskers, and his expression was what the nineteenth century would have called "imperious." This face, with its white-blue eyes, was startlingly like Dmitri's, except that the jaw was heavier. On the back was a legend in Cyrillic. I didn't doubt that this was Count Alexis Volkov, and said so to Mike.

He took the picture and studied it, his silence becoming oppressive. "Aristocrats," he said at last. "What use are they now? I reckon this grandfather was the start of Dmitri's problems."

I went on going through the box.

A number of envelopes containing loose photographs. A jade Chinese statue, old and valuable from the look of it: possibly the Goddess of Fortune. Books, two of them Russian, and dating from the last century: the works of Pushkin, and a short work of Tolstoy's whose Cyrillic title defeated me; Cossacks featured in the illustrations. Books in French: *The Outsider*, by Albert Camus; the poems of Baudelaire. Dostoevsky's *The Possessed*, in English. Many more trinkets, of little obvious value to anyone else: the sad favorite objects of a lifetime. And finally, letters: only two sets of letters.

There were two letters from Linda Holmstrom to Dmitri, dated two years before; and there were six from him to Linda, all of many pages, in unsealed envelopes, addressed but unposted. I looked at a few lines of one of them, and would not read any more. She'd have to read them, now.

I closed Volkov's trunk and found Mike still looking at me, sitting on the edge of the bed with his hands loosely clasped between his knees. For the first and only time in all the years I'd known him I saw tears in his eyes, and it disconcerted me. He blinked, but his face remained frozen and without expression. He was looking more physically drained with every moment, it seemed to me, and I guessed that until now, he hadn't had time to grieve; grief was only just beginning.

He stood up, and walked out onto the little balcony between the shutter doors, blowing his nose as he went. After an interval I followed him, and we stood there in the night's heavy warmth, looking down on the drive and the lamplit perspectives of Monivong Boulevard beyond, emptied by the curfew. It helped that we were both Australian; I knew how to judge his silence, and for how long to let it stretch.

Finally he said abruptly: "Nothing ever happened between Ly Keang and me."

I looked at him in surprise. I didn't think it had, I said. Why was he telling me this?

"I had the idea it might have been bothering Dmitri," he said.

Well, you know better now, I said. There was only one woman in Dmitri's mind, and she wouldn't get out of it.

He glanced at me with an expression that was unusual in him: a sort of defensiveness. "Have you got a cigarette, Harvey?"

I shook my head; he'd forgotten I didn't smoke.

"Shit," he said. "Why don't you take it up?"

He gave me the beginning of a grin, then turned away and leaned his forearms on the balustrade, hands locked, his long, blank face turned towards the darkness, out of which the boom of artillery could be heard at intervals. When he finally spoke, it was in the flat, jerky tones that affect the phlegmatic in the grip of emotion.

"Dmitri was my brother," he said. "And I reckon it's my fault he's dead, Harvey. I talked him into going to Kompong Cham."

No: come on, I said. Don't start thinking that way, Snow. Dmitri chose to go, the way he'd done a hundred other times. You didn't make him go.

But he went on staring at the darkness, and made no answer. For once, I was glad of his taciturnity.

His involvement with Ly Keang began very soon after this, as you probably know.

My impression was that for Langford, she became Cambodia.

You'll probably find that fanciful and sentimental. All right, maybe so. But I have this notion, Ray, that we never love another human being so completely as when that human being is part of something else. Something which we're in love with, or ready to be in love with, before we ever meet them. Something which becomes a part of our dreaming of that woman; that man. Do you see? A place; a piece of the past; a country; a half-remembered life that isn't even ours, but for which we foolishly ache. I believe that's how it was for Langford, with Ly Keang.

And the Stringer was a patriot, just to cement it. A patriot in a way that's gone out of style in the West: devoted to her country and her cause, and sworn, like some heroine out of melodrama, to avenge her father's killing by those enemies who were finally poised to seize her land and its people—a people whose suffering wouldn't end with the war, but instead would begin again, at a far more terrible level, in a frowning territory of waste ruled by the black-clad Others.

Jim Feng's right, in a way: it was as though Mike had never been in love before. Maybe he hadn't. Maybe he'd only just grown into love, on the edge of middle age. It happens. Anyway, for the next two years, until the city fell, they were seldom separated. She moved in with him in that apartment near the Old Market: a very serious thing for a young Cambodian woman of her class to do. Now she would never marry a Cambodian; now her future was with Mike.

He said very little about her to any of us—except that they'd marry when the time was right. We knew better than to try and discuss her with him. His voice and his expression forbade it: she was a creature apart.

2.

TAPE 44, MAY 10TH, 1973

—She came at about seven-thirty this evening, in the middle of a thunderstorm. The monsoon's set in early: the rain's been coming down hard since yesterday, when Jim and I got back into Phnom Penh.

—I was sitting inside the apartment on the rattan settee: sweating in the sticky heat, no shirt on, smoking and drinking brandy and doing nothing: thinking of Volkov. My head still strange, the way it's been since he died—which was only yesterday.

—Little things about Dmitri kept running through my head. The way he squinted when he shot film; the way he'd talk about music when we were drinking, describing it and waving his hands. I kept hearing his voice saying "Mon Dieu" and "as a matter of fact"—slurring the words. I wanted it to stop, but it wouldn't, no matter how much brandy I drank. He smiled at me in my head.

—The rain got harder, as though it was trying to drown out everything that had happened: drown out what I'd done. The afternoon rains go on, and the bombing goes on. Everything coming down. For the first time, the Khmer Rouge haven't pulled back with the wet season: they're still trying to take the city, fighting on in the rain, the mud. So the B-52s go on bombing, quite close: you can hear the explosions through the roar of the rain, and the thunder. Nothing but red mud and ruined villages, out in the countryside: everything being destroyed. Cambodia being destroyed.

—Tonight was like the first time Keang came. Except for the rain.

—Sary was sitting like a little brown statue on the Chinese sideboard, watching me. No lights on in the room. Through the open doors onto the balcony, over by the railings of the market, the petrol lamps of the Khmer traders were blurred and trembling in the rain. Wind, and more thunder. The top of the coconut palm next to the balcony running with water, fronds gleaming and tossing like landed green fish.

—Then she came. My door open as usual, and she walked into the room behind me, just like before.

—She told me later she spoke to me but I didn't hear, because of the thunder. A cool finger on my bare shoulder the first I knew of her. I thought Sary had come to me along the back of the settee: a paw. When I turned and saw Keang, I stood up. She began to come around to the front of the settee, looking up at me in the dark without speaking. It was as though she was accusing me of something, except that her expression wasn't quite right for that: it was more like a question.

—She's come to make me explain about Dmitri, I thought; she's going to blame me. My heart was hammering because she'd startled me, and because she was here. Her head was tilted back, her eyes never leaving my face, and she got to the front of me and took both my hands in hers. Neither of us spoke, and I hadn't planned to touch her, but I found myself holding her. She seemed to slide. Her body light yet definite against me.

—We kissed for a long time. She opened her lips, her saliva for a moment in my mouth, starting an electric tingling that would have built and built, if I hadn't let her go. Deadly, that tingling: everything being changed for us, far into the future. I could hear a mosquito whining; then it settled on my shoulder and began to drink my blood. I let it, looking at her. The sting was part of what was happening: a brand.

—Jim Feng said you'd be here. You're alive, she said. But thin, thin, Mike.

—She didn't smile. Her eyes stayed on mine, as though by staring long enough, she'd draw everything out through my head.

—Yes, I'm alive, I said. But Dmitri isn't. I'm sorry.

—But she didn't understand me.

—I'm sorry too, she said. He was your good friend for such a long time. I think you loved him.

—Yes, I said. And I think you did too.

—She turned away, shaking her head. Breath drawn in through her nostrils, clearly audible. Then she said: He was a dear friend, but you know I didn't love him. I love you: you. And you're alive.

—She was looking out through the doors at the lights in the rain. I'll be sorry I've said that, she said. But I've said it, never mind. When people said you were missing, I thought I would go crazy. I was sure the Khmer Rouge had taken you. My aunt and uncle thought I was sick in the head. I couldn't go to the paper; couldn't work; couldn't eat. And then yesterday the news came that Dmitri was dead and you and Jim were alive. But I couldn't come to the airport or the Hotel Royal to meet you with all those others. I cried for Dmitri alone—then I waited to see you without other people.

—I picked up my shirt from a chair and pulled it on; then I walked over to the sideboard and looked for the bottle of cognac. Sary stood up and arched her back. Keang came over and stood stroking her, looking at me sideways as I poured two drinks. Sary narrowing her eyes and beginning to purr.

—She likes me, Keang said.

—We both do, I said. I gave her the cognac, drank my own straight down, and poured another. My hands were shaking.

—She drank hers just as fast, and held out the glass. As I poured, she looked at me again, that long top lip of hers drawn down firm over the teeth, her expression questioning: her joker's expression. So you like me, she said. A man who likes everybody and loves no one: that's you.

—No. I love you, I said.

—So now I'd said it. And I came up close and looked down at her, but not touching her. She stared back, eyes widening. No flirtation in them, no deception: clear black glass at night. There were only inches between us: I could feel her body warmth.

—But tonight I'm thinking about Dmitri, I told her. I can't stop thinking about him, tonight. I feel very bad about him. And I should feel bad.

—She shook her head, looking at me. No, she said. No, you should not feel bad.

—I took her hand, and led her over to the settee. There was another roll of thunder; Sary jumped down from the sideboard and ran underneath it, and Keang laughed. She sipped her cognac; watched me with her head on one side. Then we both stared out at the rain and the market lamps and the swinging top of the palm tree. Water gurgled in a pipe somewhere. Everything was changed out there, the lights and wild rain belonging somewhere else: somewhere stranger than Phnom Penh, where she and I were going.

—Do you want to talk about what happened? she asked.

—No, I said. Not tonight. But it was all my fault.

—And I told her how I'd made Jim Feng and the Count come with me to Kompong Cham.

—She put her hand on my shoulder, rubbing it gently. That's what you were sitting here thinking. That's why you are sad, she said. But you're wrong, it's not your fault. Everyone chooses what they do. Dmitri didn't have to go to Kompong Cham.

—We sat for a long time in silence. A Western woman would have said more; but she said nothing more. I could feel her against me, hardly touching, but her body giving out that strong warmth. Then she said: So what will you do now? Leave Cambodia, before the Khmer Rouge come into the city?

—No, I said. I'll stay.

—She sat quite still, thinking. Then she nodded her head and said: Good. Then we'll be together. Now I must go. My uncle and aunt will be waiting.

—Don't go, I said.

—Yes, she said. Tonight you're sad for Dmitri. Rest. Meet me the day after tomorrow.

—She stood up; I could scarcely see her face. Don't turn on the lights, she said.

—She was right to go; she'd understood me. Because of Dmitri, we had to separate tonight. But now that I'm sitting here alone again, all I'm thinking of is her, and that I'll see her the day after tomorrow.

MAY 12TH

—Six o'clock: just in from the field. The rain over: another late downpour. The smells it leaves behind coming in over the balcony: mud and drains, mixed with the scent of flowers, from over in the market.

—I'll go across and buy some in a moment, to welcome her with. In an hour she's bringing her things here. She says she wonders if Sary will be jealous. I keep wanting to laugh; keep walking about the room; can't keep still. Childish.

—Rain and Ly Keang.

—On my hands the smell of paddy water that I don't want to wash off.

—We'd arranged to have a coffee at the Royal: that was all. But as soon as we sat down, she asked me to take her to the front.

—I said at first that I wouldn't.

—But I used to go out with Dmitri, you know that, she said. She was dressed in jeans and a military shirt, and carrying a Nikon: ready to go.

—Look, I'm not like Dmitri, I said. I only work alone. I never even liked to have a soundman, in the days when I shot film. I won't be responsible for someone else's life: especially not a woman's. Especially not yours.

—She pursed her lips. *Mon Dieu*, such an old-fashioned man, she said. A buffalo boy!

—It was nine o'clock. We sat on the terrace above the garden and the pool. Bright sun, and people having a morning swim, or sitting under the umbrellas. Normal and happy, as though the city wasn't at war. Suddenly she reached out and put a hand over mine. Her voice, usually pitched up a little, got low.

—You won't lose me, she said. I'm too clever. Where do you go today?

—I told her I was going north up Highway 5, towards Oudong. The Khmer Rouge seemed to be pulling back there, and I'd learned I could safely get to a Fifth Brigade enclave where there might be some low-level action. Most other highways were hopeless to drive on now, but the Government was doing pretty well on the Rice Road, and looked like re-opening it.

—So it's not too dangerous, she said. She smiled, knowing this was never true. And they have plenty of air support, she said. So please take me, Mike. Just so I can get a story for my paper, and a few pictures I might sell. If it gets too heavy, you can go forward without me. I know how you work.

—I told her no, I couldn't do that either. She could get cut off.

—Then all right, never mind, *don't* leave me, she said. We'll stay together. You should not be going out again so soon: you're meant to be resting. So if you get in trouble, better I'm there.

—Her head was cocked on one side and she was pretending to be serious: but she can never be serious for long. We laughed together, knowing she'd won. A small, fatherly Chinese waiter, standing at attention by a trolley in his white jacket, was smiling at us as though he understood.

—Why do you want to do this? I asked her. That paper of yours doesn't give a stuff about real stories from the front. They just want you to invent good news. You can write that here.

—All right, that's not my main reason, she said. I want experience of battle.

—I asked her why.

—I still believe our army can win, if the Americans help us, she said. But so many people say the Khmer Rouge will soon close the Mekong. Then we are lost, you know that. And if they win, I want to be ready. I want to get used to combat. I want to join Major Chandara, when he forms a resistance on the border.

—But that's not the way for you to help, I said, with your education. Chandara wouldn't want to see you doing that. There are better ways.

—Perhaps, she said. But perhaps the time will come when there will not be many nice ways left to fight. I can use a rifle—my father taught me. Some of our peasant girls go into battle with the men. Why not me?

—I sat and stared at her. She still had hold of my hand, but her eyes were serious, now. The Chinese waiter smiled, seeming to wait for my answer. I'll take you today, I said. But if there's too much incoming, if the troops are being pushed back, we head straight out.

—Her smile came back, as though I'd asked her to a party.

—So we headed up the Rice Road in Black Bessie, just the two of us. The sun out: no rain yet. Vora not with us: I drove myself. Probably not wise, but I wanted to be alone with her. Running beside the river, we passed the floating huts of the fishing village on the edge of town, and then we were out among the rice fields.

—I love this time of year, at the beginning of the rains. Light green rice shoots making a film across the paddies; everything coming alive. The women stooping, setting out the seedlings: peacefully planting, this close to the city, as though that sound in the distance isn't really artillery. Pink and mauve lotus flowers and hyacinths opening in roadside pools. Cambodia beginning to fill with water, shining and winking, reflecting the sky and the big May clouds. Black-and-white heron took off as we went by; marching brown ducks were driven by little boys. Everything was washed and new. So was my life, because of Keang. Both of us laughed at nothing, as though we'd drunk brandy and not coffee.

—Thank you for bringing me, she said. Drive us all the way to Battambang: let me take you home.

—After the war, I said. When the road's open again.

—After the war, she said, and put her hand on my arm.

—Ahead in the northwest, the low blue mountains seemed to wait for us: I saw her looking at them.

—A few kilometers on, we came to the Fifth Brigade enclave, just outside a bombed and deserted village in wide, flat country. Houses stood with their roofs caved in, or leaned at crazy angles on their stilts. A group of Khmer refugees passed us, some pushing handcarts, some driving pigs, others on bicycles, headed towards Phnom Penh.

—A battle was going on, but things seemed almost peaceful when we got out of the car. The Fifth Brigade had a good number of trucks and APCs here, as well as several hundred troops. A group of Khmer Rouge were dug in on a low ridge up ahead, near to the yellow shell of a ruined French villa. The sky showed through its windows, and smoke was drifting above it. Every so often the Khmer Rouge would fire a few mortar shells; but these were falling short. It was all pretty quiet: tedious even, as these encounters so often are.

—I knew the commander here, who was pretty reliable. He said they outnumbered the enemy by about ten to one, and he was confident of driving them back. So I got his permission to stay. Ly Keang moved about getting pictures of the troops with her Nikon, and talking with them. It seemed a fairly routine situation: not one that could go wrong. But after half an hour things began to change a little.

—The incoming mortar bombs got more frequent, and machine gun fire started up. The Fifth sent mortar fire and rockets back, and some of the troops began to move into the paddy fields and take shelter behind the dykes. Because of Ly Keang, I began to think about retreating in the car. But it didn't yet seem warranted, and I told her it seemed best to dig in here with the troops, and shelter in the rice field.

—We moved back down the road on foot and went into the paddy at a point where we were alone, but not too far away from the troops. The field was about two feet under water. At first we lay on the side of a dyke, but then the mortar fire got heavier, and a shell exploded quite close, the mud showering down on us like dirty snow. I took Keang by the hand and drew her down with me into the paddy water, leaving our cameras perched in a groove on the side of the dyke.

—We lay half submerged, heads down. She was trembling slightly, but that was probably the noise: I saw now that she'd never panic. A soldier's daughter.

—Then I heard the loud drone of prop-driven planes. The Lon Nol commander had brought in his air backup: two little T-28s, the old-fashioned light attack planes the Americans had donated to the Cambodian Air Force. As usual, they were skimming the tops of the sugar palms, their gung-ho Khmer pilots flying almost at ground level to find their targets. Soon we heard the bombs, and a pall of black smoke rose into the sky.

—We held hands and didn't speak, seeing nothing but the tall sugar palms rising above the dyke. After a time, the mortar fire stopped, and things went quiet. I looked over the top of the dyke. A pillar of black smoke was coming from the ridge where the Khmer Rouge were, and the two T-28s were climbing away: they'd made a direct hit. Thunderhead clouds stood on the horizon: rain coming.

—It was over. The Government troops were getting their wounded into trucks; others were moving forward in APCs towards the Khmer Rouge position. I knew I should get out and follow the troops and get film; but today I wouldn't bother. I slid back beside Keang, and put my arms around her. Just to hold her made me feel drunk again.

—Good that they had air support, she said. See? You didn't need to worry, I was right. She gave me a small joking smile: but I could feel that she was still trembling.

—We went on looking at each other. Soft mud and warm brown paddy water: a bath. Alone here: no troops within fifty yards. Big drops of rain beginning to fall, splashing in the water. The mud sucking and the water washing about us as I put out my hand and cupped her cheek. Her green shirt gone black: water and her own perspiration. Thunder rolled, and the rain came down hard.

—Water: Cambodia is water. Thousands of acres beginning to drown; rice fields and jungle submerging; fish soon breeding among the trees in underwater forests—teeming through the paddies. Cambodia was water, and Keang was Cambodia. Her mouth again: its liquor. We struggled, wrenching at blackened clothes. Fish in water. When I pulled her half out of the paddy and up against the sloping dyke, I was trembling too. Keang. Gold against smooth red mud, breasts pointing at the sky, shining and streaming. Body-hair thin black strands of silk: hollows and secret fruit left bare. So perfect I knelt in the water in front of her. Paddy water, rain and her body's juice: which was only rain?

JUNE 5TH

—The room at siesta time. Just after two: the big hot hush, when the city almost stops. The time the Nurseryman used to love.

—We keep the shutters closed: tiny white slivers of sun through the louvers. Drifting, on the bed in the heat, the roaring sun and world shut out. We tell each other that we'll drift away, here in the room.

—Sary today padding across us as we lay like statues, wet from head to foot, not able to move. Sniffing at our drying foam and suddenly staring, shocked. We laughed, and she ran away offended.

JUNE 6TH

—Scents the room never had before.

—Lime blossom I brought from the markets that she's put in vases everywhere: her favorite flower. Her scents and cosmetics, standing on the chest of drawers. All of the scents making a kind of rippling in the air, under the slow old fan. Ripples of light as well, reflected on the smudgy blue walls, as though we're under water.

—Why did you never marry?

—I told her. Told her everything.

—Listening, she sat naked in the middle of the bed, cross-legged; she's got no self-consciousness. The black silky triangle between her thighs like a figure on a pale ochre vase.

—Why do you love me? She frowned at me, warning me to make the right answer.

—I don't think I loved anyone before, I said. I only loved what I thought was there. With you, I know it's there.

—She threw herself on top of me, like a child.

JUNE 8TH

—Small things amuse her, even though she's so much better educated than me. I came in yesterday wearing a monkey mask I bought in the market: a silly joke, but she wouldn't stop laughing.

—Today she turned the photograph of Claudine to the wall, pursing her lips and glancing at me sideways. Don't want to see this Vietnamese-French lady looking at us any more, she said. Time to put her away.

—She'll always be a friend, I said. She did a great deal for me, years ago.

—But she pulled a face. No more lady friends, she said. Not even this aunty.

—Keang standing naked by the window, one arm raised to hold a shutter open. She seemed to be thinking about something very far off, lip pulled down. Watched her from the bed. A streak of hot light let in, to touch her body like a flare: her raised arm and one breast glowing apricot, her nipple a dark plum. The fan of black hair hanging to the base of her spine: almost too heavy for her to carry. Naked, she's quite small, even though her figure's a full one. To me her body's perfect, but its proportions are actually irregular: the long slender waist and then the flaring hips; the short legs.

—When will you give us a baby?

—I hadn't really meant to say this; my voice spoke the words, and I heard myself say them with surprise.

—She came over quickly and sat astride me: fierce, moist, stinging, pinning my wrists.

—You want us to have one?

—Very much, I said.

—When the war stops, she said. When it's safe. Then I will have your baby.

—Lying beside me, she explored old battle injuries: tracing them with her finger the way that Claudine used to do.

—You are really a soldier, she said. When are you going to put down that camera, and take up a gun?

—Never, I said. I won't kill people.

—But you don't want us to lose Cambodia, she said. You want to stay here. This is your home now, Mike: you said that. You love Cambodia, you said. So you have to fight for what you love, don't you know that?

—Not with a gun, I said.

—She lay down beside me, her head on my shoulder, her voice soft. I know you'll fight with us when the time comes, she said. You'll stay and fight with the Khmer Serei. Chandara thinks so too.

—I'll go on carrying the wounded, I said. I'll send out pictures to show what's happening. But I won't pick up a gun.

—Last night Keang talked about her father. Now I understand why she wants to fight, and for me to fight with her. And I wonder if anger isn't deeper than love in her.

—It was around nine o'clock. We were sitting on the rattan settee in the dark, looking out through the doors. Curfew time: the noise of the traffic stopped; quiet settling on the city. Soldiers blowing their whistles somewhere out of sight, ordering stragglers indoors. The green kiosks in the market putting up their shutters; the street traders packing up their stalls to be away before the soldiers came; the petrol lamps going out.

—Talked to Keang about the progress of the Khmer Rouge offensive. I'd been out with Bill Wall on Highway 1 today, and it looked bad, I told her. The Communists had launched heavy attacks on both sides of the Mekong, overrunning a lot of Government positions. It looked as though the Mekong–Highway 1 corridor might soon be in their hands. If that happened, I said, I wanted her to let me take her out to Bangkok.

—But she shook her head, and her eyes got large the way they do when she's emotional. I won't go, she said. I've made a promise to stay and fight until there's no hope left—and perhaps even after that.

—I asked whom she'd promised this to.

—My father, she said. I promised him in my heart. The Khmer Rouge killed him, and I've said I will find some way of fighting them, when the time comes. Never to give in.

—But your father was a soldier—he died doing his duty, I said. He wouldn't have expected this of you. He'd want you safe.

—He didn't die in action, she said.

—Suddenly she bent her head like a girl being punished, her voice muffled. I remembered what Chandara had said about her father, and waited.

—I have never told you this; now I want to tell you, she said. He died five years ago, when I was nineteen. It was the time when there was a peasant uprising in Battambang: the Red Khmer organized it. That was when they were just beginning to form their army in the countryside, and to execute village chiefs. No one knew much about them, then. The uprising was put down by our armed forces under Prince Sihanouk's orders; very many were killed. My father took an important part as a commander. He was wounded.

—She stopped for a moment. Still she kept her head down, hands locked in her lap, not looking at me. One night, she said, three men walked into the kitchen of our home in Battambang city, and they shot my father in front of us—my mother, my two small brothers and me. Then they walked out again. They were agents of the Khmer Rouge.

—She still didn't move or raise her head or look at me. I couldn't find anything to say except how sorry I was. I put my arm about her shoulders, and felt the stiffness of her body.

—I loved my father, she said. I want the Khmer Rouge to pay for what happened to him, and to others. I won't see my father die for nothing. That is what I have made my aim in life. That's why I haven't married.

—She put her head down on my shoulder. I want to marry you. But you must understand why I have to fight them.

—I understand, I said. But why turn yourself into a sacrifice? What's the bloody use of that?

—She looked up at me, and this look made what I'd said sound silly. Who was I to judge someone whose father had been shot in front of her? I was just another spoiled Western correspondent, standing on the sidelines of what was happening here. And in a way, it was all unreal to me. Here she sat in the dark, talking about revenge for her father's death like someone in a melodrama. But who was I to make judgments? These were emotions she believed in; they'd actually pulled her life apart. A lot was now explained about her: even her joking, which must often have covered pain.

—I don't want to die, I want a life with you, she said. But I must go on fighting the Khmer Rouge—even if they should win this war. You see? And if they take over, maybe your people will be looking for ways to bring them down. I could help.

—And she looked at me in the dark as though expecting something.

—My people? I said.

—I want you to introduce me to your friend Mr. Aubrey Hardwick, she said.

—I stared at her. I'd once mentioned Aubrey to her, telling her how he'd helped me to get started as a cameraman—but I hadn't told her what he did. I'd just described him as a diplomat. I should have known that she'd find out eventually he's an ASIS operative: most things get found out in Phnom Penh. I asked her why she wanted to meet him.

—Please, Mike, she said. Don't have secrets from me. I know about

Mr. Hardwick from Cambodian Army friends. Friends of my father's. They met him here in the old days before the war. They say he's a very important spy. They say he has close connections to the British and Americans. I know he'll help Cambodia, if the time comes. I want to meet him: I want to help him as you do.

—I don't help Aubrey any more, I said. I don't really trust him. I don't trust any spies—even when they're on our side.

—But she wasn't listening: she had her heart set on meeting Aubrey, and that was that. And a mean notion came into my mind: that she was making use of me. Is she? Yes and no. She loves me, and for this very reason she sees it as natural that she should get to Hardwick through me —and she thinks I should see it that way too. Cambodian women are very practical.

—Will I introduce her? I suppose so, in the end: it won't be avoidable. She'll know when he's in town. But I have a bad feeling about it.

JUNE 20TH

—Yesterday, Ly Keang got her wish. I've used a gun, and now everything's changed.

—I was out with Major Chandara down in Takeo, in that flooded flatland of grass and reeds. He was leading a company on a sweep. Late afternoon, and Chandara and I were walking a little ahead of the unit with one of his sergeants. Suddenly, a group of Khmer Rouge opened up with assault rifles. They were dug into a bunker in the reeds up ahead, and we hadn't seen them.

—In that instant, Chandara and the sergeant and I were cut off. The rest of the company was only about twenty yards to our left and a little behind us, and had a number of armored personnel carriers to give them cover—but there was no way we could get back to them across those few yards. The unit was returning fire, but because of the surprise, quite a few of them had been killed.

—We threw ourselves flat under an old mango tree, hugging the twisted gray roots. Chandara was firing with his M-16, and the sergeant was firing too; but the Khmer Rouge were well dug in. I began to be afraid that they'd soon launch one of their human wave attacks. I didn't raise my head, and made no attempt to get pictures.

—Then I saw that the sergeant was getting to his feet. He was a tough old Khmer with a weathered brown face, and completely fearless. He unhooked a grenade from his webbing, pulled the pin, and hurled it towards the Khmer Rouge bunker. Standing up was madness in the circumstances, but Cambodians are always doing it. The grenade thrown, he threw himself fast to the ground; but not fast enough. There was a burst of fire from the reeds, and the sergeant spun and cried out, clutching his left side below the ribs. A big patch of blood spread between his fingers on his shirt; I couldn't tell how bad the wound was, and I was about to move closer to help when I heard Chandara call my name, and saw him point.

—They were coming. They were out of their bunker, which had been hit by the sergeant's grenade, and were splashing towards us through the reeds, rifles at the ready: not many, perhaps a dozen in their black pajamas, checked *kramas* around their necks. Here they are at last, I thought, the Black Ghosts, and the shining, dark green leaves of the mango got very distinct just above me.

—The unit was still putting out fire from our left, and two of the Khmer Rouge fell. But the others came on, and were very close. The sergeant lay quietly, eyes half closed, his rifle beside him: a captured AK-47. Chandara leaned over and picked it up and thrust it at me, speaking very fast, shouting above the noise.

—I think you must use this, Mike, he said. Use it! And if they capture us, use it on yourself. You know what Khmer Rouge will do.

—I didn't hesitate. I took the AK, settled down against a root of the mango, and got a black figure in my sights. I'd long ago learned how to use an assault rifle, filling in time with the troops in periods when we were waiting for action, and I was glad this one was a Kalashnikov and not an M-16, remembering that the AK never jammed. Feeling the stock against my shoulder, smelling the oil, I seemed always to have been doing this.

—I fired at the man in my sights and missed; I didn't have control of the gun. They were nearly here now; I could see their faces. Chandara fired, and I saw one of them fall. Then I targeted another of them. He was a young man in his twenties with a very dark, hard Khmer face and a wild shock of hair; I fired another burst, and he threw up his hands and went down straightaway. Two more fell, one of them to Chandara; then our troops managed to land a mortar shell among them: one was blown into the air and another was spun backwards from the force of the blast.

—Silence came back, and I realized there were no more of them.

Instead of being relieved, I was let down, in those first instants. I'd been ready to go on fighting. Then I came to my senses, and put down the Kalashnikov.

—Chandara was smiling at me, wiping his sweating face with his scarf. No doubt about it, *Mean Samnang,* he said: you are the Lucky One.

—The remaining soldiers in the company began to move across to join us, and Chandara and I bent over the sergeant. He was lying on his back, a big pool of blood soaking into the ground beneath him, eyes half closed, his Buddha amulet between his teeth. He was dying. He spoke a few low words, a half smile on his face, and Chandara looked up at me.

—He says he sees her, he said. The Lady.

—I asked him what lady.

—Lady Death, Chandara said. Many of them see her, when the time comes. They say she's warm and kind.

—When the medics got to us and began to move the sergeant onto a stretcher, Chandara stood up and began to call out orders, and some of the soldiers moved out to inspect the Khmer Rouge dead and wounded. Then Chandara turned to me, and suddenly took my hand. He was half laughing, and gripped it hard.

—So we're still here, you and I, he said. I knew you'd use a gun one day, Mike. Now you're one of us. Now you've become a soldier after all.

—In that moment, for good or for bad, I felt that what he said was true. We'd fought to save our lives together, he and I, and a link had been formed like no other, which would tighten. Some day, I'd fight with him for Cambodia: it had always been going to happen.

—The motors of the APCs started up, the troops talked and laughed in relief, and everything was as always, after a battle. Yet everything had changed.

FIVE
FALL

_____

1.

HARVEY DRUMMOND

It took two more years for Phnom Penh and Saigon to fall, and my life became a tale of two cities. In this period, Langford begins to slide in and out of focus.

ABS had now based me here in Bangkok, and Lisa had joined me. I divided my visits to Vietnam and Cambodia fairly evenly, but I wasn't covering in Indochina all the time. So I wasn't in touch with Mike consistently: there were gaps. I'd see him in Phnom Penh over a period of weeks, and then not for months. Or I'd run into him in Saigon, where he'd still turn up on assignment for his American newsweekly. And as things neared their end in Cambodia, in the early months of 1975, I began to feel unsure that I still really knew him.

In that February, I'd lie awake in bed each night in the Hotel Royal, listening to the distant Khmer Rouge artillery. I'd wonder how soon it would be before I found myself on a last flight out from Pochentong Airport—and sometimes I'd wonder whether I'd be able to get on one at all.

Phnom Penh was now an island, ringed by its enemies. It was extraordinary that the city held on for so long; yet it did, and amazingly, it still had its charm. It was still pretending for much of the time that the war wasn't there; still offering all the old pleasures to those of us who could afford them. The nightclubs and French restaurants were doing good business; the afternoons were still lazy; the crowd by the pool at the Royal was still well supplied with brandy and champagne. Yet the annual Khmer Rouge dry season offensive was in full swing.

They were closing in on the last Government enclaves left in the country, and closing in on Phnom Penh. The Government troops were fighting with hopeless bravery, but the Communists were now only fifteen kilometers from the edges of the city. Their rockets were soaring out of the swamplands to the south to kill and maim civilians in the suburbs: people eating noodles at a stall; children walking to school. The power supply flickered on and off like daylight in a nightmare, and the Mekong was finally closed: the last little supply ship from Saigon had got past the fire from the riverbanks to unload its cargo on the Phnom Penh dock. But the Americans continued to airlift supplies in, and the optimists talked about a reprieve when the rains came. No one could quite believe that the end would actually arrive, even though it loomed over the city like a thunderhead cloud. There was the false tranquility of craziness in the air.

It was in that time that I began to notice the change in Langford. Before, his secret life had been peripheral; something on the edges of his personality. Now, it seemed to me to be taking over.

I first grew concerned about him through a conversation I had with young Roger Clayton.

I met Clayton by chance outside the Telecommunications Building, near Post Office Square. It was around four o'clock on a Monday afternoon: the end of siesta, and the city still drowsy in the heat. This was my first day back in the country after something like a month away, and I'd been putting a story through to ABS in Sydney on the radio-telephone circuit. Clayton and I walked towards the square together, comparing notes.

The square was half deserted: the scarlet flame trees by the white French post office burning intolerably in the sun; a couple of cyclo boys creaking by in slow motion. As we crossed the road a Cambodian Army truck roared past, and Clayton grimaced.

"There they go," he said. "They're press-ganging boys off the streets now. And there's no point at all, Harvey, is there? The Yank airlift won't save them. Nothing will."

He squinted at me: not as fresh and eager as he'd been two years earlier. There were lines of strain on his plain, sweating face, and I guessed that he was about burned out, as a lot of the press here were.

"Some of the Yank military brass are still claiming in interviews that the Government can hold the towns," he said. "Christ. Are they kidding themselves, or just us?" Without waiting for an answer, he asked suddenly: "Have you seen Mike Langford lately?"

I said I was seeing him that evening.

We were passing the curbside tables in front of la Taverne, where some French embassy people and a few foreign journalists were sitting over coffees and cognacs. Hands in pockets, Clayton glanced sideways at me, his expression a curious one: the disapproving, almost prim look of someone about to pass on news of human deviousness or corruption.

"Langford's someone who won't seem to accept the end here," he said. "It's weird. A bit of a bloody worry, in fact."

Mike's got a lot invested emotionally, I said. He regards it as his home.

Clayton shook his head. It wasn't that simple, his look told me. He seemed determined to talk about it, and I remembered how much he'd admired Langford, and guessed now that I was going to have to listen to some sort of analysis of his idol's flaws. Roger's uncritical youthful fervency was lately giving way to a judgmental earnestness I found unattractive: it afflicts a lot of journalists.

"Mike knows bloody well that Lon Nol's finished," he said.

"But he seems to be involved with this group around his mate Chandara—who's been promoted to Colonel. I gather it's the old Free Khmer revamped, getting ready to come again when Lon Nol loses. Against the Khmer Rouge! Talk about tilting at windmills: Jesus. But surely you've heard these rumors about Langford?"

Mike was a friend, I said. I didn't listen to rumors.

But Clayton ignored my tone. "You know I regard him as a friend too," he said, "and a great war photographer. Nothing will change that. But mate, he's losing his professionalism." He looked around him now as though we might be overheard. "You must have heard," he said. "They reckon that out in the field, he's picking up the gun. He's not always covering; he's bloody *fighting*, mate."

I stopped, and faced him. I don't believe that, I told him; and I didn't.

"Look, it's coming from quite a few sources," Clayton said. "A *New York Times* correspondent came on him with a platoon of Lon Nol soldiers down near Takhmau, on Highway 1, where the Government's still holding out. They'd just come out of a firefight, and Mike was carrying an M-16: he seemed to be in charge. 'Jesus,' said the *Times* guy, 'what are you doing with that rifle?' And Langford said: 'We got cut off, and their captain was killed. Somebody had to take over.'"

I laughed, in spite of the concern that Clayton had succeeded in creating in me. Any other journalist would have laughed at that story too, serious though its implications were: but not Clayton. His stare asked that I come to my senses.

He probably had to fight his way out, I said. It happens; you know that. It's happened to plenty of other cameramen. You defend yourself or you die.

"There are too many other stories," Clayton said. "And Langford doesn't hide his involvement with this bloody outfit. All he ever talks about is how Cambodia's been betrayed, and how it's got to be saved. He's losing his objectivity, Harvey."

Maybe he thinks now there are more important things in life than journalism, I said.

Clayton looked affronted, like a Bible teacher listening to blasphemy, and I patted him on the shoulder.

I'll give Mike your regards, I said, and hailed a cyclo.

I'd arranged to meet Langford for a drink that night by the pool at the Hotel le Royal. I came down from my room at about eight o'clock, and sat at a table to wait for him under one of the striped umbrellas, cognac and soda in hand.

The colored electric bulbs hung as always between the sugar palms, and the petrol lamps flickered on the tables like the fairground lights of childhood. In front of me, across the pool, rose the hotel's ranks of shuttered windows. Beyond them was the drive, with its cyclos and taxis, and then the Phnom Penh dark: dense and profoundly unsafe. All was as usual here, yet not. The garden's scented air suggested peace, but a peace in the process of mummifying: becoming as we sat here the peace of the past, masquerading as the present for a little while longer. I tried to imagine what would happen when the Khmer Rouge came up the drive.

The crowd around me was made up of embassy officials, Cambodian military officers and bureaucrats, Western correspondents, and a sprinkling of up-market Cambodian prostitutes in black silk sarongs. A small Cambodian orchestra on the café's terrace was playing "Wonderland by Night." My colleagues of the press, huddled over their table lamps, faces reflecting the flames of the lamps like those of nineteenth-century plotters, were the noisiest of the groups under the umbrellas. There was a note of hysteria in their laughter that night, and they were getting more drunk than usual. Outbursts of wild clowning alternated with emotional diatribes against the corrupt Lon Nol leaders—or simply the war itself.

One of these was being delivered at the next table by a British correspondent whose hair was held back by a red pirate's scarf. I could pick up most of his thesis in snatches. Only the American hawks wanted to keep the war going now, and a Khmer Rouge victory would be the best outcome for the country, bringing peace and stability. They wouldn't be the bogeys they were said to be: the wicked Khmer Rouge were a fiction created by right-wing war-lovers. They'd prove to be moderate Socialists, free from corruption and ready to rebuild a Cambodia at peace, with the exiled Prince Sihanouk back as head of state.

I'd heard this speech before, with minor variations. Meanwhile, in the markets, rumors of quite another kind were circulating, brought by the refugees from the countryside: horror stories about disembowelings, and heads being sawn off with the knife-edged leaf stems of sugar palms. You could take your pick: none of us really knew what the Others would be like.

There were very few correspondents that I knew here, this evening. I missed the Nurseryman, who was long gone; I missed Volkov. Jim Feng was in Saigon that week, Griffiths was back in the UK, and I expected Mike to come alone, or perhaps with Bill Wall. But when he appeared, walking down the steps from inside the hotel, I was startled to see him accompanied by Aubrey Hardwick.

Langford had introduced me to Hardwick in Saigon once, but we'd spoken very little; and that had been a number of years ago. Here in Phnom Penh, I'd seen the two of them together from a distance, at odd times—often having drinks or a meal at one of the little bars down near the Tonle Sap. They were usually alone, and I never attempted to join them. Sometimes they had Donald Mills with them, who was still Second Secretary at the Australian embassy in Saigon. Hardwick came and went, visiting our embassy here. He was said to be a military adviser, and his connection with Australia's foreign mission was left somewhat vague—which should have fooled no one who knew about such things.

As they pulled up their chairs to the table, I studied him with some curiosity. He's now quite old, as you probably know—a bachelor in his mid-sixties, belonging everywhere and nowhere. I've learned since that he has a flat here in Bangkok and a house in Melbourne; but he seems to stay nowhere for long. Like a lot of aging diplomats and Secret Intelligence people, he's developed a veneer over the years that's pretty well impenetrable. Aubrey's veneer—old-school-tie and Melbourne Club—is a sort of self-caricature: fey and dated, pre–World War Two, with a touch of Noël Coward about it. But the veneer covers a quite different interior from that of a diplomat: there's a hardness there that makes you metaphorically straighten yourself—and then feel annoyed with yourself for doing it.

Leaning back in his chair now, he looked like a military officer in mufti. Everything said it: the lean fitness; the hair—now quite white—cut to a Marine stubble; the clipped, quasi-British accent; the cotton shirt with patch pockets and the knife-edged tan slacks. He had the expected firm jaw, but the mouth was odd: pursed pink lips that were rather feminine: a fastidious elderly lady's. One eyelid drooped slightly, in a frozen wink. There was no small talk: he wouldn't allow any. As soon as he had a cognac in his hand, he turned his full attention on me, and proceeded to the only topic anyone here was talking about: the country's death. He led into it with a dose of flattery.

"Good to meet you again, Harvey. Never miss your television pieces when I'm at home in Melbourne. Constantly listen to your radio reports on the ABS overseas service as well. Excellent; they keep me abreast. And I notice your assessments are seldom wrong. So tell me: how long do you think we have, before welcoming the Red Khmer into town?"

I told him a couple of months at most.

But he shook his head, his eyes fixed on me without blinking: shrewd, unusually light eyes, arresting the attention like a glimpse of frozen water. And a little mad: the only thing in his appearance that gave him away. All spooks are a little mad; they have to be.

"Not months," he said. "Weeks."

I asked him if this was a guess, or whether he had privileged information. If he had, I said, perhaps he might care to share it.

I probably sounded a little brusque; and I saw Langford glance at me quickly. But I have something of a distaste for spooks—and as well, you have to understand that in that February, in the atmosphere of final catastrophe enclosing the city, no one felt like playing the cat-and-mouse games any more which usually provide journalists, public officials and politicians with their adrenaline rushes. We were past these games; discretion and indirectness were being dropped. It was rather like being on a sinking ship.

Aubrey wasn't put out, or didn't appear to be. But he took his time about answering, leaning above the table lamp's glass shade to light a small cigar at the flame, his tanned old face deeply shadowed. There was a good deal of the actor in him. Leaning back and blowing out a long stream of smoke in the classic manner, he gave me the unblinking gaze again.

"With pleasure," he said. "In desperate times, we scavengers should share every scrap, no? I've been talking today to my friend John Gunther Dean. Also to my old and dear friend Lieutenant General Sutsakhan."

My friend John Gunther Dean; my friend Sutsakhan. I didn't doubt Aubrey's close acquaintance with both the American ambassador and the commander-in-chief of the Cambodian Armed Forces. But I suddenly sensed something *passé* about him: something of yesterday's man. Sensed, but wasn't sure. He was pretty certainly a high-ranking ASIS operative, and close to the center of things; yet the atmosphere he gave out just now, under the bland and confident manner, was of a man trying to hold his place, and feeling the ground begin to shift. It's an atmosphere an old journo becomes highly attuned to, and I wondered why I sniffed it out in Aubrey. I still wonder, since he now proceeded to deliver some hard information of a reasonably surprising nature.

"The Government will almost certainly remove Lon Nol shortly," Aubrey said. "Sutsakhan will probably replace him as head of state. They will do this in a bid to win international approval, since Lon Nol's corruption now brings them into such dreadful odor. And what they hope then, poor things, is to get U.S. Congress approval for the major military air support they're being denied. But alas, no. It's too *late*. The troops are deserting in thousands, and almost every brigade defending the perimeter of the city has already been knocked out; you know this. The Americans have plans to evacuate the Government, and John Gunther Dean is preparing to pull the embassy out. It will be soon, Harvey, *very* soon; I can't say more. And the ambassador believes that what will follow will be what he refers to as a bloodbath."

Yes, we'd heard that often enough, I told him. Dean was always talking to the press about the future Khmer Rouge bloodbath, when he had us around to the embassy for drinks.

"True," Mike put in. "The journos have even made up a song about it. You'll probably hear it sung before the night's over, Aubrey. The 'Khmer Rouge Bloodbath Song.' "

Aubrey chuckled. "John Gunther Dean's a pessimist," he said. "I often tell him that." He turned to me again; he seemed bent on impressing me. "There won't be any bloodbath, you know— it's nonsense. It reminds one of that poem of Cavafy's—are you a Cavafy admirer, Harvey?—'Waiting for the Barbarians.' " He quoted, his voice taking on a musical cadence. " 'Now what's going to happen to us without barbarians? These people were a kind of solution.' " He gave a throaty laugh, his eyes searching mine like those of the teller of a suggestive joke. "The Americans tend to *need* monsters to frighten the children with, don't they? I love them dearly, but they do." He leaned towards me, lowering his voice slightly and checking the tables on either side: the sideways glance one grows all too familiar with, in political journalism. "The question is, Harvey, what happens *after* the defeat? That's what I've been talking about with Michael, here."

I glanced at Langford; but he was listening in silence, his face showing nothing.

"When the city falls," Aubrey said to me, "have you considered staying?"

I'd considered it, I said; but not with much enthusiasm. The Khmer Rouge didn't seem likely to respect press neutrality.

"Now you're seeing them as bogeymen, as the Americans do," Aubrey said. "But our friends speak from ignorance about the Khmer Rouge, believe me. I know a little more about them. So do some of my colleagues in Foreign Affairs: it's been our business to know. I know some of the KR leaders personally. Met them originally in Paris: just boys, then. And I maintained friendships with them here in Phnom Penh, when I was First Secretary here in the sixties. *Real* friendships: links that can be revived. You've got to realize what they're actually like, Harvey—it might surprise you." His voice took on a soothing tone, and he smiled: I began to see why Mike called him Uncle Aubrey. "They're not monsters," he said. "They're Left Bank Marxist intellectuals: idealists. Somewhat naive. In other words, the sort of people we can *deal* with. And we will."

Mike drained his cognac and put it down with a rap. He said nothing, but his raised eyebrows and faint smile caused Hardwick to glance at him sharply.

"Michael doesn't agree," he said. "I respect his experience of the Khmer Rouge soldiers in the field, Harvey, but not even *he* knows very much about the KR leadership." His voice had an edge to it, and for the first time the hardness showed clearly: a particular kind that I've usually come across otherwise in senior policemen. But still Langford sat back and remained silent, his face mild and untelling, like a dutiful son hearing his father out.

Aubrey turned back to me. "Sihanouk has said in his broadcasts from Peking that the KR will only execute those they regard as traitors," he said. "Things will settle down after that, we can depend on it. Then we'll need to understand the regime—and not only Canberra but Washington will desperately need insights. That's why a correspondent of your caliber should stay, Harvey. The links I'm talking about could be interesting to you. Links that our American friends simply can't come by." He drew on his cigar, watching me.

I'll have to disappoint you, I told him. I'm a cowardly journalist: I don't take chances. And I have a wife to consider. I'll be out on the first helicopter, when the Khmer Rouge arrive.

Aubrey's eyes remained fixed on my face, and his smile vanished. "Really," he said, and said no more; he turned away to signal for a waiter.

He'd understood me, and now wasted no more time: the topic was dismissed.

A little later, he excused himself; he had a dinner appointment with an old and dear friend from the French embassy, he said.

Left alone, Mike and I sat on in a faintly awkward silence. Then I said: Your Uncle Aubrey doesn't waste time. Does he usually try and recruit every journo he meets?

He grinned, fingering an ashtray. "Not usually," he said. "But he's dead keen to find people to hang on here, after the Khmer Rouge win. People who can report on the new regime."

I asked him if he intended to be one of them.

He stared at me for a moment, leaning back. In all these years, he and I had never discussed his association with Hardwick—and I'd never even hinted at my assumption that Aubrey was an ASIS man. But tonight had seemed a good opportunity. Everything had conspired to create it: the deepening mutter of disaster in the darkness beyond the umbrellas; the drunken, nervy laughter that came from underneath them; the sense of everything ending. And I was right; when Langford spoke again, he took my knowledge for granted.

"No," he said finally. "I'll be staying—but not for Uncle Aubrey." He looked away from me, still toying with the ashtray, and didn't enlarge on this. Then he said: "Aubrey got me started as a combat cameraman when I was young and in trouble, a long time ago. I owed him for that. So I gave him a bit of operational intelligence over the years: stuff I picked up when I was moving around—stuff that his Foreign Affairs people couldn't get. Some of it raised his stocks in London and Washington, as well as in Canberra. That was the ultimate feather in the cap for Aubrey. Our intelligence people love it when the CIA listens to them. He reckoned that some of it went as high as the Oval Office."

He looked up at me quickly, putting down the ashtray: "I know what you're thinking, Harvey. But there's never been a conflict of interest. There would have been, for a words man like you; you'd have owed information like that to ABS first. But it didn't arise for a photographer: it was nothing but background to me. And I really wanted to help Aubrey, back in the sixties. He's quite an extraordinary bloke: not just any old spook."

He felt in the pocket of his loud, aquamarine shirt and found a single, deformed cigarette there—no doubt scrounged. He leaned forward and lit it from the lamp, continuing to gaze into the flame with a faraway expression. "Aubrey's Special Operations," he said. He kept the cigarette in his mouth, which made his words indistinct, and his voice—no doubt deliberately—was softer than usual, so that I had to lean over to hear him. "He's crucially involved, here and in Vietnam. He's an adviser to the U.S. military, among other things. There's not much that old bloke hasn't been involved with, in his time. This is a man who started with British MI6 before World War Two, Harvey, when he was studying at the Sorbonne in Paris. He practically founded Australian Intelligence, under MI6 instructions."

He paused, drawing on his bent cigarette, expecting me to be impressed.

I made a suitable grunt; but to tell you the truth I found his respect quaint, considering the life he'd led himself. He was revealing things not just about Aubrey Hardwick but about himself—rather as people tend to do when they speak of a parent or a lover. Uncle Aubrey was a figure from that War of wars which had loomed over both our childhoods, and which dwarfed the present conflict as legend always dwarfs reality. For Mike, Hardwick was a survivor out of legend: a flesh-and-blood artifact of whom he'd always be in partial awe—legendary though Langford himself might have become in the eyes of others. I wonder if it's always like this, as eras give way to one another? A hall of mirrors: reality emulating some previous legend, and then itself becoming legend, while not quite believing it can be so—transfigured only by death. There's a pathos about it, don't you think?

Mike was continuing to talk. "So I did what I could for the old boy. I even used to believe I was doing some good, in a way. Helping to stop the Communist takeover in Asia. Now you'll think I'm a hawk, or naive, or both. Well, I *was* bloody naive in the sixties, Harvey, that's for sure."

You've changed your views, then, I said.

"Oh yes," he said. "I've changed them, all right." He expelled smoke with a slow, regretful hiss.

"I used to believe that the Americans would save Vietnam; save Cambodia," he said. "Well, we know now what a joke that is, don't we? The South's fighting for its life, and there's no hope left. Nixon promised the South that he'd back them all the way with money and arms, and never see them defeated. Now Nixon's gone, Congress is breaking all the promises: so the South's finished. And you know what they're going to do in Cambodia. They'll shoot through soon and leave these people for dead: leave them to the Khmer Rouge. Even the arms and the food will stop. And the politicians and the spooks will go and start a new game, after that. Aubrey's getting ready: you heard. Bloody sickening, mate."

I'd no reason to doubt the feeling behind his words. Yet the odd thing was that they were spoken with the same lack of emphasis—even casualness—as always. He would always be like this: always the mild detachment, I thought, so that you wondered how strongly he felt about anything. I never heard him sound bitter or enraged: it was what was most attractive about him; it was why so many people liked him. He seemed to have been born unable to get angry or overinvolved—and yet what he was actually saying now was totally at odds with that. It made him the enigma he still is to me.

We know all this, Snow, I said. But come on, what can you do? It's just about over now. The Lon Nol lot were too corrupt, too disorganized. They're beaten.

He leaned towards me, and put both hands deliberately on the table. In him, the action was as arresting as a more violent gesture would have been in someone else. His voice remained low, but now I thought I heard a hint of vehemence in it. "No," he said. "They're *not* beaten, Harvey. That's the lie that's being put out so that they can be finally left in the shit. But they're still holding most of the provincial capitals—right? And that's where most of the population is now: the towns are crammed with refugees from the Khmer Rouge—people who are there because they've had a taste of what's coming. If the Yanks did a real airlift, the Government could still win. Don't you see?"

I looked at him dubiously, but I wasn't going to argue. He leaned back again, stubbing out the tortured cigarette, and seemed to relax. "Maybe you think it's a government not worth saving," he said. "And I don't think much of it, either. But the ordinary Khmer troops are still fighting like tigers for their families and their homes and their temples." He gestured vaguely towards the drive. "It's all so hopeless, but they're so bloody brave. They know this government's all they have. Yes, it's rotten; but it gives them a chance against tyranny. Because what's coming is *real* tyranny, mate: so much worse you won't believe it. We're not talking about the North Vietnamese any more: they might have been tolerable, by comparison."

You think so? I said.

"I bloody know so." He pointed at our fellow correspondents around the pool. "But these guys don't know, the Government here doesn't know, even their military brass don't know—and Aubrey doesn't know. He really does have a lot of links here that go back a long way: the high officials and the military and a lot of the royal family are his buddies, from his days as a diplomat here. But he's too old to go into the field himself, and he's got no field agents who can possibly get near the Khmer Rouge. No one can penetrate them."

He was silent for a moment, and I saw that the legend, the surrogate father, was being rejected.

"He won't listen to me," Mike said. "Aubrey's living in the sixties. He thinks it can go back now to the way it was under Prince Sihanouk: his favorite time in Cambodia. He remembers the nice young students he knew then, who've grown up to be cadres. He believes that bullshit he and his Foreign Affairs mates are putting out about Khmer Rouge intellectuals. He's not in touch."

Well, we'll all be gone soon, I said.

"Not me," he said.

Surely he wasn't serious about that, I said.

"I'm staying," he said. "With Ly Keang." His voice remained unemphatic.

Why? For Aubrey? You're crazy, I said. Get out: bring Ly Keang with you.

He didn't answer for a moment. Then he looked towards the drive, speaking so softly that I had to strain to hear. "It's not for Aubrey," he said. "It's for us; for Cambodia." He looked at me. "Ordinary people get used and abused all the time in this world

—I learned that when I was young. And I'm on no one's side but theirs now, Harvey: the ordinary people here."

He drained his cognac and soda. "It's bloody politicians who-'ve destroyed this country, isn't it, Harvey? And some of them have never even seen the place. The farmers back home are right: never trust a politician." He grinned without amusement. "There's no way you can use people and save them at the same time," he said. "That's not the way."

So what is the way? I asked.

"Fight *with* them," he said. "That's what I've decided. That's where Aubrey can still be useful: he can get us some of the help we'll need. The arms. The underground backing. We'll need all of it we can get."

I suddenly felt as though I were dreaming. His manner was so normal: almost happy. And yet what he was saying was unreal.

We? I said. *We?*

"Colonel Chandara's outfit," he said. "The Free Khmer. Ly Keang and I are going to be with them when they regroup: probably on the Thai border. This is my country now, mate. I'm staying to fight."

I sat and stared at him: I've forgotten now what my next speech consisted of. Helpless remonstrances, no doubt: useless efforts at making him see what I considered to be his madness.

A few seconds later, the Khmer Rouge Bloodbath Song rose from a few tables away: looking across, we saw that the singers were Bill Wall and a couple of British correspondents. Bill was looking in our direction, beckoning to us to join them. Standing to obey, I found that I'd become fairly drunk. Langford had too, I think.

So the scene begins to distort and fade: the dark garden, the empty blue oblong of the pool, the strings of colored lights in the trees, the light tropical suits and dresses, the white and brown faces, and the old hotel's ranks of secretive windows, whose closed nineteenth-century shutters had once hidden French colonial intrigues and boredom and adulteries, and were now hiding the more frantic intrigues and ringing phones and quick fornications of my colleagues of the international press, who had made the

Royal hum like a beehive for these past five years. Soon (if I can allow myself a moment of elegy for this lost period of my life) the humming would stop, and we too would be gone; soon, any night now, we too would be nothing but after-images, hanging in the air of the old Hotel le Royal: the important ringing of our phones stilled, our jokes and all our wild urgencies and deadlines as archaic and faintly ridiculous as the concerns of the French planters. But for now, and perhaps for the last time, here we were, seated at our small round table, singing into each other's faces while a dubious and uneasy Chinese waiter watched us. The tune was "She was Poor but She Was Honest":

> Oh will there be a dreadful bloodbath
> When the Khmer Rouge come to town?
> Yes, there'll be a dreadful bloodbath
> When the Khmer Rouge come to town . . .

Langford sang well: he had a natural, pleasing voice. Opposite me, his face grew a little red, and a sheaf of yellow hair fell across his forehead. Watching him, I said to myself that his notion of belonging here was nonsense. He'd never looked more like a country Australian, and I decided that the declaration he'd just made to me was the product of a mood; a fantasy. After all, most of us were a little deranged, in that month.

2.

HARVEY DRUMMOND

Aubrey Hardwick proved to be wrong: the Khmer Rouge didn't break through in the next few weeks. The city held on through February, and all through March as well.

It was April that brought the fall; and even then, it came as a surprise. Most of us were still imagining that defeat might still be a few more months away. We can never believe in any absolute end, I suppose; we're never quite ready.

I know that was Langford's frame of mind. If it hadn't been, he'd never have come to Saigon with Jim Feng and me.

We made the short flight there on Thursday, April 10th, intending to return to Phnom Penh in forty-eight hours—and the reason we went was that it now seemed certain Saigon would fall first. It could now only be weeks—perhaps days—before the North Vietnamese Army reached the capital. Nobody knew what would happen then; there was still talk of a truce.

Our bureau chiefs were pressing us to go, of course, but that wasn't what gave the trip its principal urgency. We'd given the war a good slice of our lives: we wanted to be there at the end.

Showered and changed, Mike, Jim and I sat in the same old green wicker chairs on the Continental terrace, drinking beer.

It was five in the afternoon on Friday. We were surrounded by familiar figures from the press corps and the foreign embassies; our drinks were brought to us across the tiles by the same aged Chinese waiters. But beyond the terrace's low stone wall, nothing was the same. The Army of North Vietnam was moving south at terrific speed, and everything was going down in front of it. Sometimes there'd apparently been no resistance. The Communists were now about half an hour's drive away, on Highway 1. No one had imagined that the end would arrive so quickly.

We'd just got back from covering a battle at Xuan Loc: a province capital where the Army of South Vietnam was trying to make a final stand. We'd gone in the back of a military truck to a point as close as we could get: a South Vietnamese artillery position in a hamlet where long-range shelling was going on. Mike had taken pictures; Jim and I had done a filmed interview with an ARVN military spokesman. The spokesman had said that Xuan Loc was crucial, and that the ARVN would hold it. But we knew they wouldn't. Nothing would hold any more.

Hue was gone. Da Nang was gone. Kontum, Pleiku, Nha Trang and Cam Ranh were gone, as the North Vietnamese military machine came south. These were places that were meant never to fall: towns which the vanished American Military Command had sworn never would fall, and from where we'd reported times without number. Now they'd gone down within days of each other. Resistance was crumbling by the hour, and out on Tu Do Street, beyond the terrace, the refugees were streaming by: in battered cars, on bicycles and on foot. Peasants in black pajamas walked with middle-class families in Western dress, all of them carrying their toddlers and babies. All wore the same expressions; all carried baskets and suitcases and sad plastic airways bags crammed with possessions. Some pushed barrows. Malignant brown gusts of wind churned up choking dust about their feet.

How can I explain to you what Saigon was like, that afternoon? The smells were still petrol and diesel fumes, cordite, *nuoc mam* and spices. But it seemed to me that a new and larger odor lay over everything, permeating the whole city. It was the odor of human fear: a little like seaweed, or perhaps dying flowers. I can still smell it.

There was the usual traffic jam in the square, but a new sort of rage could be heard in the blaring horns and voices. Above the din hung impotent Government propaganda banners in red and yellow. Everything leaned and moved like the sails of a yacht, fast yet slow, fast yet slow: and as in bad dreams, the appearance of things remained slyly unchanged. But at the deep, hot core of the din, everything was changing.

Correspondents were now being visited in their hotel rooms by beautiful young Vietnamese women from wealthy families, who offered their bodies and then begged to be transported to America; Europe; Australia. One had knocked on Bill Wall's door the week before, with a briefcase in her hand. She had opened it up, and it was jammed with a hundred thousand U.S. dollars in cash. All she asked was to be taken out, Bill said. She wept when he refused.

We now watched two cars stalled at right angles, a dozen yards away: a battered blue-and-cream Renault taxi with an ARVN captain in the back, and a long black Ford driven by a man I placed as a drug dealer, in white suit and sunglasses. He and the taxi driver and the captain waved their hands and screamed at each other, their faces distorted with a rage that looked psychotic. Then a pistol shot made us jump. Leaning out of the taxi's window, the captain had drawn his Colt .45 and had fired into the bonnet of the Ford.

Mike threw back his head and laughed. "Shot him between the headlights," he said, and Jim laughed too.

But I couldn't laugh. My throat was dry, and sweat sprang from the palms of my hands. Even machines had to be punished now; and what everyone was thinking of was flight. It was in their faces, all of which seemed to look inward. Everyone was thinking the same thing: you could hear it, pulsing in the air. *Where, where can I run? Who will save me?*

We'd listened to many rumors, that afternoon: rumors of what would happen when the Communists arrived. Everyone predicted a massacre of civilians—like the one that the Communists had carried out in Hue in 1968. The first people to be killed, it was predicted, would be civil servants—and foreign journalists like us. And there were stranger rumors. All single women would be made to marry Communist soldiers—and the painted fingernails of bar girls would be torn out. There were also rumors of reprieve: the American B-52s would come back, and save the South at the eleventh hour. The Americans would not desert them.

Jim Feng suddenly spoke to me, gazing out at the crowd. "How much longer, Harvey?"

It wasn't the first time we'd discussed this question, and I knew he was asking now for a reappraisal.

Maybe a week or ten days, I said. It all depends on how hard the ARVN will fight for the city. Or maybe President Thieu will pull off a deal—although I doubt it.

Jim turned to Mike, his eyes narrow and sharp: almost elated. "We should stay, Snow," he said. "We should stay for the bitter end, when the NVA get here. You too, Harvey."

I shook my head. Beyond the call of duty, I said. I doubted that there'd be a single correspondent in town when the NVA arrived. The rumors could be wrong, I said, but I'd rather not put them to the test. All the big outfits were making their plans to evacuate already: Telenews too. No one wanted to be stood against a wall. Neither should you, Jim, I said.

But Jim shook his head, and leaned forward earnestly. "It won't happen, Harvey. A lot of journalists are pissing their pants over nothing. The North Vietnamese won't execute news people. We know what they're like, Mike and I: they're disciplined. They play by the rules. Isn't that right, Mike?"

Mike nodded. "I'd trust them," he said. "Although I wouldn't trust the Viet Cong. But I won't be staying, Jim. I can't wait here that long. Things could go down at any time in Phnom Penh. I have to get back to Ly Keang."

Jim leaned back in his chair and sighed, beer in hand, his expression resigned and wistful, his legs in their faded khaki trousers and highly polished boots extended in front of him. His white shirt was beautifully ironed as usual, and his slicked-back hair shone. But I suddenly saw the deep lines in his cheeks, and the worn look about the shrewd and humorous almond eyes; and I was looking at a double image. The young Jim Feng of a decade ago was sitting here too, in one of these same wicker chairs, in the time of Rolling Thunder.

"Sure, Snow, I understand," he said. "You've got to be with her. But we spent a lot of years covering this war, didn't we? A lot of our youth. A pity, not to see the curtain. Dmitri should be here too."

"Yes, he should," Mike said.

They were silent for a moment. Then, half humorously, half with sudden concern, Jim said: "Jesus, Mike. No more firefights. What will we do when there are no more firefights?"

He left us a little after this. Duty called him to dinner with one of his chiefs from Telenews, in town on a visit from London before the office closed down.

Mike and I sat on. He was looking out over Tu Do with a distracted eye, and the question he asked me now showed that his thoughts were with Ly Keang.

"Did you check with the AP office, Harvey? Anything new from Phnom Penh?"

AP had correspondents in Phnom Penh, and were getting stories on the wire all the time; so Jim and I made a habit of looking in at their office in the Eden Building, on the floor above Telenews, and seeing what they had. Yes, I said, we'd checked; nothing much had broken since this morning. But make sure you do come back on Saturday, I said. I've got a feeling.

"Sure. I'll come back Saturday no matter what," he said. "But there's something I have to do here first—people I have to see, at the U.S. embassy."

He didn't explain this immediately; instead he fell silent for a moment. Swallows flickered and wheeled in the early twilight; sunset was turning the sky deep red above the tower of the Caravelle. On the roof there, the usual tiny figures could be made out, looking down on Tu Do's chaos; a cameraman was shooting film.

"I want you to do me a favor," Langford said suddenly. "Come to dinner with me tomorrow night at Claudine Phan's."

This surprised me. He'd mentioned Madame Phan from time to time over the years, but only briefly; and he'd never suggested introducing me. I asked how she'd feel about having an extra dinner guest.

He smiled. "Why should she mind? She's turned the place into a restaurant: that's how Claudine survives now. The family business and the money are all gone."

He leaned closer to me across the table, lowering his voice. "She wants me to get her two sons out to the U.S. They're guys in their twenties: both up to their necks in Government circles. So you see what's in store for them. Claudine believes the VC will execute them when Hanoi takes over, and it's probably true. So I've got to do this for her, Harvey. And I want to get Claudine out as well."

I pointed over the wall at the trudging, jostling streams of refugees. They'd pay every piastre they have for what you're offering Madame Phan, I said. Some of them would kill for it. Can you actually deliver?

"Yes," he said. "No problem. The Americans are planning an airlift of picked Vietnamese nationals when they pull the embassy out. Didn't you know? They're already drawing up secret lists, and they listen to journalists. I've got a mate in the embassy: I can get the sons on the list." He leaned closer, both hands on the table. "But I've got to persuade Claudine to go too, Harvey. At the moment she's saying she won't—but she's got no more hope of surviving than they have: probably less. The problem is, she doesn't want to be saved. It's crazy."

He looked away from me, fumbling for a loose cigarette in his top pocket. "Claudine's a wonderful lady," he said. "She can't be left here to rot in a bloody prison camp." He flicked on his lighter, looking at me again. "Help me to persuade her, mate. She might listen to you."

So this was why he'd come to Saigon, I thought. It was this that had drawn him out of Phnom Penh—not the story. Yes: I understood. Phnom Penh was the present, and Ly Keang was the future. But Saigon was the past, and Madame Phan was the guardian of the past; and he couldn't abandon the past or her. It was Claudine whom he'd really come to save—not her sons.

All the candles in the room were burning low, and some were flickering out, causing shadows to tremble on the walls. Young Vietnamese women wearing the *ao dai* had cleared the debris of dinner from the table, leaving us with balloons of brandy. They had been quite noiseless, except when they spoke to each other: a soft chirruping like that of sleepy birds.

Now the three of us were alone, and the room was silent. All the customers had gone.

For some moments we sat without speaking, as though in a trance. The Phan villa had that effect, I found: a house of musing silences. One of Madame Phan's bare arms was extended at full length across the table, her hand covering Langford's. They sat looking at each other, frozen as though on a stage, with me as their audience.

Her ivory-colored arm was firm and shapely: that of a much younger woman. But her face was haggard and weary. Her appearance had shocked me, when we were first introduced. Her hair was half gray, and a long wisp of it had escaped from the chignon at the back: a touch of disarray that I guessed wasn't typical—or wouldn't have been, once. She wore a sleeveless black silk dress of Chinese cut, with slits at the sides. She was probably around fifty, and was still a handsome woman—the surprising gray green eyes in the Vietnamese face her most arresting feature. I remembered how often I'd heard in the sixties how beautiful she was; how wealthy and powerful. Now here she sat: beauty going; the money gone; the North Vietnamese Army hammering at Xuan Loc, the door to Saigon.

"Dearest Mike," she said. She had a deep, drawling voice that compelled your attention. "Tell me again," she said. "You're sure? No nasty little loopholes? They won't go back on it?"

"No," Mike said. "You know the Americans: it's done when they say it's done. Larry Hagen won't let me down. All your boys have to do now is stand by and wait."

She continued to look into his face, as though trying to discover some hint of deception. Then she blinked rapidly, and glanced at me.

"How can I thank this man, Harvey? How can I thank this Snow of mine?" Despite the old-fashioned flippancy of the words, her tone wasn't light, but serious.

Langford answered her before I could. "I'll tell you how, Claude. By letting me put your name on the list. Tomorrow. There's no bloody time to lose."

She released his hand and put a finger to her lips, closing her eyes and frowning as though at a sudden migraine. "No," she said. "No, *mon cher;* don't start that again."

Her eyes remained closed; she sat still, and both of us contemplated her face's blind mask as though for clues as to what might move her. And now Mike looked despairing, his mouth compressed, his eyes wide and exasperated: the expression of a child who tries to digest some loss that threatens childhood's roots. The silence extended, in that strange room.

There were six small round tables there, covered with lace cloths, a candle burning on each. They were set well apart, each of them provided with high-backed old French chairs. The high ceiling made the place formal and imposing, but there was a sense of dustiness, and the walls were dim and grimy. Everything looked neglected. Despite an overhead fan, it was stuffy in there. I doubt that the place had changed since the sixties, or, perhaps, since the thirties: it had the air of being stuck in time. Valuable Indochinese antiques stood on gilded cabinets; tall shelves were crowded with European books. It didn't look at all like a restaurant; Madame Phan had simply thrown open her drawing room as it was. There'd been no sign advertising the place outside, either: she catered for a small clientele, Mike had told me, who came by appointment only.

Most of the tables had been occupied, when we'd arrived. All the diners were Vietnamese, and all but one were well-dressed members of the middle class. I guessed them to be officials and business people and their wives. Langford had kissed Claudine on the cheek, while the nearest diners covertly watched; and I was struck by the way he did it. There was a kind of tender respect I can only call filial; and in Claudine's face, there was a pleasure that looked maternal. Yet it wasn't quite that: I sensed other dimensions. She had told us she'd join us later, and had gone off among the tables; finally she'd vanished to the kitchens.

The meal, served by the gliding, white-clad young women, had been delicious: a wonderful blend of French provincial and Vietnamese, accompanied by a fine Bordeaux. But we ate in a state of tension. There was no music, and the diners spoke in low, furtive voices, so as not to be overheard. Their conversation was punctuated by long, unnatural silences, during which they would toy with their cutlery, or stare into their wineglasses. Some would stop eating and stare into space, and I would occasionally look up and intercept a curious glance, which would then dart away. All of them wore the same inward-looking expression I'd seen on Tu Do Street. *Where, where can I run?* The clicking of cutlery and dishes took on an unnatural loudness, and an atmosphere grew that was amorphously sinister. But everything seemed sinister in Saigon now.

A diner sitting alone had caused me particular unease. He certainly wasn't of the middle class like the others, and didn't seem to fit here. He was a long-haired, youngish Vietnamese in a cheap white sports shirt and black trousers, seated in a corner. He had a face I didn't like at all: ascetic and cruel at the same time. At least, that's how it looked to me in the dimness, in the nervous state I was in. Every time I looked up, I would find him watching us. Nor would he look away: his dark eyes held mine with a sort of contempt. I tried staring him down, but his gaze wouldn't drop: it then became openly menacing.

I'd suddenly become convinced that he was Viet Cong: he looked the type, and I'd drawn Langford's attention to him.

"Right," he'd said. "VC for sure. I wonder why Claudine let him in? They'll have been watching her for years, of course." He'd stared past me, at bleak visions. "You see why I've got to get her out."

Madame Phan's eyes were still closed, and the silence continued.

Langford tipped his brandy balloon up and drained it; then he looked at me. "Make her understand, Harvey."

At this, Claudine opened her eyes and gazed at us both in silence; then she smiled, and waited politely for my answer.

I believe Mike's giving you good advice, I told her. It's not my business, Madame, but I really think you should do what he says. It's a chance you may never have again.

I knew it was hopeless: she'd hear me out, but purely from courtesy. She'd clearly reached that phase of life where calm and resignation predominate, in a woman of understanding. And in her case, I began to perceive an underlying spirit I won't call melancholy, but which was melancholy's sister. In my mind, it matched the spirit of her city, whose collapse was now so near; but in Madame Phan, it didn't have the effect of pathos.

I think you've got about a week, I told her. Two weeks at the most. That's the estimate my American contacts give me. Then it's all over.

"The sides may come to an agreement," she said. "The Communists may not come into Saigon. Perhaps if President Thieu is replaced with someone they approve of, they'll agree to an armistice, leaving us a little of the South. That's what some are hoping for. Even the Americans."

Do you believe that? I asked.

She smiled like a young girl caught out in a white lie. "No," she said.

"No," I said. "Because they don't have to make concessions, do they? They can take it all, and they will. They'll want unconditional surrender. And you must know what that means, Madame."

"Call me Claudine," she said. "I like you, Harvey; I can see you are a good friend to Mike." She sipped her brandy and looked at me seriously; almost coldly. "Do you think I don't know the Communists, after all this time? Everything will be taken from us: you're right. We'll be told what to do and what to think and how to think it. All real freedom will be gone. We'll be put in re-education camps, and sent into the jungle to plant rice. That's why I wanted Mike to save my sons, and he's done it: they'll start a new life in America. But not me, Harvey. It's too late for me."

Mike interrupted, his eyes fixed on her face, wide and almost imploring. "It's *not* too late," he said. "That's bullshit, Claudine! All you have to do is let me put you on that list." Hunched over the table, he held both hands out to her, fingers crooked, seeming to suspend some heavy, valuable object for her inspection. It was the closest I'd ever seen him to being agitated. "*Do* it, for Christ's sake! There's no more time," he said. "Don't you understand?"

But still she shook her head, and reached out to caress his cheek. What struck me now was that it was she who was comforting him, when logic said that it should be the other way around.

"Yes," she said finally. "I understand that. And I understand what you're offering, Snow. You put me on the list, and the Americans take me away in their magic helicopter, with all the other poor bloody runaways. Yes?"

Suddenly she threw back her head and laughed. It was a startling, full-throated laugh, boisterous and infectious. In spite of ourselves, we both smiled. But then she stopped abruptly, and her face became serious again. "But when I get off the helicopter: what then?"

We looked at her blankly.

"Then I become a refugee," she said. "And what's a refugee? Someone who belongs nowhere. Don't speak, Michael: listen. I'm too old, darling, do you see? Too old to belong anywhere else. What would I do in America? Start another restaurant? Pretend I'd created a little bit of Vietnam in a corner of some foreign city? Taste *nuoc mam* and get sentimental? That's not me. It wouldn't be enough: I won't live in a bloody bubble. And I won't be a runaway. You saw them in here tonight, looking into their wine. They were thinking: 'What can I do? Who can I trust? If I plan my escape and fail, others may denounce me to the Communists when they come!' You see them thinking that in the cafés along Tu Do, stirring their coffees, waiting for the end. I won't be like that. For Claudine Phan, business as usual!"

And again, she gave her shout of laughter: unnaturally loud, this time. Then she pointed at Langford, glancing at me.

"Look at him, Harvey! He wants to keep everything fixed, like his photographs. Yes? Fixed and not changing—nothing and no one ever lost." She leaned forward to Mike, and her voice sank. "But everything gets lost in the end, Snow—everything and everyone. Don't you know that, yet? Can't you live with it? We all have to live with it, every moment. Every moment, every day of our lives, we watch people and things being lost. And some day we'll be lost ourselves. You are so tough—can't you be tough about *that* yet?"

Mike didn't answer. He sat absolutely still, staring at her. More than ever he looked to me like a large, bemused child: a child whose immobile face was masking a response to the unbearable. Their eyes held and silence extended, broken only by faint clatterings from the kitchen. The two of them seemed to have forgotten my presence.

To break the tension, I spoke to Claudine. You could go, I said, and then wait to come back here. It may change.

She turned and looked at me. "Yes, it will change," she said, and her voice was flat, now. "But not until I am an old woman —or dead. People forget this, Harvey, when a bad regime finally ends. They say: Look, it wasn't so bad after all. But they forget the people whose lives have been taken away from them forever. How can you give those lives back?"

"There was a VC in here tonight," Mike said suddenly. "Did you know that, Claude?"

"Of course I know," she said. "I know him well. He gets his meals here for nothing. So do his comrades."

Mike's long jaw set. He looked shocked now, and the effect was faintly comical.

"And when they take over, I may get protection, if I'm lucky," she said. "My restaurant may even stay open for business, in Communist Saigon. Don't look so horrified, *mon cher*. It's called surviving. Don't you even understand that, after so long? Only a bloody fool dies for ideas, when the ideas have no more allies. You might tell that to Uncle Aubrey, if you see him sometime. And if I don't survive—"

She shrugged in a manner that was suddenly French, and reached for the brandy bottle.

A little while later, she saw us out.

We paused outside the entrance, in front of the double doors. Claudine was accompanied by one of the white-clad young women she called her orphans. This one was little more than a girl, and clearly spoke no English. Her bright, unchanging smile assumed our farewells to be just routine: no different from any other happy parting.

"Don't worry, Snow," Madame Phan said. "I'll stay afloat. That's my specialty, remember?"

Her voice now had gone soft and young, but the strand of gray hair still hung down from the chignon, making her seem an old woman. Mike stood mute, hands hanging heavy at his sides like a farmer's, and Claudine craned her head and kissed him on the mouth, one hand resting on his shoulder.

"Worry about your little Cambodian," she said; and she was speaking as though neither I nor the Vietnamese girl was here. "I'll miss you, Mike. I'll miss you. Now go back to her."

She turned abruptly to me, her hand still on his shoulder.

"Make sure he does go, Harvey. He has to understand that he can't worry about everybody."

Then she drew back into the doorway, holding the girl's tiny waist. "I have these little ones to worry about now," she said. "Who'll do it if I don't?"

Langford and I walked towards the gates. Mike didn't look back; but I did. The two women were watching us go, both of them smiling as though at good news, Claudine still holding the girl by the waist. Framed by the tall, aged doors, the orange glow of the anteroom behind them, they seemed to look out from a stage: players in some traditional theater of which both Langford and I were ignorant.

I believe Claudine Phan used to be called a dragon lady. She certainly wasn't that any more: the business empire gone, disaster flooding towards her villa's iron gates down the dark, teeming tunnel of Highway 1. But the woman I met was more impressive than any dragon lady. I understood now why Langford had been devoted to her for so many years.

The next day was Saturday the 12th. We were booked on an Air Cambodge flight that left for Phnom Penh at noon. At ten o'clock, Mike and I walked around to the Eden Building on Nguyen Hue Boulevard, to see what we could learn in the AP office. Jim had gone off on his own, shooting film about the city.

The AP office had a reception area out in front, with big French easy chairs. Correspondents from other organizations were always calling in there to see what information they could pick up, and you could seldom find an empty chair. Most of us would stand leaning on the counter that divided the reception area from the main office—mainly in order to read the clipboard. The clipboard, which lay on the counter, held teletype copies of stories that had come in on the loop from New York, and were available for public consumption. Only favored visitors—of whom I was one—were permitted to enter the main office, where we were sometimes allowed to read the original stories. These came straight off the outgoing teleprinter, and were supposed to be closely guarded until the story was edited and sent out again by New York.

Today the reception room was unusually crowded, and I knew as soon as we came in that something had happened: you can never mistake the electricity. The clipboard was currently being read by a *Washington Post* correspondent: a middle-aged veteran called Barbara Hauser. Others were looking over her shoulder. We peered over her shoulder with them, and asked her what had broken.

"Phnom Penh's fallen," Barbara said. "Finito." She had a quick, flat delivery, and her tanned face showed no emotion. She went on leafing through the sheets, frowning intently.

Voices from all sides echoed her. "Right." "It's kaput." "All over."

"Fallen?" Mike sounded disbelieving, and glared from one to the other of the surrounding faces: I can't really describe his expression in any other way.

Barbara glanced at him briefly. She'd begun to write in her notebook, and her expression was impatient. "See for yourself. Our embassy's pulling out today," she said. "I'd say that amounts to the same thing, wouldn't you? You'll have to excuse me, Mike—I'm in kind of a rush." She scribbled, hunched over the counter.

Someone tapped me on the shoulder, and I turned and found Ed Carter, who'd just come in from outside. He was an AP correspondent we'd drunk with quite often in the old days: a tall, fleshy, unexcitable man from Ohio, with a thatch of brown hair going gray. "Disaster time, Harvey," he said. "You guys better come with me."

He held open the little swinging door in the counter and ushered us into the main office, where the staff writers sat at their desks. We followed him to the frosted glass box of the telex room, where the big old teleprinter machines chattered and hummed. Here Ed halted, and pushed a teletype sheet into my hand.

"Tuck it away," he said. "The U.S. Government's asked us to put an embargo on this until eleven o'clock, for safety reasons. So I'm putting an embargo on you, Harvey, OK? This is from our stringer in Phnom Penh. The U.S. Embassy started pulling out an hour ago. They took all our people, the acting President, and a few other lucky Cambodian nationals. The Prime Minister and the cabinet didn't go: they've stayed to negotiate with the Khmer Rouge. Poor bastards: imagine what kind of negotiation that will be."

I began to read the story, while Langford simply stared at Ed. His eyes were very bright, and there were red patches in his cheeks; his chest rose and fell rapidly. He looked angry: almost accusing. He seemed to be holding in check some sort of fury.

Ed didn't seem to notice. "The Marine helicopters started lifting everyone out at nine o'clock," he was saying. His voice seemed unnaturally placid, but then it always did: he was that sort of American. "So it's already over," he said. "Bye-bye to our Cambodian allies; hello Khmer Rouge."

Mike spoke for the first time. "Are the Khmer Rouge into the city yet?" He was standing on the balls of his feet, his hands open, like a footballer about to go onto the field.

"Not yet," Ed said. "It's apparently pretty quiet right now. Weird, in fact, according to our Cambodian stringer. Most of the population don't even know yet that the embassy's gone."

Without speaking again, Mike turned, and began to move off. I took his arm, and asked him where he was going.

"To make sure we're still on that Air Cambodge flight," he said.

"To Phnom Penh?" Ed said. He grinned faintly. "No more flights, old buddy. All civilian flights are finished."

"Military flights?" Mike said.

"No," Ed said. "The airlift's over. It's all *over,* man, just like it'll soon be over here. No one's running the airport any more—and the Khmer Rouge over the river were shooting at the Marine helicopters when they lifted off."

He suddenly looked hard at Langford over the tops of his glasses.

"Jesus, Mike, I just remembered: you've got an apartment there, right? All your goods. That's tough, man. You're lucky you're out, though: look at it that way. Now all you've gotta do is get out of Saigon."

But Mike had already turned away, and was heading out of the office at a run.

Ed stared after him, pulling at his lower lip. His eyes had a faraway expression, and I imagined he was contemplating Langford's crisis. But when he spoke, I realized he'd already stopped thinking about Mike.

"Those poor sons of bitches," he said. "We sure sold them down the Mekong, didn't we?"

3.

JIM FENG

When we found ourselves locked out of Cambodia, Mike and I had nothing except one change of clothes each, and our cameras; and Mike had that small tape recorder he took everywhere. Whatever we'd left in Phnom Penh was gone forever.

In my case this wasn't much: I only had a few extra clothes in a room in the Hotel Royal. All my important possessions were now in Bangkok, where Lu Ying and I had our apartment. We'd been married for nearly two years, and I moved all the time between Bangkok, Phnom Penh and Saigon. But since Phnom Penh had been his home, Mike had lost everything: his personal possessions, furniture and art collection. There'd be no hope of seeing any of those things again, with the Khmer Rouge in power.

He'd taken only one precaution against what had happened. Some months before, when he'd realized that the Lon Nol Government had little hope of surviving, he'd given me a small bag full of his personal papers, tapes and photographs, asking that Lu Ying and I keep them safe for him in the Bangkok apartment. So that's why those things have survived. Nothing else has.

Much worse than all this was the fact that he couldn't find out what had happened to Ly Keang. He didn't know whether she was still in the city, or had escaped across the border. And no phone call or message came from her to the Hotel Continental, as he kept hoping would happen.

The first thing we did when we realized our situation was to go off to Mr. Minh the tailor to get some new clothes made. He and his assistants finished them in forty-eight hours: I think it was his last order, poor Mr. Minh. He was quite old now, and very bent. The next day he closed the shop forever, and disappeared. So many people were fleeing like Mr. Minh, using any means they could. But Mike and I had decided to stay on in Saigon, and wait for the arrival of the North Vietnamese Army.

Most of our colleagues in the media thought we were mad to do this: they told us we'd be shot or jailed when the Communists arrived, and they believed we'd change our minds at the last minute. But we felt fairly confident that the North Vietnamese would treat us correctly. We remembered Captain Danh; and I said that the sort of people who had returned my Rolex watch to me when I was a prisoner would not fail to honor our neutrality as war photographers. Mike agreed.

But despite the fact that the NVA divisions were getting closer every day, all Mike was thinking of was Cambodia. He stayed in Saigon not to cover the Communist victory, but because here he was close to the Cambodian border. He and I remained at the Continental, and in those first few days his whole attention was concentrated on getting back into Phnom Penh. He tried to find somebody who would fly him there—but nobody would do it. And when he wasn't doing that, he was trying to get through to Ly Keang on the phone—at her uncle's house, or at her newspaper. But the telephone lines to Phnom Penh, which had always been bad, now seemed permanently out of order. Nor could he get through to Aubrey Hardwick, who'd been staying in Phnom Penh at the home of a friend of his: a French diplomat. The French embassy's number didn't answer either.

I now felt more sorry for Mike than I can say. He looked sick, and hardly ate: his mind was all the time on Ly Keang. He also worried about Lay Vora and Bopha and the children: they'd become like his own family. He'd lost his whole life in twenty-four hours—and he feared that he'd lost Ly Keang as well. He wouldn't believe it, but he feared it. He blamed himself for leaving her, and he was angry with himself—even though none of us had believed that Phnom Penh would fall in those few days.

I could only imagine his pain and frustration, not share it. Not to be able to act drove him crazy; and wherever he turned, he was blocked. Then, on April 17th, the Khmer Rouge finally marched into Phnom Penh, and sealed the country.

This was no ordinary regime: that was clear straightaway. The foreign journalists who had stayed were eventually allowed to leave—but after that, no one could get in or out. The border was closed, and all communications with the outside world were stopped. No telephones; no post; no foreign embassies; no flights operating except between Cambodia and China. We were as cut off from Cambodia now as though it had been a country on the moon.

By Monday the 28th, there were sixteen North Vietnamese divisions around Saigon, some of them only eight kilometers away.

Tan Son Nhut airport was being rocketed, and although many South Vietnamese pilots went on fighting, going up in gunships to hit the Communist positions, others now fought each other for the possession of planes. They made their escape in these, flying them out to Thailand.

There were thunderstorms that day, I remember: the noise mingling with the sound of shelling. Mike and I moved about the city, getting pictures and film. Restaurants and shops were still open, but thousands of people were streaming out to the airport in cars, lorries and on foot, still hoping that they could somehow get on planes.

The Army of South Vietnam continued to defend the city's perimeter. It had fought with great bravery in these last stages, but now it was falling into panic. The South had put all its hopes on the military aid promised by the Americans: now the news had come through that there would be no more aid. The last shipment of artillery had been sent, and there were no shells. The

Government and the ARVN troops knew now that there was nothing more to hope for.

The end came the next day: on Tuesday the 29th. That morning, the U.S. embassy began its evacuation. Americans in Saigon had been told to listen for a coded message on U.S. Armed Forces Radio as the signal that evacuation had begun; it would come every fifteen minutes, followed by Bing Crosby singing "White Christmas." When this was heard, all the remaining foreign media offices began packing up—in the Eden Building, the Caravelle Hotel and elsewhere. The Telenews staff had gone the week before, taking their equipment to Bangkok, abandoning the office, and leaving me the keys. London was happy for me to cover since I chose to do it, I was told, but Telenews took no responsibility for me.

Despite the rocketing of Tan Son Nhut, Marine helicopters were being sent there from the U.S. fleet off the coast to ferry out all remaining American citizens in Saigon. They were also to take Vietnamese who worked for American agencies. But fixed-wing aircraft could no longer fly because the bombardment had closed down the airport, and this meant that fewer Vietnamese could now be taken out than the Americans had planned. The people in the city knew this, and panic grew. The Americans had told Western correspondents that places would be found for them on the choppers; special buses were picking their people up from prearranged points around the city, and journalists were told to go to these points. Only a very small number of journalists and photographers decided to stay, as Mike and I were doing.

We had made our base in the deserted Telenews office in the Eden Building. The AP office was on the floor above, and at around 11 A.M., after we'd loaded and checked our cameras, we decided to look in there and say goodbye.

Nobody had much time to speak to us. The scene was frantic, like an out-of-control schoolroom. Phones were ringing and not being answered, an American voice was coming over a radio, and all over the room people were emptying desks and files and stuffing things into bags, moving very fast. Most of them were sweating a lot; some were laughing and joking; some looked pale and scared.

One of them glanced up at us from an airways bag he was packing: he was a staff writer with a blond mustache, whose name I've forgotten. You guys coming? he said. Better move your asses.

No, we said, we were staying.

And we gave him some film to take out and deliver for us. He did it, too, and Telenews were very happy with what I sent; it was shown in a great number of countries.

You're lunatics, he said. Crazy as Ed Carter. You're gonna die.

In the middle of the jerking and hurrying and shouting figures, Ed was sitting at his desk with his feet up, reading a newspaper. Ed was always very calm.

We went over to him, and he looked up over his glasses. I figured somebody should be around to welcome General Giap, he said. You guys gonna keep me company? I've got transport.

And he held up a bunch of keys.

The correspondents going out on the choppers had only been allowed to take one bag each; they had to leave everything else. One AP staff writer had been forced to leave a beautiful Ford Mustang, and he'd given the keys to Ed, with instructions that Ed was eventually to sell the car and send the money, if the Communists spared his life. So we went out to the man's house and picked up his Mustang, and drove in it around the city.

The crowds in the streets were huge, surging everywhere. Everyone carried bags or children. Many were running in a sort of hysteria: but I don't think they knew any longer where they were running to. I saw one little gray-haired man in a white canvas hat, a small suitcase in one hand, who was actually running in circles, in the middle of Nguyen Hue: I think he'd lost his wits. The White Mice had now disappeared, and we realized there was no law and order any more: no one was in charge of the city. There was supposed to be a curfew, but that meant nothing now. It was like a crazy carnival: but not a carnival of happiness.

The American buses for Tan Son Nhut were moving about the city to their special pickup points, collecting their passengers;

and the people in the streets were following these buses in tens of thousands, begging and screaming to be let on. They saw the buses as their last hope, and they were right. The drivers were fighting them off when they opened the doors, not always successfully. Most of the windows were protected with heavy-duty mesh, but some people got in through sliding windows at the back; others pushed their babies in. Cars stood abandoned, keys still hanging in the dashboards: if you wanted a car, you just had to steal one. In many side streets, we saw ARVN uniforms lying in the gutter; the soldiers were changing into civilian clothes, and melting into the crowd. Looting had begun: people were breaking into rich villas, and the streets were getting dangerous. Many now hated the Americans for deserting them, and as we went by, and they saw the white faces of Mike and Ed Carter, they shouted: Go home, Yankees. The Saigon Cowboys were out on their Honda motor scooters, looking for what they could steal. We also saw people who did nothing; who stood crying on the pavements like lost children.

Taking the Mustang, Mike and Ed and I went around to the American embassy that evening. Mike and I shot film of the Marine Corps Sikorsky and Sea Knight helicopters landing inside the compound and on the roof, taking out the embassy staff while Marines stood guard on top of the walls. The Jolly Green Giants and the smaller Sea Knights had been coming and going since late afternoon, and it was now around seven-thirty. They would keep on coming at intervals until dawn. We got hold of an American newspaper journalist by the gates who was going out on one of the choppers, and gave him our film to deliver. You'll have seen the pictures—including the shots Mike took that were published in his American newsweekly, and which now appear in books on the war.

Thousands of people were hammering at the closed gates and on the walls with their fists, demanding, pleading, weeping, many of them holding up documents. A lot of the time it was raining, and very dark: the city's power supply had cut out at seven o'clock. The whirring and beating of twin rotors filled the blackness, and the choppers hovered and tilted, the glaring white lights in their noses guiding them down. Young Vietnamese climbed the walls and made it to the top, but the big Marine guards kicked and fought them off. Other Marines lobbed tear gas canisters into the crowd. What are you doing? I thought. You came here long ago to help them against their enemies; how can you do this to them now? And I felt ashamed to be filming.

There were some ARVN soldiers there, full of anger against the Americans for deserting them, and shouting up at the Marines. *Du-ma,* they called—meaning "mummyfucker." Yet some of the people around the walls were actually in a cheerful mood, knowing that we who were staying behind faced a new situation together, and that there was nothing more to be done. There's a sort of excitement in such disaster: a comradeship which most of us don't admit. And these people had now faced the fact that what they most wanted they were never going to have: they would never be lifted out by one of those giant green choppers that were the only things that could save them. All they could do now was to watch the white lights that kept on coming down through the dark, like lights from another world.

I won't forget those scenes; but what I find hardest to forget are certain other rooftops in the city, which we passed later in the evening. The Americans had sent some helicopters to these buildings in midafternoon, to pick up Vietnamese who'd been promised evacuation. Now, although many were still left, the choppers did not reappear. Yet little groups of people stood on those rooftops in the dark, quiet and patient, their luggage beside them. The throbbing of the choppers was gone from the air, except in the direction of the embassy; the evacuation was over. But still these people could not believe that the Americans would not come back. I heard that they were still there at dawn, watching the sky. They were waiting for helicopters that were only in their minds, coming to rescue them from tomorrow.

When tomorrow came, Saigon was very quiet. All the noise had stopped: it was the strangest quiet I've ever known.

Mike and Ed Carter and I sat at breakfast in the restaurant

of the Continental: orange juice, croissants and coffee. There were only about half a dozen others there: some Italians, two French journalists from *Le Monde,* and a Japanese photographer. It was a hot morning, calm and pleasant. The power was working again, the big ceiling fans turned, and the Chinese waiters in their starched white jackets stood by the yellow pillars.

The whole city seemed silent, and the streets were half empty. Out on the square, some military trucks went by, and a few refugees still trudged through the streets with their possessions. But there were no ARVN troops; no black market operators; no Saigon Cowboys on Hondas; no White Mice. The blue haze of exhaust fumes was dissolving, and the air was almost clean. After the din and fear of the day before, waking to this silence had been like waking from a fever to find yourself well. Saigon was waiting for the victors to arrive.

Sure is peaceful, Ed said. I can handle plenty of this. The only thing is: who's in charge?

No one's in charge, Mike told him. I never thought I'd miss those little White Mice—but not having them around's a bit creepy.

We laughed, and Ed signaled for more coffee. One of the old Chinese waiters came shuffling forward, carrying the tall silver coffee pot. He had a dignified expression, but I detected a faint frown of worry. I wondered what would become of him after today. He'd probably been at the Continental for forty years: could he even understand what was happening?

We began to discuss where we should position ourselves, to be ready for the NVA's arrival. No one could know when that would be, or where they'd head for first when they came into the city.

Right here in the middle of town seems best to me, Ed said. We might as well make ourselves comfortable. I don't want any dealings with the South Vietnamese Army, either: they're pretty mad at Americans today. Yesterday on the sidewalk an ARVN sergeant spat at me, and told me we were running out on them. I told him I was staying, and then he shook my hand. They're feeling pretty emotional.

Can you blame them? Mike asked. His face grew set and bitter, and Ed looked at him.

I guess not, he said.

We were quiet for a moment; then Ed said: The NVA are going to want to hoist their flag somewhere significant, when they come into town. Maybe at the Palace. I guess Big Minh's sitting in his office out there, waiting to surrender. But my bet is they'll go just around the corner here, to City Hall.

You take City Hall, Mike told Ed. Jim and I will go to the Palace. And twenty dollars says we're right.

We shook hands on it, and Mike grinned. He still had a little of his old spirit; but he seldom smiled. His mind was always on Ly Keang.

So he and I went to the Presidential Palace, driving the Mustang again, which had survived the night in the Continental without being stolen.

It was now eleven-thirty, and the sun was growing hot. The streets were still very quiet, and out by the Palace it was quieter still. The big wrought-iron gates in front were locked as usual, and we drove down a side street to the service entrance, where journalists had always entered in the past. This gate was open, and there was no sign of the guards who used to be posted there. We walked into the grounds and around to the front of the long white building with its flight of marble steps going up to the entrance.

Here we found an even bigger quiet than the one in the city. The Palace stands in a wide parkland enclosed by iron railings, where spreading tamarinds and other trees stand in open, grassy spaces. These spaces were empty, all the way to the road and the railings a hundred meters or so away, and the quiet here was like sleep. Nothing but bird calls, and the whirring of cicadas. There seemed to be an unusual number of dragonflies in the air, hovering and shimmering, and I wondered what this signified. They must be a sign, I thought. But of what? I guess I'm superstitious; and I was now very keyed up.

The only people we found at the entrance of the Palace were some South Vietnamese troops: members of the palace guard.

They were sitting and lying on the grass near the marble steps in a way that was very unmilitary, their automatic rifles stacked beside them, many of them with their helmets off. It looked almost like a picnic.

They no longer consider themselves soldiers, I thought. It's over for them.

When we went up to them, we spoke to them in Vietnamese. I was concerned they might be hostile to us, like those Ed Carter had encountered, but they smiled back, and were quite friendly. Most of them were young, but there was a sergeant of middle age.

What are you doing? I asked.

Waiting to surrender, the sergeant said. Nothing more to do, now.

I guess that's right, Mike said, and offered him a cigarette.

We sat down in the grass, and talked with them. Many ARVN troops had thrown away their uniforms today, they told us; but they thought it better to go on guarding the Palace until they were told to do otherwise. They wanted to do their duty. Then they would surrender their weapons.

It was very still, and getting much hotter; soon we spoke only in snatches, lying there in the grass. The whirring of the insects began to sound to me like some mechanical alarm system, warning us of what was to come.

Then I saw the tank.

I could not believe what I was seeing, at first. I don't know what I'd expected, but it hadn't been this; I squinted at it through the shimmer of the heat for a number of seconds, before I called out to Mike. It was a green, Soviet-made tank, and it was moving down the road outside the railings. It flew a huge National Liberation Front flag on a pole—blue and red, with a yellow star—and the number on the side of it was 843. A North Vietnamese trooper was looking out from its turret; others, in their sun helmets and familiar green cotton uniforms, were riding on the front. I glimpsed people running behind it; one of them was a British correspondent, and I recognized some French correspondents and photographers. As we watched, flame shot from the barrel of its cannon and there was a report; then it turned towards the closed Palace gates, and Mike and I stood up. The soldiers were standing up too, and raising their hands.

The tank smashed into the gates, and one of them came half off its hinges. Mike ran towards it across the lawn, his Leica at the ready. I had my CP16 Commag, a sound-on-film camera: I hoisted it onto my shoulder and started after him.

The tank stopped, like a big slow animal, and seemed to consider; then it reversed and charged the gates again, and I saw Mike raise his camera. This time the tank smashed straight through the gates and rolled on, lumbering across the lawn. I was still running, the camera slowing me down. I was checking my light meter as I went, my face pouring with sweat, my heart pounding. I knew only one thing: this was film I must get no matter what happened to me.

Mike was still taking pictures when the tank stopped again. Some of the soldiers were pointing at us, and beginning to climb down, and I became aware that Mike and I were alone in this space of grass; none of the palace guard had followed us. But I was shooting film now; everything else was vague: the drilling of the cicadas inside my head, the dragonflies dancing around me. Looking at the soldiers through the lens, I was seeing their faces clearly, and they suddenly seemed very familiar to me. They were very young, mostly just boys, and they reminded me of Captain Danh's unit; I almost thought I recognized Doc and Weary and Prince among them, but of course I didn't. And in that instant, I saw a soldier in a sun helmet running towards us and shouting, his AK-47 cocked. He was telling us to put our hands up.

He reached Mike first, and Mike raised his hands, his camera held in the right. I did the same: it took all my strength to suspend that heavy Commag. The soldier was standing close to Mike, the AK leveled, shouting in Vietnamese.

American! he shouted. You are American!

He had a broad brown country face, and his eyes had a fierce, hard shine: the killing shine.

Mike answered in Vietnamese, his hands still high. No, he said. Australian. Welcome to Saigon.

The soldier frowned and looked puzzled; then I saw the shine go out of his eyes. He lowered his gun, and I knew we were going to live.

4.

Now Langford begins to disappear.

There's only one more cassette in his audio diary collection. It has four dated entries on it—all of them recorded in Saigon in that April. These would seem to be the last diary passages he recorded.

After the city's fall, he went to Bangkok with Jim Feng, and stayed for a time with Jim and Lu Ying in their apartment there, before renting a place of his own. There are no tape-recorded entries for the year that followed in Bangkok, before his disappearance—or if he did make any tapes, he didn't put them among the ones he left with Jim. But my guess is that these Saigon entries are truly the last, and that with his exile from Phnom Penh and the disappearance of Ly Keang, he no longer had the heart to keep a diary.

The Saigon entries are verbal jottings, like messages scribbled hastily on a pad. They're not easy passages to listen to.

AUDIO DIARY: LANGFORD

TAPE 72, APRIL 10TH, 1975

—At the Continental: 10 A.M. Got in half an hour ago, with Jim and Harvey. All the signs are that Saigon will go soon, and I have to get to Claudine.

—Tried to explain this to Ly Keang last night, but for a while she wouldn't see it. We quarreled. I've never seen her angry like that before.

—She stood in front of me in the apartment with clenched fists. Why must you go to Vietnam? she said. Why, when everything here is worse every day? *This* is where you should be, she said, not Saigon.

—It'll hold here a while longer, I said. But Vietnam's going fast. The end could come any day now, and I might never get back there. I'll only be gone forty-eight hours. I spent a lot of my life covering that war, I said. I want to get some pictures at the end. My magazine expects it.

—She was staring at me, knowing this wasn't all there was; so I told her.

—I also have to see Claudine Phan, I said. I have to get her out with the Americans: she and her sons. I can do it; I've got the contacts. She'll be shot or imprisoned if she stays: nothing's more certain.

—That woman! she said. I knew it was that bloody French Vietnamese. Well, go to your Vietnamese, she said. Go to Vietnam, that enemy country. You won't find me here when you come back.

—And she ran out of the apartment, and down the stairs.

—I followed after a few moments, but she'd already disappeared. I looked through the Old Market, but I couldn't find her there. Felt as if I'd swallowed a load of lead.

—Went back to the apartment and sat on the balcony as dark fell. Every minute that she didn't reappear was a minute I couldn't bear. An hour went by and she didn't come. I sat drinking cognac.

—At eight o'clock, I stood up, deciding to search for her: at her uncle's house, then all through the city, if I had to. I'd cancel going to Saigon.

—How has this happened to me? Without her, there's no life. I want her jokes, I want her anger, I want the way we talk together. I want everything that she is.

—I walked out the door, and met her coming up the stairs. She was carrying a small brown paper package, and looked at me with an expression of alarm. This alarmed look was half comical, half apologetic: more exciting than a smile or a look of tenderness would have been. She threw her arms around my neck, and I backed inside the door, dragging her. We said nothing until we'd made love.

—Then she said that she'd behaved badly. I'm jealous, she said. Also, I'm prejudiced against Vietnamese. We all are, she said: all Cambodians. They are always our enemies, and never to be trusted. This isn't rational, I know, but I feel betrayed when you go there now. Now that we are almost lost, I want you only to care about Cambodia and me. I know you don't love that old aunty; I know that. You only want to save her; you want to save everyone. So go and do it, she said. But please come back quickly.

—Only two days, I said. And I told her I'd grab a flight back if there was any change. If there's any sign of trouble, I said, get in touch with Aubrey Hardwick. He's still in town; he'll help you.

—And I gave her the address of the Frenchman whose villa Aubrey was staying in.

—When I come back, I said, you and I are going across into Thailand. If commercial flights stop, we'll get out with the Americans.

—Yes, she said, and we'll take Sary, won't we? We'll get a villa on the border, not far from Battambang, and marry and make a home. We'll help the Khmer Serei, she said, and live there until Cambodia's free again.

—This was a story we told each other: half a game, half something we believed.

—The brown paper package was lying beside us on the bed, and she handed it to me. I brought you a present, she said.

—As I unwrapped it, the package made a crying noise. It turned out to be a small, furry toy cat with orange stripes, made in Japan. It mewed when you tipped it up. We both started laughing. She buys a lot of silly presents for me like that: the apartment's full of them.

—Take it to Saigon, she said. A mascot. It will protect you; I've told it to. I have Sary to look after me here.

APRIL 12TH

—Phnom Penh fallen: the Americans gone. No commercial or military flights. Tried to charter a plane. None available.

—Can't raise Ly Keang's number at home; nor the one at her newspaper.

—Phoned Aubrey at his friend's villa: no answer. The phone system between here and Phnom Penh was always bad: easier to phone New York from the Hotel Royal than to phone Saigon. Now it seems to have broken down completely. The switch at the Royal doesn't answer; no proper ring at my apartment or Vora's; none at Ly Keang's uncle's house.

—Christ. It's like a wall.

APRIL 13TH

—Tried all day to charter a flight to Phnom Penh. Impossible.

—One AP man is still there: a Cambodian, still sending wires. He tells AP on the telex that nothing's happening in the city: the Khmer Rouge still haven't arrived.

—Ed Carter asked him to contact Ly Keang for me. But he sent a message back that he can't find her.

APRIL 14TH

—Still can't charter a plane. Still can't make telephone contact with Ly Keang.

—She must surely have gone to Aubrey, as I asked her to. I've been trying to find out where Aubrey is, without success; today I rang the PR business in Bangkok. Donald Mills answered. He said that Aubrey went to Europe immediately on coming out of Phnom Penh: he rode a chopper out with the U.S. embassy staff. But Mills told me that Aubrey said that he didn't see Ly Keang at all, in the period after I left: not even on the day the U.S. embassy pulled out.

—I could try to go over the border, but I know my chances of reaching Phnom Penh would be nil.

APRIL 22ND

—Midnight. Sitting in my room at the Continental. Can't sleep. Everything ending here too: it can't be more than a week before the South surrenders. When Indochina's gone, and the war's finally over, what's going to happen to my life? And if I can't find Ly Keang?

—Just went to look for cigarettes in my overnight bag. Found the toy cat that she gave me. When I picked it up, the sound it made was like a baby crying. Why is a silly thing like that so hard to bear?

—Little things; always the little things. Like when the Count died: the odds and ends in his box. When Ken died: his Digger hat, hanging on the verandah. And when Mum died, the old chocolate tin I found in her wardrobe: inside, baby photos of all of us, and an invitation to a ball in Hobart, before she was married. Miss I. Olsen. Nothing else: she left nothing else. Why did she keep that invitation? Was that her happiest night? And why were those little things all that was left of her? The invitation's among my photographs and papers and diary tapes: a good thing I got Jim and Lu Ying to store them for me. The Khmer Rouge won't get those. But what about Sary? She'll be killed and eaten if she strays.

—Keang, where are you? I should never have come to Saigon.

SIX
THE BORDER

1.

The office of Pacific Consultants is in Ratchadamri Road, a block away from the square where the Newsroom stands. Hardwick and Mills no doubt chose this location because of its proximity to the foreign media offices.

My taxi gets here just after eight in the evening: the time of the appointment I've made with Donald Mills on the phone. I left my hotel early, to allow for the city's traffic jams. Darkness has set in, and a downpour's in progress; neons and headlights are reflected in the torrents that rush across the road. I hurry from the curb to the shelter of a glass-and-concrete cube called the Raja Damri Building: the name is fixed on the awning in heavy metal letters. But the office proves difficult to find.

It isn't included in the golden list of firms lettered in English and Thai on the glass doors, and I run down a lane at the side, the rain soaking my shirt, to find myself in a square that smells of drains, where boys running food stalls watch me from the shelter of colored umbrellas. Finally I discover *Pacific Consultants, Third Floor,* lettered on a small glass door. Another sign in English says: *Ancient Massage Parlor, Second Floor.*

I reach the third floor in an empty lift that rocks and groans. When I get out, the automatic door booms shut in a deserted foyer with grimy white walls. Opposite me, double glass doors frame what looks like a reception area: an empty, corridor-like room with leather armchairs and potted palms, softly lit. As I prepare to knock, a man in a canary yellow shirt and white trousers appears there.

Halting to peer at me through the glass, he sways a little, and I remember Harvey's remark about Mills's drinking. He opens one of the doors, and stares at me with a look of bemused suspicion. His small, somewhat slanting blue eyes are empty and glazed, like ceramic chips.

"Ray Barton? Right. You're impressively punctual," he says.

His voice is quick and abrupt, hinting at a stammer that isn't there, and the slurring caused by drink is just perceptible. He raises a hand to gesture me inside; once I'm through, he swings the glass door shut with some force. The crash makes me jump, and I turn to stare at him. He's grinning at the door, rocking on his feet. "Always forget that it's not a *swinging* door," he says. Then he puts out his hand, gripping mine with athletic vigor.

A counter here divides the reception area from a large main office that's almost in darkness; I can make out a tall set of shelves containing files. Beyond, there may be other rooms, or there may be nothing; it's not possible to see. A big lamp with a green, drum-shaped shade stands on the counter, spreading muted light. Mills waves me to one of the leather armchairs, and throws himself down in another. He and I face each other across a small round coffee table, on which stands a bottle of Johnnie Walker Black Label and two whiskey glasses. Without asking me whether I want a drink, Mills leans forward and fills both glasses halfway. There's no water. My heart sinks; I wonder whether any coherent discussion with him is going to be possible.

I imagine he's changed a good deal—at least in appearance —from the youthful diplomat Mike met in Singapore. He has high-combed, reddish hair that's still thick, but streaked with gray. The eyebrows are lighter than the hair: sandy, and getting bushy with middle age. His square face and pugnacious jaw are an undamaged boxer's, and his complexion is ruddy in a way that suggests sunburn and outdoor living; but the broken capillaries in his nose give him away. He raises his whiskey to me, and drinks off half of it at a gulp. Then he sits back and looks at me in silence, one hand spread on the arm of the chair, the other holding his glass. The yellow of his shirt is jarringly vivid. Waiting for him to speak, I hope that he's not going to prove to be one of those drunks who'll make me run a gauntlet of rudeness. At first, it seems that he may.

"You won't be able to see Aubrey Hardwick," he says. "Did you realize that?"

"That's a pity. I thought he might be in Bangkok at some stage soon," I say.

He shakes his head. "No. Aubrey and I have dissolved our partnership," he says. "No Aubrey." He waves his hand at the half-dark office over the counter, as though to prove that Hardwick isn't hiding there. "No more consultancy, either. I'm winding it up."

I adopt my dry legal tone. "I'm sorry to hear that. But perhaps you can help me, even if Mr. Hardwick can't."

"Help you find Mike Langford? Nobody can do that," he says. "I'll talk to you about him, though."

He throws down the rest of his drink; then he stares at me in silence. His stare is insistent, and in some way odd, and I sense that this isn't simply caused by the tipsiness. He has something specific to tell me: something that's important to him. I have an instinct for such things, developed over the years in dealing with clients.

"What I'm hoping," I say, "is that you can give me an informed opinion about why Langford went into Cambodia. I understand that Mike once did some work for you and Aubrey Hardwick. I thought it might have had something to do with that."

His eyes now become watchful: almost sober. I notice that his mouth is at odds with his boxer's face: it's that of an obsessive; thin and downturned. He doesn't reply to my implied question;

instead, he says: "Harvey Drummond tells me you've got a lot of Mike's papers and diaries."

"Yes," I say. "He left them to me in his will. I'm his executor, as I told you."

He nods and picks up the bottle, this time filling his glass to the brim. Mine's still a quarter full, but he tops it up to the brim as well, ignoring my protesting hand. Then, having taken a sip, he looks across at me, thin lips drawn in over his teeth, mouth a little open, head cocked.

"There's no point in trying to fool a lawyer," he says. "Even a lawyer from Tasmania." He smiles. "No offense, Ray. Yes, Mike used to pass on a few impressions to us. I'd guess you'll have seen some of his reports among those papers of his. Always very organized, Mike was. Copies of everything."

He's beginning to irritate me, and I decided to be blunt. "So he did do some work for ASIS," I say.

There's usually a lag of some seconds while Mills stares and digests what's said to him; it's the same this time.

"You'd better get something clear," he says. He looks past me, at the glass doors. "I'm out of the service now. An ex-spook. Right? There is such a thing, Ray, and you're looking at one. And I'm no longer associated with Hardwick in any way. If you want to pursue Aubrey about this, and you end by giving him trouble, that's fine by me. I don't give a stuff. Clear?" He looks at me belligerently, daring me to fail to understand, in the way that difficult drinkers do. "All I've been trying to do these last two years is to run a good PR business," he says. "But that wasn't enough for Aubrey. You understand what I'm saying, Ray?"

"I think so."

"No you don't. But you will, because I've decided to tell you. Why not you? Mike's boyhood mate: an honest man from home, and a lawyer. You want to lift the lid off this? Fine. I'll set you on your way, and you can take it from there. But if you quote me as a source, I'll deny it." He gestures towards the darkened office. "No witnesses, right? Are you reading me?"

I nod, and he stares at me in silence, breathing audibly through his nose.

"The bloody war's over," he says at last, and his voice has grown more slurred. "We lost, but Aubrey won't give up. He won't retire; he can't let go. That's why I ended the partnership. He broke promises to me regarding this firm. Promises that were very important. One of them being that it would never be used as a cover."

He's holding his glass with both hands, his small, oblique eyes glinting with a resentment that's incurable and profound; and I begin to see that his drunkenness is such that it's doubtful that he remembers from moment to moment who it is he's talking to. Perhaps it doesn't matter.

"Okay. In the old days, Mike was of help to us," he says. "I was his case officer for a while, when he came to Saigon in the sixties: but mostly he dealt with Aubrey. He was never heavily involved; never took pay. He just gave us background from time to time: things he came across in the course of his job. He was an independent source, at a time when we were sick of being dependent on the Yanks for information. We wanted to give Canberra our own picture, and he helped us do that. Langford not only knew the latest military situation in the various regions, he also knew a lot of people. An ARVN general might have a Viet Cong brother; a Cambodian politician might have a mistress working for the other side. Mike picked up things like that. And in the early years of the war in Cambodia, he gave us a more detailed picture than anyone else could have done. What sort of backup the North Vietnamese had in the villages; where their petroleum dumps were; where their rafts were bringing munitions downriver. Stuff you only get on the ground, and that only a roving cameraman could have picked up so easily. Very sexy information. Even Washington was impressed. Their aerial photography didn't give them that kind of thing. And to be able to feed the Americans was a very big deal for us." He smiles with faint fondness, like a man remembering lost love.

"Aubrey and I once tried to get Jim Feng to help us in the same way," he says. "But Jim would never do it. He was friendly; but he never gave us anything. Some correspondents are like that. They worry about their integrity."

"And what about Mike?" I ask. "What did Mike worry about?"

"Mike wasn't political, if that's what you mean," Mills says. "And as I've said, he wasn't in it for the money."

"What, then?"

"I think you'd have to say idealism." His thin mouth turns down further, as though tasting something sour. "I suppose you'd say he was patriotic, when he was young. That was always a help, in our game. Yes, Mike was an idealist. And the nature of the idealist is that he never learns—right?" He swallows most of his whiskey; then looks across at me again. "Are you married, Ray?"

Divorced, I say.

"Thought you'd be the type who'd stay married. Steady. Well, join the club. My marriage went years ago: it didn't go with the game. Seldom does. The woman doesn't know who she's married to." He picks up the bottle again, looking accusingly at my near-full glass. "Jesus, Ray, you're not much of a drinking man. Down the hatch. We've got a lot more talking to do."

"It must be an odd sort of life—intelligence-gathering," I say. "Difficult to maintain normal relationships."

I've expected him to dismiss this ploy; but the invitation works better than I could have hoped for. The expression Mills wears now is like that of a man whose sexual tastes are eccentric, and who sees that you may understand. He sits back in the armchair, and seems to search for words.

"You lose your personality, in the end," he says. "For an operative, the day comes when he's not quite sure who he is. And everyone you know becomes recruitable. You understand? The Law must be nice and simple, compared with that."

I'm surprised that he's talking to me like this; yet when I analyze it, I realize that so far he's told me nothing of any importance. But I still sense that he will. He gives the impression of being inwardly destabilized; of some huge rift having opened in his life. I only have to wait, and he'll display it.

I resign myself to a headache in the morning.

■   ■

He's very drunk indeed now. Hands in pockets, legs extended, he stares in front of him, eyes wide and fixed, looking down an endless tunnel. I'm certain that for minutes at a time he forgets that I'm here. Behind him there's a window protected by a wire grille: it frames night sky, the swaying tops of trees in the still-thundering rain, and a line of blue lamps on a distant freeway. A red neon spells out *Mitsubishi,* and lightning flashes over it. The hot, elemental excess out there is unreal, watched from this air-conditioned chamber: an image on a cinema screen.

"No life after Intelligence," Mills says suddenly. His voice is dragging but deliberate; he clearly has a remarkable capacity for liquor. "And no life outside it," he says. "That's what they made you believe when they recruited you, those old British Empire types like Aubrey. He would have made Mike feel like that. When I was young, training with MI6 in London, I felt I'd gone into a world where anything was possible; above and beyond anything the average poor bastard could imagine. A life where dullness didn't happen: a big ride through the air." He shakes his head with drunken deliberateness. "Well, it was: a big ride," he says. "And now here I am: on the ground."

His tone attempts irony, but emerges instead with a fleeting note of regret: even of sentimentality. The emotionally cold live in a sort of vacuum, I imagine, noses pressed to the window of life; sentimentality must be the closest they get to the warmth that's denied them.

"You probably imagine espionage work to be cold-blooded," he says. "Bullshit: it's the reverse. There's a lot of feeling. Love, even. A case officer identifies with his agents *deeply.* They're like his creations, Ray. That's how it was between Mike and Uncle Aubrey. He thought Mike was his, in the early days: more his than a son."

He picks up his glass again; then points a finger at me.

"Want you to grasp this," he says. "Are you listening? The hardest thing of all for an old intelligence operative is to quit. And Aubrey Hardwick really was one of the great operatives of his generation. So you can perhaps understand. Losing contact with the goodies of the Western intelligence system—cut off from the distribution list—that's an intelligence officer's greatest nightmare. The distribution list is Uncle Aubrey's life-blood. It means more to him than his Thai boyfriends, or his collection of Chinese scrolls, or the bloody knighthood he's chasing. That's why he did what he did."

I wait. I don't need to prompt him.

"I'm talking about the girl—Ly Keang," he says. "She's why Mike went back in: you must have worked that out. Ly Keang was Aubrey's stay-behind."

The term's unfamiliar to me, but still I say nothing. I'm afraid to remind him I'm here.

"Everyone put stay-behinds in place, before Phnom Penh fell," he says. "Locals who'd report on the new regime. The CIA had quite a few of them. All of them were lost, of course—every bloody one. And when Ly Keang went missing, the old bastard used her as a bait."

Suddenly I have the sensation that the air-conditioning's become too cold. "I'm not with you," I say.

"No," he says. "You're not with me, Ray. You're a lawyer from Launceston." His tone is drunken and brutal. "But you will be." Once again, he waves a hand at the darkened office behind the counter. "No witnesses, right?"

He's made me aware of how silent and empty the place is. Despite the rain on the glass and the distant hum of traffic, the sound of his swallowing as he finishes his whiskey is quite distinct. I've finished my own drink now, and he leans and pours for me as well as for himself. The bottle's almost done.

"Langford introduced her to Aubrey," he says. "Another idealist, that girl: another patriot. And while Mike was in Saigon in that early part of April, Aubrey persuaded her to stay, if Phnom Penh fell. He told her to keep her newspaper job when the Khmer Rouge took over, and then to hang on for a month or so—to send him reports on the new regime." He breaks off; drinks; wipes his mouth. Then he laughs under his breath, his eyes empty. "Report on the Khmer Rouge: can you imagine? He had her all set up as an agent. The radio he gave her was state-of-the-art: a favor from his mates in the CIA. Looked like an ordinary set: undetectable. Transmissions went out on a special band. They reached us in Aranyaprathet, up on the border."

He closes his eyes for a moment, and sits quite still. When he opens them, the whites are bloodshot, and his lids droop. "Under any other regime, she could have done it," he says. "It's done all the time. And Aubrey told her she'd be brought across the border. He had agents there who'd look after it: Cambodian sleepers." He expels breath. "And this was a man who claimed to be an expert on the Khmer Rouge. Well, the CIA made the same mistake."

He's not looking at me; he's staring down his tunnel again, leaning forward with his elbows on his knees, clasping his glass. Then he imitates a plummy voice. " 'People we can *deal* with,' " he says. " 'Left Bank Marxists.' Jesus. There are still Foreign Affairs dickheads who believe that stuff. Well, we don't know much about what's happening in there now, but we do know they've driven the whole population into the countryside. We do know that the cities are stone bloody empty. Back to basics: no Western technology, no money, no cities. Pure. A true Communist society, all in camps, all obeying orders, where you'd have to get permission to sleep with your wife. So there was nowhere for a stay-behind to hide. You see? *Nowhere*. It was all settled in a few days. If you were middle-class, if you were educated, if you even wore spectacles, you were dead. So how was a young woman like that going to function? How was she going to disguise herself? Where was she going to hide? Can you picture it?"

He looks at me for a moment, then closes his eyes again. When he opens them, he says: "Aubrey was full of regrets, of course." He imitates the plummy voice again. " 'A lovely girl. Intelligent; brave. Ly Keang was like a niece to me. A niece lost to the sharks.' "

I decide to prompt him. "You said she was a bait."

He looks at me; then looks away again. He has no expression. "Aubrey had a strong link with one of the Khmer Rouge leaders," he says. His voice is thick, but his delivery remains lucid. "One of his chums from the old days in Phnom Penh. This guy wanted to defect; to come over the border. Do you know what that would mean? If Aubrey could get this man out and debrief him, we'd have our first real insight into the regime and its leadership. London and Washington and Canberra would kneel and adore Aubrey, and his MI6 and CIA mates would revere him forever. And he'd *never* retire. He'd be in his glory. He'd get everything he's always plotted for and dreamed about. And guess what that is?" He blinks at me, and points a finger at my chest again. *"To write the definitive history of the service."*

I laugh involuntarily, but he doesn't smile. "Try and understand," he says. "That would mean an office and a desk and a travel budget in his old age: perks forever. And more: much more. The most secret files open to him: the files *no one* sees. Now do you get it? Aubrey the old master; Aubrey the historian, presenting top case studies to young recruits. The ultimate ex-operative. A senior intelligence officer's paradise."

He sets his glass down on the table, slowly and with great care. "So that's why he sent Langford over," he says.

I stare, probably stupidly. He looks up at me, seeming to read my question.

"Aubrey didn't have an ASIS agent who was capable, under the circumstances," he says. "Suicidal, to go over that border. So he wanted Langford to use his influence with the Free Khmer, and take two or three of them as guides. You probably know about Mike's buddy, Colonel Chandara. The colonel would do anything for Langford, and he made men available. The plan was to go about ten kilometers inside the country, not far from the refugee camp run by the Free Khmer. It was all set up. The Khmer Rouge cadre would be waiting at a prearranged meeting place outside a particular village. He wasn't prepared to try for the border on his own; he couldn't be sure the locals wouldn't betray him, and he was no good in rough country. An intellectual, right? The Free Khmer knew their way about the area, and Aubrey gave Mike a map and a compass. It should have been all right; but they never came back."

"But why would Mike do it? Was he really that involved with you people?"

Mills shakes his head. "He didn't give a stuff about ASIS any more," he says. "He hadn't given Aubrey or me anything for years."

"Then why?"

Now he examines my face wonderingly, as though seeing me for the first time. "Oh mate, you really have led a sheltered life," he says. "He went because he was told Ly Keang would be there too. Aubrey told him that she'd come through on the radio again. He said she was up there near the border."

I'm still staring at him, and he seems now to focus on my face, and actually to register its expression. He raises his eyebrows at whatever it is he sees, shrugs, and sighs. "I only found out about this after Mike had gone in," he says. "Want you to have that clear, Ray."

I've drunk too much of his whiskey; my head's begun to swim. "Isn't it possible it was true? Maybe she survived after all," I say.

He sinks back in his armchair, lying almost prone, legs extended, hands in his pockets. He's stopped drinking, and when he speaks, his voice has dropped so low I have to strain to hear it.

"No," he says. "No. I was up there, Ray, at Aranyaprathet with Aubrey, waiting for her to come through on the radio in those first few days after the Yanks pulled their embassy out: before the Khmer Rouge came into Phnom Penh. She only contacted us twice. The first time was when they were still waiting for the Khmer Rouge, and there wasn't much to report. She asked Aubrey to get a message to Mike in Saigon, and Aubrey said he would. But he didn't: I only found that out later. He didn't want Mike to know he'd recruited her. He got me to lie about it too. The second time she made contact—"

He stops, and for a moment he doesn't go on.

"The second time was when the Khmer Rouge had come into town," he says. "Her voice had changed; she was frightened." He draws a hand across his mouth, not looking at me. "What she said was: 'We're all being ordered out—out of Phnom Penh. Even the sick have to leave the hospitals. It's not like you said it would be. The soldiers are very frightening. They're going to every house in this street. They'll be here at my uncle's in a few minutes. What should I do?' "

He pauses.

"Guess what Uncle Aubrey said? 'Trust your judgment, my dear. Get through to us again when you can.' " Suddenly, and with startling crudity, Mills spits sideways on the floor. "I won't forget what she said then. Wish I bloody could. 'You're a fool, Mr. Hardwick. You understood nothing. They're here. They're here.' Then there was some kind of banging noise, and she went off the air. She never came back on again."

The rain still lashes the window. We stare at it: our phantom cinema. Then Mills says: "When a certain kind of man's losing the life he wants, there's nothing he won't do to save it. That's Uncle Aubrey."

I find I'm not able to speak. I'm looking at the far-off highway through the window, its blue lights strung across a country of which I know nothing.

_____

2.

The Telenews car is a new BMW: roomy, air-conditioned and almost soundless: one of Jim's perks as bureau chief here. It rolls free of the suburbs of Bangkok in the predawn dark. Out through the windscreen, an occasional house light glimmers.

It's still only five o'clock, and Jim and I are silent, entangled in the last threads of sleep, sitting in the back. Daeng, the Thai driver, is a stocky man of middle age; he lights his first cigarette now, hissing as he draws in smoke, his face reflecting the soft glow from the dashboard. He puts the pack down beside the hand brake, jerks his head at it, and turns half towards us, speaking in a voice that's hushed in deference to the hour. "Always I have kept a pack there for Mike, when he came up to the border. That way, I would not run short." He chuckles, and Jim joins in.

"He never stopped believing he would give up smoking," Jim says. "And never stopped cadging them."

"But he cadged nothing else," Daeng says.

"No. He gave things; he didn't take. That's the way he was," Jim says, and I sense that they have said these things many times before: a litany, recited now for my benefit.

They fall silent for a time, and the car hums on. Then Daeng turns to glance at me. "You think he is still alive, Mr. Barton?"

"I hope so," I say.

"Jim hopes too, and so do I," Daeng says. "But I am very afraid for him. Where can he be? Very brave, what he did, but not sensible. Inside Cambodia, you know, there is nowhere to hide. The Khmer Rouge occupy every village. Everywhere you go in the country, they are there: this is what I am told."

"Mike's alive," Jim says.

His tone is quiet, but as always it discourages speculation. After another silence he turns to me. His face has a stony look, in the dimness: one that's only appeared since yesterday. "But I've been thinking I should do something about Hardwick," he says. "Maybe put a contract on him, when he comes up to Bangkok again. It's pretty cheap to do, here."

I look at him to see if he's serious. "No. Never mind," he says. "What would be the use? Mike will be found, I know it. And maybe Ly Keang too."

We're driving northeast, and now streaks of pink have begun to appear in the sky up ahead.

"Getting light," Daeng says.

The sun rises ahead of us down the shining asphalt highway, and the calm Thai countryside is springing into being around the car. Electric pylons march across a wide green plain, receding to blue mountains in the east. Bean trees and casuarinas grow among fields of tapioca; sleeping houses pass, their Siamese eaves curved upwards; a Buddhist pagoda rises on top of a hill of white rock. Mike must have seen these images every week, riding towards his window on Cambodia. And suddenly, as though picking up a faint radio transmission, I feel his longing.

Yesterday in the Newsroom, Harvey Drummond dwelt on that longing with some eloquence, leaning forward as if I were in a witness box, one finger pointing, wanting to make me see.

I wonder if you can imagine his desperation, he said. I

watched him bottling it up in the Foxhole for nearly a year. He wouldn't stop searching for her. Every week of this past year, without fail, he'd ride up to those secret Cambodian camps. Jim would give him the use of the Telenews car, and to justify it, Mike went back to film work, acting as a stringer for Telenews, with Daeng working as his soundman. He shot film of Khmer Rouge attacks on Thai villages that were sheltering the refugees; he also did interviews with Chandara and other Free Khmer leaders. But all the time he was looking for Ly Keang. It was like some religious commitment: not to be questioned. If anyone did question it, and suggested that Langford should give up and resign himself, he got angry. One dickhead correspondent in the Foxhole kept insisting that she must be lost, and Mike punched him up—and that wasn't like Mike.

Picture it, Harvey said. For a year, he checked every group of Cambodians that escaped over the border—always hoping to find Ly Keang among them. She'd been everything to him: he'd found her rather late in life, and now she was snatched away: locked in that closed country of hers, where these bloody horrors were going on. You see? Do you see, Ray?

The country's changed. We've had breakfast in a roadside café, and have passed through Aranyaprathet, the principal town of the region. Now we're getting near to the border of Cambodia.

The road's no longer asphalt, and has turned a bright ochre red. We're coming close to Camp 008, Daeng says, and the BMW rolls through a flat red wasteland that's waterless and parched and burning, resembling inland Australia. Even the smudges of vegetation here are the juiceless gray-green of desolation.

We've been stopped at a succession of military posts. Coming to this area of the Cambodian refugee camps has needed Thai Government permission, and soldiers have checked our documents at every post. At the last of these, we waited two hours for the invisible commander of the region to sanction our proceeding any further, sitting on wooden benches beside a concrete blockhouse. The heat had a burning intensity beyond anything I'd experienced, making me grow faint and dizzy; I longed for the air-conditioning of the car.

Camp 008, the clandestine headquarters of the Free Khmer guerrillas, turns out to be a small primitive settlement of bamboo huts with palm-thatched roofs, crouching in the dry red waste. Palm and banana trees stand stricken in the windless air. Beyond, in the east, lie the hills and mountains of Cambodia: rusty, pale green, then mauve, their peaceful screen hiding the atrocious. Jim and I leave Daeng sitting in the car, and walk down brown-graveled alleyways that attempt to be streets.

There's a reek of open drains; half-naked Khmer children stare and run away from us; dark faces watch us go by, from the secret, dark interiors of earth-floored huts. It's uncannily quiet here, and the air is heavy with boredom. A light, hot breeze comes up, and lost, black-clad Cambodians drift slowly about the make-believe byways.

"There's nothing for them to do," Jim says. "For a year, they've sat here, waiting. Some hope to go to America or Australia. Others wait for the Free Khmer to give them their country back. I think they'll wait a long time." He shakes his head, limping jerkily on the gravel.

At the center of the camp is a makeshift office building: a big, stifling bamboo shed with an earth floor and no fans, since there's no electric power in the camp. Half a dozen Cambodian clerks sit poring over papers at old wooden desks; one of them gets up and comes across to the bamboo counter. Jim addresses him in French, asking to see Colonel Chandara.

The clerk looks uneasy. He speaks in French too rapid for me to follow, and Jim turns to me.

"He says Chandara isn't here—but I believe he's lying. Chandara doesn't see people easily, since he took command of the Free Khmer. He always saw Mike, though. And I believe he'll see me, if he knows I'm here." He speaks to the clerk again, repeating his name loudly, his face stern and affronted, and I wonder if this expression has developed since he lost his leg.

The clerk hesitates; then he says: *"Attendez,"* and disappears. A short time later he comes back, smiling as though he's achieved something remarkable, and speaks in English. "Colonel Chandara will see you. Please." He gestures towards the door, and then leads the way.

We sit down on crude wooden benches at a table with a red-checked cloth: Jim and I on one side, Colonel Chandara on the other. It resembles a conference table; but I suspect it's also used for dining by the colonel and his troops. There's a bowl of yellow roses on it, a mug containing pencils, a pad, and some ash trays: nothing else. The roses have come from a garden plot outside, visible through the open door behind us: a tract of biscuit-dry soil behind a picket fence, baking in the immense heat. A young Cambodian soldier in green fatigues stands at attention beside an inner door of the room, trying not to stare at us.

"I'm so sorry, Jim," Chandara says. "They didn't understand who you were. It's always good to see you."

He smiles and shakes our hands, leaning across the table. He too wears green military fatigues, without insignia. He's much as he appears in the photograph with Mike: thin and fit, with the shock of thick straight hair and black mustache. But the photograph hasn't conveyed his presence, or the intensity of his eyes, whose deep brown is almost black.

Jim offers him a packet of Winstons, and Chandara takes one. "We don't see many of these up here," he says, and leans to Jim's Zippo lighter. Sitting back again, he inhales with open pleasure. "We don't see many journalists either. I no longer trust them, Jim: my people are told to keep the wrong sort away. You will know what I mean." He looks at me. "But you and Jim are both welcome, Ray. Jim says that you knew Mike as a boy. That's enough for me."

I thank him, and look about me. The room is long and narrow, and is set up as the office of a military commander, with large maps of the region pinned to the walls. But the house plainly doubles as a dwelling for Colonel Chandara, and perhaps for some of his officers as well. On another wall, there are personal touches: a color photograph of Chandara with his wife and three children;

a Cambodian landscape in oils; pictures of Buddhist monks. In a corner, there's a small shrine, with a statue of the Buddha and a cluster of unlit candles. This is the biggest structure in the camp, but it's still merely a hut, with an earth floor like the others, and no fans. Like the office we've just left, it's at oven heat, and we mop the sweat from our faces every few minutes. Even Chandara's face glistens, and there are dark patches of sweat under the arms of his shirt.

Another young soldier appears through a door behind the colonel, carrying a tray of coffee. Moving with formal care, he sets the cups down around the table. Chandara gives a brief order in Khmer, and both soldiers hurry out. Watching, I try to keep a neutral expression. The carefully contrived formality of the situation, with its maps and conference table and roses, is like a child's imitation of the adult world. But it's easy to be amused by the dispossessed, and I feel a quick sense of shame. As I pick up my coffee, I find Chandara looking at me; when he speaks, it seems to be in answer to my thoughts.

"Few Western journalists want to know about us, Ray," he says. "And we are often misrepresented. They love to make stories about CIA plots. If only they knew how little the CIA or anyone else will help us. Only Mike Langford told the truth about us."

"He always believed in the Khmer Serei," Jim says.

"Yes, he believed," Chandara says.

He pauses, drawing on his cigarette, his eyes moving away from us; and now a look of sadness comes into his face: he appears to be struggling to mask distress. He releases smoke, and goes on.

"When I started to form our national liberation front, coming alone to Bangkok, Mike took me into his house, and later made our cause known to the international press." He looks at me. "You know this, Ray? You know how much he supported us?"

I say I have some idea.

"Who will do what Mike did for us? We so badly need good public relations," Chandara says. He pauses again, his mouth compressed under the mustache. When he continues, his calm, discursive tone seems calculated to distract attention from his emotion.

"That was what Mike understood," he says. "That was how he has helped us in this last year. We are now carrying guerrilla warfare thirty kilometers inside the border, but it is only the beginning. We need supplies, intelligence, communications. We need the big powers to believe in us. We must plan three, four, five years ahead; it will take time to win back the countryside. Not many want to fight the nightmare; they are too weak. But we must sacrifice ourselves, as the Communists do, and live as hard as they do. Nothing else will earn us our country back. We lost it through loving luxury. Now—" He spreads his hands, palms upward. "I have sent my wife and children to Bangkok," he says. "There is nothing else here but the struggle. It's the only way."

He looks at us both as though anticipating questions; but neither of us speaks. I don't feel hopeful for Chandara and his cause. Prosperous Thailand, with its cars, television, transistor radios and sexual bazaars for tourists, is waiting on his flank; and his people are waiting in their shanties to emigrate to America and Australia. He'll swelter here on the border with his refugee army, in his bamboo hut with its rose garden and its military maps, attended by his young officers and aides-de-camp, and he'll probably never give up; but it will all be worked out elsewhere in the end, by people in air-conditioned offices who have no emotional involvement with Cambodia; people who'll decide its fate with larger aims in mind.

"Mike helped us all the time," Chandara is saying. "His warmth and support meant so much to me. He and I were going to write a small book together. He did all these things out of friendship, and because he loved Cambodia." He drains his coffee cup, and puts it down. He's sitting very straight, and unnaturally still.

"Mike was my truest friend," he says. "Just as he was yours, Jim. I loved him. I trusted him from the day I first met him. My men admired him." He pauses, looking directly at Jim.

"But now his luck has gone," he says. "I know that you want me to discuss how he can be found—but I have to tell you: it can't be done." He stops abruptly, and I'm startled to see that his eyes are brimming with tears. Then he says: "It is very hard for me to speak to you about this."

He continues to sit motionless, holding the arms of his bamboo chair, his face hard and composed, looking past us out the door, neither indulging his grief nor wiping his tears away.

Jim has been sitting just as straight and still as Chandara. Now he leans forward, and I see that his good left foot taps nervously on the earth floor, in its highly polished brown boot. "His luck isn't gone," he says. "He isn't gone, Colonel. We still have to try and find him."

But Chandara shakes his head, blinking and clearing his throat. "You will not find him now," he says. He takes out a handkerchief and wipes his cheeks. "Something has happened since you were here last, Jim. It isn't good news." He turns aside, blowing his nose, and then shouts two words in Khmer.

One of the young soldiers comes in, and salutes. Chandara speaks to him quickly, and the soldier hurries out the front door, disappearing through the rose garden into the white and ochre furnace of the day. Then Chandara looks back at Jim.

"This week Lay Vora came to us," he says. "You remember Lay Vora? Mike's driver?"

"Of course I remember Vora," Jim says. "I've so often worried about him—and his family too. I had given up hope for them. He's here? They got away?"

"He and his wife and small daughter have just come across the border," Chandara says. "I have sent for him to talk to you. He will tell you about Michael."

I lean forward. "He's seen Mike?"

Chandara doesn't reply at first. Then he says: "Yes. But better that he tells you himself. I cannot be the one to tell you."

Harvey Drummond has described Vora for me as a man in vigorous middle age, always neat and lively and well dressed. But the small, bent figure that shuffles into the room is that of an old man, and the faded blue shirt, black shorts and rubber shower sandals are the outfit of a street beggar.

"Vora," Jim says. He stands up and holds out his arms.

They embrace, and Vora says in English: "Mr. Jim. It's so good to see you. They tell me you are here in Thailand."

His looks are semi-Caucasian, as seems often to be the case with Cambodians: waving hair, and eyes that are round rather than almond-shaped. Except for the deep brown skin, he could almost be an old Irish-Australian. He's somehow familiar; and his face is gentle and likable. His hair is still black, but there are white streaks in it, and his skin is very wrinkled. Looking up at Jim with an expression that's half delighted and half stricken, he has his brows raised high, and this has put a large number of horizontal corrugations across his forehead. Now in his late forties, he appears close to seventy.

Chandara waits for some moments; then he speaks to Vora in Khmer, gesturing at a bamboo chair next to Jim's. The small man hesitates, as though wondering whether he should have the temerity to sit down; but Chandara speaks to him again, his voice quiet and soothing, and Vora obeys, hunched forward respectfully on the edge of the chair. His brows are raised again: this time in a sort of pleading apprehension.

Jim sits beside him. "It's good to see you, Vora," he says. "I'm very glad you made it. And your wife and family are safe too?"

For some moments, Vora looks at him without answering, the many wrinkles in his forehead increasing. Then he says: "Bopha is with me, and our little daughter. But my sons are dead, Mr. Jim. Both dead."

Jim grimaces, staring at him. There's silence for a moment. Then he reaches out and takes Vora's hand. "Vora, I'm so very sorry. Oh Jesus, your sons."

"Better I did not educate them," Vora says. "Not send them to school."

His voice is toneless, and he looks down at the floor while Jim holds his hand. Then he goes on talking. His English has been picked up from the correspondents he's worked for: it's rudimentary, and he mostly uses the present tense, but all the things he says are clear.

"The Khmer Rouge find that my sons are educated," he says.

"They kill all educated people. So they take my sons away with their hands tied. Afterwards we are told they are beaten with hoes and killed."

None of us speaks. Vora goes on looking at the floor; then he looks up at us as though asking for something, his expression bewildered.

"It's the same story," Chandara says. "We hear it so many times." I find he's looking at me, his eyes glittering with anger. "But still many of your Western intellectuals and journalists won't believe it, Ray. It doesn't suit them to believe—so they say the stories are false. But we have refugees arriving every week who tell us these things. The Khmer Rouge are killing anyone who is educated; a little bit of education is enough. When they drove the people out onto the roads, they killed any who had books with them. They are killing not just thousands of people but tens of thousands. They make mountains of bodies. They are like the Nazis. The towns are emptied; the temples destroyed; the monks slaughtered. This is true barbarism, which wants to smash everything that is civilized."

Vora is listening to Chandara quietly, with a sort of awe, as though the loss of his sons is at last being given meaning. A soldier brings him coffee and he sips it respectfully, while Chandara goes on addressing Jim and me. The colonel's voice is low, but tight with anger; when he lights another of Jim's Winstons, I see his fingers tremble.

"Communism has been taken to its limits over there," he said. "Envy has become a religion: they call it *angka*. I have learned much about *angka,* talking to our refugees. It is a new Dark Age. No books for the people to read; no medicine to heal them when they fall ill; no law to protect them; no family life; no religion to comfort them; no music but the music of propaganda, played over loudspeakers. Oh yes, they have loudspeakers, just as they have AK-47s. They want to get rid of Western technology, but the leaders make exceptions for what is important to them."

He draws deeply on his cigarette, and I sense that he's talking partly to postpone the moment when Vora must tell us what he knows.

"Many of the soldiers are peasants as young as twelve," he says, "Children with automatic weapons. Anything they envy or don't understand must be evil: must be killed and destroyed. When executing, the Khmer Rouge don't waste bullets: they use hoes, and other simple methods. My own brother and his family must have died in this way. They failed to leave in time, and we hear nothing of them."

Out of the corner of my eye I can see Jim Feng's boot tapping again. He takes out a Winston and passes it to Vora, who smiles and bends gratefully to the flame of Jim's lighter. Sitting now with his artificial leg crossed over the other, gripping it in his left hand, Jim is showing tension in every line of his body. He clicks the lighter shut, and his voice when he speaks is strained and dry. "Vora—Colonel Chandara says you have news of Mike."

For a moment Vora is silent. He sits looking at the valuable American cigarette in his hand as though he hopes the question may drift away, like the smoke. Then he looks at Chandara.

Chandara nods, wiping sweat from his forehead with his handkerchief. He says nothing.

Vora looks back at Jim and me, and the corrugations of his forehead seem to have multiplied. "The Others come marching into Phnom Penh," he says, "down Monivong Boulevard. No one knows what they will do, what they will be like. Then they order everybody out—out of the city. We are sent too, my wife and sons and I—with all the others, onto the roads. We have seen many dead people beside the road, hands tied behind their backs. But because I pretend I am just a taxi driver, they do not kill me." He looks at Jim. "I have had to leave Black Bessie," he says.

Jim nods, still sitting rigid, waiting.

"At first we work outside Phnom Penh, digging canals," Vora says. "It is very hard; we have only rice to eat, and my wife is ill. This is when they have taken away my sons. Many they take away and execute, every day. Then we are taken with others in a train to Sisophon, up here near Thai border. And from there we go into the country and must build huts, and work in the rice fields. We have been there a long time, until just now when we escape. One night we have run away with others, and come through the forest to the border."

"You're not telling us about Mike," Jim says.

Vora's look of pleading intensifies; the effect would be comical, in other circumstances. His small, wrinkled face is really made for humor: for jokes. In the days when he drove Black Bessie for Mike, there would have been a lot of joking.

"There is a village near that place we are in," he says. "This is where the Khmer Rouge bosses in our camp have said that Mr. Mike came. They say that a Westerner and some Khmer Serei soldiers from over the border are captured there. We only hear what they say—do not see anything. People say the Westerner is an American CIA spy. The next day we have been taken out to a field near the village, and we saw them—in the distance. The Khmer Rouge guards say this is what happens to Lon Nol officers and traitors, and American spies who are enemies of *angka*." He leans and stubs out his cigarette; he looks from one to the other of us, seeming to ask to be spared from saying more.

"You saw them?" Jim asks. His tone is almost angry. "What did you see? Tell us."

"There are six executed," Vora says. "We saw them, out in that field. The Khmer Rouge have executed so many; I have seen it before. I have seen them do many bad things. This time—" He breaks off and looks at us with his pleading despair. Then he raises his arms and holds them out stiffly from the shoulders, at full length.

While Jim and I stare, Chandara speaks again. "This time their method was crucifixion. They often do this. Perhaps it's an influence of their French Catholic education."

A fresh wave of perspiration pours down my face; as I mop at it, faintness comes over me. From a distance, I hear Jim say: "And Mike was one of them? Is that what you're saying, Vora?"

"I saw a man like Mr. Mike," Vora says, "tied on one cross. I can see his white skin and yellow hair. He is wearing a black shirt and trousers, like a Khmer. It's far off, and they have fires under the crosses, so there is a lot of smoke. But I believe it was Mr. Mike."

"But you couldn't see his face." Jim Feng's voice is strained and almost accusing. He leans close to Vora with his fists clenched on his knees. "You couldn't see his face, so you don't know it was Mike!"

"Jim," Chandara says. "Jim. Who else could it have been?"

Vora has begun to cry. He cries in a way that Westerners seldom do: like a child, his mouth open, his eyes staring in a sort of sad amazement, the back of his right hand held against his cheek. When he speaks again, his voice is high and squeezed, and he's looking at the floor.

"I know it must be Mr. Mike," he says. Then he raises his face to look at us all again, blinking away his tears. "He has helped all my family," he says. "He has helped many others. He has fought for Cambodia. I will always remember him. I think of him many times. As often as I think of my sons."

Jim asks no more questions. His face is yellow and ill-looking, and dewed with perspiration. Holding his leg, he turns half away from us, looking out through the door. Across the baking white spaces out there, the green and mauve hills of Cambodia can be seen, musing and peaceful.

Chandara comes around the table, and places one hand on Vora's shoulder. He speaks to him quietly in Khmer. Vora rubs his nose and sniffs. He has finished crying for Mike, and now sits with patient dignity, in his ragged clothes and rubber sandals, looking from one to the other of us, waiting for what will happen next.

____

3.

My last duty in Bangkok before flying home is to arrange for the sale of Langford's house.

I decide to inspect it. It's only five minutes' walk along the canal from the Newsroom, standing on a section of the *klong* that's lined with giant, spreading trees. Harvey Drummond, Jim Feng and I walk there together at four in the afternoon, crossing the *klong* by a little wooden bridge.

We arrive at a plain, two-story villa made of cement sheeting, with a gabled iron roof, set among banana and mango trees. A middle-aged Thai housekeeper and her husband live downstairs; Mike lived alone in the two rooms upstairs. The housekeeper lets us in and leads the way up there, opening the shutters of a window looking onto the *klong,* and turning on the overhead fan.

We stand in the middle of the room, which is close from having been shut up; there's a smell of dust and tobacco. It's very hot and still, and a bird outside the window keeps repeating the same call. Harvey and Jim begin talking to the housekeeper, whose name I haven't caught. Harvey speaks a little Thai; she speaks no English.

While they talk, I walk about the room. It's plain and featureless as a motel room, with a bamboo settee and chairs, a dining table, a desk and a sideboard of Thai teak. Langford evidently hadn't begun to decorate the place in any way, nor to replace any of the art works he'd lost in Phnom Penh. There are no personal possessions in evidence; Jim Feng long ago removed them. A couple of scraps of paper lie on the desk: bills for film. The only individual touch here is a cork notice board on one wall, bare except for two photographs, which I go up and examine.

One is a picture of a group of Cambodian peasants walking through the countryside: men and women in pajamas and sarongs and checked *kramas,* their faces stoical, the infants and bundles they carry showing them to be refugees. The other is a picture of Mike and Colonel Chandara. They're walking away from a helicopter that's just landed.

"I took that shot," Jim says. He's come up to stand behind me. "It was the last picture taken of Mike in Cambodia. The other is one Mike took a long time ago. I have copies. You should keep them both." He pulls out the drawing pins and hands me the prints. "I have his three cameras at home," he says. "There wasn't much else here, but I've itemized it for you. He lost everything he had in Phnom Penh."

"The cameras are yours," I say. "He left them to you in his will."

Jim's face sets. "I will keep them for when he returns," he says.

The housekeeper and Harvey are still in conversation in the

middle of the room. She's a short, solidly built woman in a purple-figured blouse and brown sarong; her face is round, reminding me of a tabby cat's. Harvey has to bend from the waist to hear her: she seems to have been speaking for some time, her flat voice low and mournful, and I begin to get curious.

"What does she say?" I ask Harvey. "Are there any problems about the house?"

"No problems," Harvey says. He straightens up, rubbing his bald head, his expression uneasy.

The housekeeper is looking at Jim and me with an insistent, sad expression. She speaks briefly to Harvey again as she does so, obviously asking him to translate.

Harvey hesitates. "She wants me to tell you this," he says. "A couple of times lately, she's heard Mike come in here. The last time was two nights ago."

Jim and I stare at her, and the woman speaks more rapidly, her voice rising, her face becoming stubborn and defiant.

"She says on quite a few nights when she and her husband are in bed, they've heard Mike's boots on the gravel outside," Harvey says. His tone is neutral, but I sense his embarrassment as he meets Jim's gaze. "They know it was Mike, she says, because he always wore those jungle boots. They were used to the sound they made; they also knew it was Mike's walk. They heard him go up the stairs; then they heard him walking overhead, in this room. He walked up and down, she says, like somebody worrying about something. One night her husband came up to investigate, but there was no one here."

Jim draws breath between his teeth with an impatient hiss, his expression scornful. "They're superstitious people, these Thais," he says to us. "This is just bullshit. They didn't hear Mike's ghost, because Mike isn't dead."

He swings around and walks quickly to the door, his limp more pronounced than usual. Harvey and I look at each other, listening to his uneven steps going off down the stairs. I start to follow, but Harvey takes my arm and shakes his head.

"Let him go," he says. "We know where he'll be."

When we come out of the house and cross the little bridge, we walk along the path above the *klong* that leads back to the News-room. It's still daylight, but twilight's gathering. Swarms of small birds are twittering in the huge tropical trees on the canal: trees for which I still have no names. The hum of invisible traffic from the big main avenues is deepening in volume.

The Newsroom isn't very full at this time, and Jim is seated at our usual table, a beer in front of him, his artificial leg stretched stiffly into the aisle. The moment he sees us, he smiles. It's a curious smile, expressive of tender contemplation. As we sit down, he signals for one of the waiters and orders two more beers. When they come, he pours for us from the bottles, and then raises his glass. "Cheers," he says. We drink, but none of us speaks.

Harvey and I are on one side of the table, Jim on the other. I watch through the white iron grille as the first colored lanterns come on in the stalls under their awnings across the road. We've talked away so many afternoons here, Harvey and Jim and I, living mentally over the border in those countries that are now locked off. Passions fermented in Europe more than a century ago created such a long agony there: passions of the mind. Now the war's over, and all that's left is a flavor of empty longing: a flavor I suspect that Harvey and Jim will taste for the rest of their lives. I turn back from the window to find Jim looking at Harvey, an unlit cigarette in his mouth.

He still smiles, wearing an expression that perhaps signifies the recollection of something touching, and he plays with the Zippo lighter that's a relic of youth and Vietnam, turning it over in his fingers. When he speaks, his voice is reminiscent; he seems to pick up a broken conversation.

"You took risks only when you had to, didn't you, Harvey? You were never crazy. Snow and Dmitri and I took them because we wanted to: that was what we were hooked on."

Harvey smiles back. "You always denied that until now, James."

Jim takes the cigarette from his mouth and looks at it; then he clears his throat. "It belonged to the time when we were young," he says. "And we went on doing it too long. Yet since I lost my leg, I've been eating at myself because I couldn't go back to it." He releases a breath of laughter like a sigh. "That means I'm a bloody idiot, of course. Ying tells me so all the time. She also tells me I'm lucky; lucky I lost my leg and didn't die. Maybe she's right. I often think so when little Meiping comes running to me, holding up her hands."

He finally lights the cigarette, narrowing his eyes, his face becoming empty. When he speaks again, his voice is dry, as though he's discussing business. "Of course the rest of you are right, Harvey—Mike's gone. When I first told Ying that he was missing, she cried out. 'Oh no, not him, not him!' She knew straightaway that he was lost; she knew he wouldn't come back. I have never wanted to believe it—partly because I loved him, partly because I can't bear to know that he died in the way he did."

He breaks off and sits back. He removes a fleck of tobacco from his lower lip with his index finger and studies it, not looking up when he speaks again.

"So I will stop telling myself and others that Mike is still alive," he says. "Even though in a part of my heart, I'm still not sure that he's dead."

"Maybe you never will be sure," Harvey says. "Neither will any of us. But that's all right, brother."

Harvey and Jim have gone home now. But I sit on in the Newsroom, reluctant to leave. Tomorrow will be my last day in Bangkok.

I go on looking through the grille: past the Chinese owner's Mercedes, past the new Japanese motorbikes and cars that are turning and whirring on the square. Over by the canal, as darkness creeps in, black-haired figures by the row of little stalls are busying themselves among earthenware jars and baskets: cheap goods from another age. I imagine that they and their stalls will soon disappear, like a mirage: they don't really fit with the new Bangkok.

I reach into the airways bag beside me, and pull out one of the photographs that Jim took down from the board in Langford's house, in that room that was like a waiting room.

Mike walks away from the helicopter behind Colonel Chandara, his hair fluttering in the draft from the chopper blades. He looks different here: different from the way he appears in any other picture. He's haggard, and for the first time seems less youthful: an appearance that's emphasized by the shirt he's wearing, which appears almost black. Perhaps the unit's been through some difficult action; or perhaps he's simply showing the strain of the past year. But certainly he looks older: another, interior face has emerged through the skin, and a trick of the draft gives the thick, lifted hair a nineteenth-century appearance, which his sideburns accentuate. The long, hollow white cheeks and far, washed-out eyes are a mid-Victorian gentleman's: an image from the birth of photography. And suddenly I see his great-great-grandfather, whose portrait now hangs on my study wall at home. It's Robert Devereux's face.

In a region of Dis beyond the Thai border, a row of crosses rises from the paddy field's red earth, in the motionless and terrible heat. I see flames reach up for him, like the heat's choking essence. But then there are other upright poles about him; and now he's somewhere else.

Orderly wires stretch away, and hidden voices murmur among bright leaves. Walled and roofed by green, by a green like light itself, he hangs in a blessed coolness: the underwater cool of the hop glades.

Home.

FOR THE BEST IN PAPERBACKS, LOOK FOR THE

In every corner of the world, on every subject under the sun, Penguin represents quality and variety—the very best in publishing today.

For complete information about books available from Penguin—including Puffins, Penguin Classics, and Arkana—and how to order them, write to us at the appropriate address below. Please note that for copyright reasons the selection of books varies from country to country.

In the United Kingdom: Please write to *Dept. JC, Penguin Books Ltd, FREEPOST, West Drayton, Middlesex UB7 0BR.*

If you have any difficulty in obtaining a title, please send your order with the correct money, plus ten percent for postage and packaging, to *P.O. Box No. 11, West Drayton, Middlesex UB7 0BR*

In the United States: Please write to *Consumer Sales, Penguin USA, P.O. Box 999, Dept. 17109, Bergenfield, New Jersey 07621-0120.* VISA and MasterCard holders call 1-800-253-6476 to order all Penguin titles

In Canada: Please write to *Penguin Books Canada Ltd, 10 Alcorn Avenue, Suite 300, Toronto, Ontario M4V 3B2*

In Australia: Please write to *Penguin Books Australia Ltd, P.O. Box 257, Ringwood, Victoria 3134*

In New Zealand: Please write to *Penguin Books (NZ) Ltd, Private Bag 102902, North Shore Mail Centre, Auckland 10*

In India: Please write to *Penguin Books India Pvt Ltd, 706 Eros Apartments, 56 Nehru Place, New Delhi 110 019*

In the Netherlands: Please write to *Penguin Books Netherlands bv, Postbus 3507, NL-1001 AH Amsterdam*

In Germany: Please write to *Penguin Books Deutschland GmbH, Metzlerstrasse 26, 60594 Frankfurt am Main*

In Spain: Please write to *Penguin Books S. A., Bravo Murillo 19, 1° B, 28015 Madrid*

In Italy: Please write to *Penguin Italia s.r.l., Via Felice Casati 20, I-20124 Milano*

In France: Please write to *Penguin France S. A., 17 rue Lejeune, F–31000 Toulouse*

In Japan: Please write to *Penguin Books Japan, Ishikiribashi Building, 2–5–4, Suido, Bunkyo-ku, Tokyo 112*

In Greece: Please write to *Penguin Hellas Ltd, Dimocritou 3, GR–106 71 Athens*

In South Africa: Please write to *Longman Penguin Southern Africa (Pty) Ltd, Private Bag X08, Bertsham 2013*